DARK SONG

Titles by Christine Feehan

The GhostWalker Novels

LETHAL GAME

TOXIC GAME

COVERT GAME

POWER GAME

SPIDER GAME

VIPER GAME

SAMURAI GAME

RUTHLESS GAME

STREET GAME

MURDER GAME

PREDATORY GAME

DEADLY GAME

CONSPIRACY GAME

NIGHT GAME

MIND GAME

SHADOW GAME

The Drake Sisters Novels

HIDDEN CURRENTS

TURBULENT SEA

SAFE HARBOR

DANGEROUS TIDES

OCEANS OF FIRE

The Leopard Novels

LEOPARD'S WRATH

LEOPARD'S RUN

LEOPARD'S BLOOD

LEOPARD'S FURY

WILD CAT

CAT'S LAIR

LEOPARD'S PREY

SAVAGE NATURE

WILD FIRE

BURNING WILD

WILD RAIN

The Sea Haven/Sisters of the Heart Novels

BOUND TOGETHER

FIRE BOUND

EARTH BOUND

AIR BOUND

SPIRIT BOUND

WATER BOUND

The Shadow Riders Novels

SHADOW FLIGHT

SHADOW WARRIOR

SHADOW KEEPER

SHADOW REAPER

SHADOW RIDER

The Torpedo Ink Novels

DESOLATION ROAD

VENDETTA ROAD

VENGEANCE ROAD

JUDGMENT ROAD

The Carpathian Novels

DARK SONG

DARK ILLUSION

DARK SENTINEL

DARK LEGACY

DARK CAROUSEL

DARK PROMISES

DARK GHOST

DARK BLOOD

DARK WOLF

DARK LYCAN

DARK STORM

DARK PREDATOR

DARK PERIL

DARK SLAYER

DARK CURSE

DARK HUNGER

DARK POSSESSION

DARK CELEBRATION

DARK DEMON

DARK SECRET

DARK DESTINY

DARK MELODY

DARK SYMPHONY

DARK GUARDIAN

DARK LEGEND

DARK FIRE

DARK CHALLENGE

DARK MAGIC

DARK GOLD

DARK DESIRE

DARK PRINCE

Anthologies

EDGE OF DARKNESS
(with Maggie Shayne and Lori Herter)

DARKEST AT DAWN
(includes Dark Hunger *and* Dark Secret*)*

SEA STORM
(includes Magic in the Wind *and* Oceans of Fire*)*

FEVER
(includes The Awakening *and* Wild Rain*)*

FANTASY
(with Emma Holly, Sabrina Jeffries, and Elda Minger)

LOVER BEWARE
(with Fiona Brand, Katherine Sutcliffe, and Eileen Wilks)

HOT BLOODED
(with Maggie Shayne, Emma Holly, and Angela Knight)

Specials

DARK CRIME

THE AWAKENING

DARK HUNGER

MAGIC IN THE WIND

DARK SONG

A CARPATHIAN NOVEL

CHRISTINE FEEHAN

BERKLEY
NEW YORK

BERKLEY
An imprint of Penguin Random House LLC
penguinrandomhouse.com

Library of Congress Cataloging-in-Publication Data

Names: Feehan, Christine, author.
Title: Dark song / Christine Feehan.
Description: First edition. | New York : Berkley, 2020. | Series: A Carpathian novel
Identifiers: LCCN 2019059049 (print) | LCCN 2019059050 (ebook) |
ISBN 9780593099834 (hardcover) | ISBN 9780593099827 (ebook)
Subjects: LCSH: Paranormal romance stories. | GSAFD: Fantasy fiction. | Occult fiction.
Classification: LCC PS3606.E36 D3896 2020 (print) |
LCC PS3606.E36 (ebook) | DDC 813/.6—dc23
LC record available at https://lccn.loc.gov/2019059049
LC ebook record available at https://lccn.loc.gov/2019059050

Printed in the United States of America
1   3   5   7   9   10   8   6   4   2

Jacket image of woman by Michael Nelson /
Trevillion Images
Jacket design by Judith Lagerman

For my amazing team:
Denise, Domini, Brian, Sheila.
You are the best of the best.

For My Readers

Be sure to go to christinefeehan.com/members/ to sign up for my private book announcement list and download the free ebook of *Dark Desserts*. Join my community and get firsthand news, enter the book discussions, ask your questions and chat with me. Please feel free to email me at Christine@christinefeehan.com. I would love to hear from you.

Acknowledgments

As with any book, there are so many people to thank: Brian and Sheila, for competing with me during power hours. Domini, for always editing, no matter how many times I ask her to go over the same book before we send it for additional editing. Denise, for staying up nights and letting me write while she did the brunt of the business I never want to do. I can't thank you enough.

DARK SONG
By Caedyn Feehan

Through the howling of the wind, a whisper can be heard;
A soft serenade, pine sarnanak, feel my words.
A slumber for the ages, hidden within your retreat;
Awaken from your nightmare, feel the ground beneath
    your feet.

There's light in the darkness, waiting to be seen;
Just as I wait for you, a king for his queen.
The earth may shake, and rivers may swell;
Yet here I stand, ready to break the spell.

The fog along the ridge, drifting through the trees;
A shadow in the distance, nothing but a breeze.
The rain upon a fire, frenzied and in need;
A blessing for all life, and fortune for the seed.
What once was a blaze, grows stronger than before;
A metal in the forge, turns a sword for the war.

A life of hope sings to you, melodies of devotion;
A world of love awaits, vaster than the ocean.
As the hues of the sky, shift upon the shore;
The reds once gray, a spectrum once more.
The waves among the rocks, music of the sea,
Thunderous harmonies carry you to me.
Hand in hand we are strong;
Sing with me, it's to you I belong.

I'll be the bright star, in the dark hour of night;
When you're feeling lost, I will be your light.
I am by your side with every step you take;
Fighting every demon, your love I won't forsake.
When evil seeks a place, deep within your mind;
I will be your shield, protecting what's inside.
I can't heal your scars or take away the pain;
But I can be your shelter, a refuge all the same.

I'll teach you the words, and show you the way;
You're strong on your own but tell me you'll stay.
A symphony of power rolling through the land;
You and I together, here we make our stand.
Once blinded by the wicked, now your eyes are clear;
Look inside yourself, there's nothing left to fear.
The cage has collapsed, the prisoner stands tall;
The battle is ours to end, once and for all.
Now tell me this and tell me true;
Say you'll choose me, as I chose you.

What once was a blaze, grows stronger than before;
A metal in the forge, turns a sword for the war.
A life of hope sings to you, melodies of devotion;
A world of love awaits, vaster than the ocean.

THE CARPATHIAN FAMILIES

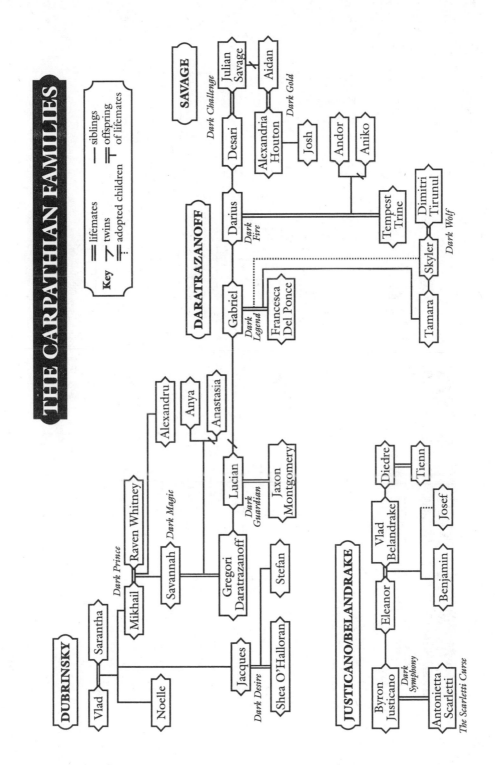

Key
= lifemates
⌢ twins
⊤ adopted children
— siblings
⊤ offspring of lifemates

DUBRINSKY

Vlad = Sarantha

Mikhail = Raven Whitney
Dark Prince

Noelle

Jacques = Shea O'Halloran
Dark Desire

Stefan

Savannah = Gregori Daratrazanoff
Dark Magic

Alexandru

Anya

Anastasia

Lucian = Jaxon Montgomery
Dark Guardian

DARATRAZANOFF

Gabriel = Francesca Del Ponce
Dark Legend

Darius
Dark Fire

Tempest Trine

Skyler
Dark Wolf

Dimitri Tirunul

Tamara

SAVAGE

Desari = Julian Savage
Dark Challenge

Alexandria Houton
Dark Gold

Aidan

Josh

Andor

Aniko

JUSTICANO/BELANDRAKE

Byron Justicano = Eleanor
Dark Symphony

Antonietta Scarletti
The Scarletti Curse

Vlad Belandrake

Diedre

Tienn

Benjamin

Josef

THE CARPATHIAN FAMILIES

Key

═ lifemates	⅄ cousins		
⅄ twins	⋁ parents not		
⅋ triplets	lifemates		
⌣ offspring	⁓ offspring		
⊤ offspring	* monastery ancients		
of lifemates	^ converted male		
─ siblings			

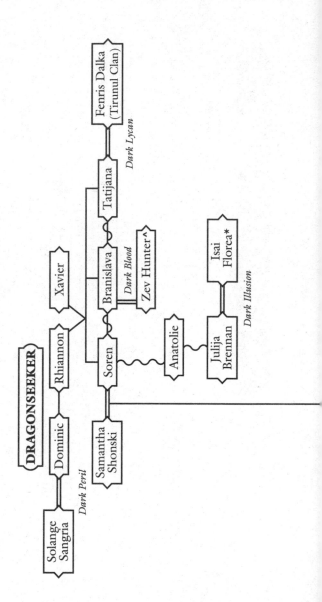

DRAGONSEEKER

Solange Sangria — Dominic — Rhiannon — Xavier
Dark Peril

Samantha Shonski — Soren — Branislava — Tatijana — Fenris Dalka (Tirunul Clan)
Dark Lycan

Branislava ═ Zev Hunter^
Dark Blood

Soren ⁓ Anatolie

Julija Brennan ═ Isai Florea*
Dark Illusion

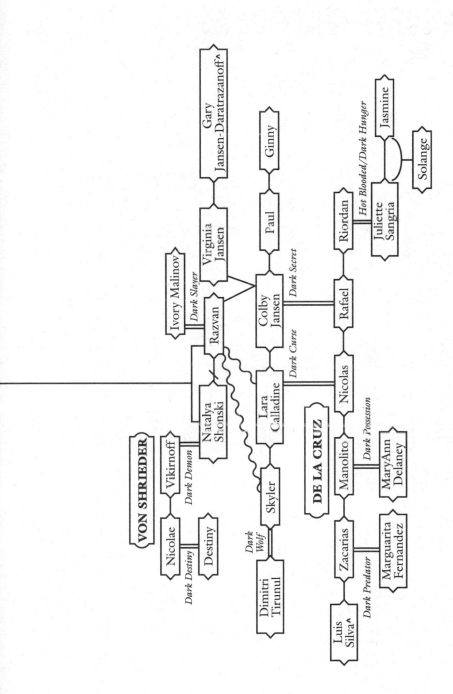

VON SHRIEDER

Nicolae — Vikirnoff
Dark Destiny

Vikirnoff — Natalya Shonski
Dark Demon

Destiny

Ivory Malinov — Razvan
Dark Slayer

Razvan — Lara Calladine

Virginia Jansen — Gary Jansen-Daratrazanoff^

Virginia Jansen — Paul

Ginny

Colby Jansen — Rafael
Dark Secret

Lara Calladine — Nicolas
Dark Curse

Skyler — Dimitri Tirunul
Dark Wolf

Rafael — Riordan

Riordan — Juliette Sangria
Hot Blooded/Dark Hunger

Juliette Sangria — Jasmine

Jasmine — Solange

DE LA CRUZ

Nicolas — Manolito

Manolito — MaryAnn Delaney
Dark Possession

Zacarias — Marguarita Fernandez
Dark Predator

Luis Silva^

OTHER CARPATHIANS

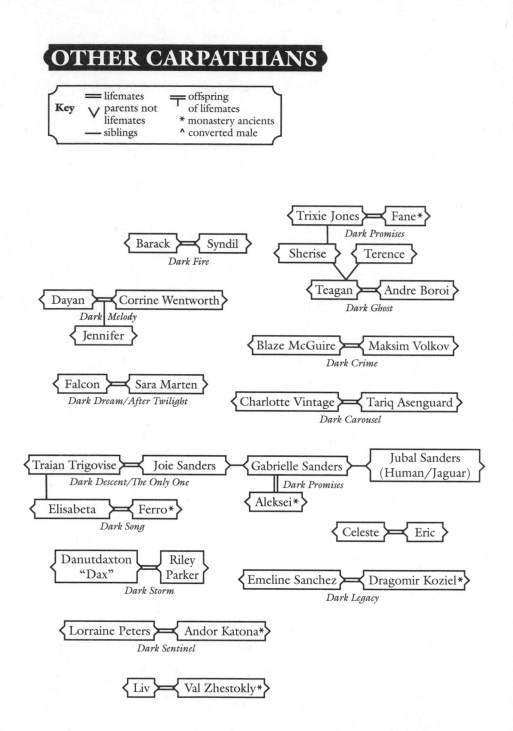

Key
═══ lifemates
⋁ parents not lifemates
— siblings

⊤ offspring of lifemates
* monastery ancients
^ converted male

Trixie Jones ══ Fane*
Dark Promises

Sherise — Terence

Teagan ══ Andre Boroi
Dark Ghost

Barack ══ Syndil
Dark Fire

Dayan ══ Corrine Wentworth
Dark Melody
Jennifer

Blaze McGuire ══ Maksim Volkov
Dark Crime

Falcon ══ Sara Marten
Dark Dream/After Twilight

Charlotte Vintage ══ Tariq Asenguard
Dark Carousel

Traian Trigovise ══ Joie Sanders — Gabrielle Sanders — Jubal Sanders (Human/Jaguar)
Dark Descent/The Only One   *Dark Promises*

Elisabeta ══ Ferro*   Aleksei*
Dark Song

Celeste ══ Eric

Danutdaxton "Dax" ══ Riley Parker
Dark Storm

Emeline Sanchez ══ Dragomir Koziel*
Dark Legacy

Lorraine Peters ══ Andor Katona*
Dark Sentinel

Liv ══ Val Zhestokly*

DARK
SONG

I

Through the howling of the wind, a whisper can be heard;
A soft serenade, piŋe sarnanak, feel my words.

S ound woke her. Elisabeta Trigovise didn't want to be awake. She wanted to sleep forever, but those weeping notes refused to allow her to succumb to her need to hide from the world. Like the drops of rain drumming softly into the earth, feeding the soil, those notes slipped into her mind with a song of rising. More and more that gentle melody awakened her on each rising, became more insistent that she comply more fully. That she more than just wake to feed and go straight back to slumber.

Whereas before, the song was in her mind, now it sank into her body, her blood and bones, her heart and soul, calling to her persistently, and she knew it was the call of her lifemate—one she couldn't ignore. She didn't dare ignore. It didn't matter how terrified she was of him. She had to answer.

There was safety beneath the ground. Solace. No one could get to her. She was alone and no demands could be put on her, but she had known all along it wasn't going to last. Every rising, each time the sun set, the danger began. She tried to sleep, but they came to feed her. At first many had come. Different ones. That had been frightening, but the blood had revived her, made her stronger, and no one had asked anything of her. She was allowed to go back to sleep in the healing soil to repair her body and fractured mind. Now, only *he* gave her blood.

Elisabeta tried not to waken, but it was too late, the song had played through her mind, those beautiful weeping notes of rain. The sun had set, and the moment it did, her body had tuned to it. She was Carpathian, that ancient race paralyzed during daylight hours and needing blood to sustain their lives. There were few of them left in the world, and the fight to keep from dying out was made worse by the vampires trying to kill them.

A little shudder went through her body. Elisabeta had been tricked by a friend when she'd been young and naïve, and she'd been kidnapped, taken from her home and family and hidden away by one such vampire for centuries. She no longer remembered that young girl, or her family. She'd been reduced to this woman who hid herself away in the ground, too terrified of everything and everyone to show herself. Sergey Malinov— the master vampire—would come for her and he would use her to destroy everyone who had shown her any kindness because that was what he did. He would never let her escape him. Never.

The moment she surfaced, he would use her, and they had no idea how powerful he was. They had rescued her, and he was angry, whispering to her, trying to get past the barriers and shields they had erected to protect her, but he was there, crouched and waiting to strike. She knew him, knew he was wholly evil. There were children in this compound, this place her rescuers thought safe. No one was safe from Sergey, least of all children.

The world had passed her by while she lived in a cage, with only her sadistic captor for company. One moment he could be falsely sweet; the next, savagely ugly, torturing her, starving her, hurting others in front of her. Leaving her alone for long periods of time so that she thought she would slowly starve to death and even welcomed that end. He was her only company. She couldn't speak unless he gave her permission. She made no decisions for herself and so, after centuries, no longer knew how to make them.

She had been rescued, put in the healing grounds to recover from the wounds to body and mind, but there was no recovery from centuries of captivity. She had no idea how to fend for herself. She was terrified of having to talk to strangers. They had told her she had a brother and that he had searched for her for centuries. She had thought of that often, ashamed that when she tried to remember him, her mind seemed to explode with pain, rejecting the idea of her past. She knew they would expect her to remember him, but she didn't.

She didn't remember herself as a young Carpathian woman, nor did she remember her parents. Her mind had been fractured, and no amount of healing in the earth was going to change that. She wasn't that same girl who had been taken from her home. She was—nothing. No one. She wanted to remain where she was, hidden away from everyone, but she knew her time was fast running out. Her lifemate had found her. Just thinking of him made her heart pound out of control. She knew better. She knew to control herself. That simple sound would alert him, and of course it did.

Elisabeta.

His voice filled her mind. Calm. Soothing. A masterful voice. One always in control, unlike her. Her heart accelerated even more. Panic began to set in. At once the ground above her opened before she could begin to struggle for air. He did that for her. She hadn't done it for herself and it shamed her that she always had to be taken care of. The least little detail of her life had to be arranged for her because she didn't know how to do it.

She couldn't provide herself with clothing, and if her lifemate knew, he might be angry. If she spoke without permission, he might be angry. Punishments could be terrible. She didn't know the rules in this new world or with this man. She only knew what she sensed of him—that he was an ancient, far older than Sergey and much more dangerous. He terrified her on so many levels, but then everything did.

She had been befriended by a woman, Julija, a strong woman who walked her own path, walked beside her lifemate and made her own decisions. Elisabeta had dared to defy Sergey and secretly talked with her. She wanted to be strong like her but knew she never would be. Hundreds of years of captivity and silence, of having someone telling her what to do, of punishments and fear, had shaped her into this terrified being she had come to despise. She no longer knew who she was or what she was, only that she had no purpose, and she was so tired of being afraid.

She stayed very still and remained silent, terrified of being tricked. She kept her eyes closed tightly, even with the ground above her open, afraid of seeing where she was. She hadn't been out of a cage in hundreds of years. Open spaces made her feel sick and disoriented. She didn't know how to process space.

Speak to me, lifemate.

Her heart sank. That was a direct order. The first he had ever given to her. It mattered little that his voice was so different from Sergey's. He was her master and could torture her, deprive her of food, kill others in front of her. Her heart pounded out of control. *What would you have me say?*

There was a small silence that terrified her even more. Had she angered him? She really didn't know what he wanted from her.

Elisabeta, listen to my heartbeat. You are panicking for no reason. We are merely having a conversation. Breathe with me. Listen to my heartbeat and follow with yours.

She made the mistake of lifting her lashes, just for a second. Surrounding her, she could see what appeared to be balconies where people could stand and look down onto the healing grounds where she lay. They could see her. Full-blown panic had taken hold and she couldn't find air. Her body nearly convulsed. She tried to curl into the fetal position, to sink deeper into the healing soil, allowing the rich minerals to blanket her body and hide her from any prying eyes.

She sank into waiting arms. Strong arms. She had always fantasized about being held when she needed it most. She longed for human contact—was often desperate for it—and now, somehow, she had made her fantasy so real she felt a very hard male body surrounding hers, holding her safe. With her eyes closed tight, she felt him surround her with his warmth, his heat. His breath was in her ear, his chest rising and falling behind her back.

Breathe with me, piŋe sarnanak, follow the rhythm of my heart.

Her heart tuned almost automatically to his, before she could do so intentionally. The breath moved in and out of her starving lungs, pulling air into her. The air smelled of rain, of rich soil and unexpectedly of juniper and allspice mixed together. He had called her "little songbird." That didn't seem so bad, an endearment in the ancient Carpathian language. Her heart stuttered a little at the gentleness in the way he treated her.

That's good, Elisabeta. Now tell me, while you feel safe, what is your greatest fear of rising?

She did feel safe. She burrowed deeper, imagining being held in those strong arms, feeling them tighten around her, feeling the warm breath in her ear, so steady. Breathing in and out. His heart rate never faltered. Never rose or slowed but remained that same steady rhythm, as if he could always be counted on. Did she dare voice her concern aloud? Already she was terrified that she had been awake long enough to alert Sergey.

He will never give me up. He will use me to kill everyone who helped to take me from him. He's so cruel. If I don't go back to him, he will burn this place to the ground with everyone in it right in front of me.

As soon as she gave voice to her concerns, even if it was only in her mind, panic again began to burst through her. What if Sergey heard? What if he was able to monitor her in spite of the safeguards the Carpathians had so carefully woven around her? She didn't dare utter his evil name just in case the vampire was able to latch on to that.

A hand pressed into her hair, a soothing stroke down the back of her head. Like a caress. It was so strange, so unusual, such a rare, shocking feeling she'd never experienced, it stopped the welling panic before it could take her over.

Thank you for telling me your greatest fear. I know it frightened you just to tell me. What else has upset you? Be truthful with me, Elisabeta. You will not be punished for telling the truth to me no matter what you say.

Could she believe that? She had to answer him truthfully, no matter if she was punished or not. One didn't lie to one's lifemate. He would know. She took a deep breath. *You did not claim me as your lifemate. You know I am not worthy. I accept that, and I understand. I am not the same woman I was born to be. I have been corrupted by the vampire who took me and held me captive for so many years. I do understand but . . .* She broke off.

It was the truth. She didn't even know if she wanted to be claimed because she had no idea what she would do as a lifemate. Carpathians only had one. When a man was born, his soul was split in half. He carried all the darkness in him. The light was placed in a woman who was born either at the same time or later. Around the age of two hundred, Carpathian males began to lose their ability to see in color and emotions began to fade. As time went on, if they didn't find their lifemate, their world became gray and emotions retreated completely.

Men were born with the ritual binding words imprinted on them. Once they found their lifemate, their emotions and color were restored to them. They said the vows to the woman when they found her, binding them together. No man waited, especially an ancient hunter who had lived long and suffered greatly.

Still, she *did* understand. She was conflicted about her feelings. If he claimed her, it would be another layer of protection for her against Sergey. Ferro Arany was a very dangerous man. She could feel that even beneath the ground. He was older than so many of them, and most had been on earth a long time. He was a skilled warrior. She was a little humiliated that he didn't want her, even if she did understand.

It had been drilled into her almost from the moment of birth that somewhere was her other half and he would be actively looking for her. Always looking for her. To know that he had found her and didn't want her was another blow to her. Although, if he had claimed her, she would have been even more terrified, so that made no sense at all. She just needed to stay in the ground, where she could lose herself and not have to face the world she didn't understand.

I intend to claim you now, piŋe sarnanak. You are going to leave these healing grounds, and to do so, you will need my protection. I feel your fear of the unknown beating at me and wish to protect you from that, but most of all from him. He cannot get to you here, and he will know, once we are bound together, that he cannot have you unless he destroys our bond. He can only do that if he kills me. By protecting you, and shielding you, this vampire cannot use you to harm anyone here at the compound. You have no need to worry about him using you to that end.

His heart rate never rose. His voice was as calm as ever. He didn't seem to fear Sergey in the least or to be impressed that the master vampire had outsmarted his four older siblings and even powerful mages. The vampire led an army against the Carpathians, yet Ferro seemingly wasn't worried about him.

I do not know what a lifemate does. I have forgotten so much.

He was claiming her to protect her from Sergey. While his last statement brought tremendous relief, it also brought her clarity. He was an ancient hunter. He had spent several lifetimes sacrificing for his people. Binding himself to her would be nothing in comparison to what he had suffered on behalf of the Carpathian people. That made perfect sense to her.

I will have no trouble telling you what I expect from you.

She hoped so, because she wasn't good at thinking for herself. Julija was trying to help her with that. Julija had told her she had a couple of friends who would love to meet her, and they would be as welcoming as Julija, but even that scared Elisabeta. Everything scared her.

Hands circled her arms and began to rub up and down them. *You are shivering. There is no need to be so afraid, piŋe sarnanak. You have only to look to me and I will help you when you feel you cannot find your way.*

She wanted to cry, but she had long ago run out of tears. *I lost my way a long time ago. I have no knowledge of any way. I cannot talk without permission. I do not dress myself. I cannot do my hair or find my own food. I cannot be out in the open. I am lost, a burden to a man who does not want the responsibility of a prisoner.*

Sas, piŋe sarnanak. I am an ancient, not a modern warrior. I am your lifemate. My soul calls to yours. When you have a question, you are to ask me immediately. That is an order. Do you understand?

Without permission?

You always have permission to talk to me or to your female friends. If the vampire tries to reach you, and for some reason I do not feel him, you must come to me immediately no matter what he threatens. That is an absolute rule. Do you understand?

She swallowed hard. The rules were certainly different, but she felt better that there were rules. She understood structure. *Yes. I will obey.*

Once she gave her word, she would never go back on it. She liked that he gave her permission to talk to Julija. She wouldn't have to sneak, and she would have tried to. That would have been difficult. Once he tied them together, he would be slipping in and out of her mind easily. She wouldn't always know he was there.

Te avio päläfertiilam. You are my lifemate. Éntölam kuulua, avio päläfertiilam. I claim you as my lifemate.

Her breath caught in her throat. The ritual binding words. His arms were real. She felt him there, surrounding her, but she still didn't have the courage to open her eyes and look at him, to see what her lifemate looked like. He felt big. All muscle. When her heart began to hammer, his immediately tuned to hers and once more slowed her rhythm.

Ted kuuluak, kacad, kojed. I belong to you. Élidamet andam. I offer my life for you. Pesämet andam. I give you my protection.

His lips slid into her hair, nuzzled the side of her neck right over her pounding pulse. His tongue touched her skin. It felt . . . erotic. Her pulse jumped. He made her feel things she didn't know were possible. His arms felt safe when she'd never been safe, not even in her own home.

Uskolfertiilamet andam. I give you my allegiance.

Was that even possible? It was a vow. More than a promise. A vow between two souls. His allegiance was to her. Her eyes burned. More than anything she wanted to be strong for herself. To stand on her own two feet and be a partner to her lifemate. Maybe not the kind of partner Julija was, but at least someone Ferro could be proud of. Not some shrinking ball of terror hiding under the ground.

Sívamet andam. I give you my heart. Sielamet andam. I give you my soul. Ainamet andam. I give you my body. Sívamet kuuluak kaik että a ted. I take into my keeping the same that is yours.

His heart was given to her. His soul. His body. And he took hers in return. Her mouth went dry. She could handle it if he took her heart and soul, but her body? Even the vampire hadn't taken that. He couldn't. That was all she had left of herself that belonged to her. Her pulse jumped under his touch and he soothed her with a soft brush of his lips. His hands continued to rub her arms gently.

Ainaak olenszal sívambin. Your life will be cherished by me for all time. Te élidet ainaak pide minan. Your life will be placed above mine for all time. Te avio päläfertiilam. You are my lifemate. Ainaak sívamet jutta oleny. You are bound to me for all eternity. Ainaak terád vigyázak. You are always in my care.

His lips wandered down the side of her neck, and then he was suddenly shifting his body out from under her, so she lay in a fine mattress of rich minerals with his heavy body blanketing hers. His lips kissed both closed eyelids.

"Are you ever going to look at me and see your lifemate, *pipe sarnanak?*" There was the faintest trace of amusement in his voice.

She pressed her lips together. *Only if you command me. I mean, yes. But . . .* She couldn't. Not yet. As long as she had her eyes closed, she could enjoy his touch. Pretend her world was going to be all right. If she opened them and the world was too big or she panicked, and everything frightened her, he would realize just what he had tied himself to for all eternity.

He didn't command her to open her eyes. His lips continued a slow travel from her eyelids along her left cheek to the corner of her mouth. Her heart stuttered as he brushed across the curve of her lips and then down her chin and throat. He continued lower over the curve of breasts. For a moment she thought to bring her hands up to cover herself, but it seemed a little silly. Her body belonged to him. She had scars. He had already seen them. He had already seen how thin she was.

His lips moved back and forth in a mesmerizing way, pushing out coherent thought. She didn't know what he was doing. She was feeling, but she wasn't quite certain what. She wanted to bring her arms up and touch him, to put her hands in his hair. She could feel it sweeping over her skin, a thick mass sliding over her, sending ripples of awareness and adding to the slow heat building in her veins caused by his mouth moving on her body. The scrape of his teeth sent a dark shiver down her spine. Unexpectedly, her sex clenched. In all her years of being alive, that had never once happened. It was shocking. Maybe even a little mortifying, mostly because she didn't know what it meant.

His teeth sank deep and she bit back a gasp at the shocking wave of pain that instantly turned to erotic pleasure, spreading flickering flames through her body. She could have sworn flames licked at her skin and the insides of her belly, smoldered between her legs and threatened to build an inferno in her deepest core that could never be put out if he didn't stop.

She couldn't stop her arms from creeping around him, no matter how hard she tried. She cradled his head to her, needing him to feast on her, to sate himself on her blood. Nothing in her life had prepared her for the way it felt with him taking her blood. He could drain her dry and she would be happy. When Sergey had taken her blood, it had been painful; a terrible, torturous experience. With Ferro, it was a wonderful, sensual, shocking encounter. He held her in his arms as if she meant something to him. His mouth moved over her like she was priceless.

Again, her eyes burned, when she had no tears to shed. No one had ever treated her the way he did, not that she could remember. If she had to have a new master, no matter if he turned cruel later, she had this mo-ment, this one moment, to hold on to and treasure. Did she believe that he would stay kind to her? No. Not really. She'd lived with terror for so long that she didn't know how to live without it, but she was determined to hold on to every decent moment life gave her. This one was unexpected— a true gift.

His tongue swept across the pinpricks, closing them, and he shifted back and to one side, taking her with him, lifting her as if she weighed no more than a feather and settling her onto his lap. He swept her hair back and pressed her face to his chest.

"Drink, *piŋe sarnanak*. You need to take my blood in the way I took yours."

Her eyelashes fluttered before she could stop them. Curiosity was one of her worst traits. It always had been. Sergey Malinov had known that about her. She had tried so hard to suppress that need to find out every little thing, and she still couldn't help herself at times. Like now. Her lashes lifted and she found herself staring into her lifemate's face for the first time.

She had known he was dangerous. Lethal even. His face could have been carved from the stone, etched out of the hardest rock known to man.

His jaw was set, stubborn, his eyes the color of iron ore, a light, almost silvery color, although she could see streaks of the lightest blue and just the faintest jagged lines of rust spread through the irises. His lashes were dark like his hair, although his hair had streaks of silver running through it. He had high cheekbones, an aristocratic nose and a dark shadow along his jaw where most Carpathian men were clean-shaven.

His gaze drifted possessively over her face. He didn't smile at her, but he bent his head and his lips moved over her eyes, pressing kisses over them.

"You're very brave, Elisabeta."

She wouldn't call it bravery. The moment she opened her eyes and saw his face, saw all that male power, she knew she was in trouble. She'd had to fight her first inclination to hurl herself to the ground and try to burrow into the soil fast. She knew from experience there was no running away. She was always captured, and the repercussions were terrible. Still, the admiration in his voice, that respect, was totally unexpected and caught her off guard.

"Take my blood, *piŋe sarnanak*. You are very pale. I can feel your hunger beating at me."

She was so used to being hungry she barely noticed anymore if she'd gone weeks without blood. He pressed the back of her head very gently, urging her face toward his bare chest. She transferred her gaze there. He had a thick chest, with heavy, defined muscles. He wore ancient ink, the kind etched into his skin. It was difficult to tattoo a Carpathian. Ink didn't stay. Carpathians rarely scarred. Ferro had ink pressed into scarring on his chest, arms, shoulders and, she was certain, his back.

The back of her head fit into his palm easily and he pressed her close to his skin, to those heavy muscles. At once she caught his intriguing scent and drew it deep into her lungs. Something about the way he smelled got to her on a molecular level. She instantly wanted to taste his skin—no, *needed* to taste him. Without thinking, she lapped at him with her tongue. An exotic, perfect flavor burst in her mouth on her tongue and slid down her throat, bringing a heat to her belly. She almost keened with delight. Nothing tasted like he did. Nothing.

Her teeth scraped back and forth over his pulse while she contemplated what his blood would taste like. Would it be that good? Would it live up to the promise of his scent? The mere flavor of his skin? He had fed her before, when she was beneath the ground and he slept above her, but he hadn't claimed her, hadn't joined them together. Was there a difference? She had been too terrified to notice then. She was terrified now, but . . . He groaned. It was just a soft sound, but it went straight to her sex. Like an arrow.

"Elisabeta, take my blood." He growled the command at her. His voice was velvet soft, but still, it was a growl. An order.

She sank her teeth instantly. Deep. Without preamble. Shocking him. Shocking her. He threw his head back, his hand locking her head to his chest while the other pinned her hip to his, holding her still, forcing her to realize she was squirming on his lap, her bare cheeks sliding over his fully erect cock. She would have been mortified, but already his blood was in her mouth. Not just any blood; an aphrodisiac, the finest thing she'd ever tasted in her life.

Ferro would never have enough blood to give her. Never. She would forever crave his blood. Nothing would taste this good and she knew it. She tried not to be greedy. She'd been trained not to take what she needed. If she tried, Sergey beat her into submission. Twice, she tried to pull back, but Ferro murmured his displeasure and held her to his chest. She continued feeding, grateful he allowed it, grateful for the rich sustenance from a true ancient, but more importantly, grateful for the amazing gift a lifemate's blood provided.

"That's enough, Elisabeta," Ferro said finally, gently stroking her hair. "In all the years of my existence, no one has ever tasted the way you do. I hope it was the same for you."

She reluctantly slid her tongue across the pinpricks to close them and lifted her head away from temptation. She nodded. "It was."

He continued to stroke her hair. "That is a good thing. I want you to come to me when you are hungry. If you can't find me, reach out to me. Don't wait until you feel starved. You will need extra feedings for a while."

At once panic set in. "I won't be with you? If I'm not with you, won't

I be in the ground? I can't be on my own. I won't know what to do." Her heart rate had gone crazy and her lungs burned for air. She couldn't do this. She really couldn't. She couldn't even look around her, let alone be on her own. Just because he held her and gave her blood and gave her permission to speak didn't mean she could maneuver her way through a world she didn't know or understand.

She clapped a hand over her mouth to keep from blurting out another word. It was already far too late. He could read her mind anyway. She'd gone from appearing half normal—or at least she hoped she looked that way—to looking insane. He was stuck with crazy. She did try to crawl off his lap back to the welcoming soil. It was impossible to move when Ferro didn't want her going anywhere. He simply clamped his arms around her and held her to him.

"You are having another panic attack. Breathe. I am not going to leave you on your own until you are ready. Stay still, *piŋe sarnanak*. Just breathe while we go over a few more rules."

She could do that. Rules made her feel safe. She liked rules. He stroked her hair in that soothing way he had, and she found herself following his breathing pattern. She liked that he called her "little songbird." It sounded a little like an endearment. He wasn't making fun of her, or taunting her. He seemed only gentle when he could crush her so easily.

"I know that you are very afraid of Malinov attacking this compound."

She gasped at his audacity in naming the master vampire. She even put her fingers up to cover his lips before she could stop herself. It was a terrible transgression, and the moment she did it, she knew she should be punished. She dropped her hand into her lap and bowed her head.

"I'm sorry. Truly. I shouldn't have touched you without permission. There is no excuse. Whatever you deem is a fit punishment . . ."

Ferro caught her hand and returned her fingertips to his lips. "I am your lifemate. You are allowed to touch me when you wish or have need. Sometimes those needs will be for comfort, other times they might be sexual. You might just want to feel close. Whatever the reason, there is no need to ask for permission. I intend to touch you at will."

She was confused, frowning at him. "But I belong to you. You have the right to touch me when you desire to do so."

He shook his head. "I belong to you as well, Elisabeta, but we are lifemates, not master and prisoner. Not master and slave owner. Not vampire and captive. Those days are over for you. He will not get you back. You have every right to say no. To me or to anyone else."

Elisabeta was more confused than ever. Shocked even. She didn't understand what he was telling her. It sounded so farfetched she was afraid he was trying to trick her. The inevitable panic began to well up and she pushed her fist into her mouth, biting down hard on her knuckles. She didn't understand anything. The cool earth looked so good to her. She understood the richness, the wealth of the soil. The way it surrounded her body and eased the pain in her joints the tiny cage had caused when she couldn't exercise properly or get enough blood to sustain her. This world she found herself in now was so foreign to her that she didn't understand even one small part of it.

Ferro stroked more caresses in her hair, soothing her. "We are going to start with simple things. Do you remember how to clothe yourself or is this something the vampire insisted he do?"

That shamed her. "He did if he allowed clothing. He always made decisions."

"Do you prefer to wear dresses or trousers?"

Her heart accelerated. Was it a trick question? What did he prefer? She'd never worn trousers in her life. Not once. She knew Julija wore them, but they looked as if they might be uncomfortable. Would Ferro want her to wear them?

"Do you want me to wear dresses or trousers?" she countered, trying not to sound as timid as she felt.

"This is about what you want. There is no right or wrong answer, *piŋe sarnanak*, only what you would really prefer."

She couldn't possibly choose. There was no way. She hadn't made a choice in hundreds of years. Not one single choice. She shook her head, refusing to look at him, refusing to answer.

Elisabeta expected him to be angry, frustrated, to lose patience with her, but his hand continued the gentle strokes in her hair. She realized her long, thick hair—hair that had never been cut—was clean, and as he burrowed his strong fingers into it to massage her scalp, the strands slid through his fingers free of tangles.

"I prefer dresses, but I am an ancient warrior, Elisabeta, not at all modern. I have not had time to catch up to this world. I do not want to color your choices with my own. Still, if you prefer me to choose for you at this time, I will show you two different dresses that I really like, and you can decide which one to wear this evening and which you will wear next rising. Is that acceptable to you?"

She would still have to make a choice, but he liked both dresses and, in the end, she would wear both of them. Her only choice was which to wear tonight and which the following rising. The thought of making that decision was still difficult but exciting. It was a decision. *Her* decision. Ferro was letting her choose.

"Yes, I like the idea very much," she agreed.

"But it is still a little scary to you," he said.

Of course he would know. There was no hiding her pounding pulse from him. She bit her lip and nodded slowly, daring to lift her lashes and sneak a peek at his face to see if he was exasperated with her. She wouldn't blame him if he was. He looked so invincible, as if nothing in the world had ever frightened him. Nothing. How could he sit there so calmly in the middle of the healing grounds, taking his time as if he had nowhere else in the world to be but right there with her, sorting out the terrifying new world she found herself in?

"When you get very frightened, *piŋe sarnanak*, always remember that you have only to look into your mind and I am there with you. You can hear our song. It soothes you every rising. The sound of the rain calling to you to awaken. When you hear that, it is our combined heartbeat. No matter even if I am holding you, if you wish to soothe yourself first, our song is there in your mind. I will admit, I prefer to be the one to care for you, but I want you to know that you are capable of standing on your own two feet always. The vampire took that from you, but I intend to give it back to you. You are not without your own power, Elisabeta. You will

learn, with time, to believe in yourself. To know you're strong. I want that
for you."

She was his lifemate. More, she had spent centuries tuned to the
slightest nuance of her master's voice. His body language. His breathing.
"You do want that for me, but you do not want that for you." It was utterly
daring of her to state what she knew to be truth aloud, to basically con-
tradict him. Had she done so with Sergey, it would have earned her such
a beating she wouldn't have been able to move for a month. Maybe she
was testing Ferro's limit. The truth of his rules.

To her utter astonishment, he nuzzled her shoulder, turning his face
into her neck, his breath warm against her wildly pounding pulse. "I am
ancient, Elisabeta, and more, I have always thought my woman would
obey my every wish. That is what you see in my mind. Having seen what
this vile creature has done to my lifemate, I am determined that the two
of us will learn more modern ways. We will not be as the others living in
this compound, perhaps. We will find our own union, but we will not be
as I envisioned long ago, because I no longer want that for either of us."

She turned his statement over and over in her mind. He was willing
to change. To grow into someone different. She had to find the courage
to do the same. She took a deep breath. "I would very much like to see the
dresses, um . . ." What was she supposed to call him? How was she supposed to address him?

"Ferro," he supplied. "I am your wedded spouse. You will call me
Ferro."

She pressed her lips together to keep them from trembling. He was
her wedded spouse. He'd said the ritual binding words and there was no
going back from that. Not ever. He'd tied them together for all eternity.
For whatever the reasons, they were bound together.

"Say it, *piŋe sarnanak*, say my name. I wish to hear how it sounds coming from your lips." His mouth was against her ear, his breath warm,
teasing, wreaking havoc with the blood in her veins.

Elisabeta wasn't certain she wanted to call him by his given name.
"Ferro," she said softly. "But you call me *piŋe sarnanak*. I think you are
kont o sívanak, strong heart, and this songbird will learn to fly because you

have a heart big enough for both of us." She felt very daring to tell him what she was thinking.

Deep inside, she was desperate for it to be true. They were lifemates and she could look into his mind, but she wasn't brave enough for that yet, nor was she strong enough, if he deliberately kept her out, to push beyond any shield. She had learned, over the centuries, to do so with Sergey, but subtly, so he was unaware. She had the feeling that Ferro would always be aware.

His teeth tugged at her earlobe and then released her just as abruptly, but not before the sudden gentle bite caused a spasm in her sex that sent a shock wave through her entire body.

"Take a look at these dresses. Lorraine, lifemate to my brethren Andor, had several books she called catalogues she allowed me to look through for clothing styles. She has been very helpful."

Elisabeta tried not to stiffen at the underlying affectionate note she heard in his voice. Up until that moment, Ferro had little expression in his voice. It was by turns gentle or soft or commanding, but there was definite affection for this woman. Another woman. Not his lifemate. She didn't like it.

His hand waved in the air and two dresses floated in front of her. She tried not to gasp, but—well—they were just a little bit formfitting. She had rarely been seen by anyone other than Sergey, and then he had covered her body in shapeless gowns. She'd never worn anything like either one of them. It wasn't that they wouldn't cover her adequately—they weren't low in the front, they went to her ankles, and both had three-quarter-length sleeves—but they weren't the shapeless, boxy dresses she was used to wearing.

One was a soft shade of cool forest green with accents of a lighter green in blocks on the bodice and skirt, the material thin and clingy, so she knew it would emphasize her curves. She was thin, and not all that curvy, so maybe her bones would show more than her curves, but it was still a little risqué.

The second dress was black with gray accents. It was also made of a soft material she'd never seen before. The bodice came to a vee at the waist and the skirt dropped in a series of lacy ruffles to the ankles. It was the bodice that gave her pause or she would have chosen it immediately. She wasn't certain how comfortable she would be in a dress that clung to her body that closely.

Ferro didn't hurry her. He waited patiently. In fact, he seemed more interested in her hair and the nape of her neck than he did the dresses and her dilemma. He kept distracting her with his breath, with his lips moving against her pulse, with the way his fingers on her skin and scalp felt, until she was desperate to stop the unfamiliar feelings he flooded her body with.

"The black-and-gray one," she said. "I'll wear that one."

"Excellent choice."

His large hands spanned her waist and he lifted her off his lap and to her feet, setting her to one side. When he stood, he was fully clothed. He waved his hand and she found herself in the long black-and-gray dress. The material clung, just as she knew it would.

"You look beautiful, Elisabeta. Are you used to wearing shoes at all?"

She looked down at her feet and shook her head. "I was never allowed to leave the cage for any length of time."

He waved his hand again. "If these shoes become uncomfortable you are to tell me immediately. That is an order. Am I clear on that?"

She nodded and looked down at the slipper sandals on her feet. They were black and gray to match the dress she wore. She had no idea what they were made of, but it didn't feel like stiff leather. Whatever it was, they were comfortable, and she wiggled her toes. His hand brushed hers. She looked up at him expectantly.

"Take my hand, *piŋe sarnanak*," he said. "We're going to walk around the compound together. I want to show you where everything is and where we'll be staying."

She blinked at him, trying to process what he'd just ordered her to do. What he'd just said. He wanted her to let him take her hand. He was going to walk with her and take her outside the safety of the healing grounds. Outside, where there were people. Walk. When she didn't know how. She swallowed hard and tried to remember the mechanics. She'd seen it enough times. She was intelligent. She could shuffle along.

"Ferro . . ."

He reached for her hand, curling his fingers around hers, bringing her palm to his chest. "You will be with me, Elisabeta, and therefore safe at all times. My brethren will be close, and they will protect you as well. Julija, your friend, is here with her lifemate. Lorraine, my sister-kin, is here and anxious to befriend you."

She remained frozen, staring up at him, too terrified to move. He brought her fingers to the warmth of his mouth, his strong teeth scraping the very ends of them, sending spirals of heat dancing through her veins.

"If you become overwhelmed, just look to me. I will shield you. I am your lifemate, Elisabeta. Everyone we come across, including my brothers, will expect me to be old-world and overbearing." He showed her his teeth again, this time looking for all the world like a predator. "We can communicate as we did earlier, just the two of us. You tell me what you need, and I will provide it. I do not expect you to suddenly, after centuries of captivity, know how to speak with strangers or handle situations unfamiliar to you. I am proud of you for just choosing to rise and face your lifemate. I am told I am quite intimidating."

She glanced up at his face. He was walking her across the healing grounds toward the exit, not striding fast but setting a leisurely pace, enough that she could slide her feet, one in front of the other, not lifting them, her heart beating as if it might fall out of her chest. His tone invited her to find amusement in his statement. She wished she could laugh, but she was too scared. Still, just having him so close gave her courage. Thus far, Ferro had shown her nothing but kindness. She had to believe he would continue to do so.

2

A slumber for the ages, hidden within your retreat;
Awaken from your nightmare, feel the ground beneath your feet.

Ferro looked down at the top of Elisabeta's dark, gleaming head of silky hair. He could feel fear coming off of her in waves. His woman was no mouse. She thought herself closed off to him, terrified that he would think she wasn't worth anything at all to a man as "ferocious" as she thought him. She considered him a true Carpathian warrior and he supposed he was, although he didn't think much about it. He had passed far too many centuries hunting and destroying vampires. It was simply what he did.

She had been little more than a child when Sergey Malinov had taken her from her home and placed her in a cage away from the world. Everyone had thought she was dead. Her brother, Traian, had searched for centuries for her, but no trace of her had been found. No one suspected the Malinovs were in any way connected to her disappearance. Sergey had hidden her from his own brothers. Not even they had suspected she existed.

The little glimpses into the past Ferro had caught in her mind were more than disturbing. They were horrific, and he'd encountered many terrible things in his lifetime. She was so alone and could only rely on the vampire who had taken her prisoner for everything needed to sustain her life. It was no wonder she was terrified to go out into the world.

Right now, as they paused before stepping from the healing grounds into the actual gardens of the compound where the main house, the lake and the smaller homes were located, he knew the wide-open space, without the bars of her cage, made her feel a little sick and disoriented. He pulled her close to his body, beneath his shoulder, to give her more of a feeling of being surrounded. He locked his arm around her waist while they stood there, just looking over the gardens.

"It's really quite beautiful, isn't it?" he asked, to distract her.

He'd never really noticed the beauty of nature, at least not in centuries. He hadn't seen in color until he'd heard her voice, that low moaning beneath the healing grounds when she'd called out to try to keep from having to emerge to be fed. Now, the various shades of color on the leaves intrigued him. The blue of the lake, the surface shimmering silver and frost in the moonlight.

What he really wanted to do was pick her up in his arms, take to the sky and carry her back to the monastery secreted high in the Carpathian Mountains. He would have no problem telling his beautiful, fractured woman what to do and guiding her gently into the world they would create together, but he was her lifemate and he provided what she needed. She needed to know that she had her own power.

After centuries of being enslaved by a vampire and treated so cruelly, Elisabeta would never be like Andor's wife, Lorraine, a very modern woman who Ferro respected and admired but would never be compatible with. He wouldn't want that. He couldn't live with that. He was too protective, but he didn't want Elisabeta to feel fear, not of the world around her and never of him. He would seek every solution possible to figure out a way to help her find what was taken from her—her own power.

Already a plan had formed in his mind. He'd allowed Elisabeta to stay hidden in the healing grounds longer than was strictly necessary while he thought out his strategy to find a way to empower her. In the beginning, he knew the world around her would be too big for her. After being in such a confined space, just being out in the open would be disorienting and frightening. He would have to go slow, introducing her to small portions of the compound rather than all of it at once.

Everyone was eager to meet her, but she couldn't be overwhelmed with too many people. He would have to shield her, although he knew others would misinterpret what he was doing, thinking he was keeping his fragile lifemate from them because he was an ancient and held to the old ways. Opinions didn't bother him in the least. He was ancient and he did hold to the old ways.

Ferro also had a strange foreboding. Elisabeta had been given blood by several of the ancients before he had discovered he was her lifemate. That had been an accident. He had heard her moaning. That soft little sound of distress had opened an entire new world for him, but it had also triggered his very sensitive alarms. There was danger stalking his woman—and it wasn't coming only from the master vampire. He felt a vague threat to her coming from *inside* the compound. From someone he trusted. Someone who should be protecting her. The threat was so vague, almost as if it wasn't fully formed, but it was enough to put him on alert.

Ferro felt a small shudder go through Elisabeta's body and he wrapped his arm around her tighter, pulling her front to his side. "Just look at the beauty surrounding you, *piŋe sarnanak*. Tariq Asenguard found a place to build his world a long time ago. The others have been securing the land around his compound to add to this fortress. We weave safeguards together to keep everyone protected."

She tilted her head up to look at him. "No one will ever be safe from him as long as I'm here. I think you know that." Her voice trembled.

He realized it took great effort for her to speak to him at all, to voice her concern. Just talking was a strain on her when she hadn't done it in so many centuries. She didn't think herself brave, because she didn't understand true courage. Just the fact that she could stand there beside him instead of staying crumpled in a little ball in the earth the way she wanted was a testimony to her mettle.

Ferro brushed his lips on the top of her head in a little caress, trying not to frighten her. He was feeling his way with her. Elisabeta had had no human contact other than when Sergey punished her for infractions.

Now, he was surrounding her with—him. He wanted her to get used to relying on his strength until she found her own. He was determined she would find it, even though, for him, it would mean she would most likely not want to remain with him. He couldn't think too long on that or what it would do to him. That way lay insanity. Elisabeta deserved a chance at life after all the centuries she had endured as a prisoner, and he intended to give her that chance.

"You are now bound to me, Elisabeta. I will build a shield in your mind he cannot get through. He cannot command you as you fear. He cannot use you to spy. You will never give him information on anyone here as you have been so afraid of. I have been alive far longer than he has been, and I am more powerful."

He felt the quick shake of her head, but she didn't speak. In fact, her hand came up to press her fingers against her lips to hold back whatever was on her mind.

He gently captured her wrist and pulled her hand down. "Speak to me, *päläfertiilam*. I wish to know what is on your mind."

Her long lashes fluttered, but she didn't look at him. She shook her head twice before she finally spoke. "Is this a command?"

"If it needs to be."

The tip of her tongue came out to moisten her lips. For some reason he found that little action much more sensual than it should have been. He waited, holding her close to him, staring down at her instead of at the beauty of nature surrounding them. The gardens and lake seemed to pale in comparison to her.

"Everyone always underestimates him. His brothers did. The mages have done so. He has slivers of them in his head now, so that gives him access to their knowledge. He has created spies using human psychic males. He has an army of vampires here in this country and abroad. He planned for centuries so quietly, allowing others to make fun of him and to treat him as if he wasn't bright. He never quite lost all of his emotions because he thought, ahead of time, to take me prisoner. If you underestimate him, the way everyone has, simply because you're older and have more fighting experience, you will lose."

Her voice was so low he could barely hear her, but it was impossible not to catch the notes of fear, of weeping, of utter hopelessness. She didn't believe he would listen to her. Men were arrogant. She had seen so many die over the centuries, men who had been intelligent and had risen to power only to be defeated in the end. Sergey was the last of the Malinovs, the last of the five brothers and the only brother no one, Carpathian and vampire alike, thought would ever be leader, yet he had proved the most powerful of them all.

"I did not live this long by underestimating my enemies, *piŋe sarnanak*," Ferro said gently. "I appreciate that you would worry about me, Elisabeta. Always tell me when you have concerns."

Her lashes lifted again, and this time he found himself staring into her dark, liquid eyes. His stomach did a strange clenching. His groin tightened. It would not be good for either of them if that liquid spilled over onto her high cheekbones. He wouldn't know what to do with tears. He had never dealt with such things.

"You aren't going to punish me for the things I said to you?" Her hand tightened in his shirt as if she were bracing herself. He felt a little shudder go through her body.

"I might have to kiss you now and then," he said. "That is the closest you will get to a punishment and only because it is difficult to resist you."

She blinked up at him as if she couldn't process what he'd said. He took a step out of the healing grounds, forcing her to move with him. That instantly took her mind off what he'd just said and put it back on the world around her. He kept her in the gardens, avoiding the playgrounds where the children might be or the homes where the women often gathered to talk on the front porch. He wanted to just walk with her in the beauty of nature so she could feel air on her face and freedom surrounding her.

Ferro knew she couldn't be out of the ground too long. They were going to have to start their life together in baby steps. So many people were waiting to meet her. Tariq, the owner of the compound—the man the prince of the Carpathian people had appointed to take his place in the United States—wanted Gary Daratrazanoff to examine her for signs that

Sergey had left something of himself behind in her to spy on them. He wanted that done as soon as possible. Although he understood why Tariq felt it was needed, Ferro would rather take Elisabeta and leave than subject her to that.

Ferro was very uneasy subjecting Elisabeta to Gary's examination. Both Carpathians had given Elisabeta blood numerous times. Ferro's soul was tied to Gary's through Andor and Lorraine, a tie that bound them together with several other ancients. Ordinarily, that would have assured that Gary's first loyalties were the brethren, but Gary was second-in-command to Tariq. His lineage, the Daratrazanoff line, had always been second-in-command to the prince. Gary had been sent by the prince to guard Tariq, and that would put his loyalty to Tariq first. Ferro knew the strange, vague threat was emanating from one or both of the two men he should have every reason to trust.

Women were sacred, particularly Carpathian women. Lifemates were held as cherished treasures. In a time when children were so scarce their people were on the very verge of extinction, the last thing a Carpathian male would do was threaten a female, especially a lifemate. Ferro couldn't even say if there was a concrete threat, only that he had the vague impression of one and that it seemed to emanate from a man tied to him soul to soul. Even that he wasn't one hundred percent certain of, but to a man like him, it was enough to make him wary and to want to take his woman and leave.

Her brother, Traian, had arrived with his lifemate, Joie, from the Carpathian Mountains. Traian was very eager to see his sister after so many centuries. Ferro knew it was natural to want to see her, but she was nervous and didn't clearly remember him. Sergey had deliberately stamped out her memories of her past as much as possible. When she tried to remember, there was pain involved, although she didn't associate the emotional and physical pain with the vampire anymore. It was going to be a long road back for her.

The moment Ferro had heard the sound of Elisabeta's voice and knew she was his lifemate, he had taken over her care when he wasn't hunting the enemy. He very gently moved through her mind to examine the fragmented pieces of her memories each rising as he fed her. He hadn't been invasive on purpose, not wanting her to associate him with Sergey. The glimpses he caught of the vampire's punishments had set the predator in him snarling and ready to hunt down Sergey until the task was complete. He knew, right then, Elisabeta needed him more, and he would have to wait to hunt the master vampire.

Elisabeta stumbled as she walked, every step hesitant, like a small child relearning her steps. She didn't take her eyes from the ground and her fingers dug into his arm and rib cage as if those were her lifelines. The ground was very uneven on the path through the gardens, unlike the healing grounds made up of soil rich in minerals smoothed over every day by the Carpathians. Ferro inwardly cursed himself for not considering that Elisabeta wasn't simply having a difficult time walking because she wasn't used to shoes, it was because she hadn't walked.

"*Kislány piŋe sarnanak*, I want you to look into my mind."

She gasped and shook her head, halting, her hands gripping him so hard he thought her fingers might actually meet in the middle of his skin. He very gently pried them open and held both hands to him.

"Only so you can see how to move your feet. It will help you. I will teach you so many things this way. You do not remember, but it is the way Carpathian people instruct one another. We pass information back and forth in this manner. I am your lifemate. You have nothing to fear when your mind touches mine. I will shield you from too much information at once."

Elisabeta pressed her lips tightly together, refusing to meet his eyes again. She kept her lashes stubbornly lowered and her mind as blank as possible. He wasn't a man given to smiling. He had forgotten humor over the centuries, if he'd ever had a sense of humor in the first place. He didn't have a soft side, either, but his little songbird was fast bringing one out in him.

She had a will of iron, which was how she had managed to survive for so many centuries living in the conditions she had. Sergey must have come up against her stubborn nature often, at first beating her into submission, or at least trying to. When that didn't always work, he had switched tactics, trying to starve her. She showed him her willingness to die, so again, he found her weakness, bringing others in front of her, torturing them, until she did as he wanted.

"Tell me why you fear to learn from me this way." He kept his voice as gentle as he was capable, making certain not to in any way frighten her more. Just the way he phrased it made it an order to her, not a simple request.

She hesitated, clearly weighing what a refusal to comply might cost her. He brought both her hands to his mouth and scraped his teeth on her knuckles.

"Do not fear me, Elisabeta. You can choose not to answer me, and nothing will happen to you. I wish to make it easier for you to walk. That is all. There is nothing else. You will not learn anything else of me by touching your mind to mine. Not of my past, not of what I intend for us in the future. We are going slowly. I want only to help you with this one simple task. If you are not yet ready for this, you have only to say so."

While he spoke to her, he rubbed his chin back and forth across her knuckles, scraping her sensitive skin with the shadow on his jaw just the way his teeth had. Intimate. Provocative. Tying the two of them together in a way he'd never known—in a way she had never known. It was a small thing, but it felt huge. She didn't pull her hands away and he didn't want her to. He wanted those small, slender fingers to remain in his, keeping a physical contact between them while she decided what she was going to do.

Her lashes fluttered again, drawing his attention to them, and his groin tightened. She could move him with just the smallest feminine gesture. "I do not know how to make choices. They confuse me."

"Yet when I give you a command, you choose to disobey me." He kept his tone mild, without reprimand.

Faint color stole into her cheeks. She touched the tip of her tongue to her lip again and he wanted to groan. That was clearly a nervous habit. She had quite a few of them, each more endearing to him than the next—and maybe a little sexy. He had never thought in sexual terms, and it was the last thing he needed to be thinking about right then.

"Mind-to-mind contact can be . . . intimate. Or ugly. Or really pain-ful. Three things that make it very scary to try."

He brought her hands to his chest. "You are my lifemate, Elisabeta. I am sworn to see to your happiness and protection. Mind-to-mind may feel intimate between us because it is supposed to. I will shield you from any ugliness you might find in my past, and touching my mind, you will never feel pain." He waited, wanting her to make up her mind.

The touch was tentative at first, so light he barely felt it. She brushed against his mind and retreated, running, almost like a child might. He didn't go after her or reprimand her. He simply waited, sliding his arm around her back when he felt her sway. Standing was becoming difficult for her. He sank to the ground, taking her with him, sitting her on his lap in the midst of Tariq's wild garden.

All around them, plants rose up toward the sky, leaves looking various shades of dark green and silver. The moon slipped in and out of the gray clouds as the wind pushed them across the sky. Elisabeta shivered and curled into the warmth of his body, as if she couldn't control her own body heat—something every Carpathian learned to do as a child. Had that fundamental ability been taken from her as well? It would be like Sergey, giving him one more thing to hold over her head. If she didn't cooperate with him, he could make her freezing cold, or so hot she would be burning.

"I've got you, *piŋe sarnanak*." He began to hum softly.

He didn't like to sing in front of others, but he could soothe with his voice. When things in the monastery became too difficult for one of the brothers, he would sometimes use his voice to calm them, although he never acted as if that was what he was doing. He simply would pace away and sing softly as if to himself, just as he did now. He hummed at first, and then imitated the rain. He was good at pouring various sounds into music. He heard music in all things nature and re-created that for her, waiting for her to relax in his arms.

It took a few minutes for Elisabeta to settle. She was really afraid. He let himself slip into her mind, not far. He never went too far, which went against everything he was. His personality demanded he take what was his. He was dominant by nature. His word was never questioned. He was a law unto himself. He hadn't sworn allegiance to the present prince of the Carpathian people, nor had he sworn allegiance to Tariq Asenguard. He went his own way and he expected his woman, his lifemate, to go his way with him. He would need that.

He sighed as he rocked Elisabeta gently to the tune of the rain in his mind. There was sorrow in his song. He couldn't help that. He felt emotions now, when for so long he hadn't. This woman had become the center of his world so fast. Lifemate. For so long she held the other half of his soul. She had guarded it from Sergey at a great cost to herself. The vampire had tried every way possible to take it from her. Ferro didn't have to get into her mind to see; he knew from the scars on her body and more in her mind. The utter terror carved so deep in her that he knew it would always be ingrained in her.

Had Sergey managed to wrest his soul from Elisabeta, the vampire would have controlled Ferro, made him a servant, used him ruthlessly to prey upon the Carpathian people. Ferro was a skilled hunter; a legendary, feared hunter. Sergey hadn't known who Elisabeta's lifemate was, but had he managed to take his soul from her and control Ferro, he would have had a weapon even the ancient hunters would have had difficulty destroying.

Elisabeta touched his mind again, and this time he felt that light feminine touch as much more than a tentative, fearful brush. Elisabeta felt his sorrow and she reached for him the way a lifemate instinctively would. The way a woman would. Gentle. Caring. Soothing. Questioning. He felt her filling the emptiness of those lonely spaces he'd revealed to her inadvertently when he'd started his song for her.

He had his shields up so there was no way for her to see into his past, all those kills, the battles with master vampires, the mortal wounds that should have taken his life so many times. He gave her none of that, or the way humans and Carpathians alike shrank from him in fear. He didn't give her the battle he fought with the whispers of temptation to feel something after so many centuries of not feeling, or when those whispers stopped and he had nothing at all—the terrible emptiness that followed and the need to sequester himself in the monastery to protect everyone from him. Instead, he gave her the instructions on how to walk and how much he loved being with her, that his intent was to protect her from any harm.

Elisabeta absorbed the information the way a Carpathian did, telepathically, almost automatically, her brain tuning itself to his, but her hands came up to his head so gently, it felt like her palms were the lightest of butterflies sliding up from his jaw to frame his face. His breath caught in his throat.

"Tell me why you feel such sorrow."

Her eyes were looking straight into his for the very first time. Straight into his. He swore he was falling into a cool, dark pool, a deep well. Her soul. He was her lifemate and that demanded honesty. Either he told the truth or he refused to answer.

"I am not the man I once was, *minan piŋe sarnanak*. Like you, the centuries and circumstances have changed me, and not for the better, I fear. You are a beautiful, deserving woman." He couldn't help pushing his fingers deep into the thickness of her hair. "I am not so deserving. For you, I wish that were not so."

He couldn't look at her any longer. She was too innocent for a man like him. Innocence had nothing to do with sex and everything to do with the kind of man he was. She belonged with the women in Tariq Asenguard's compound. They were good women, if not a little beyond his understanding.

There was Lorraine, the one he called *sisar*—sister. She was lifemate to one of his brethren, Andor, from the monastery. She had done what no woman, Carpathian let alone human—which she had been at the time— had ever done or thought to do. She had bound her soul to Andor's brethren in order to save his life. If they died, she died. If they turned vampire, they would be able to find her and destroy her. He doubted if any other women would have had that kind of courage—to tie themselves to the unknown on the chance that they could call their lifemate back from the other world.

Julija was the only friend Elisabeta had that Ferro knew of. The little mage had risked her life, allowing herself to be captured by Sergey in order to try to free Elisabeta. Ultimately, she was the one to bring Elisabeta to the Carpathians' attention, allowing her to be rescued. Julija was a strong woman and lifemate to Isai, another one of his brethren from the monastery. Julija held great power and she went her own way in life.

The two women were modern-day examples of what Ferro knew Elisabeta would be comparing herself to and most likely aspiring to be. While he wanted that self-confidence for her, he knew he was not a man who would be compatible with either Julija or Lorraine, as much as he might respect them.

The way her mind moved in his was delicate, feminine, wholly beautiful, a whisper of a touch rather than a bold demand. It was unexpected, her soft, womanly presence that seemed to fill every lonely place in his mind. The experience of her sharing his mind was beyond intimate. He had spent centuries alone, lost in that gray void of nothing.

She brought life to him. Scent. He could inhale and bring her into his lungs. He would know her anywhere. Her scent was distinct. Exotic and rare. She had a faint fragrance of orange, the Italian bergamot he had encountered but never thought about. The orange held a note of lime, and the two citrus fragrances mixed with rare camellias, adding just a touch of spice to the blend. The scents mixed with sandalwood and vetiver, an Indian grass root. For Ferro, that scent would always be associated with Elisabeta.

Color. She brought vivid, bright color into a world of gray. He hadn't known there were so many shades of green. Or blue. Just looking at her hair, that dark silk, shining in the moonlight, he could see so many colors, and she had given him that. The garden, the lake, the sky, the birds and even the ground itself. She had made him see the world again in an entirely different light.

Touch. He had never allowed anyone to touch him unless he planned to use them for sustenance, or he planned to kill them. Elisabeta showed him that touch could be something different, something warm and gentle. Tender even. Touch could mean so many things other than the precursor of death. Then, there was the feel of her skin, like the finest satin.

Her hair, like silk. In a very short amount of time he had learned the beauty of touching.

Sound. Her voice was like music to him. Soft. Intimate. Pouring over him like a gentle summer breeze. When she spoke, her voice was pleasing, moving through him, equally as effective as the touch of her fingers on his skin. That soft sound was that potent. He could almost feel the notes dancing over him, brushing his skin intimately, first there and then here, stroking and caressing, one moment soothing him, the next making him want to go up in flames.

Ferro had lived centuries, much longer than most, and yet he had not tasted many things. Blood was blood. One needed it to survive. There was no taste. No rush. Nothing whatsoever other than when he was wounded and starving that made him crave or need more blood. Until he had tasted his lifemate's blood. It was exquisite. Almost beyond comprehension. He could barely make himself stop feeding once he'd started. Her taste was some kind of aphrodisiac, something beyond description he would always crave. He thought about it, and the taste would come to him, vivid in his memory and then in his mouth.

"I do not like you feeling sad . . . Ferro." She stumbled a little over using his name but was brave enough to say it. "We are both changed. You have been very kind to me, more than I imagined anyone would ever be. I have never had a rising such as this one. For that I have to thank you."

The pads of her fingers swept over his jaw, her touch light, sending ripples of heat moving through his veins. Her voice was very sincere. He had merely taken her across the healing grounds and into the gardens. The kindness he had shown her was so basic that he wanted to weep for what little she expected. She was more concerned with his sorrow than what she was feeling. In fact, she was completely focused on him now, all thoughts of herself and her fears were gone. She had immersed herself completely in him, in an attempt to find a way to ease his sadness.

Carpathian healers shed their bodies to become wholly spirit, losing all ego, all sense of self, in order to heal. In a sense, Elisabeta, while retaining her body, did something very similar. She lost all ego, all sense of herself, and thought only of Ferro, moving gently through his mind, seeking ways to brighten his spirit.

Those gentle fingers of hers on his jaw, stroking heat into his veins, wreaked havoc with his emotions, with his physical control, when for centuries he had always been completely disciplined. Abruptly, he rose, taking her with him, setting her onto her feet, giving his body some respite, a little shocked that he would need that.

"I want to show you our home, *minan piŋe sarnanak*. Hopefully it will be a place of solace and happiness for you. It does not have bars on the windows or doors, and you can walk out of it when you wish, but if I am not with you, I prefer that you let me know when you wish to leave the safety of the walls. I have woven strong safeguards into it so the vampire and his puppets cannot penetrate from any direction in his attempts to get to you. If you choose to visit your friends, as you will naturally wish to do, if you let me know, I can safeguard you."

That was difficult for him. Much more so than he had thought it would be. He wanted her to have freedom. He told himself that a million times. She needed to know she wasn't a prisoner. He never wanted her to feel that way with him. He wanted her to feel cherished. Treasured. Always. But he wasn't the type of man to have his woman casually leave a place of safety when she was in danger. Not at her preference. Not on a whim. Not when he could so easily command her to stay. Her friends could visit her there if she wanted to see them.

It made no sense to him to leave such a dangerous decision in anyone's hands but his own. He was the one who would have to fight Sergey Malinov. He would not use his lifemate as the bait to draw the master vampire to him. He would choose the time and the place of the battle. It would not be where there were children around. Or women. Or his woman. Not when he had so much to lose.

"Have I angered you?" Elisabeta asked.

Ferro realized he was striding along the path and immediately shortened his steps to accommodate her. "No, Elisabeta, I was thinking of you leaving the house and what that might entail."

She gave a quick shake of her head. "Please do not ask me to do such a thing, even to see Julija, not without you. I know I am not capable of that."

Not only did her voice tremble, but so did her entire body. That shamed him. Ferro didn't want that for her. He didn't want her so frightened she was nearly paralyzed with terror at the mere thought of venturing out on her own. He wrapped his arm around her and pulled her thin, shivering form under his shoulder for protection.

"Elisabeta, I have told you that you do not have to do anything that is frightening to you. I do not intend to leave you alone unless it is strictly necessary. In that event, I will put you in the ground where you will sleep, or I will leave you with Julija or someone you feel very safe with. You are not expected to entertain or go off on your own at any time. In fact, I would not like it." Ferro felt the instant relief flooding her mind.

He had always been a decisive person. He knew exactly how to conduct a battle. He avoided humans and Carpathians alike. He was direct when he wanted something and commanded others, expecting instant compliance with his orders. He didn't bother with niceties. He had no need and no time for such things. Now, with Elisabeta, he was feeling his way, completely at odds with not only his own personality but his own character and needs.

He stroked a caress down the back of her head as they stepped out of the protection of the gardens into the open. Elisabeta gasped aloud, stopped and actually turned to flee. The yard ahead of them seemed to be filled with people when there was only Isai Florea and his lifemate, Julija, standing on the front porch of a little Victorian replica of the main mansion, talking with Emeline and Dragomir Kozel. Both Dragomir and Isai were Ferro's brethren from the monastery, as was Andor, the third male who was standing on the stairs of the little Victorian house with his lifemate, Lorraine.

Ferro caught Elisabeta around the waist and pulled her tight against him. She moaned and buried her face against his ribs. *I can't. Too many. Too many. Do not ask me to do this. It is too big. Too much. Hurts my eyes. My stomach. I can't. I can't do this.*

She repeated the chant, a mantra in her mind, in his, over and over until he realized she didn't know he could hear her. He felt her tears.

Heard them in her voice. They dripped in her mind, yet his clothes, his skin, remained dry.

Ferro tried to assess what was happening to her, all the while breathing calmly for both of them. His heart remained steady. He pried her fingers off his shirt and placed her palm over his heart so she could follow the rhythm.

Breathe with me, sívamet. I am with you. We do this together. You do not have to speak. You do not have to look at them. I stand in front of you at all times. I will simply tell them I do not allow you to speak to others yet. We are new and you are getting used to a new master. A small well of humor he didn't know he had welled up at the thought of the modern women hearing him state that. He didn't know Emeline and Julija very well, but he was very familiar with Lorraine and her ultra-forward thinking. Her head might explode.

I do not want this woman's head to explode. This does not seem kind.

It will not literally explode, Elisabeta. She will not like me referring to myself as your master. Nor will she like me saying you cannot talk to anyone else but me.

Why? Elisabeta tipped her head up to look at him curiously, her dark eyes roving over his face as if he were her anchor.

Ferro couldn't help himself. He bent his head and brushed her lips with his. It was the briefest of contacts, but her lips were quivering, just that little bit, just enough to break his heart, and he wanted to reassure her he would take care of her.

"Did you notice how well you were able to walk? I did not feel you stumble once. You learned simply by looking into my mind and taking what you needed from me. Just keep putting your trust in me, Elisabeta. I know that is difficult when you have had no reason for centuries to have faith in anyone, but if you keep looking to me, I give you my word, I will not let you down. Lifemates cannot deceive one another. You can hear lies if you listen for them."

She didn't answer him, but her body felt as if it might shake apart any moment.

"Tell me what you fear the most. What is the worst of what is happening to you right this moment, *piŋe sarnanak*?" He phrased the question as a command because she responded and was most comfortable with an outright order to answer. She didn't seem to like room for making her own decisions under stress.

She moistened her lips, glanced around her and then quickly buried her face again in his ribs. "It is too much. Too big."

He was in her head, careful to keep his touch light so she didn't feel as if he was being intrusive. Her mind was in chaos and he could hear her weeping. At once he began to set that sound to the beats of rain in their song, the one he'd composed for her. The one he'd used to draw her from the safety of the earth's embrace.

"Don't look around you as I take you to our home, Elisabeta. We will cross the open space, but you can anchor yourself in my mind. I can carry you if you prefer." He hadn't wanted to embarrass her, but she wasn't a modern woman who would worry about what others thought of her.

"Why are all those people staring at me?"

"They are my brethren. Julija has been waiting to see you." He felt her instant withdrawal and then the self-loathing. "You are not a coward. You have already done far more than I expected this rising. They can wait until you are settled."

"I don't want any of them to feel as if I am rejecting them, especially Julija. She has gotten me through so much. Without her I wouldn't have made it," Elisabeta confessed in a small voice. She still kept her face tucked against his chest to keep from looking at the open spaces around them.

"I will tell them you are not ready yet and I have forbidden any contact at this time."

At that, she pulled her head free from his shirt and looked up at him, her eyes searching his. He could see a breathless kind of hope on her face. Again, he couldn't stop himself. He bent his head and brushed his lips over each eyelid before he lifted her in his arms, cradling her close to him.

I am taking Elisabeta to our home. She will not be visiting at this time.

He sent the decree on the pathway forged between the monastery brethren rather than the common Carpathian pathway. Sergey Malinov had once been a Carpathian and he would have access to that pathway. If, for some reason, there was a breach in their safeguards, there would be no chance that the master vampire would know Elisabeta had risen from the healing grounds.

The women have been waiting for some time to speak with your lifemate, Ferro, Isai said. There was no inflection in his voice. Not even one of protest.

Ferro. Lorraine had no problems objecting. *You can't keep her to yourself. This isn't the Neanderthal days.*

Ferro didn't bother to answer. He gathered his lifemate into his arms and took to the sky. She muffled a startled cry and clutched his shirt, her face once more buried tight against his chest.

Did the vampire transport you through the air? He must have had you fly.

No. I would wake up in new places.

Ferro was not used to the emotion gathering in the pit of his belly, a dark ugly rage that simmered like an explosive volcano slowly gathering force. He breathed through it and let it go. Rage had no place in his life. Malinov was going to pay for the crimes he'd committed against the Carpathian people, and against Ferro's lifemate, but his death would come from a place of justice as Ferro had been delivering for centuries. There was no other way.

He took his lifemate to the house his brethren had purchased for him, a property that had been added to the growing acreage of the protected compound. The site was nestled in between Isai and Julija's property and Andor and Lorraine's land. The hills were gently rolling and the land had groves of trees on it and, more importantly, water that added to the colors of all the various plants scattered around the property.

The house had been built by a famous architect, at least that was what Andor had told him, a man whose vision was to keep the landscape so pristine that the house would be difficult to see until one actually walked up to it. Andor and Lorraine had also bought property with a home designed by the same man. Ferro had viewed the property and home with an eye toward defense, escape and the ability to get to the ground undetected from anywhere above the house.

Now, as he brought his lifemate to the Spanish-looking home, he thought he should have consulted with the women to see if the house met with their standards. Elisabeta would entertain her friends there, make a life there. She might sleep beneath the master bedroom, but she would live within those walls. He set her feet very gently on the wide verandah, his hands on her waist to steady her.

3

There's light in the darkness, waiting to be seen;
Just as I wait for you, a king for his queen.

Open your eyes, *piŋe sarnanak*," Ferro said in his soft, command-ing voice.

Elisabeta took a deep breath and forced herself to obey. She liked his voice, and no matter how afraid she was of her new life and the huge terrifying changes, so far, although things had been overwhelming and emotional, they had all been good. She loved that he called her "little songbird" or, even better, "his little songbird." Those variations created a strange new feeling in her, an affection that seemed to be growing the more she was with him.

She found herself looking at a tall massive door to a house. Ferro stood directly behind her, his hands at her waist, holding her close to him. She was grateful for his presence. She had no idea why they were standing on that cool, wide verandah, but suddenly her heart was beginning to ac-celerate again. Something new. Something she was going to have to learn.

"Ferro." She whispered his name in a kind of protest.

"No one is here. Just the two of us."

"It is too big." It was. The door was gigantic. For Ferro it wasn't, be-cause he was a big man. His shoulders were wide, and he would go through that door so easily, but she was thin and felt insignificant. The door was tall and wide and seemed enormous to her. What could it possibly lead to?

"This will be our home. You will be mistress here. Not a prisoner, Elisabeta, but mistress."

Already she was shaking her head. She knew nothing of taking charge of a house. She couldn't possibly entertain his friends. Or clean a place that size. How did one know what to do? When she was little, did she live in a house? She tried to remember, and immediately her head exploded with such pain it nearly drove her to her knees. She knew better than to cry out, but both hands flew to her head and she hunched in on herself.

Ferro instantly shielded her, taking the pain away and soothing her mind. "The vampire placed a block on your memories so the moment you try to access anything to do with your family or childhood, you experience pain," he explained.

She had come to realize that some centuries earlier, but that hadn't stopped the occasional times when, unbidden, she reached out to try to remember something important to her.

Ferro wrapped one arm around her shoulders, pulling her back to his front. "He took so much from you, Elisabeta. We will get it all back, but you need to be patient with yourself. He had you for centuries. This process will take time. Do not judge yourself so harshly. This house is merely that at the moment—a house."

"But you want it to be a home for you." She pressed her lips together and then tried again. "For us."

"I lived in a monastery, a shelter of rocks in the Carpathian Mountains shrouded by the mists. This place we will claim in small increments, one room at a time. As for caring for it, just as you learned about walking and you will learn about dressing yourself, you will learn to clean each room, taking the information from my mind, or Julija's mind. Whoever you are most comfortable learning from."

He was so matter-of-fact. So calm. Ferro never seemed in a hurry or in the least bothered by having to reassure her constantly. He simply provided a solution in his gentle voice.

"You will make it a home for us. I have no doubt about that. I have every faith in you. There is no time period that you must accomplish these tasks in. This is our journey together and we will make it ours as slow and as leisurely as we want. We both have had centuries of dancing to others' tunes. This is our time and our song. I do not want anyone to dictate to us what we should do or when or how we should do it. We do not even have to open that door if you want to just make the verandah all we explore for this rising."

He meant it. There was no lie in his voice. He didn't seem to mind in the least standing there staring at the door while behind them was perhaps a view of nature. She didn't know because she was too afraid of wide-open spaces. That made her feel like such a coward.

He bent his head and, when he did, his thick salt-and-pepper hair slid over the side of her neck, making her shiver with awareness. His hair was very long and thick, tied with a cord, but it felt soft against her skin and the slide along her neck was actually sensuous. His breath was warm in her ear when he spoke.

"You are no coward and I do not want you to think this of yourself again, Elisabeta. This does not please me. I have told you: I find you brave to face an entire new world the way you are doing. I am your lifemate and my opinion of you should matter."

Instantly Elisabeta looked over her shoulder at him, worried that she'd upset him. "Your opinion really does matter to me, Ferro, that is why I worry so much that I cannot do the things I think I should be able to do." She took a deep breath. "I want to go inside." She realized she had dug her nails into his arm. "I really do."

He waved his hand at the tall door. "If it is too much for you, just tell me and we will find the smallest room in the house and start there. I imagine the room we are going into will be the largest because it would be the room company would come into. At least, in the houses I've stepped into, that is the way the layout has been."

Elisabeta stared into the cool darkness beyond the open doorway and tried not to hyperventilate. She told herself it was no different than entering a cave, or even going underground. There were no lights on. It was dark inside and she could feel the cool air coming out of the interior. Ferro didn't try to hurry her. He made no move at all, just kept his arm locked around her shoulders and his front supporting her back.

There was a part of her that knew she was far too dependent on him. Julija wouldn't approve of that. She had talked to her about a new start, about being her own person, standing on her own two feet, and already she was a failure. She didn't want to be without Ferro's support. Not without his strong hands and his tall, warrior-like demeanor that gave her confidence, his body that gave her strength and his voice that directed her, by turns gentle and commanding. She needed those things from him as much as she wanted them.

A shocking bite of pain flashed through her and then eased into something darkly erotic, a soothing blend of moist heat and rasping velvet. She gasped, realizing Ferro had nipped her neck right over her pulse and then pulled the injured spot into his mouth and sucked gently, his tongue stroking little caresses. He lifted his head, but as he did, his lips brushed several little kisses over the spot.

"Julija does not dictate to you what you are to be as a woman, *minan piŋe sarnanak*, any more than I should dictate this to you. You will find your own way in time. If you prefer my company and support and I do not object, and in fact like it, then it is no one's business. Our relationship is ours alone."

It wasn't the first time he had said this to her, and she knew it wouldn't be the last. His advice had to sink in and take hold. She had to believe she was really free to choose her own way. Her brain refused to believe, and anytime there was a choice to be made, she shut down and became paralyzed with fear. Ferro didn't seem to mind. He showed endless patience with her.

"Thank you." She took a deep breath and slid her hand along his very muscular forearm down to his wrist, as if that could give her the necessary strength to take the step toward the door, and maybe it did. She forced one foot in front of the other. She expected him to let her go, and he did, although he turned his hand and caught hers in a tight grip, so they were still connected.

"I will go in first and you stay right behind me," Ferro said.

The relief she felt was so tremendous that for a moment her legs felt rubbery. She dropped back by a couple of steps, allowing his larger frame to step in front of her. She kept her head down, not daring to look around her for fear of seeing too much and getting dizzier than she already was.

"Once inside, if the room is too big and you want to keep moving to a smaller one, you tell me and we will do so, otherwise we will stop there, sit down and just take small pieces of the room to look at and familiarize ourselves with. I want to attempt to remove the vampire's barrier on your memories."

Elisabeta reacted, both with fear and with hope, tightening her fingers in his, knowing he was in her mind, although his touch was so light she could barely feel him there.

"*Sívamet*, do not let your hope grow too much." His voice was very gentle. "After so many centuries of not remembering, you most likely will not be able to on your own. Your brother, Traian, is here with his lifemate, Joie. He did search centuries for you, refusing to give up when everyone else did. He will return as many memories to you as he is able."

She didn't want to think too much on what her brother would expect of her and how much she would disappoint him. Instead she considered that it was twice now that Ferro had called her *sívamet*. His heart. An exact translation was "my heart." For some reason that made her stomach do a slow-rolling pitch and then continue into a complete somersault. He was slowly stealing her heart when she thought she no longer possessed one. She thought Sergey had chopped her heart into little pieces and removed them from her one by one. He had taken her trust and stomped that into those pieces and then strewn them across the ground like so much trash because he had no use for such things. Somehow, Ferro was finding them. She didn't know how he could do that. Just that he could frightened her more than everything else combined.

"Sergey is a vampire, Elisabeta, but in his own twisted way, he felt something for you. You provided him with some emotion, which is why he survived so many years when others completely failed. He needed your heart, *sívamet*, and your ability to allow him to feel if just a little emotion, twisted and obsessed as it was."

She kept her eyes closed, one hand in his, the other fisted in the back of his shirt, matching her steps to his as they entered the house. It was cool inside, and she pretended it was just another cave. Another cage. She wasn't lost, and a monster's puppet with wicked serrated teeth wasn't going to jump out at her and tear at her flesh and try to devour her alive while her master laughed in amusement.

Abruptly, Ferro spun around and swept her into his arms. "Elisabeta, you are breaking my heart. Why would this vampire treat you so cruelly to make you so frightened to enter a new dwelling? Your mind is consumed with terror. I feel every one of your senses flaring out, seeking his puppets, certain they will set upon you at any moment to try to rip as much flesh off you as possible before he calls them off. Why does he do this to you?"

She pressed her forehead to his chest, refusing to meet his eyes. Refusing to answer.

Ferro caught her chin and forced her head up so that she was looking into glittering iron-colored eyes. Those eyes had gone hard and scary. "He did this too many times. I command you to answer me."

Elisabeta touched her tongue to her suddenly dry lips. "I refused to give him access to your soul. I told him I would suicide first. He allowed his puppets to consume children and I carried out my threat. He was barely able to save me that time. Twice more he did things to others I couldn't tolerate, and I suicided. After that, he only punished me. I knew you would survive if I died. I would be reborn with your half of our soul intact, but if he was able to take it from me, you could be made his servant, and he would have been able to corrupt or harm you in other ways. I couldn't take the chance."

She rushed the confession, ashamed that she couldn't think of any other solution than to suicide when she had been told the Carpathian hunters in the monastery had endured for centuries and locked themselves away because they hadn't believed in meeting the dawn and giving up on their lifemates. That was only showing him once again that she was a . . .

"*Do not.*" He hissed the command at her in obvious displeasure. "If you persist in thinking you are a coward, I will insist on punishing you, Elisabeta, and I promised myself I would not frighten you. Still, it is there in your mind. I see the image as clear as day. You continue to view your-self as a coward in spite of my dictates to you. This is a clear rule I have set for you. One of the very few I have given you."

She tried to duck her head, but his hand under her chin refused to budge. It was true. He hadn't really given her too many rules. That was probably part of the problem she was experiencing. She needed clear lines at all times. She couldn't help trembling a little, wondering what her punishment was going to be. Ferro was a very big man and extremely strong.

The pad of his thumb slid gently over her bottom lip twice. "I told you what your punishment would be, *piŋe sarnanak*. Surely you listened to me."

Panic rose. What had he said? Had she blocked it out because it was so terrible, she couldn't face it? Over the centuries, Sergey had subjected her to so many punishments, she was fairly certain she had managed to encounter all of the nonlethal ones.

Ferro bent his head toward her, a faint smile in his eyes. "I do not think *minan piŋe sarnanak* listened at all," he murmured, not sounding angry.

He sounded velvet soft. Like faint paint strokes brushing gently over her mind. Something else she couldn't identify, something that turned her inside out. His lips brushed hers with such exquisite gentleness her heart turned over. Everything else in her froze. He kissed the corner of her mouth and then his teeth tugged at her lower lip and every nerve ending in her body leapt to life. She had never been so aware of herself as a woman. Her breasts ached and felt swollen and hot. Her nipples tingled and felt like hard pebbles. Lower, between her legs, she went damp and her sex clenched.

"Do not think you are a coward, Elisabeta. You are a very courageous woman. You are *my* woman. I am one of the most feared hunters on the planet. You are my lifemate for a reason. You are *hän ku vigyáz sívamet és sielamet*, keeper of my heart and soul, and you did just that. You guarded both for centuries under the worst of circumstances. I want you to remove my shirt, *piŋe sarnanak*. I have something to show you. Something that is for you alone."

He stepped back and she actually felt the loss of both his strength and heat. Her hands went to the buttons, little squares she recognized as old-fashioned. Her lifemate hadn't caught up with the times in his clothing as he had with hers. She pushed the little squares through the buttonholes and the edges of the material fell open so that he could shrug off the shirt. She took it automatically, rather than allowing it to fall to the floor.

He had tattoos scarred into his body, inked in the ancient language. He turned so she could read what he had so painstakingly put into his skin when Carpathians rarely scarred.

Olen wäkeva kuntankért. Staying strong for our people.

Olen wäkeva pita belső kulymet. Staying strong to keep the demon inside.

Olen wäkeva—félért ku vigyázak. Staying strong for her.

Hängemért. Only her.

Elisabeta read the lines several times, wanting—no—needing to commit them to memory. Seeing the words inked into his skin, knowing he had to have had them done repeatedly in order for the scars to actually take effect, nearly brought her to her knees. *Staying strong for her.* She had tried to stay strong for him. It was the only thing she had held out for. The only thing she had managed to keep from Sergey—Ferro's soul. His light. She had that in her keeping and she had steadfastly refused to give it up no matter what he had done to her or to others.

Ferro slid into his shirt easily, and turned back to her, standing still, as if waiting for her to button it for him. Elisabeta did so with shaking fingers.

"That is the creed of our brethren, our code," he said, as she slowly slid each button through the buttonhole. "It is what we sometimes chanted through the nights to keep ourselves from stepping off the path and losing honor. Always, our lifemates saved us. You saved me many times, Elisabeta, in my darkest hours. So many times through the centuries, I can't even tell you. Never say to me, or to yourself, that you are a coward."

She dared to look up at his glittering eyes. She'd never seen eyes so piercing, as if they could look right through her and see right into her—and she knew he could. He was in her mind as all lifemates could be. He was polite about it, gentle, but he was there, providing a shield because both of them knew Sergey was going to strike at her soon. He would know she had risen and he would insist she answer him.

Elisabeta shuddered at the mere thought of Sergey using her to bring down the compound and killing anyone there—especially the children.

"We will take care of that first. Come sit with me, here in this room. Do not try to look beyond this small area. I do not want you overwhelmed. This room is where our visitors will eventually come to see you. Julija and perhaps Lorraine."

Lorraine was someone he really admired and wanted her to get to know. He thought of Lorraine as a sister. She was the closest thing he had to one. Elisabeta made up her mind that she would not only get to know Lorraine, but for Ferro, she would do her best to establish a good relationship with the woman.

Ferro took her hand and again walked in front of her, allowing her to keep her eyes closed in the large room. "You do not have to have a relationship with anyone, *piŋe sarnanak*, not for me. I am happy only with you. Others do not matter so much to me. I wish them in your life in order for you to be happy. If we left this place and went somewhere alone together, it would suit me just fine. I have no need of excess company."

He sank into a large chair and pulled her onto his lap. One hand forced her head to his chest, tucking her face against him. "I am going to examine your mind and see what the master vampire has left behind that allows him a gateway, a path to reach you."

"Centuries," she whispered, appreciating that he rarely called the vampire by name. That would have frightened her more. Naming him would make her feel as if it gave the vampire even more power over her. "He had me for centuries. He knows my mind. He can find me anywhere."

Ferro brushed a kiss on top of her head and then brought his hand down the back of her skull in a long caress, his strong fingers massaging her scalp as he did so. "Perhaps that is so, Elisabeta. But you have a lifemate, so you are changed. Your mind is changed. Your life is changed. You have accepted my claim on you and our soul is once more fully formed back together. I am older and more experienced than he expects his opponent to be. He will find it much more difficult to take on your lifemate."

Elisabeta didn't want her lifemate to have to take on a master vampire's wrath. Sergey would never give her up and he had an army at his disposal. She knew his cruelty. Ferro had proven to be a kind man. She wasn't certain if he could match Sergey's ferocity in battle and she didn't want anything to happen to him.

Ferro didn't try to reassure her, nor did he reprimand her for not believing in him. He didn't seem to have any kind of ego at all. She felt him moving in her mind, a more forceful presence than he had been, but not necessarily one that was taking her over. He was still gentle, but she felt him searching, making certain Sergey hadn't left anything of himself behind. She knew mages could take small slivers of themselves and plant them in others to use them as spies. Some vampires had learned how to do the same. Sergey held the dark mage, Xavier, within him as well as his brothers. That gave him access to their knowledge, although, on his own, Sergey had never accessed those slivers.

"I am going to build a shield in your mind that he cannot penetrate. If by some miracle he managed to slip past all the safeguards woven by the warriors here as well as my brethren, he will not be able to get to you."

She moistened her lips. She had to confess to him. "When I was in the healing grounds, before you came to me, he spoke to me every rising. He wouldn't stop. I couldn't make him stop. He told me to come to him or he would kill everyone harboring me."

Silence met her disclosure. His body didn't change in the least. He didn't stiffen. His breathing didn't change in the least, his hands didn't tighten on her, but she was very tuned to him and she knew he definitely hadn't expected the revelation.

Ferro's hands came up to her hair again, stroking those gentle caresses, as if they not only soothed her but, in a way, brought him a type of peace as well. "That changes things a bit, *sívamet*. Anything to do with this vampire, or any of his suspected servants, you are to tell me immediately." He poured command into his voice. "*Immediately*. First thing."

"I'm sorry." Clearly that oversight had been a mistake. She hadn't wanted to think about Sergey let alone talk about him. She detested that she hadn't said anything to Ferro. She had told Julija sometime earlier, when they had spoken in secret, but since then, she hadn't communicated with anyone. Now she felt guilty and very distressed, almost as if by not telling Ferro, she had betrayed him in some way.

"There is no need to be upset. I did not think there was a possibility so I did not ask you or give you an order. That is my failing, not yours." He was silent again. "You disclosed this information to Julija?"

Again, there was no inflection in his voice, but she had the feeling he condemned her friend for not telling him.

"She was sworn to secrecy. I spoke to her only on the condition that she never let anyone know I was communicating with her."

"This was a matter of your safety."

There was no threat in his voice. No understanding, either. A shiver went down her spine and she was uncertain why. She was suddenly very, very uncomfortable and a little afraid, not for herself but for her friend.

"What did the vampire say to you?"

Ferro's arms slipped around her body, holding her closer to him when she shivered almost uncontrollably. She couldn't stop the trembling. She never should have told him about Julija, although it hadn't occurred to her to keep anything from her lifemate.

"He said to come to him or he would kill everyone. He repeated it over and over each time I was awakened to feed. I didn't want to open my eyes and rise even to get blood. It was terrifying to hear the things he said, and his pull was very strong. I was so afraid all the time. I didn't know what was expected of me. And I knew there were children close. He was especially cruel to children."

"What stopped his calling to you?"

"You, I think. Once you began sleeping close to me, I couldn't hear his voice anymore."

Again, there was a small silence while his hand moved in her hair and his arm remained locked around her, giving her strength. "That's interesting," he said finally. "I wove safeguards around the two of us, but you had safeguards around you at all times. I wonder what the difference was. Or is. I have to speak with Tariq about this."

Her heart jumped. Did that mean he was going to leave her? Or would she have to go with him to face the unknown leader of the compound where the children were protected and she'd brought danger? There was no way he couldn't hear her heart pounding. His hand slipped from her hair to massage the nape of her neck.

"Elisabeta, you have to have faith that I am going to take care of you. I will send for Tariq and also Julija and her lifemate, Isai, one of my brethren. Julija will be able to give us a clear timeline. It is necessary because with all the safeguards woven by so many of us, the vampire should not have been able to get through to you. We need to know when he was able to do so and why, for the safety of everyone here." His fingers kept moving on the nape of her neck, feeling like magic. "You do understand that, right? And you know that I will not allow anything to happen to you."

The last was a statement. It was difficult not to believe him. She had been lied to so much that she had stopped believing anything, but in a short period of time Ferro had managed to overcome every defense she had. He had shown her kindness when no one in her life that she could remember had, other than Julija.

Tentatively, because she was still afraid to do anything without express permission, Elisabeta wrapped her fingers around Ferro's wrist. It was a strong wrist, a large bone covered with muscle and skin. She felt the connection of his veins, the blood running there, his heartbeat.

"Julija is the only person besides you who has ever cared for me, that I can remember, *kont o sívanak*." She whispered the name for him she had in secret places of her mind. Strong heart. It was there beating under the pads of her fingers. Sometimes beneath her ear when she laid her head against his chest. It was in the sound of the rain and in his song.

"Julija seems to be so strong, and she is. A mage and a Carpathian. A modern woman, and yet she was raised a prisoner just as I was. Cruelly used and horribly treated. She risked everything to save our people and to save me. She has been waiting for me to rise to meet everyone. Please, if I can ask one thing of you—and I know I do not deserve it, but it is not for me—she is with child and she has been through so much, do not be angry with her."

She didn't want Ferro to upset Julija or her lifemate. What if Isai forbade Julija to speak with Elisabeta or refused to allow them to be together because Ferro was angry?

"Elisabeta."

She recognized the soft command in Ferro's voice and her stomach did a slow roll. It was strange to her how her body reacted just to the various tones of his voice. She knew he expected her to meet his eyes. That was one of the most difficult things for her to do. She had been taught never to look at her master. Never to raise her eyes. Centuries of keeping her gaze downcast made it nearly impossible to force herself to look into Ferro's eyes, but he was *isänta*—master of the house—and he was never to be disobeyed.

Silence stretched between them while she gathered her courage and then dared to lift her lashes and look into his amazing iron-colored eyes. She had dared before and it seemed the color was different every time. Right now, the color was almost gold. For the first time she noticed the long, dark lashes ringing his eyes.

"I will not jeopardize your friendship with Julija," he promised solemnly. He bent his head and brushed a kiss over her forehead. "She is on the way. Tariq approaches with several of the brethren as well as the healer, Gary Daratrazanoff."

Elisabeta stiffened. She couldn't help it. *Several* meant more than one. Tariq was the leader of the people there in the compound. Daratrazanoff was a name even Sergey cursed often. The lineage was always second-in-command to the prince of the Carpathian people. They were very powerful, not just as healers but as warriors. More, these were Carpathians who had given her blood, and she'd sensed both Tariq and, especially, the healer trying to penetrate the shields in her mind.

She wanted to retreat into the ground, find a corner of the room and slide into the shadow, disappear into the wall itself, become part of it as she had for so many centuries. Ferro's arms prevented her from disappearing, but she ducked deeper into them.

He nuzzled the top of her head. "You do not need to speak unless I ask you to. If you need to answer, you can speak to me on our path alone. No one else needs to hear the sound of your voice. You do not need to look at them. I will shield you at all times."

Elisabeta was shivering again and there was nothing she could do to stop it. She wanted to be brave for him, especially since he continually persisted in calling her courageous, but already she felt the power building around the dwelling. They were coming. It wasn't one or two. There were several ancients and they carried power easily, so easily that the house and ground fairly crackled with it.

Ferro waved his hand casually toward the door and the heavy oak swung open. A tall warrior strode in. Elisabeta kept her head buried in Ferro's chest, her hand over her eyes, but she opened her fingers just enough to see him. His hair was a true black with strands of gray, much like Ferro's only not quite as long. His shoulders were wide and he looked very muscular. His eyes were brilliant sapphire, almost startlingly so. She recognized him from Julija's description. This had to be Isai, her lifemate and one of Ferro's brethren from the monastery.

He came straight to Ferro's side and reached out. Ferro's arms abandoned her for one moment, reaching toward Isai, clasping forearms in the way of the Carpathian warrior greeting.

"*Sívad olen wäkeva, hän ku piwtä,*" Isai greeted.

May your heart stay strong, hunter, Elisabeta interpreted. Ferro was her lifemate. His heart was *very* strong. She called him *kont o sívanak*—strong heart—for a reason.

A faint stirring of what could have been amusement brushed a velvet caress in her mind. *My fierce little protector.*

A little shiver crept down her spine that had nothing to do with fear and everything to do with the strange way he made her body and mind feel. The fingers of one strong hand had gone to the nape of her neck and he massaged there, a slow, deep movement that eased the tension from her in spite of the fact that Isai was towering over the two of them. Ferro didn't seem concerned. He was more relaxed than ever.

"Julija," Isai called and turned toward the open door and held out his hand.

Elisabeta's heart beat very fast. At last. Her friend. The woman who had risked everything to save her. She started to sit up straighter, but Ferro's arms tightened a fraction in warning.

Wait until she is in the house and the door is closed behind her. You can sit up straight but stay on my lap in the shelter of my arms.

That was a clear order. It was also Ferro looking out for her. He was leery after she had revealed that Sergey had managed to speak to her before her lifemate had slept above her in the healing grounds, adding the weave of his safeguards over the others. She had thought the master vampire invincible, wholly powerful. It hadn't occurred to her that something other than Sergey's power had been the reason he had been able to reach out to her every rising until her lifemate had come to her. Now, with Ferro's reaction, she wasn't so certain.

She waited quietly, still on the outside but a mass of nerves on the inside. Her gaze was riveted to the door. A small woman with delicate features, dark eyes and hair, and a curvy figure came into the room, taking Isai's outstretched hand. She recognized Julija immediately. The only thing different about her was the deep scar on her where Sergey had deliberately ripped at her throat in order to kill her. Or if not to kill her, then at least to prevent her from speaking to her lifemate.

Julija's gaze was fixed on Elisabeta and she broke out into a wide smile. "At last. It's wonderful to see you, although it's very dark in here. Don't you want some sconces lit?" Julija was mage-born and excelled at spells. "I can provide some beautiful ones that are quite dim, Elisabeta. They won't hurt your eyes."

Elisabeta couldn't help the small little shudder that ran through her mind at the idea of the others coming. They would see her clearly. Stare at her.

"No," Ferro said firmly. "I do not wish others to look upon my lifemate until we have a chance to bond. We have business to discuss or no one would be invited to speak with her this rising."

Elisabeta was a little shocked at the sound of Ferro's voice. He didn't sound like the same man at all, so much so that she had to sneak a quick glance up at his face to make certain it was really him speaking. His expression could have been carved from stone. He looked remote. Not at all the gentle, kind warrior who had been so patient with her. Where his voice had held command before at times, his tone had always been firm but gentle. There was no trace of that now. He was in charge and no one dared cross him.

Julija took a step back toward her lifemate and glanced over her shoulder at him, lifting her eyebrow as if to say "I told you so."

Ferro gestured toward the chairs across from them. "The others will be here very soon. Already they are on their way. Isai, Elisabeta has indicated to me that a short while ago she told your lifemate that Sergey was speaking to her each rising when she woke to take blood, trying to force her to communicate with him. Time is lost for her. It is possible your lifemate can help with the timeline."

Isai's head went up alertly. "Safeguards were put in place, both by those ancients already here within the compound and the brethren as well. How is this possible, Ferro?"

"I do not know, but it happened each time she was awakened to get blood. I heard her cry out and knew she was my lifemate. I began to sleep above her. When I did, I wove safeguards around her. Only then did his voice cease to call to her."

Isai leaned toward Elisabeta and Ferro. "Has Sergey managed to call to you this rising?"

Elisabeta curled closer to Ferro, drawing her knees tighter into her chest. The two Carpathian hunters kept using Sergey's name. There was power in names. They knew that. She also didn't like the way those sapphire eyes pierced through the veil of darkness and shone right at her like a beam of light. She had too much to hide. Too many scars. Too many terrible things in her past she didn't want brought to light. Too many things she was ashamed of.

"Speak only to me," Ferro said. "I do not allow others to speak to my lifemate."

Julija hissed out her displeasure. "Of course you don't," she muttered under her breath.

Isai turned his head toward her, his eyebrows coming together in a frown. Color rose in Julija's face as her lifemate clearly reprimanded her telepathically. She sank into the chair opposite Elisabeta and crossed her arms over her chest.

"Ferro, has Sergey contacted her this rising?" Isai corrected himself. *Has he?*

It shamed her a little that Ferro had to ask her. He should have known that she would have shared everything immediately. *No.* She kept her head down, not even looking at Julija. This reunion wasn't going the way she had hoped it would but she didn't know how to make it better. She was just so uncomfortable in the presence of others. She longed for the coolness of the earth.

Ferro's hand came up to her ear, his fingertip tracing her lobe and sending little tingles of fiery heat spreading like electricity through her. *This is not your fault. Let Julija answer the questions and then the two of you can talk together on your path while the others come in. We will try to ascertain where the breakdown occurred.*

You do not mind if I speak with Julija?

Of course not. She is your friend.

She does not like you.

She does not know me and I do not expect her to like me, nor do I care. I am your shield, piŋe sarnanak, yours alone. I will ask the necessary questions and then you two can talk while the others decide the best course of action.

Elisabeta could barely contain herself. She glanced at Julija, found her gaze on her and sent a quick, reassuring smile. It was the best she could do before ducking her head.

"Sergey has not contacted her since I have been safeguarding her. If your lifemate can give us any kind of details regarding the timeline it would be helpful."

"My understanding is that Sergey continued to plague Elisabeta every time she was awakened and given blood. He called to her every rising, whispering to her that he would kill everyone in the compound and torture the children in front of her if she didn't come back to him. I believe he had done so since she was first brought to this place."

Even to Elisabeta's ears, Julija sounded disrespectful.

Is that so, piŋe sarnanak? If Ferro was upset with Isai's lifemate, he didn't sound it. *Do you recall that the vampire always whispered to you?*

I cannot recall a time that he did not until you stopped him, but time no longer means anything to me. She was frustrated that she couldn't give him a definite answer.

He stroked a caress down the back of her head. *You have given me all that I need, Elisabeta.*

4

The earth may shake, and rivers may swell;
Yet here I stand, ready to break the spell.

Ferro wasn't a trusting man. He had never been one to trust, not that he could remember. He had his brethren from the monastery, and even with them he was wary. Careful. Now, with Elisabeta to protect, he was even more so. He had thought to bring Isai there first, knowing that Elisabeta would be uncomfortable with visitors, but he needed to get to the bottom of how Sergey had managed to reach out to her in the compound, in the healing grounds, when she should have been protected.

He had that feeling of a threat coming to her from either Tariq or Gary, perhaps both. Now that he'd been in Elisabeta's mind, he knew she was uneasy at the mere mention of the two Carpathians coming near her. He would have thought her anxiety was due to just being around others, but it was more than that. The healer had tried to examine her mind. He may have been trying to repair some of the damage the vampire had caused, but it would be unusual to do so without consent—and Elisabeta had closed herself off.

Ferro called Isai *ekä*, brother. Isai's loyalty would be first to his lifemate, Julija, but he would fight with Ferro if need be, to get Ferro and Elisabeta away from the compound. Ferro also thought that having Julija there would help to calm Elisabeta when the others arrived.

He should have known that when Tariq Asenguard arrived, as the leader appointed to represent the prince in the United States, he would be closely guarded, and that meant more than Gary Daratrazanoff came with him. Chairs formed a loose circle around the large room, Tariq sitting directly across from him. Gary sat to his right. He was a strange man. At one time he had been fully human, but he had been turned and the blood of the Daratrazanoffs ran in his veins, and their knowledge of healing and battle experiences filled his mind. His eyes carried the peculiar, bluish-silver color only their particular line held. Power clung to him and he gave the impression that he saw everyone, including Elisabeta, which didn't sit well with Ferro. The battle experiences and skills of every warrior that had come before in the Daratrazanoff line lived in every cell of his body and resided in his brain. He would be a difficult opponent and the one to kill first. Ferro didn't want that to happen. He felt a kinship with Gary, but if his lifemate was put in jeopardy and he had to fight his way out, it was the healer who would have to go first.

Maksim Volkov sat on the other side of Tariq. Maksim had run with Tariq on and off for centuries. They hunted together as loose partners just as Ferro had with the brethren. Maksim was a force to be reckoned with. He could be very still and then explode into action with blurring speed. Maksim was a man never to be discounted under any circumstances, no matter how much he liked to fade into the background.

Valentin Zhestokly had been in the monastery on several occasions but the call of his lifemate had been strong and he had left several times to hunt for her. He had found her when she was still a human child. She had been taken by a vampire and given to a puppet to use as food. When she was rescued, eventually, the Carpathians had to convert her in order to save her. Valentin watched over her now, staying close to the Asenguard compound, where Liv resided. He sat in one of the chairs and it was impossible to know where his loyalties would be, so Ferro didn't count on him.

Elisabeta huddled into herself, retreating further and further into her mind. She seemed light, almost insubstantial in his arms. He knew immediately it had been a mistake to have her be present for the discussion on how Sergey might have accomplished reaching out to her while she was safeguarded in the healing grounds. There had been an attack on her once, using one of the children. Now, it seemed, there had to be a second breach in security.

Talk with Julija and pay no attention to those coming to discuss this security matter, Ferro advised his lifemate as gently as possible.

He didn't want to draw any more attention than necessary to his very frightened woman. She had curled up so small in his lap that he doubted she was even visible in the dim lighting of the room, although all Carpathians could easily see in the dark. If her trembling got any worse, he feared she might really shake apart.

He kept his hand curled around the nape of her neck and his gaze fixed on Tariq, as if he wasn't in the least concerned with his lifemate huddling on his lap. His fingers gently massaged in an attempt to ease the tension out of her. He knew that Elisabeta hadn't been exposed to so many people in centuries. It had to be a terrifying experience for her. This rising was proving to be far worse than he had expected for her.

Seven men had come with Tariq. Ferro knew they had come as guards because he was considered dangerous and he had never sworn his allegiance to the reigning prince. Tomas, Matias and Lojos, triplets who were always together and had been for centuries, had been sent by the prince to help guard Tariq whether the man wanted it or not. They took their job very seriously. Ferro knew they were a force to be reckoned with.

The seventh man who had come to protect Tariq Asenguard was Afanasiv Balan. Most of the Carpathians simply called him Siv. Like the brethren, he was a true ancient and he was considered extremely dangerous. He had thick, long blond hair and strange eyes that by turns could be green or blue. More than once, Siv had sought respite in the monastery when demons had been too close, but he left to hunt vampires and eventually ended up in the United States, guarding Tariq. He had the creed of the ancients inked onto his back, just as the brethren did. If he turned on them, he would be forever branded a traitor among them. Ferro had no idea whether or not he had sworn allegiance to the prince.

"After what you've told us," Tariq said, his voice soft but carrying, "there is very little choice but to have our healer examine Elisabeta for signs Sergey has left behind that would allow him access to her."

Ferro had known that the moment he revealed to the others that Sergey had tormented Elisabeta even while she was in the protected sacred healing grounds, until Ferro had woven his own safeguards for her, Tariq would insist that she be subjected to their examination. He didn't blame them. There were children to protect. All along, many had speculated that she could have been used as a spy by the master vampire. Even his own brethren had considered the possibility. He also knew Gary wanted to examine her. He just didn't know why.

Elisabeta heard Tariq's soft declaration and her instant rejection was immediate and visceral. She made no sound but he knew if she could have run, she would have. The thought of strangers violating her mind, seeing the cruelties Sergey had subjected her to over the centuries, was humiliating to her. She was Ferro's lifemate. Already she felt she was embarrassing him by not being a warrior woman, a fitting mate for a man like him. To have the others see what the master vampire had done to her, keeping her in a cage, forcing her to beg him for everything—it was too much for her to bear.

Ferro glanced around the room at his brethren. They had come at his call. Isai, of course. He had his mage lifemate with him and she was powerful in her own right. Sandu, with his black eyes that could burn with red flames, was only a few feet away. Petru, eyes the color of pure mercury, standing as still as a statue in the corner so that one forgot he was even in the room. Dragomir, lifemate to Emeline, one of Tariq's own, there in the compound, but Dragomir with his golden eyes would always back the brethren if it came down to it.

Andor, lifemate to Lorraine, one he called *ekä*, brother—Ferro had tied his soul to Andor's to save him—sat in the circle looking alert. Andor would stand with him. Benedek lounged as if he were barely paying attention, very close to the door, ensuring they could fight their way out if necessary. Nicu, worn and grim, who moved like lightning in a fight, was the last of Ferro's seven, and he also sat in the circle, but was close to Ferro, close enough to block the others with his body if Ferro took to the air to leave with Elisabeta. They would give him the chance to take his lifemate and flee the compound with her if Tariq pushed his authority beyond what Ferro believed it should be.

"I have searched for anything Sergey may have left behind and found nothing," Ferro said, keeping his tone mild. He didn't protest Tariq's decree, but made it clear that Tariq was going to have to challenge his abilities. That would be difficult in light of the fact that he was an ancient and few could match his skills.

He waited for the leader of the compound to make his next move. *There is no need to shake until your body falls apart, piŋe sarnanak. No one is going to harm you. My brethren are here to protect you. Look carefully around the circle. I want you to try to determine which stayed with me in the monastery in the Carpathian Mountains.*

Perhaps that would take her mind off the fact that Tariq and his guards were regarding his lifemate with piercing eyes, as if they could see beyond her flesh and bones to what lay beneath. She shivered again. He didn't want to be like Sergey, hiding her away in a cage from others, but he felt she was going to be sick if this kept up.

Elisabeta, I can shield you from their sight if you prefer, although I do not wish to do so. You are no longer a prisoner in a cage to be hidden from the world.

Her fingers pressed into his arm. *So many eyes staring at me. I feel their scrutiny, as if I could be their enemy.*

No one thinks this of you.

Yes. I can feel that they do. They think I harbor . . . him. She couldn't even say his name. Sergey. The master vampire. Her captor. The one who had stolen her life.

Ferro lifted his head, his gaze sliding around the circle of men facing his woman. A low, feral sound slid from his throat, and when it did, the brethren immediately went on visible alert.

"I suggest you shield your thoughts from my woman," he said, his tone even softer than normal. "If you have doubts about her, that is your prerogative, but she does not need to feel them, hear them or know of them. Just staying aboveground is difficult enough." There wasn't a single hint of a threat, and yet the air vibrated with it.

Tariq looked around at those seated. "I'm certain all of us in this room know that Elisabeta was taken against her will, held and subjected to untold cruelties by a master vampire. She is not responsible for anything that hideous monster visited upon her, nor would I hope any here would think that she would be. If you do, I would ask you to leave immediately. This is a delicate matter and she is very brave for allowing us into her home on her first official rising."

Honesty rang in his voice. Tariq was not a man to mince words, and there was an underlying tone of anger. He continued to look around at those guarding him. No one moved.

"Forgive us, Ferro," Lojos said. "We should have been guarding our thoughts more carefully. Your lifemate is Carpathian and very sensitive. We do not think your lifemate is in league with our enemy or in any way wishes to aid him. We have seen the way the Malinov brothers can use innocents to wreak havoc here in the compound. They plan far in advance for every situation."

Matias nodded. "It is so. We did not mean disrespect. Your lifemate has been through enough without any of us making it worse for her."

Tomas steepled his fingers and regarded Ferro over the top of them. "Your woman deserves only admiration, Ferro. If Sergey was able to speak to her while she lay protected in our healing grounds with safeguards woven around her, there is a major problem in our fortress. We continue to have security breaches, over and over. We need them addressed. Our worries were never about considering that your lifemate might be a spy sent here by the master vampire to aid him, but rather concern that he has found a way to keep his eyes on her as well as on us."

She is your lifemate, Ferro, Siv said, using the pathway only the brethren shared. *Without emotion, using only the logic of the hunter, what they say holds merit. I see and feel her distress. Only you can determine how this is going to play out.*

Siv was pragmatic about issues, and he hadn't given any indication of whose side he would come down on. Ferro couldn't very well take exception to the triplets' apology. Their logic made far too much sense. He would have looked at every angle without emotion as well.

"Sometimes, Ferro," Gary said, "as you well know, the smallest irregularity can be overlooked. We are tied together. I ask that you allow me to examine your lifemate just to ensure that Sergey cannot get to her. Once you know for a certainty that she is safe, I offer freely to aid you in safeguarding her until we find the security breach."

Ferro had tied his soul to Gary's, along with Sandu and Lorraine, in order to save Andor. It was impossible not to know another when entwined at that level. Gary had laid it on the line for him—and yet Ferro still felt that vague uneasiness and knew the threat came from the healer. He just didn't know why. Very gently he ran his hand down the back of Elisabeta's head, over the thick silky hair.

Minan piŋe sarnanak, Gary can see things that perhaps I cannot. I do not want to take the chance that the vampire has left some part of himself behind that allows him access to you. I will be with the healer while my brethren guard us.

No. No. No. She shook her head and tried to pull out of his arms, a wild, terrified bird trying to escape. *He will see me. He is searching for something damning . . .*

Ferro wrapped her up easily, feeling as if his arms were like the thick bars of the cage she had been prisoner in for so many centuries rather than something that gave her comfort and peace. He despised that.

"I will take my lifemate and leave this compound. Thank you for the offer, Gary. It is appreciated." *Sas, Elisabeta, you will make yourself sick. We will leave this place.*

"Sergey's spies have surrounded the compound," Tariq objected. "They will know the moment you leave and they will pursue you, Ferro. You cannot hope to outrun them with her."

Ferro knew he was right. He had to take control of Elisabeta. She responded to firm control. He didn't want to resemble Sergey in any way, but it wasn't in his nature to allow his woman to hurt herself, throwing her thin, fragile body against his strength like a broken bird because she was so panic stricken she couldn't think straight. He had to think for her.

Stop this immediately, Elisabeta. Get a hold of yourself. You will do as I tell you to do. He poured absolute authority into his voice. Absolute steel.

Elisabeta froze. He caught her chin and tilted her face up to his. She had her eyes tightly shut. *Look at me now.*

Her long lashes fluttered and then lifted. He looked into that well of dark despair. He could see absolute terror.

You were told that I would take care of you. I have done so. I have not allowed anything to hurt you. Is that not so? Answer me now.

Elisabeta swallowed hard but she nodded her head. *Yes.*

There is no reason for all of this fear. You are in my care. I want the healer to search for anything the master vampire has left behind, and so you will allow him to do so without objection. Do you understand me? I will not allow him to find anything else. I will be right there with him the entire time.

Her heart beat so fast and loud, Ferro knew the others in the room couldn't fail to hear. They were used to hunting. Carpathian males were predators and his little songbird sounded like cornered prey.

I am isäntä—master of the house. Your master. You will answer me.

Holding her gaze captive, Ferro could see that the firmness of his commands did have an effect on her fears. Her eyes stared into his, clinging as if he were her lifeline. The tip of her tongue touched her lips to moisten them, but she was far calmer, stilling in his arms. Although the shivering was continuous, she had ceased struggling.

Yes.

I will hold you here in my lap and my brethren will remain close to guard my body. I will enter with the healer. You will not fight either of us, do you understand?

He did not release her gaze. Liquid filled her mind but not her eyes. She didn't weep tears. He tightened his arms around her.

Elisabeta, do you think I am less than the others in this room because I have shown you kindness? You are my lifemate and capable of going into my mind and looking into my past. I was careful to keep you from seeing what I thought might frighten you, but if you persist in thinking your lifemate cannot protect you, then look quickly. These warriors have other things to do this rising than wait on us.

Deliberately, he allowed his voice to grow colder.

Her lashes fluttered again and then she capitulated completely. *I will not fight.*

He would have liked it better had she referred to him by name, but at least he managed to get her cooperation, and her fear level had dropped tremendously. She was governed by rules—the stricter they were, the more she understood. It wasn't right, but he was going too fast with her, trying to force her into a world she didn't yet understand because he didn't want to appear anything like Sergey. He was her lifemate and he had to be what she needed. Right then she needed someone to tell her what to do and to allow her to lean completely on his strength.

"She will submit to your examination, Gary, but only yours. I will be with you." He kept his voice as neutral as possible, knowing no matter how he worded it, the threat was there.

The healer didn't hesitate, moving out around the others and coming closer to crouch beside Ferro. The moment he did, Sandu came up behind Ferro's chair and Siv followed the healer to stand behind him. Ferro and Gary both shed their bodies at the same time, becoming pure healing light. Gary's light was blazing, a strong beacon that was hot and powerful, moving through Elisabeta's body slowly, meticulously, starting with her brain.

The high mage had left tiny slivers of himself in others in order to spy on his enemies before he realized that by doing so, it diminished him. It was known that Sergey had at least two slivers of Xavier, the high mage, in him, giving him access to the knowledge of dark spells and trickery the mage had practiced for centuries before he died. Gary methodically began the inspection of Elisabeta's brain to try to find the tiny dark splinter that would signal Sergey had left a little piece of himself behind in her.

Ferro stayed very quiet, keeping back as Gary inspected her systematically and carefully. As the healer finished each section, Ferro went over it a second time just to be certain. Gary was thorough, never considering that Tariq or anyone else might be waiting. He moved slowly, sometimes going over and over the same place.

Ferro watched every movement as the healer pushed close to Elisabeta's memories. Each time, prickles of unease slid through Ferro's mind.

He couldn't tell if it was his own warning system or Elisabeta's going off, but he was uncomfortable with Gary's inspection. Still, he observed no wrongdoing, nor did either of them find anything suspect no matter how hard or how long they looked.

In the end, when they both emerged, they hadn't found any evidence of the master vampire in Elisabeta's brain. Both men were weak and needed blood. Siv and Sandu offered their wrists immediately. Gary looked at Tariq and shook his head as he took what Siv offered. He sat on the floor beside Elisabeta and Ferro's chair while he consumed the nourishing ancient blood.

"Did you access her memories?" Tariq asked.

Ferro shot him a fierce glare. Elisabeta's entire body went rigid at the inquiry. Gary glanced up at Ferro. He had been in Elisabeta's mind so recently that it was impossible not to feel her emotions. Her feelings were chaotic, all over the place, and her terror filled the room, impossible to contain. Tariq's question added to her growing panic and his growing distrust. She was cooperating because Ferro had commanded her to do so, but he feared she was going to pass out soon just from lack of air.

Gary might tell them all that he was searching for evidence of the master vampire, but Ferro was certain that Tariq and the healer were looking for something else—something they might be willing to kill his lifemate for. He glanced around the room, a quick assessment once more, just to assure himself he was in a position where he could fight his way to the door if there was need.

Breathe with me, piŋe sarnanak, Ferro ordered. *Let your lungs follow mine. You are beginning to hyperventilate. There is no evidence of the vampire hidden in your brain. That should make you happy, not more upset. We are clearing the possibilities one by one.*

As he directed her lungs to follow the rhythm of his so her breathing would slow to a more normal pace, he continued to ease the tension from her, massaging her scalp, the nape of her neck and her shoulders. His touch was gentle but firm. She needed to know that he was in charge.

"You may access only her memory of the risings when she is in the healing grounds," Ferro said aloud. "There is no need to see anything else."

Tomas, Lojos and Matias stirred as if all were in the same body. Clearly, they were of the same mind. Ferro's gaze jumped to them. He wasn't the only one. Sandu, Benedek, Petru and Nicu all turned their heads, their eyes going red and feral. At once the tension in the room mounted again.

"You have an objection you would care to voice?" Ferro asked softly—making it a clear challenge. He moved then, gently shifting Elisabeta as if to set her to one side.

She shook her head almost wildly, her arms sliding up around his neck tentatively as if she could hold him there. *Ferro. Please. I cannot stop myself. I know I am making things worse for you. You do not have to defend me. Let me go into the ground. Send me away. Do not fight them because I cannot control myself.*

"I think that is more than reasonable," Tariq said, his voice mild, as if there were no tension whatsoever in the room. "Does your lifemate agree, Ferro? I know this must be extremely difficult for her."

Ferro framed her face with his hands, tilting her chin so she was forced to look into his eyes. *You do not have to subject yourself to anything more. You did what I told you to do. We can go. The brethren will go with us.*

He is out there waiting beyond the safeguards of the compound.

Ferro knew Sergey was there, or at least his spies. They all felt him. They'd been feeling him since Elisabeta had been brought there. *That is so.*

A delicate shudder ran through her body, but her gaze never left his, clinging there, as if he were her safe anchor in a terrible storm. *Then have the healer access my memories.*

"Gary," Ferro said, still holding Elisabeta's gaze. "But you will be merged with me at all times, healer." He decreed it. If Tariq and Gary were looking for anything but what they were telling the others, or they planned on hurting his lifemate, he would be there to stop them. He glanced at Sandu, then to Andor. Both men were tied soul to soul with him.

Ferro felt Elisabeta's unshed tears, but there were none in her eyes as she stared directly into his. He saw her make a tremendous effort to pull herself together. To still her mind. To let her heart calm along with her breathing. She took her direction from him, choosing to follow his lead. He was very proud of her, knowing how difficult it had to be and knowing she was doing it for him to avoid him having to fight their way out of the compound.

Gary was already shedding his body, once more becoming healing light. Ferro didn't want to leave her alone, but he didn't like the idea of anyone entering her without giving her his protection. *Piŋe sarnanak, I must watch over you. Sandu and the others will guard my physical body and yours.*

Her nod was barely perceptible. He didn't wait. He shed his body and followed the healer, not trusting Gary with his lifemate. The healer knew him well enough that he waited, and the two of them flowed together to her brain once again.

She is very afraid of Sergey. I think looking in the amygdala is our best choice to access any memory she might have of his calling to her.

That made sense to Ferro. The amygdala was the part of the brain that regulated emotions like fear, which Sergey had trained Elisabeta to have in abundance. Again, Ferro stayed back, allowing Gary to take the lead, but he merged with that hot spirit in order to know any piece of information the healer discovered. He had no idea what he was doing and didn't want to disturb the healer while he sorted quickly through Elisabeta's memories, but he was determined to see each memory as it came to light.

Here, Gary said. *I have found her memories of his communication to her.*

The recall of the vampire's voice whispered to them, filling her mind, filling theirs. He sounded commanding. Menacing. A snarling, ugly broadcast that hurt the ear.

You will return to me or I will skin those children alive in front of you and allow my puppets to tear the flesh from their bones.

Every man, woman and child will be burned alive when we are finished torturing them.

Come to me now. You cannot exist without me. You do not know how to exist without me.

Come to me now or when I get you back you will be punished for a thousand years.

Each different refrain from rising to rising was repeated in a grating voice that was much like nails on a chalkboard. Ferro could imagine that someone as sensitive as Elisabeta would suffer endlessly just hearing his voice, let alone from the vampire's actual punishments. Sergey's threats weren't empty ones, either. He had shown time and again that he would carry those intimidations out. Ferro had seen glimpses of her memories and knew that Gary had as well. They had gone through her brain, hunting for evidence that Sergey may have left a sliver of himself behind, and had to examine her so closely that they could see many of the terrible things the vampire had done to her and to others in order to force her to comply with his wishes.

Elisabeta had been in the healing grounds for several weeks before her moans and cries had been overheard by Ferro and he had realized she was his lifemate. At that time, he had taken over feeding her, sleeping in the ground with her and weaving his own safeguards around her when he was hunting vampires. Each time he was with her, Sergey was unable to get through, or at least he had gone quiet. There was no evidence of him speaking to Elisabeta. On the occasions Ferro was gone, Sergey whispered more viciously than ever. Each threat became worse than the next, and with it, a memory of something horrendous he had done to her or someone else. Once, it had been the annihilation of an entire village.

Ferro wanted to wrap Elisabeta in a silken cocoon, and at the same time he wanted to become what he was born to be, the fierce predator, hunting the master vampire until he found him and destroyed him. Such a vile monster couldn't remain on earth where, eventually, as his power grew, his insatiable cruelty would demand more and more victims.

Without Elisabeta, the decomposition of his body would begin to accelerate quickly. The memories of emotions would already be fading. If he didn't have access to her, not even short visits to threaten her, he would unravel and become desperate to reacquire her. It was no wonder that he was stepping up his terrorization tactics. It was Sergey who was becoming frantic, but how could Ferro get Elisabeta to see that she was the one with the power?

Sergey had beaten her down for centuries, making her so dependent on him, taking all power away from her. She was Carpathian and yet she didn't know how to do what even a young human child could do, let alone a full-grown Carpathian woman. Ferro had been told that as a young girl, Elisabeta had the reputation for bringing peace to the Carpathian males. Ancient hunters would often visit the Trigovise household just to be in the same room with her to get a respite from the terrible emptiness of their lives. She had no idea of the gifts she held because Sergey had made her feel as if she were nothing, and yet he had targeted her, kidnapped and imprisoned her for those gifts.

How is it possible he is getting to her? Can you see in her memories where he is getting in? This does not answer the question of how he is getting around the safeguards.

I am well aware of that.

Ferro could see that Gary was moving backward through Elisabeta's memories, trying to find where Sergey could have planted something of himself in her to allow him to penetrate the defenses of the ancients inside the compound.

No matter how hard either of them tried not to see the ugliness of Elisabeta's life in order to spare her the humiliation of having others see things she didn't want seen, there was no getting around it when shuffling through the years of her life. Ferro found he couldn't be as detached as he thought he could be. He'd had centuries of no emotion. He could switch emotion off to hunt, and yet he found when it came to his lifemate, it was nearly impossible not to feel.

His gut churned, knotted, an unfamiliar sensation that made him very aware the woman was getting inside him, a dangerous thing for him when he might have to leave her and go to the monastery after she gained her independence. The ties between lifemates couldn't be broken. He knew that. He understood what they were, but he also knew he wasn't the same man born to be Elisabeta's lifemate any more than she was the same woman. They had both changed over the centuries. He had to provide her with what she needed because everything in him demanded he do so. Once that was accomplished, he would not be what she needed.

He stayed merged with Gary as they moved through her memories, and while Ferro was wrapped up in emotion, unable to distance himself as he should have, the healer remained completely without feeling as he searched to find where Sergey was able to break through the safeguards. He was positive Tariq's second-in-command was searching for more than that, but if he found anything, it wasn't anything Ferro could identify.

At once he found himself back in his own physique, weak, disoriented, a little shocked that he had all but been thrown out of Elisabeta's body. He had gone from pure spirit back to his own ego, thinking of himself in that moment and the consequences of his actions. That had been enough to send him back to his own physical form. At once, Sandu was there again, giving him blood, as traveling as spirit depleted him.

Gary hadn't returned, and immediately Andor shed his body and entered Elisabeta to guard her while the healer continued to sift through her memories.

Ferro? I can feel your sorrow.

Elisabeta's voice was like a breath of fresh air, a cool breeze moving through his mind, clearing away all doubt and the deep sadness that always took him when he thought about losing her after centuries of searching for her. He felt her fingers on his face, brushing along the lines carved deep there from centuries of wear, soothing him as nothing else ever could.

I am here with you. I may be afraid of everything, kont o sívanak, but for you I will always find the courage needed to walk by your side, if that is what you decree, for as long as you want me.

She sounded humble. A gentle woman, turning him inside out because all she thought of was him. There was no thought in her mind for herself at all. He knew that was a major part of her gift. She had to have been that way as a child, to be able to bring such peace to the ancient warriors.

She called him "strong heart" and yet, after looking at what she had endured for centuries, often the worst of her punishments on his behalf, guarding his soul, he thought his little songbird should be the one called *kont o sívanak*, strong heart, not him. She filled his soul with light, sweeping the darkness in him aside just with the brightness in her.

I will always want you with me, he assured her. That was the strict truth. Lifemates didn't lie to each other.

What did they see in my memories? Is he there? Inside me? Her voice trembled, but she continued stroking caresses on his face and in his mind.

How did one answer that? He closed the wounds in Sandu's wrist, politely murmuring his thanks, and shifted Elisabeta in his arms, holding her much more firmly to him. Sergey had been her entire world. The vampire had made it that way, ensuring there was no one else for her to talk to or interact with. Julija was really the first person she had ever connected with, and Sergey had held Elisabeta captive for centuries before that happened.

He is there in your memories, but I saw no evidence that he left anything of himself behind. Do you recall him casting spells? He has slivers of the high mage, Xavier, in him. He would have access to Xavier's spells.

A little shudder ran through her body, but she had calmed. He realized it was because she was no longer thinking about the others in the room, or the healer examining her memories. She was focused on Ferro and the sadness that had swept through him. She was still trying to find a way to alleviate the dark melody that played repetitively through his mind. Ferro was still connected to Gary, a presence in his mind, staying very still but watching closely, just as Andor was.

He is not very good at casting spells, but he practices. It scares him because there are severe repercussions when mistakes are made, and he makes many mistakes.

Ferro considered that. If Sergey had access to Xavier's spells but didn't have the ability to actually cast them properly and was afraid of the consequences if he reproduced them incorrectly, then it was doubtful he used a spell on his favorite toy. Elisabeta had become necessary to Sergey. He had developed a need for her. Although Elisabeta had been his prisoner, in more ways, he had been hers.

Her breath hitched in her throat and her head tilted toward his. He looked down into her dark eyes. *What do you mean, Ferro?*

He liked that she wanted to enter into a discussion with him. She had a good mind. Sergey had convinced her she couldn't use it.

He was totally dependent on you all those centuries. He may have had his brothers around him, but remember, they had turned vampire. They no longer had emotions. He felt emotions only through you and he didn't share you with anyone. He was afraid to and for good reason. The others felt he was less than they were. Only you had the knowledge that he was more. Only you could see that he was the strategist capable of biding his time to take the ultimate prize. He became dependent on the way you brought him peace. On the way you made him feel. He will be losing his mind now, unable to function without you.

She was silent, turning his opinion over and over in her mind. *How could you know that?*

If I lost you, even now, having you for such a short period of time, the loss would be . . . difficult beyond measure. Ferro told her the truth so it would sink in how valuable she was.

I am your lifemate.

He framed her face with both hands and stared down into her eyes, feeling as if he could get lost there. *You are more than my lifemate, Elisabeta, which should tell you something, because a lifemate is everything to an ancient hunter. Everything. And you are so much more.*

It humbles me that you think that of me, Ferro. I will try to be worthy of your opinion.

He could feel her resolve and wished the others were gone, so he could kiss her. Instead, he brushed kisses in her mind, telling her without words what she meant to him, trying to give her courage to face whatever the healer was going to say when he returned from his examination. He knew there was a part of her that she held back, wary that his kindness was an act and at some point he would turn on her. He didn't blame her for that worry. She had lived with treachery for too long. She had seen Sergey deceive others over and over. It would take time for her to trust Ferro fully.

You are already worthy. Sergey needs you and knew that he would when he decided to follow along with his brothers down this path they chose. You were the one he depended on for the strength to get him through. His brothers beat him down, made fun of him and used him. They never acknowledged that he had the Malinov brilliance, that he was every bit as intelligent as they were. He feared them, not because they were any smarter but because he knew how vicious they were, and all his life, being the youngest, he had been the one they teased and made fun of.

That is so. I was often stashed in a corner, part of the wall when one came in, and they would be quite cruel to him. He would talk to me and feel very smug and superior because his brothers never had a clue that I was there right in front of them. They could never detect me, although they often wondered how the master stayed so young and composed.

He is not your master. Ferro couldn't keep the clipped, fierce note from his voice. He went directly to dominant in seconds, without thinking. Just the idea that his woman would think of Sergey that way set his teeth on edge. *He was never your master. He was a cruel Carpathian who kidnapped an innocent young girl. He will pay for what he did to you.*

At once that soothing breeze swept through his mind, clearing out his need to find the vampire and rip out his heart. There was only Elisabeta and her sweetness, that gentle soul with her light and the courage to guard his soul for centuries.

You are right, she agreed. *He is not my master. The point is, I can look a little closer at him with you here holding me and see things I could not before. I would not have the courage if you were not with me. I would fear he would find me the way he did when I was in the healing grounds. He always told me he could find me anywhere.*

Gary's spirit emerged from her body, his light much dimmer than when he had entered, and his body jerked with weariness as he reentered. Siv immediately offered him his wrist and the others waited in silence for the healer's verdict while he fed.

Andor followed Gary out and fed as well, slipping into the background with Benedek. Ferro met his eyes and Andor shook his head, indicating he didn't think Gary had found anything Sergey had left behind in Elisabeta. Ferro frowned. If the breakdown of safeguards wasn't in Elisabeta, where was it coming from?

5

The fog along the ridge, drifting through the trees;
A shadow in the distance, nothing but a breeze.

*E*lisabeta, *you do not have to obey every single order your lifemate gives you. A woman can talk to other men. Some of the men in this room are barely out of the caves the way he is, but others are very modern and would address you themselves. They would treat you with the respect you deserve.* Julija was totally indignant. *Isai swore to me that Ferro would take good care of you and be whatever you needed.*

For the first time that she could ever really remember, Elisabeta felt what it was like to really know what humor was. What it felt like. *Ferro is exactly what I need. I told him there were too many people and I could not have them looking at me or talking to me. He said he would take care of it if that was what I desired, and he did. He asked Isai to bring you to me so I would have you to visit with because he knew you did not frighten me.*

Elisabeta kept her eyes fixed on Julija's face as she told her what her lifemate had done for her. Julija's expression was priceless as her gaze flicked from Elisabeta to Ferro and then back to Elisabeta.

Wait. Are you saying that Ferro deliberately made himself look like an asshole in order to protect you? Julija scowled at the ancient hunter.

Ferro didn't deign to look her way. The healer had gotten to his feet and once more had taken a chair beside Tariq.

Yes. I do not like being in the open. This room is too big for me. He is protecting me so I do not have to look at the entire room. I do not like all these people seeing me but he does not want to hide me away like the vampire did, so he holds me in his arms where I can hide my face. I did not want to answer questions so he told them not to talk to me directly.

"I did not find anything in her memories to indicate that Sergey placed anything in her to spy on this compound or that would allow him access to her remotely," Gary announced.

Elisabeta nearly sagged with relief, but the fact that Ferro didn't seem relieved prevented her from doing so. She felt every one of his emotions, even when she was certain he didn't feel them. He seemed to distance himself from emotions, as if, because he was incapable of feeling for so many centuries, he still didn't process sentiment at all. He simply didn't acknowledge emotion unless it was in regard to her. There was a part of her that got a tiny secret thrill from that, although like everything, it frightened her as well.

That amazes me, Julija said. *That's like some kind of hero, Elisabeta. Everyone thinks he's a first-class jerk, at least all the women do. Lorraine, Andor's lifemate, is going to give him a lecture to end all lectures. I'd better warn her not to make a fool of herself.*

Ferro had a very specific feel to him. Strong. Very strong. A predator's edge. Almost feral. Not almost, Elisabeta had to acknowledge, but definitely feral. Untamed. He felt like a law unto himself, and when he surrounded her, she could identify him instantly not only by his scent but by that distinctly powerful feel to him.

The moment Julija told Elisabeta she was going to have to tell Lorraine not to lecture Ferro, Elisabeta felt him in her mind. He had been there all along. Quiet, monitoring, just to make certain she was all right and didn't need him. Now, he poured himself into her, surrounding her. To her astonishment, there was a bite of humor.

Tell her not to say anything to Lorraine. I want to hear Lorraine's lecture.

She didn't want all the women in the compound to have a poor opinion of her lifemate because he was shielding her, but she didn't want to disobey him, either.

Julija, please do not say anything to Lorraine. She wasn't good at deception, and Julija glanced at her sharply and then at Ferro, who appeared to be listening to Tariq question the healer.

He's paying attention to our conversation, isn't he? Julija asked.

Reluctantly, afraid she was doing something wrong, Elisabeta nodded her head. *I do not feel comfortable without him. I am afraid.*

You do not have to apologize to anyone for the way you are, minan pinye sarnanak. Ferro sounded fierce. *There is nothing wrong with needing your lifemate to get you through these first risings.*

This time, Elisabeta knew Julija could hear him and that had been deliberate. It was also a threat. *I fear my need of you being with me will be far longer than just these first risings, Ferro.*

She wanted Julija to know it wasn't Ferro at fault. His staying in her mind even when he was present in the room with her was all on her. He wasn't monitoring her to know what was said between them. She was terrified that if he wasn't sharing her mind, Sergey would find his way inside her again.

Pinye sarnanak. His voice softened, was so gentle it turned her heart over. *As long as you have need of me, I have the need and privilege to protect you.*

Elisabeta looked up at him. Ferro seemed to be paying attention to Tariq and the others as they discussed the possibility of Sergey having another spy in the compound, but she knew his focus was on her. She felt him surrounding her with his strength, and that gave her the courage to sit up straighter. She dared to take a look around the room that she hoped to call her home one day.

The first sneak peek was dizzying, and she hastily closed her eyes and pressed back against Ferro's broad chest. He felt like a rock, steady and immovable, something she could count on when she felt the smallest breeze could knock her over.

Julija chose to ignore Ferro's interruption. *What does he call you? Pinye sarnanak? What does that mean? Or minan pinye sarnanak?*

Elisabeta wasn't sure she wanted to share that private name. "My little songbird" felt intimate to her. Theirs alone. She knew any Carpathian who heard him call her that would know what it meant, and Julija was her friend, but that name represented far more to Elisabeta than she'd realized. No one had ever been kind to her, or made her feel special. No matter how she acted, terrified or not, Ferro accepted her.

It is a sweet name he calls me sometimes, she managed. *I am very fond of it. I do know the Carpathian language, but that is very ancient, isn't it?*

Elisabeta nodded. *What is the healer saying about the vampire now?* She wanted to change the subject until she understood her emotions better.

The rising had already been too overwhelming for her and she didn't want to add anything else to it that she didn't have to try to cope with if she didn't have to. Both women immediately turned their attention to the conversation between the healer, Tariq and the others.

"We have no option but to once again examine those in the compound who have been near the healing grounds," Maksim said, sounding weary.

Tariq sighed. "The children have been put to the test repeatedly. I am not certain how much more they can take. Certainly Charlotte will be very distressed by the idea of having to examine them again, but we cannot risk everyone here."

Sívamet, there is another answer, one that will be difficult for you to put to the test, but these are children who you saw the vampire torturing. Do you remember?

Yes. How could she forget? Julija had allowed herself to be taken prisoner in the hopes of rescuing her. There were children down in the tunnels, and they were used cruelly by Sergey and his brother. Elisabeta had been in a tiny cage, hidden in the room, unable to do anything but watch the horror unfolding before her eyes.

You would have to be very brave and trust me. I know it would be difficult for you, but if I am right, it would spare these children more pain and Tariq would not have to tell his lifemate he has no choice but to once more subject their children to examination.

Aloud, Ferro interrupted the discussion. "Before you call the meeting,

Tariq, and put the plan into action, I have one more idea, but I need my lifemate's permission. I am discussing it with her now. It will be very frightening for her and she will have to be extremely brave to cooperate, but if I am right, we can spare the children this examination."

Tariq had begun to rise but at Ferro's statement he dropped into the chair and nodded, steepled his fingers and waited. He glanced at Maksim and then Gary. Both men shook their heads. Neither had any idea of what Ferro might be thinking.

Tell me what you would have me do. Already Elisabeta was trembling. She despised herself for being such a coward when she caught so many glimpses of him acting with such courage, facing master vampires and defeating them in terrible battles.

Ferro's hand was very gentle, stroking her hair. *Julija is in the room with you. She is in your mind. My brethren are here. All are ancient hunters. They will weave safeguards. Look around you at those in the room. These are all powerful Carpathian hunters, each with their own gifts. I will have them weave the strongest safeguards over and under and around this room with you in it. Sandu, Andor and Gary, those I call ekä, my brother, will be in your mind, secreted there waiting quietly to see if the vampire creeps in.*

Elisabeta gasped and pulled into an upright sitting position, facing him, shaking her head, uncaring that the others would see her visceral reaction. She already knew what he was going to do. Leave her. He was leaving her. Panic set in and she couldn't catch her breath. The moment she knew he was going to abandon her, she felt the vampire pressing close. She felt his glee. He was there, just waiting for his moment.

"You promised me," she whispered. "You promised me."

"Yes, Elisabeta, and I always keep my promises," Ferro agreed. "I am not abandoning you. You are mine. I protect you first above all others. This is only to see if I am right, and if I am, it will keep the children safe and from having once more to suffer through examination. It is up to you. I will abide by your decision."

Elisabeta rocked herself back and forth, trying to self-soothe. Nothing helped. He caught her chin and forced it up, forced her eyes to meet his. He had the strangest-colored eyes. This time they seemed to be more silvery-blue with that strange rusty stain, like a lightning bolt arrowing through them. His gaze was steady on hers.

I am asking for your trust, Elisabeta. I will never abandon you. Never. This will only take minutes. I know it will feel like hours, but I swear it will be minutes and I will be close.

There was such a force in him. She couldn't see or hear a lie in him, but he was her courage. He was the reason she was able to be aboveground and she was still terrified, even with his physical presence. She couldn't do what he was asking of her—but there were those innocent children. Was she going to be so selfish that she would let fear conquer her and allow the children to suffer because she couldn't overcome her terror?

I cannot make decisions, Ferro. You know that. You have to decide for me. You have to choose what is right.

You know what the right thing to do is. He never looked away from her, his eyes on hers the entire time.

Her heart dropped. She knew he was going to choose the honorable path. He had always chosen honor. He had secreted himself in the monastery because he was honorable. Honor was inked on his back. She wanted to live up to that for him.

What are you going to do?

I will explain to everyone. If you have an objection, state it to me alone on our path, but know I will be leaving your mind and physical presence for a few moments only to leave the way open for the vampire so he can be traced.

Again, he did not look away from her. She heard a moan escape and she quickly cut it off, pressing her forehead into his chest, unable to continue looking into his eyes. He couldn't possibly understand the terror sweeping through her.

Elisabeta? he prompted.

She couldn't say the words. She wanted to, but she couldn't get them out.

Make the decision for me, Ferro. If you decree it, I will follow your lead. She wanted to curl up into the fetal position and just disappear.

"I would ask that Andor, Gary and Sandu once again silently observe by joining with Elisabeta." *You will allow my brethren to merge with you in my place.*

They cannot protect me from him. They couldn't. She didn't care how powerful he thought his ancient brethren were, they couldn't stop the master vampire, not when he was coming for her. Only Ferro could do that.

Nevertheless. Ferro made it a decree. "Before they do, every ancient in this room, with the exception of me, together must weave the strongest safeguards to keep Sergey out. Do not leave a single loophole. Once that is done, the three of you who are bound with me, so I know that you will guard my lifemate, will merge with her. I will leave until summoned to return. In the time I am gone, we will see if Sergey manages to find his way to terrorize my lifemate."

They cannot stop him from getting to me. Only you can do that. You have to stay with me. If you are not with me, he will come. She couldn't help pleading with him.

Elisabeta found her fingers were twisted into two fists in his shirt and she was astonished at her audacity. She would never have thought she could possibly have taken such liberties, but Ferro didn't seem to mind. If anything, he seemed proud of her. When she tried to pry her fingers loose, he brought up his hands to cover hers. As always, he was exquisitely gentle.

Then we will know how he comes and we will be able to stop him, Ferro stated calmly. *You will do this, lifemate, because I have asked it of you.*

The rules. The guidelines she understood. That discipline she'd had for hundreds of years. She closed her eyes. She could do this if she had to. She could endure as she had for centuries.

"That makes no sense," Maksim said. "How could he possibly get in if we all weave such strong safeguards?"

"We have woven them around the compound," Tariq pointed out.

"I see where you're going with this, Ferro," Gary said. "It makes perfect sense." He stood and nodded to the others. "Before it is too much for Elisabeta, let's hurry."

Elisabeta wanted to tell him she was already at her limit; still, she gathered her courage. This wasn't for herself. *Ferro, you said I could ask anything of you.*

Yes, piŋe sarnanak.

Please have Julija leave. I do not want her here. That is the one thing I ask of you. With you gone, I fear Sergey will come and he will strike at me through her. She carries a child, and he will harm that child.

Ferro leaned over her and pressed a kiss on top of her head. "It is Elisabeta's wish, Isai, that you remove your lifemate for her safety while we conduct this experiment. I would ask that you honor her wish."

Isai rose immediately and held out his hand to Julija, who stood reluctantly. "Are you certain, Elisabeta? I would help you through this."

"She is certain," Ferro said. "This is difficult for her," he added when Julija continued to hesitate. "I ask that you go."

Julija nodded and went with Isai from the house. Elisabeta didn't look at her. She couldn't. She already felt abandoned by her lifemate. The moment Julija and Isai were gone, the remaining Carpathian males immediately began weaving safeguards.

Ferro continued to hold Elisabeta while her mind went crazy with all sorts of possibilities that this was the moment when the axe was going to fall and she would see what was really in store for her. Was it possible that this was one of Sergey's many cruel tricks? He'd played so many over the centuries he'd held her. Was Ferro an equally vicious master and now was the moment when he would reveal his true character? She couldn't stop the thousands of likelihoods from pushing forward.

Very slowly Elisabeta uncurled her fists from Ferro's shirt and forced herself to sit up on her own. She could only try to prepare herself against the pain that was going to come. It was already creeping into her mind and heart, stealing in like a thief. She was familiar with the feeling. So many times, over hundreds of years, she had tried to make herself numb, to not feel anything at all, but for some reason, that wouldn't work for her.

Minan piŋe sarnanak, I do not blame you for trying to protect yourself. You do not know me, and so far, you have chosen not to merge too closely in my mind. I can only reassure you that you are my true lifemate and I have bound us together with the ritual words. Those ties are sacred and cannot be broken. They not only affect you, but me as well. I meant every word I said to you. I am not abandoning you or playing some elaborate hoax on you. I am searching for a way to protect you from this monster. We will see if he can slip through the safe-

guards the ancients have woven without me. If he dares come, sívamet, you have only to reach for me. Call to me and I will be there with you.

Ferro sounded so sincere. So strong. So real. How did one know the truth? She had been deceived all her life, and she had lived long.

"We are ready, Ferro," Tariq announced.

Ferro tipped her chin up and leaned his head down to brush his lips across hers. *My brethren will protect you, and I will come the instant you call to me. That is all you have to do, Elisabeta. Simply call to me if he comes. I will drive him away.*

She couldn't answer. She didn't know how to answer. She felt his withdrawal and then she was alone. He was gone from her mind, and she'd never felt so isolated as she did in that moment. She'd been alone for hundreds of years and with him only for that rising, and yet having him merged with her, even staying in the background, made her feel safe. She hadn't known how much he was giving her until he was gone.

His physical presence was gone as well and she found herself sitting alone in the chair. She kept her eyes closed tightly and her hands clenched so tightly on the arms of the chair her knuckles hurt. She knew when his brethren merged with her, but it didn't alleviate the terrible emptiness she felt. They shifted almost as one to the back of her mind and stayed so still she couldn't feel them in her. She didn't want to feel them there. They weren't Ferro.

Her heart began to accelerate. She tasted fear in her mouth. Thunder roared in her ears. There was no understanding the passage of time because each second without Ferro was like years moving at a snail's pace.

The sound of ugly laughter crept into her mind, one slow note at a time, as if the sender wanted to prolong the agony of suspense. The noise was grating and harsh, scraping deliberately along nerve endings, a vile, sickening sound meant to hurt—and it did.

He fears me, Elisabeta. Your magnificent lifemate runs like a coward from me, leaving you behind to face your punishments. You have accrued so many now with your stubbornness. Your friend Julija. The mage. I will tear the child from her body first and feed it to my puppets while you watch. While she watches, knowing you caused her the loss by your stubborn behavior.

Sergey sneered and threatened by turns, his voice quickly deteriorating more and more into a growling animalistic noise that could barely be recognized.

Elisabeta put her hands over her ears to try to drown out the ugly threats that kept getting worse and viler if she could even make them out, but it was impossible because they were coming from inside her head. In desperation, she reached out, hoping her lifemate had told her the truth.

Ferro. She couldn't say anything else. Just his name.

Instantly, he poured into her mind. Strong. An untamed warrior. Utterly confident and invincible. He filled every lonely place in her mind, every tiny crack Sergey might think he could slip in and hide. He strode in, bigger than life, taking over, a fierce hunter few dared to cross. As Ferro merged with her, his brethren joined them, tracking the master vampire as he rushed to try to evade them, throwing himself out of Elisabeta's mind.

Ferro and the other hunters followed. "He is in the room. He cannot leave with the safeguards intact. Be careful, he can strike at us, even from a distance. We need to shed light on him. It is only a small replica of him, but it is enough to diminish him if we destroy it. I will shield Elisabeta."

She knew Sergey would try to hurt her by going after Ferro. She was so grateful she had insisted Julija leave the house. By weaving the safeguards, they had contained Sergey's shadowy replica there in the room. She couldn't stop shaking, her gaze darting around the room, forgetting to be overwhelmed by the amount of space.

The Carpathian males waved their arms to cast a brilliant light throughout the entire room, leaving no corner with so much as a shadow in it. Ferro stood in the center of the room as the ancient warriors spread out. He spread his arms wide, encompassing the entire room.

"Muonìak te avoisz te." His deep voice was commanding, pouring centuries of sheer strength and control into his tone. Few could actually command a vampire to reveal himself, let alone a master vampire, but it was impossible to ignore Ferro's absolute authority.

At once a dark shadowy form began to creep toward Ferro, stretching across the wall and then the floor in the shape of a tiny insect that began to grow as it slid down the wall and touched the hardwood floor. At once, Sandu, Dragomir and Andor hurled wooden darts carved from ancient wood, pinning the shadowy feet to the wall.

The figure's mouth gaped wide in a silent scream. The empty eye sockets turned toward Elisabeta where she huddled as small as possible in the chair. Ferro took one step to place himself between the shadow figure and his lifemate so that it was impossible for the thing to see her. Benedek, Petru and Nicu formed a wall behind Ferro, standing shoulder to shoulder, making it doubly impossible for the shadow to even lay eyes on Elisabeta.

The moment she was taken from its line of sight, the creature began to twist and turn in desperation, seemingly not to get away from the ancients but in order to keep looking at Elisabeta. It stretched farther across the floor toward her, its shape thinning, until it looked like a ribbon of gray with nothing but feet and outstretched hands.

"What is it?" Tariq asked. "I have never run across such a thing."

Sandu and Andor pinned the shadowy shoulders into the hardwood floor so it couldn't move. Again, the mouth gaped wide but there was no sound. The empty holes where the eyes should have been darted back and forth. More than ever the creature resembled a cross between an insect and a vampire.

Gary crouched beside the shadow, touching it with one of the pegs made from the ancient wood Sandu handed to him. "It was referred to as a *kod lewl kuly* in ancient times—a shadow spirit worm or demon sent to devour souls or bring messages. It is brought forth from the netherworld, and the conjurer—in this case, Sergey—has to give it something of himself, some part of his own spirit, in order to give it any kind of direction."

"It is fixated completely on Elisabeta," Maksim observed. "Not on escaping."

"Were you able to see how it got in?" Lojos asked. "With all the safeguards, how could it slip in?"

Gary glanced at Ferro and then he calmly took the ancient wood and plunged it into the heart of the creature, careful to avoid touching any part of the gray shadow. The thing wiggled obscenely and then slowly went still. The healer stood and brought the light to bear on the pinned worm. The edges of the shadow began to darken and curl. Flames licked at it and eventually consumed it. When the entire creature was reduced to ash, the door to the house opened and the breeze carried the ashes outside. The light in the room dimmed and then receded completely.

"What did you find?" Tariq asked. "How did the *kod lewl kuly* slip through our safeguards? The three of you were sharing her brain when he managed to penetrate Elisabeta's mind."

Ferro once more went to Elisabeta and lifted her into his arms, surrounding her with his strength. *I am here, minan pipe sarnanak, just as I said I would be. The vampire is gone. He cannot get to you. But you must be very brave and continue to believe and trust in me as you have done.*

You know how he did it. Her heart began to beat harder in trepidation.

Ferro's arms tightened even more around her, as if she would need even more courage to face what the healer was going to disclose to the others.

"Sergey has held Elisabeta prisoner literally for centuries. She knows no other life. No other keeper. He has terrified her all those centuries, and held her away from any other contact, vampire, Carpathian or human," Gary explained to the ancients in the room. "Ferro is her lifemate. She has a strong connection with him and the belief instilled in her from birth that he will shield her, if necessary, from all harm. Through the centuries, when Sergey tried to force Elisabeta to give up Ferro's soul to him, she refused, no matter what torture he subjected her to. She knew what strength it took for lifemates to hold out against evil."

Elisabeta tilted her face up to Ferro's. *Why is he telling them these things?* She was very confused. The healer had merged with her several times. He had searched her memories trying to find evidence of Sergey planting spies, so he had been able to see so much of her life in small vignettes, but she didn't expect him to champion her or to reveal to the others anything about her.

There are things in my memories he found that no one here will ever accept. They will cast me out.

There is no need to be alarmed, Elisabeta. You are with your lifemate. I am keeper of your soul. Your heart. No one will ever harm you again. If those in this room cannot accept us, then we will find our way. Some of our brethren will travel with us, others may stay here. What matters is that we are together and that I can keep you safe.

He didn't exactly answer her. She took a deep breath and forced herself to turn her head and look at the ancients who had merged with her. Sandu, Andor and Gary. These men were bound to Ferro soul to soul. They had tied themselves together, along with Andor's lifemate, Lorraine, and the bond would hold until all of them had lifemates. Only then would they be able to break those ties. What happened to one happened to all of them. Now, she was a part of that brotherhood.

It was very difficult to look at the three men without the bars of a cage between her and them. The open space made her feel vulnerable but it helped that she could feel Ferro's strength surrounding her. He was extremely strong and felt that way to her, like one of the ancient hardwood trees that was forever unbending even in the fiercest storm. He was back in her mind, merged with her but unobtrusive, just providing her with the confidence to stay there instead of running away.

She resolved that she wouldn't embarrass him. He had come instantly at her call, just as he said he would. There had been no deception, nor had he gotten angry with her because she hadn't wholly believed him. Right now, his hands were soothing on the nape of her neck and then moving in her hair, rubbing her arm, always reminding her of his presence.

His brethren faced the other ancients in the room stoically, without expression, but she felt them standing with Ferro—with her. For what reason? How had Sergey gotten past the safeguards?

Stay with me, Elisabeta. Let your heart and lungs follow the rhythm of mine. Every warrior in this room can hear any change in your breathing or your pulse. I am impressed with your bravery. Your courage. They have no right to pass judgment on you, nor do I think they will, but you are harsh with yourself. You are to think only of me. You represent me.

His hands framed her face very gently and turned her to look at him. Her gaze couldn't fail to meet his. *Do you understand? I am giving you an order you cannot disobey. You are to concentrate on your lifemate. Keep your heart rate exactly in tune with mine. Keep your breathing the same as mine. Look only at me. See only me. Think only of me. Know that I am the only one you are to please.*

The guidelines were very clear and she was very good at following rules. She moved in his mind, looking for anything that was disturbing to him. She always felt that faint note of sorrow running through him. The song was there, the one she was beginning to think of as their song. Hopeful one moment and despairing the next. As if in the distance, she heard the healer speaking to the ancients.

"Elisabeta is fully Carpathian. She is powerful in her own right. She may not have had the opportunity to develop every one of her gifts as most Carpathian women do over the centuries, but those gifts are in her. She can bring peace even to one such as me. There are few like her in existence."

Elisabeta heard the praise as if from a distance but felt Ferro's pride in her, and it warmed her that he felt that way. She didn't like him to feel that deep sorrow that she couldn't reach and remove. It was important to her to take care of his every need.

"Her fears drive her. Sergey has terrorized her for centuries, and without Ferro to shield her, he continues to do so," Gary explained. "Her very fears summon him. She opens the doors for him. Obviously, nothing from this world can come through and Sergey knows it—the safeguards are woven too strong—but not one of us thought to keep anything from the netherworld from creeping in. Elisabeta summoned him with her fears and Sergey responded to the summons by sending in the only servant he could get inside. The *kod lewl kuly*, the spirit shadow worm, could only stay so long in this realm, which is why it slipped away the moment she was put back in the ground."

Complete silence greeted the explanation. The ancients looked at one another. "You are certain of this?" Tariq demanded.

"We observed it happening within her mind," Gary said. "Ferro suspected. She is so terrified of Sergey yet he was her only contact throughout the centuries. She expects him to come after her. She knows nothing but his threats. It is natural for her to believe he will do exactly what he told her he would. When she is not with Ferro, she believes she is wide open for Sergey's assault. And she aided us in uncovering yet another hole in our defenses."

"That is insane," Maksim said. "She actually *summoned* the vampire? Could he resist her call?"

"I doubt it," Gary said. "As he was the constant in her life, she was the constant in his. More, he needed her to provide emotions and keep his body from decomposing. Right at this moment, he is deteriorating at a rapid pace. That has to be very shocking for him when he is used to getting his way in all things. He may have acted as if he was going after other women to take her place, but no other woman will do for him. There is only Elisabeta for him. He had to have put something of himself in the worm in order to direct it to her specifically. His hope was to intimidate her into coming back to him."

"You believe Elisabeta can actually summon Sergey at will?" Tariq asked.

"Yes," Gary said.

"I believe we are done here, gentlemen," Ferro said. "My lifemate is exhausted."

Immediately Tariq stood. "I appreciate you allowing us into your home, Elisabeta. I know this was difficult for you."

Elisabeta didn't look at him. Ferro had told her to look only at him. See only him. She took in what they were saying, but only from a distance, and that allowed her to process the information without reacting to it. She would do that later, when she was alone or with just her lifemate.

"Will she summon Sergey into this compound again?" Tomas inquired. "If he was able to slip the worm in, could he do so with some other creature once she calls for him?"

Ferro's cold gaze moved over Tomas. It was a legitimate question, and one that all the warriors would be asking and preparing for, but he didn't want it asked aloud in front of his lifemate. He had no choice but to answer honestly.

"It is my hope that she will summon him," Ferro said. "When I am ready, we will make certain she does, in a place of my choosing."

"She will summon him if Ferro isn't with her unless he can convince her that Sandu, Andor or I can protect her the way he can in his absence," Gary said. "And that means, Tomas, that every ancient in this compound had better do exactly what I told you to do when I first arrived, find every point of weakness and fix it. This is not her failing, it is yours, mine and all of ours in this compound. We have not safeguarded against the netherworld well and we must do so immediately."

Tariq walked to the door, followed closely by the healer. Immediately, the others filed out, leaving only the brethren.

"If you have need of us, Ferro, call. We will come. Should you have to leave this place, we will accompany you," Sandu said.

Ferro inclined his head. "Thank you."

Elisabeta found it interesting that Ferro felt deep affection for those who had stayed to protect them but didn't seem to acknowledge it to himself. None of the ancients recognized their emotions or admitted to those feelings.

The moment they were gone and the door shut behind them, Ferro waved his hand toward it and murmured a few words, sealing the thick oak closed. He bent his head and brushed his lips over hers.

"You did very well, Elisabeta. You were in this enormous room, surrounded by strangers, and you allowed yourself to be examined by the healer in order to keep young children from having to undergo another inspection. I am very proud of you."

The moment he spoke, that barrier that had provided a distance between her and everyone in the room was gone and she understood exactly what had occurred. "I summoned the vampire? I did that? Is that really possible? Why would I do that?" She was horrified. More than shocked. Sickened. She pressed a hand to her churning stomach. "I really did endanger the compound and everyone in it. I not only allowed him in, I *invited* him in."

"That is not what the healer said, *piŋe sarnanak*," he said gently. "You did not listen properly. You summoned the vampire with your fear. That is not the same thing as inviting him in. He could only send the *kod lewl kuly* from the netherworld and with it some tiny part of his own spirit, which we destroyed. He cannot get that back. That worm couldn't live in this realm so it would not do him any good as a spy. He could only plague you with it. In truth, you summoned your own tormentor."

"The healer says I will do so again if you are not with me." Her nervous fingers plucked at his shirt.

"I believe he is correct. Over time, you will gain confidence and that will not happen. In the meantime, if I have to be gone, you will be in the ground where you are safe. I will also see to it that you become more comfortable with Julija and Lorraine. Sandu, Gary and Andor are tied to us. Eventually, it is possible we both will be comfortable with one of them guarding you when I am not available."

He wasn't certain that was true, especially regarding Gary. He still felt that vague threat toward his lifemate. No matter that the healer had stood for her. He had examined her properly and told the truth, but that faint alarm was still present no matter how much Ferro wanted it to be gone. It was possible that because he was from ancient times, when Carpathian males kept their lifemates hidden away from other males, and he was a throwback to that era, he was in some way casting the healer in a villain light because he was powerful—or because Elisabeta didn't trust him. She caught all those thoughts and couldn't help shaking her head, although she knew if he decreed it, she would have to abide by his decision. She felt his rejection of the idea in his mind and she was happy for it.

"Have no fears, *piŋe sarnanak*. I am an ancient and still live the ancient ways. That means I do not like other males around my woman unless I am right there."

She found that she was extremely happy that he was an ancient and preferred the older ways. She didn't want anyone else around her. She definitely preferred it that way as well.

6

The rain upon a fire, frenzied and in need;
A blessing for all life, and fortune for the seed.

T
he call of the rain woke Elisabeta, a dark drumming that beat in her heart and lungs, forcing her to come to the surface regardless of her determination to stay safe beneath the soil. Above her, already, the earth had opened at her lifemate's command and she knew she had no choice but to obey his summons.

She wanted to come to Ferro whole, her mind free of the vampire who had been her constant companion for centuries, but he had damaged her in so many ways, she didn't know where to start repairing herself. She did know, and accepted, that her lifemate was a good man. A kind one—and he deserved her trust, although a part of her couldn't quite believe she really was in good hands.

She lay in the earth waiting, but Ferro made no move to bring her to him, and she realized he wanted her to come to him. At once, familiar panic gripped her. Her heartbeat accelerated. Her breathing turned ragged.

You are afraid, minan piŋe sarnanak. Tell me what disturbs you.

His voice. Gentle. Velvet soft, sliding over her skin and into her bones. She felt him pouring into her mind, directing her heartbeat to slow to the steadier rhythm of his. Her breathing took on a calmer, much more even pace. Still, for all his gentleness, it was a clear order, and for that she was grateful.

I do not know what you want from me. I do not know what to do.

She felt him stroke a caress through her hair as if he were there with her. The touch of his fingers on her face. Barely there, but felt all the same. Her body reacted strangely to his touch, coming alive in ways she had never known previously. Little goose bumps rising on her skin. Her nipples tightening. Butterflies taking wing in her stomach.

When I call for you to rise, Elisabeta, and come to me, you will float to the surface, freshen your body and hair, and clothe yourself if you wish. I will call you after I have fed. I will take your blood and then feed you. I do not want you feeding from anyone else unless I am unavailable, and then one of my brethren will see to your needs in my absence.

She couldn't think of him being away from her. The idea was terrifying. Sergey would come immediately. He would know. She would somehow send for him. She jammed her knuckles into her mouth and bit down to keep from letting a single sound escape. She'd used the trick often to keep the vampire from knowing he'd gotten to her.

You have forgotten I am merged with you, päläfertiilam, there is no hiding your thoughts from me. I am not going to leave you alone until you are strong enough to keep from summoning the vampire. I have woven a shield and that will keep his shadow worms from invading should an accident happen. For now, rise and come to me.

I have never clothed myself. It was humiliating to have to admit such a thing.

It is time for you to practice, sívamet. He sounded very matter-of-fact. Calm. Normal. Not at all judgmental or impatient. *You are Carpathian and you are powerful. I want you to feel your power. The vampire could not steal it from you. By taking your control he could make you believe you were helpless. You were young, a child when he took you, but you are no longer that child and you will learn how strong you are with time. Think in terms of small steps. While I enjoy every aspect of caring for you, Elisabeta, to have you do this would please me.*

She took a deep breath. She wanted to please Ferro. She had a nature that naturally needed to bring peace and comfort to those around her. She recognized that that was the biggest part of herself. It was a gift she had, and she actually had to control it in order to keep from giving Sergey too much comfort. She had been ashamed that she couldn't stop herself when his brothers had cruelly taunted and made fun of him, acting as if they were so superior.

She knew Sergey retained some of his emotions because of her. He felt the vicious, derisive insults his brothers heaped on him. They had from the time he was young, even before he had followed them, choosing to give up his soul. Elisabeta knew Ferro would see that she had given Sergey comfort and it shamed her even more. There were so many terrible secrets she had that her lifemate would find out, merged as he was with her. Even the healer and possibly his brethren had already discovered some of her shameful secrets in her memories.

Elisabeta, you will stop this instant. Ferro snapped the command in a fierce, curt tone.

She instantly jerked to attention. She had never heard him sound like that, but it stood to reason when everyone around them seemed to regard him as the most dangerous man in the room that he could command with such a frightening voice.

You will obey me at once and stop this nonsense. I will not have my lifemate ashamed of who she is. Your greatest gift is to bring peace to those of us without solace for centuries. Hunters live in the utter gray of nothingness and yet just your presence relieves that terrible burden. It matters little if you speak. Your voice adds to the length of time your gift lasts, but you were born with a trait few have. I will not have you in any way demeaning what is one of the most highly prized and rare gifts our people have. Do I make myself clear?

She knew he was right in that she couldn't stop herself from reaching out when someone was distressed. In the room the rising before, when there were so many ancients without lifemates, she had felt their lost emotions when they had not. While they talked to one another, discussing her, she had huddled in Ferro's lap most of the time, silent, but she had done her best to send out soothing waves to bring as much peace as possible to those in the room who would be receptive.

She wasn't in the best of shape, weak from the long years of being kept half-starved. Her mind was fragmented, so scattered that at times it was very difficult to think for herself. She knew Sergey had deliberately tried to beat that ability out of her. He didn't want her thinking. He wanted to control everything in her life. He was furious that she refused to turn over her lifemate's soul to him, too afraid of losing her to push her beyond what he'd already done.

Elisabeta, I require an answer immediately.

Ferro wasn't going to drop it. He didn't sound angry, but she knew he bordered on something close to it. He really didn't like her self-derision over her talent. They were connected, and she dared to touch his mind. He really believed that her ability to bring peace to the ancient hunters was worth more than any other talent others held. He took pride in her gift and took pride in her. The fact that she felt shame offended him in some way, as if her poor opinion of herself reflected on him. She didn't like that at all.

You are very clear, päläfertiilam. I will always remember. I am coming to you now.

She would never forget that he took pride in her ability. She would do so as well. He was right in that she couldn't control her need to soothe those around her. That energy radiated out of her without her consent whether she wanted it to or not. She had to accept that about herself and know that as long as her lifemate took pride in her, she would, too.

I want you to feel pride in yourself because you deserve to feel it, not because I feel it, Elisabeta. You are important on your own.

She wanted to be the woman he seemed to need as his lifemate, but deep down she knew it was impossible and she was always going to disappoint him. If he compared her to Julija, she would always come up short. The comparison would be laughable. She tried not to let herself feel as if there was no hope. She would learn the things she could. Rising on her own, cleaning her body and dressing herself couldn't be that difficult—and yet it was.

She could float easily enough out of the ground. She made herself lighter than air. That wasn't difficult. It took several tries to clean herself to her satisfaction, and she was very self-conscious, aware Ferro was merged with her and could see everything she did. She felt like a child attempting to do the same task over and over. At some point, when she was a toddler, her parents must have shown her how to do these things, but she had no memory of the lessons. Sergey had managed to destroy her memories of her earlier life with her family. The flashes of recollection were always accompanied by pain.

Ferro didn't show impatience. In this instance, she almost wished he would. Her hair was thick and far too long. It fell nearly to her knees and weighed heavily on her head. It felt a tangled mess and she wanted to cut it and wear it short so she didn't have to learn to manage it.

You will not.

That was a decree. Hard. Fast. A gut reaction that almost made her smile in spite of her frustration with the mass. Ferro definitely preferred long hair. At least she'd gotten that admission out of him. Not only had she gotten that out of him, but her hair was suddenly shorter, more to her bottom than to her knees, and now clean, untangled and neatly braided.

Thank you. It was a relief not to have to figure out how to do that task.

Now there was the matter of the dress. That long dress he'd shown her. It was a more modern style than she had ever conceived of wearing. She'd made the choice to wear the black-and-gray one the rising before because, although it did cling to her figure, it wasn't quite as thin as this one was. She had the vision stored in her mind. She had set every detail of the dress in her mind so that she would be able to duplicate it when he asked it of her. Now, she was so afraid. How could she wear it?

May I ask you anything?

I have said so. There was no impatience in his tone, but his words implied that she should have remembered.

Will others see me in this garment?

Yes. Andor is bringing Lorraine to meet you. And Traian, your brother, is very impatient to see you.

She couldn't help pulling back in horror, trying to distance herself from him. He refused to let go of their merging. She clenched her fists. This wasn't going well at all and she'd promised herself she would do so much better this rising. Lorraine. The woman he felt affection for. How could she face her in such an indecent garment? And Traian? A brother she didn't remember who would have expectations she couldn't meet. She would hurt him without meaning to. It seemed she was doomed to fail everyone, especially her lifemate.

This wasn't going to work. As much as she wanted it to, as much as she thought Ferro was the most heroic man in the universe, she couldn't do this, not even for him.

"You are panicking for no reason, *piñe sarnanak*," Ferro said, his arms sliding around her waist from behind. "When you have need of me, you are to call out. Reach out. Hear our song. You have choices, Elisabeta, and one day you will remember that you have them. In the meantime, I will make your choice for you. Your choice is always me. I am your shield."

He bent his head, his hair sliding against her bare skin, sending a shiver of awareness down her spine. His lips trailed over the side of her neck from her earlobe to the pulse pounding so temptingly there.

"You have not seen modern women and the way they dress. The dress I have chosen for you is extremely modest by comparison. You will look beautiful in it. I would not provide garments for other men to stare at your body. When we are alone, I can show you the types of clothing you can wear only for me."

His teeth scraped over her pulse, and between her legs her sex clenched unexpectedly. Hotly. Her stomach did a slow roll.

"You must have more trust and faith in your lifemate, Elisabeta. I am ancient and I do not care for other males to be around my woman, especially those I do not know. I am more dominant than many of the other ancients. I was born that way and the centuries only amplified that trait in me. I worry that you will find me . . . difficult to live with."

His teeth sank deep and she couldn't stop the little cry of pleasure that escaped. His hands came up to cup the weight of her breasts, his thumbs brushing over her nipples. She felt as if flames flickered and danced over her.

You will wear the dress with confidence because I will find you beautiful in it. If you do not wish to meet Lorraine, you do not have to do so. I wanted you to have friends, but it is not necessary. Only if that is your desire.

His fingers and thumbs began tugging on her nipples, gently at first and then a little rougher, so that streaks of fire seemed to go straight to her center, which had turned to liquid heat. How could she think straight? There was no thinking when his mouth and hands were wreaking such havoc with her body. It felt to her as if every nerve ending in her body had come to life and was on alert, just waiting for him, desperate for his attention. She found herself wholly focused on him. Acutely aware of him as a male. A man. Her man.

She couldn't see him, but knew he was dressed and she wasn't. It seemed—decadent. There were images in his mind that came and went so fast she could barely keep up, but they were all erotic and seemed indecent, and yet she wanted them to slow down so she could see them more clearly. She knew each image had to do with Ferro and her. That sent a secret little thrill down her spine.

His tongue slid across the vein in her neck and he turned her around, opening his shirt, tipping her chin up as he did so. His lips brushed hers, the briefest of touches, but again, a spontaneous frisson rushed down her spine and spread through her body. Her nipples pushed against his bare chest as he locked her close to him, his tongue teasing at the seam of her lips.

"Open your mouth for me."

She knew if she did, she would lose herself in him, but she couldn't resist him. It wasn't just his demand, made in that soft, commanding voice. It was Ferro. He mesmerized her. She parted her lips and his tongue swept into her mouth, bringing fire. Bringing chaos. Bringing a passion she hadn't known existed in her. The emotion swept over her so fast and so deep, welling up like a volcano, colliding with his overwhelming feelings so that it seemed as if they would both go up in flames.

He kissed her long and deep, until a firestorm roared in her belly and the junction between her legs burned and turned to liquid. Her sex clenched emptily. Her breasts felt swollen and achy. Her entire body was suddenly restless and needy. Tension coiled deep and a different kind of urgent hunger awoke in her.

Ferro lifted his head, his hands tracing the curve of her cheekbones. "Feed, *sívamet*. You are pale and I hunted this morning to take care of our needs."

She suddenly had other needs she knew little about but wanted him to take care of as well. She managed to lift her gaze to his, hoping he would see. He brushed a kiss over each eyelid.

"One lesson at a time, Elisabeta. You have to be very sure I am what you want. An ancient dominant ruling your life may sound good to you now, but in a few years, when you get your confidence back and know your own power, I will be a weight you would have to bear around your neck."

He pressed her face to his chest, not giving her time to answer him. She wanted to protest. She knew herself better than he did. She knew how the centuries had shaped her, but right then the sound of his heart was like the drumming of the rain on the earth's soil. Like the sound of it in their song when he woke her. Temptation, and so close. She already had the taste of him in her mouth.

She was a little obsessed with taking his blood just from the times he'd fed her. Now that addiction had grown worse. His taste was not just about his blood, but was wrapped up in him as well. His sheer personality. His sensuality. The way he made her feel about herself as a woman. As lifemates, the way his blood tasted was already an aphrodisiac to her, but she found it was so much more.

She stroked her tongue over his pulse and then bit down, sinking her teeth deep, her body clenching wildly as his unique flavor burst into her mouth and down her throat. She found it strange that the act of feeding was no longer just that, but more sexual in nature. She didn't even know that much about sex, only what Ferro was slowly showing her with the images in his mind, but her body was already reacting to him and had been all along. It was as if her body had been asleep all those centuries and he had come along and woken it up. She moved restlessly against him even as she took his blood, her arms stealing around his waist.

He let her drink more than he should have, she was certain, but when he stopped her, she still felt deprived, although she obeyed him instantly. He bent his head to brush her mouth with his as if in reward for her obedience. He ran the pads of his fingers from her shoulders over the curves of her breasts to her nipples, raising goose bumps on her bare skin and setting her heart pounding all over again.

"Clothe yourself in the gown, Elisabeta."

She blinked up at him. He was still going to make her put the dress on herself. It was so awkward. One moment she felt like a sexy woman, the next like a helpless child unable to do what any Carpathian could do. She moistened her lips and visualized every detail of the garment he meant her to wear and then pictured it on her body. She had thought to make it a little larger on her, but didn't want to disappoint him and she knew it would, so she made it exactly as he had shown her.

To her absolute astonishment, the dark forest-green gown clung to her body, falling to her ankles in soft folds of material. The fabric felt amazing on her skin. Too nice. When she moved, it slid over her, rubbing sensuously, inflaming her already aroused body. She wasn't certain that was a good idea. She wasn't wearing any undergarments. She hadn't thought to add them. She had never worn them and didn't know what women wore, but Julija had once told her that women did wear them.

Proving he was still merged with her, Ferro shook his head and leaned close to catch her earlobe between his teeth. "You do not need to wear anything else to make you uncomfortable. You are properly covered, Elisabeta. When you are ready for different clothes, we can experiment to your heart's content, or you can do so with your female friends. Right now, we do only a few things at a time so you are not overwhelmed."

"I like the material," she admitted. She couldn't keep the shyness from her voice. Running her hands up and down her thighs so she could feel the softness of the exquisite fabric, she suddenly panicked. "What about tomorrow? What am I going to wear next rising?"

"We will look at Lorraine's catalogue together and choose two dresses."

She felt her throat start to close in her anxiety. He would expect her to make choices. There would be too many. She brought her hand up in an effort to rub away the coughing fit as it began. He caught her wrist and very gently brought her hand to his mouth.

"I will allow you to look with me and I will choose two of my favorites. Hopefully, you will approve of them. We will continue to do that until you feel capable of aiding me in choosing a gown as well."

She nearly slumped against him in relief.

"We will go into the house and you are to look around the room we were in last rising. I want you to try your best to take in a little more than you did. If it is overwhelming, simply close your eyes and see only me in your mind. We will start with a small area and work our way around that room. It will be our entertaining room."

She was determined not to detest that room. Eventually, it would represent something good to her, she was certain of it. Right now, it was just too big. She nodded.

"This is a good time for you to practice moving on your own from one area to the next. You floated from beneath the ground, so you know you can do that. I want you to practice walking once we're inside the room. You have to be able to move both as a Carpathian and as a human with equal ease. No one will be in the house but the two of us, so if you have a misstep, no one will see."

She swallowed hard. "*You* will see."

His smile was slow in coming. It stole over his face, heating the iron in his eyes to a bluish-silver warmth that took the air right out of her lungs, leaving her unable to catch her breath. The way he looked down at her made her feel as if she were the most important person in his world—and for that moment, she believed she was. His hands cupped her face with such exquisite gentleness that her heart turned over. The pad of his thumb slid back and forth over her chin, mesmerizing her as his eyes looked down into hers.

"I will always see you, *minan piŋe sarnanak*, and everything you do. The way you try the things I ask of you pleases me. There will come a day, maybe soon, maybe a century from now, when I will have to hunt the vampire and you will be left to watch over our children, and I will go with confidence because of the tenacity and bravery you show me right here. You are terrified each rising, and yet with determination, you tackle every task put before you. I could not ask more from our greatest warriors. You humble me."

She heard the sincerity in his voice, saw it in his mind, and it gave her the determination to learn the things needed to exist in the new world she was in. She wanted to do that for him, but also, because he was right; she would have to be alone with their children at some time and she needed to know she could do whatever was necessary. It didn't seem possible, but Ferro was an ancient hunter and he seemed to have every confidence in her.

She nodded. "It is easier to walk without shoes," she said, to try to cover the emotion welling up like a terrible raw burning sensation in her throat and eyes.

He bent his head and brushed her lips with his. It was a brief, barely there contact, but heart-stopping all the same. She felt the butterfly wings fluttering in the pit of her stomach and pressed her hand hard over the sensation.

"Nevertheless, since it is an accepted practice to wear shoes outside, it would be better to practice in the privacy of our home with them on."

He lifted her into his arms, cradling her close to his chest. He felt enormously strong and, although she was tall like most Carpathian women, he made her feel delicate and small. He was a very big man. She knew Sergey had purposely kept her starved to prevent her from possibly growing too powerful, which was silly when she'd never had the chance to learn anything. Now, it seemed, her lifemate was just the opposite. He was willing for her to learn everything. He wanted her to have confidence and feel her own power. She was both exhilarated and terrified by that because she knew Ferro had expectations of her and she wasn't as certain as he was that she could meet them.

Ferro set her down inside the front room of what would eventually be the home base they would live in when they stayed in the United States; at least, she could see that was in his mind at the moment. She kept her eyes closed tightly, afraid of getting too dizzy. She needed to put the images from the rising before solidly in her mind as a reference.

"You are in front of the chair where I sat with you," he said, his hand sliding from her waist to her hip.

The gesture felt . . . intimate. He was never heavy-handed. His palm barely skimmed her body, so light over the thin material of the formfitting gown, but she felt that touch all the way to her bones. She felt branded. His.

"I am not facing the window, am I?" She felt very daring to ask him. In a million years she would never have asked such a question. Elisabeta still wasn't certain whether she was testing her freedom or his reaction.

"No, *sívamet*, I would not make such a mistake with the one who is *hän ku vigyáz sívamet és sielamet*. I cherish you, Elisabeta, and protect you."

She liked that Ferro called her the keeper of his heart and soul. She had kept his soul safe for so long, struggling against Sergey's continual assaults, his trickery and tortures over the centuries, that she felt she truly had been and still was the keeper of his soul. She wanted to be the keeper of his heart as well. That was much more difficult to believe. His soul had been entrusted to her by fate. By destiny. But his heart . . . if she held it, that was given to her by him and all the more treasured for the freely given gift.

His hands slid back up to her waist. She felt him grip her there. Steady her. He was there in her mind, adding to her courage. She could do this for him. He had that ink on his back, the one that said he had kept his honor for her. She could become brave for him. Maybe, eventually, it would be for herself, but for now, if she could do it for him it would be enough.

Elisabeta took a deep breath and forced her eyes open. She expected to feel sick and disoriented but she should have trusted in her lifemate. He had her facing a corner wall. A sconce was lit, the light flickering dimly, casting shadows over an area larger than she'd really taken in the night before. It seemed, at first, a sweeping space, but she made it a grid in her mind, viewing it as if she were seeing the wider corner through bars.

"Very clever."

His breath was warm on her ear. He transferred his hands to her shoulders and began that slow, soothing massage she was coming to really enjoy. He had big hands with strong fingers and he got every tense knot. With just the two of them in the house, it seemed so much easier to let herself have a panic attack if that was what had to happen in order to see the room.

"Think of this as your home, *piŋe sarnanak*. It is only this one room. This space. This is what we have together. A fireplace to keep us warm if the weather turns cold on us and we do not want to go to the trouble of regulating our body temperatures."

She liked the way his lips brushed her ear when he spoke to her. The way his breath warmed her and yet teased her senses at the same time, making her so aware of him. He had come even closer to her, so that she rested against his chest. She could feel his groin pressed tight against her. The long, thick columns of his thighs.

"We will have warm rugs in front of the fireplace. We will have furniture. Chairs to sit in for us and for our visitors. What do you envision in your home? Just in this space for us?"

Her heart pounded against the thick bar of his forearm. She moistened her lips several times before she dared to speak. "I have never been in a home. I do not know what one looks like. If you could show me what you mean . . ." She trailed off, uncertain if even then she could envision what she wanted.

To her utter astonishment, she felt amusement fill her mind. Not at her—at him. He laughed at himself and then shared it with her. "It has just occurred to me, Elisabeta, I know nothing about this subject, either. I avoided humans as best I could for centuries, using them only for sustenance. I certainly did not go into their homes. I did not enter into any homes of Carpathians other than Tariq's and Dragomir's, and then only briefly for meetings. I did not walk through their home but went straight to the meeting room in another form."

Elisabeta found herself relaxing completely, his shared laughter at himself turning what had been stressful into something altogether different. She had never known a sense of fun. Merged as she was with him, even though she wasn't moving very far into his memories, she knew he didn't really remember having fun, either. Together, they were discovering that even the things neither of them really had knowledge of could be amusing if shared.

She let her body rest against his. Immediately a feeling of tranquility and peace flowed into her. She had never known anyone could have his strength, either physical or spiritual.

"Lorraine has catalogues with clothes. Perhaps . . ."

She tried not to feel the annoyance at the other woman's name. He relied far too much on the unknown Lorraine. "I do not know what a catalogue is."

"A magazine. A book with pictures in it."

There was that same amusement in his mind, but this time, she was certain, the humor he felt was directed toward her irritation at the absent oh-so-perfect Lorraine.

"Lorraine is anything but perfect, *piŋe sarnanak*, and I thank the stars that she is Andor's problem and not mine. She is *minan sisar*. To save Andor we bound our souls together. She was not Carpathian at the time and yet, knowing she could die, she still allowed us to bind her to us in order for her to go into the netherworld to find Andor. It took Sandu, Gary, Lorraine and me to be strong enough to bring him out, so yes, I respect her. She is a warrior. She is Andor's lifemate, his problem, and he is *ekäm*."

By claiming Andor as his brother and Lorraine as his sister, he was telling her that the couple were his family and, therefore, family to her.

She turned over every word he had said. She could find no lie. No inflection that would tell her he felt any differently than his words implied. "Why do you say you thank the stars she is Andor's problem when you clearly respect and admire her?"

"She would not suit a man like me at all, nor would I suit her."

That told her nothing at all. He was still, giving her the choice to search his memories, but she couldn't go that far. She was taking one small step at a time. He wanted her to look at this space and make it a home for them. She didn't know what was in a home. He wanted her to meet Lorraine and she would do so as graciously as possible, even though she felt at such a disadvantage. She shied away from thinking about meeting with her birth brother, but knew she had that to do as well. Even if Ferro took her far away, Traian could appeal to the prince and Ferro would be forced to bring her back. He couldn't shield her forever.

"I can, you know. I care little for what others think of me. I have not sworn allegiance to the reigning prince. He cannot order me to do anything, as I am not under his command. Most of the brethren have not sworn allegiance to him, either."

Elisabeta didn't know if the relief sweeping through her was a good thing or a bad thing. She only knew she didn't want to start a war. Still, the idea of so many demands on her when she was barely able to open her eyes without placing imaginary bars in front of her sight was daunting. It was impossible for others to understand.

"I am proud of you, *sívamet*. You have already come such a long way. You do not realize how much you have accepted me into your life. It humbles me that you do so." He rubbed his chin on the top of her head.

"Why have you not sworn allegiance to the reigning prince?"

"I have not sworn allegiance to a prince I have never had the chance to get to know. His father betrayed his people by keeping his eldest son alive when he knew he should destroy him. He set many things in motion that should not have been just to please his lifemate. His duty was to his people, to all of us. His hunters were doing all we could to live with honor, and yet he chose a path knowing the Carpathian people would come to the very brink of extinction if he didn't kill his son. He left a mess to his son Mikhail."

"How could he possibly know that?"

"Vlad had precognition. He knew. He might not have wanted to know. He might have tried to tell himself that what he saw in the future didn't have to be, but he knew. He was a ruthless leader until it came to his own children. The rules he applied to everyone else he didn't apply there. I will not make the mistake of following a leader blindly."

She heard the ring of absolute truth in his voice. Ferro had gone his own way for so long, relying on himself and then his brethren, becoming such a force to be reckoned with, that even seasoned Carpathian hunters were wary of him. She understood him better and his reasoning made sense to her. He had been betrayed by someone he had believed in, just as she had been betrayed by her childhood friend. She understood betrayal and the long-term consequences.

"He is still the prince, Ferro, and unless I am misunderstanding what I overheard from the Malinov brothers, he is capable of wiping out anyone with his power. That is why he is the prince. He is the vessel for all power of the Carpathian people."

"That is true, *sívamet*. Tariq is appointed to stand for him, but he is not a prince and cannot do what Mikhail can do," Ferro admitted. "Sooner or later, the brethren will have to decide if the reigning prince is worthy of our support and defense. We have not had time to meet him for ourselves, but when we do, we will make that decision as many have done before us."

Elisabeta thought that was fair. If one was going to fight to save a prince, or go to war for one, they should believe in him.

"So, I am looking at our space here," she said, hoping to once again lighten the mood between them. "I like the chair we had last rising. We both fit nicely into it. Was it comfortable for you?" She felt very daring asking. She had no idea what the chair looked like. She hadn't seen any of the furniture.

He bent his head until his lips were once again against her ear, where she could feel his warm breath. The way he did that turned her insides to melting butter.

"Are you going to drop the bars of your cage, *minan piŋe sarnanak*? You are my little songbird, but you can fly free in our home with me by your side."

She liked being his songbird, although she'd never sung for him. She heard his song playing in her mind when she was nervous or upset. He had a beautiful and soothing singing voice. "I'm not quite ready to fly. I have not learned to walk that well."

She realized she had covered his forearm with her hand and was stroking his bare skin over and over. He hadn't protested, but she still forced herself to stop. She was taking more liberties with him than should be allowed. Worse, if she relied on him and then lost him . . .

"Elisabeta, you are my lifemate. Unless you decide you cannot be with me, I will stay by your side in this life and the next one. You will grow in confidence as you are each rising, and we will work together on building a relationship that works for the two of us regardless of what other couples think we should be."

Ferro was always so steady, so calm and matter-of-fact. Some of that was beginning to make its way through her seemingly endless fears. He gave her the impression that he could always be counted on. That he was unchanging and no matter what happened around him, he would come through. She wanted desperately to believe that. She needed to in order to let go of terror, get out of survival mode and learn to live.

Very slowly, keeping her eyes open, she removed the bars one by one. At first, she took the ones in the middle off, allowing just a little more of the open spaces in. She waited a few heartbeats to see if she became disoriented or sick to her stomach. The outer bars helped to keep her feeling as if she were still in a smaller space.

Ferro's arm, locked around her, tightened just a fraction, reminding her that he was there. She felt his warm breath against her ear. He stayed quiet, allowing her to work at her own pace, something she was beginning to value in him as a partner. He never hurried her, nor did he seem impatient with her. That trait in him gave her more confidence.

She drew in a deep breath as, for the first time in centuries, she was able to look at an open area without bars in front of it and not feel as if she were going to be sick or fall forward into space. It was exhilarating. A small step maybe, which no one else would even acknowledge, but for her it was huge, and Ferro had given that to her.

Elisabeta turned her head up toward his, looking over her shoulder. "You really are rather wonderful."

His smile was slow in coming, but when it did, it lit his ever-changing eyes to that bluish-silver she loved. He bent his head and brushed her lips very gently with his. "I am honored you think so, as I believe my lifemate is rather wonderful."

Heart beating fast like the little songbird he always called her, she turned back to examine the area in the corner, now much wider without the bars in the middle. She didn't want to fail at the last minute, but she really wanted to take the outer bars of the cage down and be totally free of Sergey's captivity. The vampire had done that to her. Forced her to look at everything in her life through bars. She was never a participant but always a watcher. Ferro gave her the opportunity to become a participant but only in what she wanted to do and at her own pace. She might be frightened, but he stood with her, giving her courage.

Gripping Ferro's forearm tight, she brought down the last of the bars, the two on the outer edges of the cage she'd constructed in front of her eyes. First the one on the right side. With that curved bar down, far more space was allowed into her line of vision, or at least it seemed that way. She forced air through her lungs and pressed as close as possible to Ferro, refusing to close her eyes.

Her stomach lurched just for a moment but Ferro leaned down, his hair sweeping over her bare neck, sending delicious little shivers of awareness through her body, totally distracting her. His teeth scraped back and forth over the pulse pounding in her neck.

"You are so incredibly brave, *sívamet*. I think you should be called *kont o sívanak* instead of me."

Strong heart. He thought she should be entitled to such a name. Her heart soared. Every time his teeth slid over the pulse in the side of her neck, she nearly forgot her own name, let alone to be disoriented by the space in front of her. Every nerve ending in her body was alive and entirely aware of him.

"I think we will leave that title for you," she murmured. Encouraged, she brought the last of the bars down.

The view of the room in front of her opened wide, spreading out so she could see so much more that it seemed enormous, far larger than anything she'd ever been in that she could remember. Her first inclination was to close her eyes and turn to hide her face in his chest. Before she could, pain and pleasure burst through her simultaneously, so close together the two sensations couldn't be separated. Then it was the most erotic feeling she'd ever experienced in her life, so much so it was overwhelming. She could barely think straight, let alone worry about what she was seeing.

I could not resist tasting you again. You are . . . exquisite. Ferro stopped himself and immediately closed the wound with the healing saliva from his tongue. *You are such a temptation, lifemate. Your blood calls to me. Your body calls to mine. If you have need, I will give you my blood. I was careful not to take too much.*

She wouldn't have cared if he'd drained her dry. He made her feel so beautiful and sensual, things she hadn't known were possible. She liked that her blood called to him, but the fact that he said her body called to his made her want to hug that statement to her and hold it tightly to examine later.

"Now that you have looked at the space, Elisabeta, what do you think we should do since neither of us has a clue what a home should look like?" His chin moved back and forth over the top of her head.

She froze, unable to give him an answer. It didn't seem to matter to him.

"Perhaps you can practice your walking and I will call Andor and his she-devil lifemate, Lorraine, to come meet you. She can bring us some ideas to look at as well. I will warn you, do not take anything she says as something I would have you do other than when it comes to house decorating. Her lifemate gives her free rein; I would not be so lenient."

He sounded stern, but she was merged with him, and although he believed Andor should take a firmer hand with Lorraine, Ferro felt unfailingly gentle toward Elisabeta.

"That sounds like a good idea," she agreed, feeling his hint of amusement and letting it wash over her, knowing it was just for her alone.

7

What once was a blaze, grows stronger than before;
A metal in the forge, turns a sword for the war.

J osef arrived with Traian and Joie, and he's already begun to work on
updating the programs for Tariq," Andor said. "He brought tablets for
the brethren and is going to be giving lessons." Andor smirked.
"Sandu is first. You know how resistant he is to learning actual technology. He does not mind in the least picking it out of someone's mind, but
to use it on a computer, no way."

Lorraine laughed. "As if you're any different. And Ferro won't even
look at a computer."

"What is the need when I can look into the mind and get the same
information?" Ferro asked. "I learn how to use one, and retrieve the information I am seeking at the same time."

Lorraine rolled her eyes. "You need to come into this century, Ferro.
And why isn't Elisabeta allowed to speak for herself? You introduced us
and yet she hasn't spoken a word. Andor told me that ancients do not
always want their lifemates to speak with other men. We're family, right?
Andor is your brother and I'm your sister, so what's with the old ways?"

Ferro shrugged his shoulders, no expression on his face. He looked
down at the woman he held close to him. Elisabeta was tucked tight

against him, his arm around her, nearly swallowing her, making it almost impossible for Lorraine and Andor, positioned on his other side, to see her clearly. He had set up the chairs deliberately for Elisabeta's comfort, not for that of their visitors. So far, Elisabeta hadn't given any indication that she wished to engage with the couple. Until she did, he was going to shield her.

Lorraine gave an exaggerated sigh while Andor coughed behind his hand, amusement lighting his eyes. She glared at her lifemate. "Don't encourage him. Elisabeta, really. Ferro only acts like he's tough. He's really a sweet teddy bear. A little gruff sometimes, but he would never, under any circumstances, hurt you. If you want to talk without his permission, go right ahead. If he glares at you, I'll kick him in the shins for you."

Ferro not only heard the ring of truth in her voice but knew she had the audacity and courage to back up her threat with action. More, the smallest sound escaped Elisabeta, just in her mind, but he could swear it was a girlish giggle. That pleased him to no end. He knew his larger-than-life warrior-sister would bring his submissive lifemate a completely different perspective, one he wanted her to see. He had no idea Elisabeta would find Lorraine as amusing as he did.

"You, I cannot put over my knee, but my lifemate, I assure you, I can, and will." In his mind, he made certain that he was rubbing Elisabeta's bottom sensuously, massaging her buttocks, not in the least hurting her. To Lorraine, he sounded archaic, as if he would spank his lifemate, but he didn't want his little songbird to fear anything in the way of punishments other than what he'd told her would happen—his kisses.

Lorraine leapt to her feet and paced across the room, all restless energy. "You horrible brute of a man. Don't you dare threaten that poor defenseless woman." She stalked right up to him, both fists clenched at her side. "I really am going to kick you in the shins. She needs care, not threats, Ferro." She drew in air, clearly struggling to calm herself down. "I understand that you're as old as dirt, but seriously, do you have any idea what she's been through?"

"Lorraine," Andor cautioned. "She is his lifemate. That means that they merge minds, just as we do. He knows everything that has happened to her. You are reacting as a human and thinking with your human mind. Think as a Carpathian. Lifemates must provide what the other needs. Ferro knows exactly what his lifemate needs."

Ferro narrowed his gaze at his brother. *You do not need to ruin all my fun.*

Lorraine's hands went to her hips and she stood in front of him for a long while, just staring down into the expressionless mask he wore. "You are such an ass, Ferro. You purposely let me believe you were forbidding her to talk to us just so you could see my head explode, weren't you?"

"I do not believe you will ever find your Zen, woman. You jump to a conclusion before all the facts are in. My woman needs time to process things, including new people. Now she most likely thinks you are insane, although I did try to prepare her by telling her you are a hothead."

Lorraine's eyes narrowed on him. "You did not just call me a *hothead*."

"It was difficult trying to get her to understand what that means, although now I'm certain she knows." Ferro kept his tone droll.

Lorraine burst out laughing. "You're so impossible. Elisabeta, I love this man like a brother, but I want to wring his neck most of the time. I hope eventually you can come to accept me as a sister in spite of the faults Ferro believes I have." There was vulnerability in Lorraine's voice, even though she was smiling.

Beside him, Elisabeta stirred. Ferro threaded his fingers through hers, hoping to give her courage. He could feel that she wanted to speak, but she was so timid.

I would wish you to reassure her if at all possible.

Ferro felt her steeling herself, gathering her courage.

"Ferro admires and respects you so much, Lorraine. He speaks very highly of you always and told me he regards you and has affection for you as his *sisar.* For an ancient without a lifemate to bind his soul to a woman, especially a human woman, it is a sign of the highest esteem."

Tears shimmered in Lorraine's eyes. She blinked them away rapidly and then turned to her lifemate as she quickly went back across the short distance to throw herself in the chair beside Andor. He immediately held his hand out to her and she took it as if catching a lifeline.

"Thank you, Elisabeta. That's the nicest compliment. Ferro would never have told me he thought any of those things about me."

"There is no need," Ferro said. "You should have that confidence already."

Lorraine shook her head. "Ferro, you, Andor and the others have all the confidence in the world. Women aren't the same way, at least the ones I know. We try to be confident, but we need a little reassurance now and then."

"You are Andor's lifemate. That is enough," Ferro decreed.

Lorraine made an exasperated sound that caused Elisabeta to give Ferro another little girlish giggle in their merged minds.

"Just because you decree something doesn't make it so, Ferro," Lorraine argued.

He lifted an eyebrow. "Do not listen to her nonsense, *minan piŋe sarnanak*. When I decree something, it makes it so for you. I set the rules and you must follow." He knew rules made Elisabeta comfortable, where as they would really make Lorraine's head explode. Just to make her really crazy, he kept going. "My word is absolute law to you."

Lorraine removed her shoe and threw it at him all in one motion, proving she'd been working at the techniques Andor had been giving to her since he'd converted her. Ferro stopped the missile in midair, not taking a chance that it would come near Elisabeta.

Andor burst out laughing. "They are like this all the time, Elisabeta. We will have to be the sane ones. If Julija and Isai are around, it only grows worse. Julija takes Lorraine's side, and Ferro taunts them all the more."

Ferro didn't have the relationship with Julija that he had with Lorraine, but for Elisabeta's sake, he knew he would need to develop one. Something. She had to know that in the end, he had his lifemate's best interests at heart.

I will tell them, Eisabeta assured. *I do not like them thinking you are treating me in a way that is considered bad when you are really taking good care of me and doing what I ask of you.*

"My woman worries that you and Julija think badly of me when I am protecting her. I do not care what others think, only what she thinks. I do not want her upset, Lorraine. Everything is new to her. Everything. She must learn the smallest thing that even children take for granted, and she has taken on this daunting task. I do not want anyone to make her feel less because she does not know something or because she has need of me to shield her while she takes the time needed to get used to a different world. I would ask that you and Julija aid her in this, not make it more difficult by expecting her to take on the modern rules of society, which she cannot possibly comprehend all at once."

Lorraine stilled, as if realizing he was reprimanding her as gently as Ferro knew how.

"She can barely breathe in the open without fear. She must learn to walk, and it goes without saying all the skills of a Carpathian must be learned. She does not know how to see without looking through the bars of a cage. Making a decision has never been done. These are things she has to conquer. Expecting her to know people she does not remember, such as her birth brother, is ludicrous. She was tortured for centuries and she never gave up my soul. She has immeasurable courage and a stubborn streak a mile wide. You do not have to fear that I would ever look down on her or treat her in a way that was disrespectful to her. I ask that you would not, either. I need you to be a *sisar* to her. To aid me in guiding her through this time so she knows she is not alone. It is important to me."

Ferro had never really asked anything of anyone, and yet he found, for Elisabeta, he was willing to ask quite a lot of anyone he trusted. He wanted her to have female friends. He had thought quite a long time over the choices there in the compound. Julija was the first choice simply because she had sacrificed so much just to give Elisabeta the opportunity to escape. She had laid her own life on the line. She was truly Elisabeta's first real friend.

Lorraine was his choice because he trusted her. She would guard Elisabeta as carefully and as fiercely as he did. She made him laugh, and she would make Elisabeta laugh. Other than her penchant for trying to modernize Elisabeta too fast, she was a perfect selection. He also knew Lorraine put his relationship with Elisabeta at the most risk. If she influenced her too heavily and his lifemate eventually became like her, they would cease to be compatible. Still, he knew Elisabeta needed Lorraine in her life.

Emeline was his third choice as a female friend for Elisabeta, and he wanted to find a way to bring her to the house. Dragomir kept Emeline and their daughter very close to their home. She was the most like Elisabeta in personality, and Ferro wanted to show her that it was okay to be different. That everyone was different and each relationship was their own.

"Of course I would be happy to help Elisabeta if she'll accept my friendship," Lorraine said. "I know I can get all about women's rights, Ferro, but in the end, I really am all about sisterhood. I believe that whatever is right for a woman, whatever she chooses, I can support as long as it really is her choice."

"You do understand Carpathians are not human, Lorraine," Andor said gently. He brought her hand to his mouth and kissed her knuckles. "We do not have choices. Not the male. Not the female. Or should I say, very few real choices. Once we are tied together, there is no way to break those ties. We are committed to one another's happiness." His thumb stroked caresses back and forth over her knuckles as he brought her hand to his chest. "Our laws and customs are very different from human ones and it can be difficult to remember that."

"I am aware of that," Lorraine admitted. "It is hard to keep it in mind sometimes, especially around certain ones, like Ferro." She sent him a quick apologetic smile. "He never changes expression so it's hard to tell when he's teasing me, and he does act all feudal with Elisabeta."

"Even so, *mica*, should Ferro act the part of a feudal lord, it is what his lifemate requires or he would not do so."

There was such tenderness in Andor's voice when he addressed his lifemate as he beautifully and gently pointed out the truth of their ways to her, that Ferro felt he needed to find a way to get that particular tone for his woman.

I like the way you speak to me, Elisabeta said. *And I like that you call me your songbird. She struggles to understand the ways of the Carpathians and he is gentle with her.*

Perhaps I should stop teasing her.

She likes that from you. She needs you to act like a brother, to feel as if she has family surrounding her. I can sense that she lost so much.

His woman had so much empathy for others. He could feel her reaching out to Lorraine, soothing her. They all had lost so much, not in the least, Elisabeta.

She lost her entire human family before meeting Andor.

"Traian is insisting that he meet with his sister, Ferro," Andor said. "He has gone to Tariq and Gary and made his appeal to them. Gary has explained that she is very fragile and you are introducing the world to her slowly. He is claiming his rights as family."

Ferro shrugged, in no way perturbed. "When she is ready, we will meet with him."

"He has indicated that he wishes to take her back to the Carpathian Mountains where she might be near more familiar things." Humor crept into Andor's voice. "Apparently your reputation has preceded you and he worries that you might have, over the centuries, turned into something— how shall I put this delicately—*beastly*, no longer fit to be a lifemate, especially for one as delicate and fragile as Elisabeta. He wishes to take her back to the prince and have him decide."

Elisabeta drew back, her breath catching in her throat, terror roaring to the forefront. *Can he take me from you? Can he do that?*

Breathe, sívamet. No one will ever take you from me. Very casually he lifted Elisabeta out of the seat and into his lap, his arms settling around her shivering body.

"I have a certain reputation for a reason, Andor. Should anyone try to take my lifemate from me, the ground would run red with their blood. I will never give her up as long as she wants me. I have given her my word of honor and I will keep it." Deliberately, he was very calm and matter-of-fact about it. He felt that way because it was a fact of life, but he needed his lifemate to know he meant it. "Her brother will understand and be reassured once he meets me. He is only concerned because he cares so deeply for her."

You already can feel that you are growing into your own power, Elisabeta. When you learn to wield it, and you will, together, we will be unstoppable. He wanted her to know he wasn't the only one with power. She was capable of stopping others from forcing their wills on her—even him.

"It is best that you meet with your birth brother, Elisabeta," Lorraine said gently, addressing her directly. "I know it will be difficult, but with Ferro there, nothing could harm you. Andor and I will stay close in case you need us."

Andor nodded. "Know that Traian searched for centuries for you. When others gave up, he did not. There was no trace of you. You simply vanished. The moment he heard the news that you were alive, that you had been rescued, he arranged, with his lifemate and young Josef, to travel here to see you. He wants only to know that you are in good hands. Tariq has assured him that Ferro is doing right by you and can protect you from the vampire."

A little shudder went through Elisabeta's body, but Ferro was in her mind and he felt her gather her courage—and she had it in abundance. She might be terrified to face the world that had passed her by as it had him, but she forced herself to do it.

If Tariq reassures him you are protecting me, why would he want to take me to this prince? I do not understand.

Ferro knew she wanted him to ask the question of Andor. He sent his brethren a faint smile. "My lifemate is logical. She wants to know why Traian would want to take her from me if he has been reassured by the prince's choice to rule here."

Andor sent him a small grin back. "She's quick, isn't she?"

"She's in the same room," Lorraine pointed out, making a face at them. "Elisabeta, men are annoying. I don't know how you don't find them so. Either I'm laughing or I want to kick them."

"She means kiss me," Andor stated. "She really likes kissing me."

"I did, until you decided to start acting like Ferro, who thinks he's some feudal lord in a castle and we should all bow at his feet."

"Not everyone, Lorraine," Ferro corrected with a straight face. "Only the women."

He shared his amusement with Elisabeta, hoping his teasing of Lorraine would help his woman realize that it didn't matter what others might be plotting or planning, their world remained theirs. He would see to her happiness and safety. Immediately, his little songbird relaxed in his arms. Her spirit slid against his, an intimate connection that was becoming more sensual in nature the more time they spent together, which would be every rising.

Without warning, a white-hot rage burst through his mind. At the same time he came to his feet, putting Elisabeta behind him, both Lorraine and Andor were also on their feet, facing the door, feeling that same threat as well.

"Sandu," Lorraine whispered. "He does not feel. Why would he suddenly be experiencing such intense emotion?"

Ferro didn't wait, waving toward the door, blasting it open, curling one arm around Elisabeta, clamping her to his side as he hurled himself outside and into the air. Andor and Lorraine were right behind him. They flew together straight into the middle of the yard in the center of Tariq's compound, where Sandu towered over a young Carpathian male.

Sandu was a powerful ancient with broad shoulders and a thick, broad chest. He was tall, with long flowing hair tied back with a leather cord. His arms were corded with muscle and his thighs were twin, powerful columns. He was the kind of man others stepped aside for. Ordinarily, Ferro knew, Sandu wasn't bothered by nuisances. Where a few of the ancients reacted to the rude modern-world behaviors, Sandu wasn't one of them. It made no sense that he aggressively stood with his white teeth drawn back in a snarl as he faced the young Carpathian who looked no more than a teenager.

Josef had very pale, almost porcelain skin, made more so by his extremely black hair. It was spiked with the tips dyed bright, almost neon blue, something one might see in human teenage boys but never in Carpathians. He might look like a human boy, but he was in his twenties, had shrewd intelligence in his eyes and didn't back away from Sandu as the ancient stepped close to him.

"You need to have patience when you're learning this kind of technology." Josef kept his voice very low, not in the least demeaning.

Ferro could tell the boy was being careful not to sound patronizing.

It didn't seem to matter. Sandu ripped the tablet from his hands, broke it in two and hurled it across the yard. It was such an out-of-character action for any ancient hunter that it shocked Ferro. He glanced uneasily at Andor and then at Gary, who had silently come up behind Sandu.

There was chaos in Sandu's mind. A red haze that burned like a terrible fire. Ferro tried to reach him through the bond they'd established in the monastery. Andor tried through their soul bond. Gary reached out as a healer. Nothing seemed to penetrate that ugly churning mass, that need for violence.

Sandu stepped closer to the boy and Ferro's heart sank. He would have no choice but to destroy the man he thought of as brother. Sandu had suffered too long and finally was turning. Around them, women and children were being hastily taken to safe rooms. The Carpathian males pressed closer, but this was Ferro's task. No one else would touch his brother.

"Do not tell me what I should do. I have been alive centuries. I need only to take this from your mind. Why should I waste one moment of my precious time on pressing buttons and staring at a screen? You wish only to look superior."

Ferro willed the boy not to respond. There were deep red flames in the middle of Sandu's black eyes, burning out of control, reflecting the wildfire blazing through his body, raging through his mind.

"Sandu," Josef began, his tone placating.

Ferro inched closer, knowing he had to insert himself between Sandu and the boy, and the moment he did, Sandu would defend himself. That was when he felt her. They all felt her. Gary. Andor. Lorraine. And most of all Sandu. Peace and tranquility surrounded all of them but encompassed Sandu, as if enfolding him in a cocoon of sheer serenity. Elisabeta flowed gently into Sandu's mind through Ferro, using his path, her touch so gentle it was barely felt, and yet so powerful, she was breathtaking.

Each of those connected to Sandu felt Elisabeta's compassionate, selfless giving. Her spirit was like a cool summer breeze, moving through the red haze in the ancient's mind, clearing away the vampire-turning tendencies in the ancient and replacing them with peace. Somehow, in a short time, she managed to restore Sandu's normal balance. His mind was once again free of all rage and chaos and he was able to think clearly.

Ferro looked down at his lifemate. She stood very still in the middle of the extremely wide-open yard, surrounded by houses, warriors, mostly strangers, but her entire focus was on Sandu. She didn't see the night sky or the huge area that would have frightened her beyond measure. She saw only a Carpathian hunter in need and she reacted the way her gift demanded. He was extremely proud of and humbled by her.

Thank you, piŋe sarnanak. Sandu matters to me very much. He knew she would have aided any of the Carpathian hunters, but his brethren, Sandu in particular, he held in great affection, although he was only beginning to acknowledge that. He wrapped his arm carefully around her and pulled her under the shelter of his shoulder. It wouldn't be long before she would realize where she was and how many others, including her birth brother, were staring at her.

"So, Sandu, I take it you are far too old to learn technology," Dragomir said, his grin taunting. "I always knew your brain was a bit addled. Apparently, it matters little what songs are sung around the campfire in honor of a great warrior if one's brain can no longer learn."

Sandu narrowed his dark eyes at Dragomir. "*O jelä peje terád.* You try this demon tablet and see how you fare with it."

The other hunters laughed, smiled or smirked as Sandu told Dragomir *sun scorch you*, swearing in their ancient language. Mostly, the humor was from relief that Sandu had been spared from turning, but now the doubt had been planted and he would be watched closely. Ferro knew he would have to monitor his friend at all times.

"We all have to learn it," Gary said. "We can't just know how it works and take the information from one another. We have to be able to use it if we need to. The Malinov brothers have been light-years ahead of us in the use of technology and we have to catch up with them fast if we are going to survive. They are attacking us on every front and they will win if we don't get out ahead of them. Josef is our best hope to do that and we need to pay attention to him."

"Who is brave enough to be next?" Sandu asked. "You, Dragomir? Or you, Petru? I see you, Isai, slinking away into the shadows."

Josef held up his hands. "I will work with one of you next rising. I need to go through the rest of the system, or at least get through as much as I can before dawn comes."

He does not show it, but he was very shaken by Sandu's reaction, Elisabeta reported to Ferro.

Just the size difference alone would have been enough for anyone to be shaken, but the fact that Sandu had so much battle experience was enormous. He was considered one of the best hunters the Carpathian people had. The boy had to have realized that he had been very close to death, although not once had the knowledge shown on his expression or in his voice.

A man holding the hand of a woman with a cap of rich brown hair and cool gray eyes came toward Ferro and Elisabeta. Ferro recognized that this man had to be Traian Trigovise, Elisabeta's brother. His eyes held piercing intelligence and also a determination that meant Ferro might really have to fight his way out of the compound if this man had his way. He wasn't alone in that assessment of the situation. The brethren, including Gary, shifted positions, spreading out to cover the grounds and exits, giving Ferro and Elisabeta a clear path, if necessary, to escape.

"You were gracious, Josef, in spite of my brief outburst," Sandu said. "I apologize for breaking your demon device, although I should have crushed the thing much sooner and been done with it when I realized it was making my head pound. Call, should you have need, and I will come to your aid."

That was a huge promise, and one not lightly given by one of the brethren. Josef had earned not only Ferro's respect, but that of Sandu.

In spite of his modern appearance, Josef was well versed in Carpathian etiquette. He bowed in a courtly manner, showing he could be as elegant and old-world as the ancients. "I accept your astonishing offer, although it isn't necessary. I have thrown my share of tablets."

Every Carpathian could hear lies, and Josef wasn't lying. Ferro liked him all the more for his confession. Sandu gripped the boy's shoulder for a moment and then stepped away from him, turning as Tariq and Maksim came up on either side of Josef. Ferro didn't like that Tariq had once again put himself in harm's way by stepping between Traian and Ferro.

Now that Sandu was safe, Elisabeta's gaze shifted around her. Ferro felt her instant retreat. Her vision shimmered, wavered, as if her eyes couldn't focus properly on the large area her sight encompassed. Her body began shivering uncontrollably. He wrapped his arm tighter around her, pressing her front to his side, his large body nearly hiding hers from the others.

You are completely safe. The brethren are here with us. Sandu will never allow anything to happen to you, not after what you did for him. You saved his honor. Andor and Lorraine are close. Do you feel them? Julija and Isai are to our right. Julija is not only Carpathian but mage as well. We have the ability to go back to our home, stay and talk, or leave this place. Your brother has only your best interests in his heart. Feel that flowing from him.

She moaned in his mind and he knew immediately she had made as many decisions as she was going to make for this rising. She'd come through when no one had asked it of her and she hadn't even realized that saving Sandu had been her choice alone. In saving Sandu, she had saved Josef and she had also spared Ferro from having to kill his friend and brother.

This decision will be mine to make, piŋe sarnanak. You will abide by what I decree. She was back to needing firm guidelines and he would provide them.

"Traian and his lifemate, Joie, have come a long way to see his birth sister," Tariq said. "Traian, this is Ferro, Elisabeta's lifemate."

Ferro inclined his head. "I realize you would like to speak with her, but she does not do well out in the open. It is too much for her. I invite you and your woman back to our home. I am taking her there now. Tariq and Maksim can show you the way if it is your wish to spend time with her."

Ferro didn't wait for an answer. Abruptly, he swung his lifemate into his arms and took to the air. He felt the brethren rise with him. They were silent, unseen, but he knew they were there. Niceties mattered little to him when his lifemate was near to having a breakdown.

You gave us a miracle, sívamet. How did you know you could pull Sandu back from turning? I have never seen anyone come back once they were that far gone. Even the healer could not reach him. None of us could.

For a moment he didn't think she would answer him, but his question distracted her enough that her mind turned the query over and over as if it were a puzzle she was trying to figure out. That kept terror at bay. *Something was at work there, Ferro. Something beyond Sandu and his dislike of modern technology.*

He knew what that something was. Sandu, like the ancients from the monastery, no longer even heard the whisper of temptation to feel for one moment that rush when they killed. All of them had thought that was the worst, but when the whispers stopped, and there was only the terrible void, they knew the danger had increased tenfold. No one but a hunter who had survived centuries on their honor alone would know what it was like to fight every minute of every rising, especially without hope. Sandu had ceased to hope.

He took her straight to their home and immediately set the room for company. "You have done this several times, *minan pine sarnanak.*" He ran his hand down the back of her head and then dropped his fingers to the nape of her neck. "Should Tariq and Maksim accompany them, and most likely they will in order to prevent them from in any way misunderstanding me . . ."

"Why would they misunderstand you?"

Her dark eyes looked straight into his. She rarely did that, and his heart clenched hard in his chest. He began a slow massage. "I am not an easy man, you know that. If I do not like something said, I do not use diplomacy. I am trying to learn, just as you are, but I have not lived among even my own kind in centuries. Tariq will counter what I say so there are no misunderstandings, especially with your birth brother."

Ferro was unsure what he expected, but faint amusement lighting her eyes was definitely not it. She reached a trembling hand up to his mouth, the pads of her fingers very soft as she traced his lips.

"You like to look very scary to everyone."

Deliberately, he captured her fingers and bit down gently, staring down into her beloved face—and it was beloved now. He didn't see, in spite of how he had tried to keep his heart guarded, how he was ever going to be able to do without her if she could no longer tolerate him.

I am scary. He tried to make her laugh.

Ferro had left the door open and Maksim strode in first, followed by Tariq and then Traian and Joie. Behind them were Gary, Sandu and Benedek. Ferro waved them to the chairs he had formed in a semicircle facing the chair he was in. Sandu sat at his right, Benedek at his left. Gary closed the door and lounged against it, but not before Petru had drifted in unseen. He was secreted somewhere in the room, at Ferro's back, making certain Elisabeta was safe. Saving Sandu from turning vampire had cemented her position with all the brethren whether or not she was Ferro's lifemate.

"Elisabeta will not always talk," Ferro said. "I do not force her to do so. She has been forced enough these last centuries. If you ask a question and she wishes to answer, she will, or I will do it for her."

Traian's eyebrow shot up, but he refrained from speaking.

Joie frowned. "How do we know if you're the one answering the question or she is?"

Silence followed her question. Tension filled the room. Ferro didn't speak, nor did he deign to look at her.

It was Gary who broke the uneasy stillness. "You cannot insult the honor of an ancient warrior, one who has lived by honor alone for centuries, and expect his cooperation. I think this meeting is over before it has begun."

Joie instantly shook her head. "You misunderstood me. Or I didn't word my question correctly. I meant, when Elisabeta wants to give her brother an answer, will you indicate to us that she is the one answering?" She leaned toward Ferro. "Please forgive me for the unintended insult. This means so much to Traian, and I was trying to get clarity only."

Ferro inclined his head toward the woman, studying her without seeming to do so. She was a smart little thing. He could see she was far more than what she wanted people to see, and that made her dangerous. Traian and his lifemate were used to working with one another, and did so with ease. He wondered if, when in telepathic communication, their energy would be barely detectable. Ferro shared his conclusions with his brethren, warning them to do as little as possible in the way of talking to give nothing away to either of these two.

Are you willing to answer your birth brother's questions? Do you have any questions for him? He knows things about your past that might be important to you. Deliberately, Ferro enticed his lifemate, wanting her to make a connection to her Carpathian roots. She didn't identify as a Carpathian. She didn't see herself in that light as of yet. He wanted her to have the confidence that came with knowing who she was and where she came from. He also wanted her to see that she had a family that cared for her.

Elisabeta's fingers dug into his arm. *I will listen to him. He is sad. Very sad. He weeps inside and she is filled with sorrow for him.*

Ferro knew that Elisabeta was naturally compassionate, but he hadn't realized the full extent of her gift. It was becoming clear to him that she could read the emotions of those near them. She didn't need to be in their minds. That would mean she could read intent as well. It also meant that her need to help others would always have to be checked by him so she didn't overextend her strength.

"I will, of course, indicate which of us is answering your question." He gave his answer to the couple aloud.

At once the tension eased in the room.

"I searched for you, Elisabeta. I do not want you to think I abandoned you. When I met my lifemate, I was still searching," Traian said. "You vanished so completely. There was no trace of you, no sign of violence. Nothing. No path to you." He shook his head. "I am sorry I failed you."

Elisabeta sat up a little straighter, shaking her head and then pressing back against Ferro, her fingers once more digging into his forearm as if he were her only anchor. Ferro felt the sharp eyes of Joie penetrating the shadows. She was watching Elisabeta's every reaction; the tiniest detail would not escape her. She noted that Ferro massaged the nape of her neck and shoulders. The intimacies he gave to his lifemate in order to give her the necessary courage to face the terrible challenges she had to overcome were for the two of them alone, but he wasn't going to cease giving them to her because Traian's lifemate had piercing eyes.

It was never his failing. No one was ever going to find me. Sergey hid me from even his brothers, and often I was in the same place with them.

Ferro repeated what Elisabeta's response was verbatim. "I wish I could give you her exact inflection because she has a way of speaking that makes you understand exactly what she means. Hopefully she will become comfortable enough that she will be able to talk to you."

"Do you know why she is afraid of us?" Joie asked.

Ferro nodded and kept his voice matter-of-fact, no accusation, although he wanted to let them both know that they had added to Elisabeta's fears. "You both made your intentions very clear when you arrived. You did not like the fact that I am her lifemate and you made that known. She fears that you will try to force her as the vampire did and attempt to separate us. I have assured her that I would fight to the death for her, but she has lived in terror for so many centuries that she cannot conceive of another way of life. She wakes every rising with such fear I must coax her from the ground. She is extremely courageous and comes to me when I call to her, but her new fears have only added another layer of terror for me to wade through."

Traian frowned and leaned toward his sister. "I want only to know that you are safe and happy, Elisabeta. That is all that matters to me. I want to be in your life, of course, but your safety and happiness come before all else. After centuries of not knowing what happened to you and fearing the worst and then knowing it was even worse than I ever imagined your fate could be, I want only to protect you. Wrapping you up in a cocoon is not what you need, and that is what I would want to do. I see your lifemate appears to know what you need, as lifemates are prone to do." He said the last reluctantly.

He pressed his fingers to his forehead as if his head hurt. "I wish you could talk to me. I need to hear your voice. I need to be reassured that it is your will that you stay here and not someone forcing you. I don't mean to sound insulting, I just have for so long been searching for you, and giving you up without knowing . . ." He trailed off.

Merged as he was with Elisabeta, Ferro felt her shivering but gathering her courage, determined that she would speak to this man she couldn't find in her memories because each time she reached for him, pain flashed through her, causing some kind of near seizure in her brain. Sergey's work, which Ferro tried to repair, was a scar on her brain that was centuries old and difficult to remove. He flicked a quick glance at the healer.

Gary nodded once, indicating he had felt Elisabeta flinching away from her past memories.

"It is difficult for me to speak," Elisabeta said, her voice so low it was a mere thread of sound, although soothing and soft, spreading through the room in that peaceful way she had.

Still, Ferro caught the underlying notes of distress. He was certain anyone paying close attention would hear them as well.

"Ferro is my choice. He stands for me when I cannot do so myself, no matter what I ask of him, even if it is abhorrent to him, even if it makes him look bad to others. He does it for me. I do not want to be with any other. I would like to get to know you, but in truth, when I try to remember . . ."

Ferro slid his hand gently over her face, feeling the tears in her mind, feeling the dampness on her lashes. "The vampire has made it impossible for her to recall her past without pain. The healer and I have not been able to address this adequately but will attempt again on the next rising. That particular scar is deep and may not be removed entirely. We have been taking things as slow as possible, giving Elisabeta as much time as she needs to learn the steps of survival. Simple things we take for granted, such as regarding the space around us without looking through the bars of a cage. She has to learn the things Carpathian children learn as toddlers. She is very determined, and if you are patient with her, she will be very happy to establish a relationship with her family."

Traian reached for Joie's hand. "I would welcome that opportunity no matter how long it takes." He glanced at Tariq. "Is there a place for us here?"

"Of course. We have several guest homes." Tariq stood. "Ferro, thank you both for allowing us to visit with you."

Ferro inclined his head and waited for them all to leave so he could once more be alone with his lifemate. "I am very proud of you, Elisabeta. You handled the entire night far better than anyone could expect from you."

"I am tired." She laid her head back against his chest and closed her eyes, exhausted, both mentally and physically.

Ferro didn't need to be told twice. He took her to the sleeping chamber far beneath their home and opened it, floating them both into the rich healing soil.

8

A life of hope sings to you, melodies of devotion;
A world of love awaits, vaster than the ocean.

The sound of the rain woke Elisabeta, but this rising, there was a new note in the beat of the earth's music. Entwined with that dark, persistent drumming was a sensual call that tugged at every one of her senses, bringing her entire body alive whether she wanted to feel those sensations or not. The moment she was aware, *he* poured into her mind. Ferro. Her lifemate. There wasn't room for anyone else. He was larger than life, an invincible warrior of old. An ancient Carpathian hunter calling her from the soil, where she would have stayed to avoid having to learn what was expected of her in her new existence.

Trepidation filled her, yet at the same time a thrill of anticipation such as she'd never felt before. She actually looked forward to this rising, and she could honestly say she couldn't remember feeling that way in all the centuries of her past. She wanted to go to him the way a lifemate would go to her spouse, but she knew little of the concept or what was expected.

They hadn't gone over any other clothing, as they had discussed they were going to do, mostly because so many unexpected things had happened the rising before. She was uncertain what to wear and still couldn't make the decision to clothe herself, especially after seeing how Julija, Lorraine and then Joie dressed. She'd paid particular attention, trying to figure out if she would feel comfortable in their modern attire, but she didn't think so.

The soil opened above her and then she was in Ferro's arms, her body clean, her heart beating too fast, her lungs dragging in air and his wild scent. He was as naked as she was, and she'd never been so aware of herself as a woman. Her breasts rose and fell in time to her ragged breathing. She couldn't seem to control the way she reacted to his closeness, as much as she tried. He felt so strong and in control. He smelled good, filling every one of her senses as they floated together somewhere he wanted to take her. She didn't care, as long as she was with him. Once they settled, she was on his lap, his arms around her, cradling her close.

"Look at me, *sívamet*."

His commanding voice sent a shiver of need down her spine, arrowing from her breasts to her feminine channel. The reaction was shocking. She lifted her lashes immediately and found herself looking into his strangely colored eyes. One moment they seemed bluish-gray and the next a gray-rust. Right at that moment they were a deep blue-silver and so intense, so focused on her with a dark hunger, she could barely breathe.

"Always remember, *te avio päläfertiilam*. You are the keeper of my heart and soul." He drew his palm very gently, very slowly and very possessively down her body, from her neck, over the curves of her breasts, to her mound and then the junction between her legs. His touch was barely there, but it was definitely a claiming.

Her sex clenched, a liquid heat, an awakening of a hunger she hadn't known existed, as if by touching her, claiming her, he'd suddenly awoken the woman in her. Need spread through her, a strange tension coiling deep. Her hips would have squirmed restlessly had she allowed it, but she was far too disciplined for that. She lay passive, looking up at his face, wanting to touch him, to trace the lines carved deep, the strong jawline. He could become an obsession if she wasn't careful.

"Every rising, when you wake, know that you are in my keeping. As my lifemate, you are first in my thoughts on rising and last when I close the soil over our heads. There are no lies between lifemates. You can hear them, Elisabeta. Believe in your ability to hear lies. You are Carpathian and you are powerful in your own right. You can hear anyone lying to you, especially your lifemate. I want you to have confidence in your ability to hear lies always. Once you know that, once you believe that, you will recognize all lies told to you in the past."

He was beautiful. His face was so rough no one else would ever call him that, but she knew he was. She knew Julija didn't altogether approve of him and would never have accepted him as her lifemate, nor would Lorraine. She also knew that she was seeing only one side of Ferro. He was showing her unfailing kindness and it was all very real. Eventually, she would reach further into his mind and see more of him. She wasn't ready. She wasn't strong enough yet; she would have to build up to that. For now, he didn't seem to mind caring for her, and while he did, she would learn. She learned fast.

"Piŋe sarnanak." His voice was soft. Amused. The sound played over her like the touch of fingers. His hand slid back up her body to cup her breast. "I love the way you look at me, as if I mean something to you rather than being a man to be afraid of." He bent his head toward her, his eyes on her face, and then she lost sight of him as his lips touched her chin and then her throat.

Her heart jumped wildly. The sensation was truly without precedent. His lips were firm yet soft. His jaw had the smallest bristles that scraped along her skin, setting nerve endings alive. His teeth teased her senses into heightened awareness. He trailed more kisses down her throat to the curve of her right breast. His hand cupped her left breast, his thumb setting a mesmerizing strumming back and forth over her nipple. Each light brush sent a dark fire streaking to her clit, inflaming it until blood pounded and she could count her heartbeats there.

His teeth sank deep and she cried out at the sheer ecstasy of the erotic bite. In spite of her discipline, her hips shifted restlessly in his lap, the cheeks of her bottom sliding over his groin, rubbing, feeling the shape and size of his heavy erection. That added to the hunger coiling so deep and tight in her body. His thumb and finger tugged at her nipple while he drank, the combined sensations spreading flames through her body unlike anything she'd ever known.

Images poured into her mind. His body moving in hers. Sharing the same skin. Her legs wrapped around his waist. Her body bent over a bed while he took her from behind. On her hands and knees, his arm around her waist while he took her hard and fast. Spread out on the floor with his mouth pressed between her legs, devouring her. Her on her knees, her lips stretched wide around his cock. She felt his need. His hunger mixed with her own until she couldn't tell who felt it more. She only knew her body was slick, hot and aching. He filled her mind and every one of her senses.

Ferro's tongue swept across the twin holes his teeth had made in the curve of her breast, and he shifted her in his arms. "You need to feed, *sívamet.*"

She was already addicted to his taste. She wondered if the moisture she felt on her bottom, where his cock leaked his essence, tasted as wonderful as his blood did. The moment those images had entered her mind, she wanted to explore them one by one. Her teeth slid into place and her mouth watered at that mere thought of feeding, yet already it was so much more.

Even as he shifted her in his arms, he bent his head to her right breast, his mouth drawing the soft curve deep, flattening her nipple to the roof of his mouth, stroking and caressing and then sucking while his fingers tugged at her left nipple. His teeth scraped erotically and then nipped, a small sting his tongue soothed instantly. He kissed the upper curve of both breasts and then lifted his head, giving her access to his chest.

Elisabeta took one look around her. They were no longer in the ground beneath the house he had said would be their home. They were on the rooftop, or a balcony on the roof, where there was a large square area fenced in by a thick wooden rail. They lay together under the stars on a thick fur that felt very sensual on her legs. Everything seemed to feel sensual to her sensitive skin.

She looked at his bare chest and her breath caught in her throat. His chest was wide and thick and very muscular. She rubbed her face over the heavy muscles and then dared to kiss the spot she'd chosen to sink her teeth deep. Her tongue tasted his skin. He didn't hurry her. He shifted her again, widening his legs so that she nestled between them, and one of her hands slid down his chest to find his thick, long cock.

She couldn't stop herself from looking. His shape was both intimidating and thrilling. He took her hand and wrapped it around his shaft and began a slow pumping motion, guiding her fist up and down. More slick heat spread through her body and gathered at the junction of her legs. He had draped one of her legs over his thighs, opening her body to him.

"Drink, *minan piŋe sarnanak*," he coaxed softly.

She scraped her teeth back and forth gently, almost in time to the rhythmic pumping of her fist on his erection, and then she bit into his chest. He threw his head back and she instantly felt his cock swell more, even as that seemed impossible. His taste was even more than she'd remembered, a spicy addiction that added to the sexual hunger spreading through her like a wildfire.

His free hand slid up the inside of her thigh draped over his lap. He rubbed back and forth for a few moments and then his fingers crept steadily closer to her slick heat.

Tell me what you are feeling. It was a command. One he made impossible to ignore.

I feel as if I am on fire.

That is how you are supposed to feel. There is more. I want you to feel more.

His hand crept higher, slowly higher up her thigh, until his fingers found her clit at the junction between her legs, where the blood pounded like mad. He circled there and then gently tugged and flicked. She jumped and cried out in her mind. It felt delicious. Scary. Unbelievable. She wanted more.

Good?

Very good.

His fingers stroked and caressed, dipped into her and then tugged and flicked again until she couldn't breathe. She had to stop feeding. She couldn't process the alien sensations and allow her organs to absorb the much-needed sustenance he was providing to her. She ran her tongue across the twin holes she'd made in his chest, closing the wounds.

"It gets so much better," he promised. "Lie back for me."

With her heart accelerating to the point she thought it might burst, Elisabeta did as he instructed. She hadn't known her body could feel so much pleasure. Just like the songs of the earth, her body sang, so the notes were mixed together in a wild melody that couldn't be separated now. She lay back on the thick fur while he once more shifted position. Her hand was forced, albeit reluctantly, to let his cock go.

She had loved the shape and feel of it. She wanted to believe that he belonged to her as much as she did to him. The sacred vows that had tied them together had proclaimed it so. He had given her his heart, his soul and his body. He had taken hers into his keeping. He seemed to be claiming what was rightfully his.

"Each rising, *piŋe sarnanak*, I will give you a lesson in something new, something important for you to learn and remember. This one is about your body and the pleasure it can feel. The pleasure I can give you and how I feel when I am giving it to you. I want you to stay merged with me the entire time so you feel everything that I am feeling. Do you understand me?"

Elisabeta gripped the fur with both fists as Ferro wedged his wide shoulders between her thighs, spreading her legs. It made her feel very vulnerable, but at the same time very excited.

"Elisabeta, I asked you a question."

"Yes, I do understand."

"Good. We will practice what you have learned often, and those things you enjoy I will expect you to gather your courage and ask for or initiate the act between us. Do you understand my expectations of you?"

She couldn't imagine being that brave, but she didn't want to disappoint him. She made up her mind that she wouldn't ever disappoint him. "Yes."

He lifted her legs at her knees and looped them over his arms. "Very good. This is one of the most important lessons of all. I have thought of this for centuries, Elisabeta. I studied technique and practices so I would bring my woman the greatest pleasure. Relax for me and let me show you what can be truly beautiful between spouses."

His eyes were intense, a molten lava, almost glowing red, a cross between a liquid volcano and a carnal predator set on having her. He bent his head and his tongue swiped over her heated center. Her entire body jerked as a flame so bright and hot swept through her, encompassing her. Her sex clenched, making her wholly aware of how different her body was in comparison to his. The shape. The texture. The way they fit together.

Ferro stroked her inner thigh with his tongue and nipped with his teeth, then kissed his way up to that heated entrance that was now pulsing with her need. She tried to stop squirming, but that one swipe of his tongue had left her drenched in liquid flames. In anticipation. Her pulse beat through her clit. Through her sheath. In places she hadn't known she had. He turned his head, the bristles on his jaw sending more sensations skittering through her body as he gave her other thigh the same attention.

Then his mouth settled between her legs, his tongue moving like a butterfly, fluttering, stroking, gentle at first, driving her out of her mind, roughening and then stabbing deep to pull at her honeyed liquid contents, to devour as if it were his favorite meal. She couldn't stop the muffled cries from escaping. She grew hot all over as the flames spread through her body, outward from her center to her breasts and down her thighs. Nothing in her life had prepared her for such a feeling. Nothing. She tossed her head back and forth, gripping the fur until her fingernails met her palms, unable to control herself no matter how hard she tried.

Ferro. This feels like I might die, it is so good. I'm scared and happy at the same time. She had no idea what to do, and that terrified her. She didn't want him to stop because she was doing something wrong.

You will not die. Relax. Just let yourself enjoy what I do to you. Stay merged with me. Feel what it is doing to me as well. Taste yourself on my tongue. Feel how my body reacts when I am devouring you, the pleasure it brings me to see you writhing under me this way.

Elisabeta loved his instructions. She had felt lost and now she could do exactly what he said. She kept her mind in his, allowing herself to feel his pleasure as well as her own. He loved what he was doing. Suddenly, she could taste herself, and it was like an aphrodisiac to him—orange with hints of lavender honey. He couldn't get enough. His cock was full and aching. So hard he pulsed with need. His pleasure was heightened by the sight of her naked body writhing under his mouth, her breasts jolting, her hips bucking, the sounds of her cries escaping when she tried so hard to suppress them. Her reactions fed his own pleasure.

She did her best to relax, although deep inside that tension coiled tighter, winding together with her need and hunger for him like a strongly bound spring. She feared after a time that she might go out of her mind.

"Ferro." She gasped his name in caution. She couldn't stop him. She was his to do with as he pleased, but he was really going to drive her insane with pleasure. Her body didn't know what to do.

Let go, piŋe sarnanak. Trust me to catch you. Just let go.

She wasn't certain what he meant but she took a deep breath and forced her body to relax into the strokes of his tongue, the thrust of his finger, the sudden flick of his thumb on her clit. Her body seemed to gather into a great force and then she was swept over a giant waterfall, dropping, dropping, free-falling, the rippling waves rushing over her in rolling heights of pleasure so intense she heard herself giving him a low, keening cry of pure shock.

He rubbed his shadowed jaws on either side of her thighs before lifting his head and looking at her with his silvery-blue eyes. "Did you feel how much I loved devouring you, Elisabeta? It is important that you know I want to feed not only on your blood but on the honey between your legs. That is mine as well."

He moved cautiously into a sitting position. She was merged very firmly in his mind and knew his cock was full and aching. He had visions of her bent over the railing, or on her hands and knees taking him hard and fast into her body, or her kneeling in front of him, his cock stretching her lips, yet he gave her no instructions. Asked nothing of her. Gave her no commands. He ached, and yet he didn't ask or demand relief from her. That instantly took away all the pleasure she'd received.

She sat up slowly and scooted a little away from him, dropping her gaze from the length and girth of his cock. There were pearly drops on the broad head of it that she longed to taste, but he wasn't giving her that opportunity, although she saw so clearly in his head that he wanted those things from her.

"Elisabeta?" His voice was very gentle. "What is it? Did you not enjoy what we just shared together?"

She moistened her lips. "You know I did." She detested that he was forcing her to speak aloud. She was merged with him, which meant he could read her as easily as she could read him.

"I want you to tell me why you no longer feel the pleasure you felt moments ago."

"You know why." She was horrified that she sounded mutinous. There was silence. She knew instantly that he had issued her a command couched in nicer terms. He had said he wanted her to tell him. He had still decreed she tell him. She took a deep breath. "I am in your mind and can tell you are in need. I would very much like to learn how to please you."

"That lesson is for another rising. This was for your pleasure, for you to learn about your body and the pleasure I can bring to you."

His voice said it all. He didn't expect her to argue with him. There was even dismissal in his mind, and it hurt. Really hurt. She felt as if he was rejecting her as a person. As a lifemate. As a lover.

"*Piŋe sarnanak.*" His gentle voice was nearly her undoing. "Look at me."

She wanted to disobey him, but she couldn't. She forced her lashes up and met his eyes. The color had gone from that blue-silver to more of a darker iron ringed with rust.

"I do not understand why you will not allow me to see to your needs. I wish to serve you, to make you happy. Your cock is full and aching. I want to learn how to use my mouth to bring you to happiness the way you did me. Or my body the way I see in your mind."

"Women no longer have to serve their men, Elisabeta. This is a modern world and women choose when they wish to have sex with their men and when they want to accommodate them. The men do not do the choosing."

His voice roughened, turned almost harsh, and she knew from being merged with him that her suggestions had made his cock even fuller and more demanding than it had been. The need to serve him was nearly a physical pain she couldn't stop.

"I do not understand." There were tears in her voice. Tears in her mind. But she didn't shed them. They weren't in her eyes, although she wanted to weep forever. "You said I did not have to be like the other women and yet you are trying to make me into one of them. I *need* to serve you. It makes me happy. It makes me feel fulfilled. I cannot contribute any other way to our relationship. That is who I am and yet you do not want that person. You want one of the more modern women like Julija or Lorraine. I will never—ever—be modern, nor do I want to be. I would try for you, but I know it is not in me and I would fail you."

Ferro's arms swept around her and he pulled her tight into his body, at once offering her comfort. "The last thing I want is for you to be a modern woman, Elisabeta."

There was no denying the sincerity in his voice.

"Then I do not understand what you are trying to make me become."

"I want you to have the opportunity to choose for yourself to grow into what you want to be. Over time, being around other women, you will learn things from them, and you will see that a life with me will not make you happy. I want you to have all the choices that were taken from you from the time you were a young girl. You deserve to be able to have every option available to you."

Elisabeta lifted her chin in the air, her gaze fully meeting his. Challenging what he'd said to her. He sounded sincere. He said lifemates didn't lie and that she could hear lies if they did. She heard no such thing. Then he wouldn't, either.

"I want to be able to make you happy, Ferro. To see to your every need, almost before you know what you need. That would make me happy. When your cock is full and aching and I can feel it in your mind, that need to have my mouth around you, or have you buried deep in my body, that is what I *need* to do for you. It isn't just a want. That is my happiness. That is what makes me feel good about myself. That might not be what other women feel good about, but knowing I make you happy is what makes me feel important and confident. More, my body aches for yours.

I want to know of these things I see in your mind and I want them with you. If I really get to make a choice, my choice is to have you teach me to please you. That would be my choice."

Ferro groaned, the sound breaking from him as if he were really being torn in two. "Woman, you are making this difficult for me. If you give me everything I could ever ask for in my lifemate and then, as time passes and you prefer to be a modern woman, and I cannot be a modern man, I will return alone to the monastery a broken and extremely dangerous being. You see the danger, do you not?"

"Ferro, you are my lifemate. My heart and soul. I will never be much different than I am now other than, I hope, more confident in myself and you. I wish to be with you and make you happy. Teach me how to do these things for you. Teach me to be your woman, the one you prefer me to be."

"I want you to be yourself, Elisabeta."

"I do not know who I am, other than that it is in me to bring you peace and that I need to see you happy at every level."

His hand stroked caresses down the back of her head. "You are certain this is what you want above all else, *minan piŋe sarnanak*? You can take the time to find out who you are. Once your mouth is on my cock or it is in your body, I will not be able to resist instructing you to keep me happy every rising, perhaps more than once."

She loved his hands in her hair and the way he sought to warn her of his intentions should she decide to continue on her set course of action. Merged within his mind, it would be impossible for her to step back. Already he was consumed with erotic images. His breathing had changed. His body was harder than ever. *She* had done that, just with her conversation. She loved feeling as if she had power when her Carpathian ancient was considered by so many to be so dangerous.

"More than anything, *isäntä*." Deliberately, she called him "master of the house." He was "strong heart" to her. Lifemate. *Sívamet*. Beloved. But she wanted to honor him with "master" so he would know she meant what she said.

He tipped her chin up and bent to kiss her. Gently at first. So gently. Then his arm locked around her back and his lips roughened, his tongue gliding into her mouth, stroking. Dueling. Flames erupted all over again. All at once her body felt on fire, her veins feeling as if he had poured red-hot magma into them and that liquid flowed straight to her center, creating a firestorm of absolute need.

Lifting his head, he put one hand on her shoulder, creating pressure until she dropped to her knees in front of him. He stroked his hands over her face, her jaw and chin. "The instructions will be in images in my head. You will follow them. I will tell you when I want you to do something different. If you are frightened, you are to tell me immediately. If you do not like something, you tell me immediately. That is a command, *piŋe sarnanak*. Is that understood?"

"Yes." Kneeling before him, she thought his cock looked enormous and intimidating, but so gorgeous. So much a part of him as a male. Her heart beat too fast, but she was determined to learn everything she could in this first lesson. She wanted this more than anything she had ever wanted, and kneeling on the fur under the stars, between the twin columns of his massive thighs, made her feel as if she belonged to him. She needed that feeling as much as she needed to breathe.

She could already see the pleasure she was bringing to him just by the submissive pose, her naked body, her breasts with her hard nipples showing him she was excited. Instinctively she widened her knees so he could see that between her legs, her liquid desire glistened at the mere thought of him allowing her to do this for him. She wanted him to see the signs on her body as well as read them in her mind.

Tentatively she reached out and lightly cupped his heavy sac. It was much softer than she'd expected. She stroked caresses lightly over him and then followed the images in his head. Leaning in, she stroked her tongue over the velvet folds. He reacted with a little shudder of pleasure.

"That is good, Elisabeta. Feels very good." His hands dropped to her head.

Encouraged, she took her time exploring, lapping at him, tasting and gently sucking him into the warmth of her mouth, jiggling gently with her fingers and then tracing her way up to his thick shaft.

It seemed from the images in his head that the wetter his cock, the better, so she took her time with that as well, using her tongue to get the thick girth as wet as possible while learning the shape and heaviness of the length of him. His breathing had gone nearly labored and she felt the difference in him, as if a great, aggressive beast were rising in him. That was both exhilarating and intimidating. Her tongue found the drops leaking from the broad, velvety head, and just as his blood was an aphrodisiac and she couldn't get enough, so was the taste of his essence. He had claimed that her body was his, and she felt the same ownership of his.

Her mouth closed over him, feeling the weight of him, the heat of him on her tongue. At the same time, she heard his roar of thunder in his mind and felt the burst of fire streaking through his body. Immediately she tightened her mouth, sucking strongly, wanting to intensify the feeling for him. Her tongue began a slow dance up and down his shaft as she took turns setting different rhythms, sucking and then stroking and caressing with her tongue. Each time she tried to take him a little deeper in her mouth to get more of him wetter, to get more of him to feel the snug, hot tunnel.

His hands fisted on either side of her hair, pulling her head back almost aggressively, and the little bite on her scalp only served to send her own body into a kind of unexpected meltdown. Her nipples felt like twin flames, her breasts felt swollen and achy. Between her legs was a living fire, one she doubted could ever be put out, but it didn't matter to her. The only thing in her mind was making Ferro feel good. Not good. Great. Not even great. She wanted him to feel the way he'd made her feel.

She gave herself up to that purpose, putting all thoughts of herself aside. She devoted every touch, every stroke of her tongue and mouth, her lips and hands, to his desire alone. She concentrated on the images in his mind, on the reactions of his body, on the pleasure she felt in their merged minds. His rising lust felt like a reward. When his hips began to thrust shallowly and his fists held her head still, happiness burst through her.

His hips jerked and bucked. He actually growled, the sound harsh, sending shivers of excitement down her spine. Each thrust of his hips sent his cock deeper, filling her mouth so that for a moment she couldn't breathe, and her heart pounded, her eyes burned, but the burning pleasure in his mind and body overrode her own discomfort. Her own body reacted to the fierce needs of his. She could feel his lungs burning for air. She moaned around his shaft and the vibrations drove him nearly insane, every nerve ending centering on his cock in the tight, scorching cauldron of her mouth.

If we continue, I will spill my seed down your throat. You would have to swallow all of it and it would be an enormous amount.

His voice, in her mind, was hoarse with need and hunger. She didn't need to ask him if this would bring him pleasure because she knew it would; she could feel it in his mind. He wanted it, but would never ask her for it. She wanted all of his essence. It belonged to her in the way his blood did. If that made her primitive and old-fashioned, she didn't care. He tasted delicious and she wanted all of him.

Please. She lifted her lashes, looking up at him to show him her eyes just in case he couldn't read her mind through the passionate chaos of his.

He didn't wait, or better yet, he couldn't. He took a tighter grip in her hair and his hips thrust into her, pressing his cock deeper into her mouth. His girth stretched her lips to accommodate his size, but it felt sensual, erotic and so perfect to her. The weight of him was heavy on her tongue. The heat of him seemed to burn her mouth. He felt like a living flame. She felt the boiling in his velvety sac as his balls tightened to the point of near pain. The scorching burn rose as he neared his fiery explosion.

Look at me. Do not close your eyes. Stay merged with me so you feel what you do to me.

The fire was moving through him, through her, like magma in a volcano. She felt the thrill in him, the elation, the domination and pride. The love wrapping her up in safe arms even as he couldn't stop the thrusts of his hips that seemed to push deeper into her mouth as his cock grew heavier and hotter, expanded wider until she was so filled with him he was everywhere, like that fire deep inside. And then he was pouring down her throat, jet after jet of his essence she tried to keep up with. So much. So good. All for her.

Each time her lashes started to drift down, his fists tightened in her hair and he tugged, forcing her head up so she stared directly into his fierce, claiming gaze.

I want you to look at me. See me, Elisabeta. See what you do to me. See what you mean to me. What a gift you are to me.

She felt tears burning behind her eyes. Not because his cock was so large and stretched her ability to take him in her mouth. Or that his essence poured down her throat in such a thick, hot torrent that she could barely swallow fast enough to keep up. It was that look of adoration on his face. The soft look in his eyes she knew had never been there for anyone else. Just her. He worried she would not want him, yet how could she not? He towered over her, strong, frightening to the rest of the world, but giving her this—his vulnerability. Letting her see that she was his world and what she meant to him.

Never think that you are not cherished. Or that you have no value. No one has ever cared for me so selflessly the way that you have.

Ferro slowly withdrew his cock from her mouth, the weight of him sliding sensuously over her lips, all the while his nearly silver gaze blazing possessively down into hers. She sank back onto her heels, staring up at him, unable to look away, drowning in her own desire for him, drenched in her need of him. Sensual hunger beat at her now and she knew it wasn't his alone. Hers was every bit as strong. He had awakened a need in her she didn't want to stop. She tasted him on her lips. In her mouth. Down her throat. She wanted to hold this moment to her forever.

She had given Ferro the greatest pleasure he'd ever experienced, just as he had done for her. She had done that for him and she wanted to do it again and again because in doing so, she found there hadn't been one moment of fear. She'd been totally focused on him, only on him, and she'd refused to allow anything else in to mar this new and beautiful experience between them. She had felt as if he belonged to her and they were in their own world together.

Ferro's hand framed the side of her face, his thumb sliding gently along her jaw, easing away a soreness she hadn't realized had been there. "You are a treasure beyond any price, *piɲe sarnanak*. I had studied the erotic arts in the hopes of one day pleasing my lifemate, but there is no way to experience such a thing, and certainly not when my emotions are as passionately wrapped up with the sexual act as they are with you."

That pleased her. His thumb slid from tracing along her jaw to strumming over her lower lip. "You have so much passion in you, Elisabeta. So much giving. You are so willing to please me."

She kept her gaze glued to his face. He sounded brooding. Moody. He looked it, too. Those beautiful eyes had gone from the silver-blue to iron-rust, and his mind was closed off and once more sorrowful. This time, she was certain she knew his musings. He still believed that she would grow out of her need for one such as her ancient lifemate. She knew better. She also knew that as the centuries had changed them both, so would this journey they were embarking on together.

"You will obey me in this, *sívamet*. When you have needs, or you have hungers, you are to ask for what you want of me. Do you understand?" He waited.

Elisabeta nodded. "Of course, Ferro."

His thumb continued back and forth again over her lips in a mesmerizing slide. "I do not want you to meet my needs at the expense of your own. Is that understood?"

She frowned, trying to comprehend what he meant. "When I meet your needs, mine are met as well."

He shook his head. "You are happy and content in that you pleased me. You are more confident as a woman and as my lifemate, both good things. You even felt powerful that you could make an ancient warrior feel the things you made me feel, but your body screams for mine. You are now ignoring your own needs, Elisabeta. Slide your hand down your belly and curl your fingers between your legs. I want you to feel your dampness."

She frowned, unsure what he meant. He knelt behind her, pressing close to her, wrapping his arms around her. She didn't really have to touch her sensitive skin to react; his words alone made tension coil tightly in her. That didn't stop her from wanting to obey him. She placed her hand on her belly a bit tentatively, looking back at him for approval to see if she was doing what he wanted. He wrapped his fingers around hers and gently guided her palm down her belly, and then skimmed them over her mound. Her breath caught in her throat as little sparks of electricity seemed to dance all over her skin.

Elisabeta let her weight rest against his body. It had become one of her favorite positions and she had begun to feel at ease with him so close to her. As he moved her fingers over her clit, he circled and then flicked the inflamed, very sensitive bud. Her entire feminine sheath clenched. Spasmed. The tension coiled tighter. Deliberately, he curled two of her fingers into her slick entrance.

Ferro's breath was warm in her ear. "That is you, needing me. You cannot neglect your needs, *sívamet*. It is just as important to me to keep you happy as it is for you to keep me happy."

His teeth tugged on her earlobe. His fingers began a slow, steady assault on her senses, using her own hand, using his. His thumb brushed her clit. He flicked hard and then brushed the sensitive bud, all the while building and building that tidal wave inside her until her body shook with tremors, and the only things holding her up were his powerful arms and the support of his body. Then he dropped his face into her shoulder and nuzzled there for a long, heart-stopping moment, his teeth scraping as his fingers plunged and receded deep inside her.

He bit down, at the same time flicking her clit with his thumb. The sting of his teeth combined with the tap of his thumb and the surging of his fingers drove her right over the edge. She heard her own keening cry. Her head fell back against his chest as the waves raced through her, rippling strongly, a million stars bursting behind her eyes as the orgasm rushed through her.

Ferro held her until it subsided and then turned her gently in his arms to allow her to bury her face against his chest. His palm stroked the back of her head, calming her, waiting for her heart to slow to the rhythm of his.

"That is what I mean, *piŋe sarnanak*. Your needs are every bit as important as mine. Do you understand now?"

"Yes." She did, and she was very much on the same page about taking care of her needs as well as his.

"There is much more I will show you in future risings." He caught her chin and tipped her face up so that she was looking straight into his eyes. "As you come to trust in your lifemate more and more, we will build on these lessons."

Ferro, we have need of you and Elisabeta now. Dragomir and Josef are in heated battle. We need Elisabeta to calm Dragomir down. Gary reached out to him.

Merged as they were, Elisabeta heard the healer call out to Ferro. Ferro swore in the Carpathian language under his breath. *O jelä peje teräd, healer, we are busy at the moment.*

Frowning, Ferro helped her to her feet. It was very clear he wasn't happy at the intrusion, and that gave her some satisfaction. Telling the resident healer "sun scorch you" was considered very bad diplomacy, although apparently Ferro had never been considered diplomatic. Nevertheless, trepidation crept in. If they left the safety of their home, she would once again be exposed in a way she didn't want to be.

Ferro waved his hand to clothe both of them. He chose a modern dress for her, but again, one that fell to her ankles. This was also form-fitting, a teal color he particularly liked. He had certain colors that appealed to him. She knew he chose the more formfitting dresses because he wanted her to get used to the idea that her figure was pleasing to him. He thought she was beautiful. He wanted her to feel beautiful and to move with confidence among the other women.

Dragomir has a lifemate. He does not need Elisabeta to stop him from turning. She knew Ferro didn't want to put more pressure on her than she already had. Each rising he hoped to practice the small things she'd worked on the rising before and add new ones. *She doesn't need to continually be thrust into the drama of Tariq's insistence on the training of computer skills to everyone in the compound. She has enough things to worry about.*

It gave her a secret little thrill that he was looking out for her, so much so that he would put her needs before his brethren. She hugged that knowledge to herself, even though she had the sinking feeling that they would have to go. Knowing he didn't want to made it easier.

She knew from being in his mind that Ferro hoped to introduce her to Emeline, Dragomir's lifemate, this rising. Once he did, he wanted her to be able to sit with all three of the women without him, even if just for a few minutes, and see if she could do so without summoning Sergey. She didn't want him to leave her, even for a few moments, and take the chance of endangering the other women, no matter that he had assured her that even with her summoning Sergey, the vampire could no longer send his worm from the netherworld.

I believe this is necessary, Ferro, or I would not ask this of you, Gary said.

He was asking it of Elisabeta, but Ferro wasn't going to point out to the ancient healer what he already knew.

"I am sorry, *minan piŋe sarnanak*, it seems that once again, your gifts might be needed."

Elisabeta wrapped her arm around his waist and nodded, uncertain what to think. No matter what, if Ferro asked it of her, or commanded it—which to her was the same—she would go.

9

As the hues of the sky, shift upon the shore;
The reds once gray, a spectrum once more.

W hat went wrong this time?" Ferro asked Gary. "Surely Dragomir didn't throw a tantrum the way Sandu did."

"I do not throw tantrums," Sandu denied with great dig-
nity. "Dragomir, however, has long been jealous that down through the
ages no one has sung his praises over the campfires. He most likely was
bemoaning the fact, and young Josef could no longer listen. I believe it was
the young Carpathian who flung the tablet at him."

Ferro turned his attention to Dragomir. "Is this true?"

Dragomir gave his blackest scowl to Sandu. "Of course, it isn't true.
Why would I care whether songs are sung over the campfires of my ex-
ploits? Ancient hunters do not expect songs of their legendary battles.
Only those vain carry on about them."

"I was referring to young Josef throwing a tablet at you," Ferro said,
striving for patience.

"Yes, well. That part might be true. He muttered something along the
lines of 'dim-witted blockheads' and flung the tablet at my head. Fortunately, I am very fast and caught it before it could fall to the ground. The
little upstart thought he might go toe-to-toe with me."

Ferro ignored the taunting amusement in Dragomir's voice. He could see that Tariq, Maksim and Traian found the young Carpathian's behavior laughable, but he found himself uneasy. He had known Dragomir for centuries and never once had the ancient had that particular mocking, almost snide tone when he was referring to the young tech. Ferro tried to change the sound in his mind but it always came out slightly sneering. The others around him didn't seem to hear it, or at least if they did, no one reacted.

"You thought this warranted calling for Elisabeta to calm the situation? Dragomir, you have a lifemate, and unlike Sandu, there is no way for you to turn. Josef is not yet fifty years of age, his emotions have not begun to fade. When using any psychic gift there is a price the user pays. What about this situation did you feel made it worth Elisabeta paying this price?"

The amusement faded instantly from Dragomir's expression to be replaced by pure ice in his golden eyes. He straightened to his full height, the lines deepening in his face. "What are you saying, Ferro? That I would hold your lifemate in less esteem than my own? Or that this *child* the new prince sent to force us to learn technology he didn't bother to learn when he should have should be able to call me names? I should put up with the indignity of that after centuries of serving my people? I should have torn his head off his shoulders and thrown it into the lake."

His voice was so cold that ice particles drifted in the air between them. Sandu coughed and moved back, away from the specks, and Ferro turned Elisabeta around.

Do not breathe those in. See if you can connect with him as you did Sandu and tell me what is happening to him.

"Dragomir." Ferro pitched his voice very low even as he flicked his gaze around to his brethren.

They closed in around Dragomir, walling out Tariq and the others. To his relief, Gary removed Tariq altogether, although the leader the prince had chosen to represent him there in the United States stayed within viewing distance of the unfolding drama.

Emeline, Dragomir's lifemate, raced unchecked from their home toward them. Dragomir saw her coming and stepped back, frowning. Shaking his head. Ferro felt Elisabeta instantly reach out to Dragomir and surround him with her soothing peace. He knew the moment all the brethren felt her gift and then when it encompassed Emeline as well. Emeline shot her a grateful glance. She'd skidded to a halt when Gary raised his hand and then stepped between her and her lifemate.

"Dragomir, your lifemate will breathe ice into her lungs. Get a hold of yourself. Let me in to aid you. Let the healer in." Ferro kept his voice pitched very low.

Dragomir shook his head again, his gaze on Emeline. She held out her hand to him in entreaty. He pressed his lips together to keep from breathing ice particles, and then those golden eyes jumped to Ferro and the healer. He nodded.

Ferro and Gary used their blood-bond with Dragomir to enter. Elisabeta, merged with Ferro as she was, slipped in as well. Ferro found weird streaks of color in a ferocious red across Dragomir's mind, almost like the vicious claw marks a cat might make. The lines were thin and already fading. Elisabeta's gentle breeze sent them drifting away, thinning until the claw marks wore away to nothing. Gary's healing spirit moved through Dragomir's brain carefully, looking for any sign of damage or an intruder that had somehow managed to slip past their safeguards. Other than them being uneasy, they could find nothing.

Dragomir scowled and shook his head several times as if he could shake loose whatever was inside his mind. "What happened to me, Ferro? I cannot turn vampire, and yet I could not stop wanting to rip that imbecile child's head off, or worse, yours."

Elisabeta, you said something to me about Sandu, and I dismissed it thinking, rather arrogantly, that I knew what you meant. You said there was something else at work here other than a dislike of modern technology. What did you mean?

Josef didn't have a dislike of modern technology, and Dragomir could not possibly turn when Emeline was his true lifemate. Gary had not found even the slightest shadow in Dragomir's brain.

The feel of evil was prevalent in Sandu's mind, an overwhelming need for violence. It was there in Dragomir's but not nearly as bad. She hesitated. *Not evil exactly. That taint was there faintly, but more like malevolence. The need for violence.*

Ferro turned what she said over and over in his mind. Ancients had no emotions. Sandu was incapable of feeling a need for violence. If Elisabeta said that was in his mind, then it had to have been there.

What do you think, Gary? he asked the healer.

Women often feel the emotions in the ancients that we cannot.

Ferro heard the speculation in his voice. Elisabeta didn't say anything more. She didn't weigh in one way or another, nor did he expect her to. He kept his arm firmly around her, holding her close there in the middle of the compound, trying to decide what was the best course of action, because something was very much off.

"Has anyone examined the boy?" he asked. "This is now two of our ancient warriors that have had a similar reaction after an encounter with him."

Traian frowned. "Do you believe that Josef has managed to do something to introduce something evil to ancient warriors that would make them turn even if they had lifemates? A boy? A Carpathian boy who has worked hard to identify potential lifemates for those without them before the vampire can get to them? He's placed himself in danger numerous times and proven himself over and over."

"No one has accused him," Gary said, his tone, as always, mild. "But something is wrong here. We have to make certain this compound is safe for our women and children, including Josef. There is no question that he is a valuable asset to our people. Like with Sandu and Dragomir, it is best, given the circumstances, that we examine him. I will need Elisabeta, Ferro. We will need to go to Tariq's home to conduct the examination."

Ferro gave an exaggerated sigh in order to make his woman laugh when he knew she would be nervous. "Of course you will. Is there anyone here who does not need my lifemate?"

He flicked his gaze at Sandu and Benedek, two of his brethren from the monastery. Entering Tariq's home with his bodyguards close meant exposing Elisabeta to danger without anyone at his back. Gary was Tariq's second-in-command and sworn to protect Tariq. As much as he would

want to count on the ancient and the fact that their souls were tied together, he couldn't do that, not when it came to Elisabeta's safety, not
when he still felt that strange, vague threat to her.

"I will need Sandu and Benedek with us," he said.

Tariq had started toward his home but he spun around, his face darkening, as if his honor had been called into question, which—Ferro
conceded—it had. "You do not feel as if you can bring your lifemate into
my home, where Charlotte resides, without two of your brethren with you?"

It was a direct challenge and one Ferro hadn't expected. Tariq was a
man born to lead, one very careful of his tone and his wording. He wasn't
a confrontational man. In all things, he was diplomatic. He was also an
ancient with an ancient's patience. Having Sandu and Benedek in his
home seemed a small thing and something often required when examining for any type of evil entity, especially if a lifemate was close. It was not
an unreasonable request.

Do not answer him, Ferro, Gary said immediately. The healer glided in
between the two ancients. *Something is going on here that I do not understand.*

"Tariq, you must have misunderstood Ferro. Elisabeta will have to be
present when we examine Josef for any hidden evil intrusion. That pre-
sents a danger to her. Naturally, she will need to be guarded, as will you.
Your safety is paramount and he knows that. We all know you chafe
under the restrictions placed on you by the prince, but it can't be helped.
You must have guards."

Tariq rubbed at his temples in much the same way Sandu and Dragomir had. Ferro and Gary exchanged a quick, uneasy glance. Something
malevolent was invading the compound and it was spreading among the
ancient warriors, even those with lifemates to anchor them. How could
they possibly examine Tariq without offending him deeply and triggering
the aggression that seemed to be pervading his mind?

"Yes, of course. I don't know what got into me. Forgive me, Ferro."

*Sandu, make certain none of the brethren take their turn learning this new
technology from Josef until we know what is going on,* Ferro warned.

He used their private telepathic pathway rather than that of the brotherhood or the one established by the soul-bond. He didn't know why he wanted to exclude the healer, but for the moment, he needed to count on those he had formed a bond with in the monastery. Gary, sent by the prince, was loyal to Tariq.

Until we know what is going on, we cannot go outside of our circle. Something is not right and the danger is spreading.

They had to know where each of the brethren stood. Dragomir was the biggest question mark, as he had a child with Emeline and she wanted to stay in the protection of the compound. If his loyalties were to Tariq rather than the brethren if they decided to leave, they would have to withhold that information from him. That would forever weigh heavily on him.

As they walked across the compound grounds, Elisabeta clamped to his side, her face buried in his ribs so she didn't have to look at the wide-open spaces, he scanned continually, searching the ancients surrounding them for signs of emotions that shouldn't be there, whether they had lifemates or not. He didn't need to be able to get into their minds, just read the energy surrounding them.

Maksim seemed fine to him. He walked with Gary, Tariq between them. Dragomir sat on his porch with Emeline, holding hands. Ferro could no longer detect any surge of violence in Dragomir. Benedek hadn't been near Josef, nor had Petru or Nicu Dalca. The three had spread out, but kept pace with Ferro and Elisabeta as they made their way to Tariq's home. Ferro found himself slowing his steps, reluctant to enter and put his woman in the position of danger he had a feeling she would be in.

I do not like this, Sandu. Something feels very wrong to me.

A trap? Is it the vampire? We know he will come for her. The safeguards on this compound have been woven and interwoven again and again. We provided extra layers over those after Tariq and the others used their strongest. We provided for every eventuality we could conceive of.

And yet Elisabeta summoned him and he was able to slip in like a worm from the netherworld right under our very noses, Ferro pointed out. He still had that feeling that Gary and Tariq regarded Elisabeta as a threat to them. He just wasn't certain how or why.

Elisabeta winced. He tightened his arm around her. *That is not a condemnation, piŋe sarnanak. We are grateful to you for showing us one of the many weaknesses a fortress this size holds. We need to find them all.*

Ferro let his mind expand, reaching as he had done for centuries, looking for hidden ruses, a deception or illusion that his eye might miss. He knew the brethren at his back were doing the same.

Elisabeta, we are not necessarily safe. I want you to be very alert at all times. If you feel anything you are distrustful of, no matter how small or elusive, you alert me. Do you understand? Even if you think it is coming from someone I trust. That is an order and I expect obedience. He poured command into his voice. He disliked sounding as if he was controlling her, doing anything that in any way resembled Sergey, but this was too important and she responded to clear guidelines. *Tell me you understand.*

Yes, of course, I will tell you.

Pay particular attention to the healer, but be cautious, Elisabeta. He is extremely powerful and he will know if you are touching his mind. Anyone or everyone in that room is a potential enemy or they may be marked by the enemy to use against all of us here. We have to know to be able to help them.

They were right at the door, the entrance to Tariq's home, and Ferro knew he couldn't hesitate to enter. He'd already gotten Tariq on edge just by making a common and proper request. He stepped across the threshold, lifting Elisabeta as he entered so that her feet didn't touch the floor. She didn't protest. If anyone noticed and became upset, he had the perfect excuse; he could tell them that she was unused to walking. He was certain Gary would notice.

Tariq and Maksim led the way to the conference room and took their places at the large oval table where often they had to hash out war plans against the vampires who were already in place, doing their best to stamp out the existence of the Carpathian people.

"We've sent for Josef," Maksim said. "Traian and Joie both have said they are willing for Gary and Elisabeta to examine them if Gary feels it is necessary. They traveled together."

"If it comes to that," Gary said smoothly. "I think all of us are in trouble, Tariq. I think there is something working against us within this compound that is not yet known to us."

Tariq rubbed at his temples. "Something is happening. We never seem to be able to have five minutes before we're attacked by something new." There was an accusation in his voice, as if he blamed Gary. He even narrowed his eyes at the healer. His face was flushed. His heartbeat accelerated. It was clear to those in the room that his blood pressure was rising and his body was preparing to take physical action against some unknown threat.

Elisabeta's hand slid up Ferro's chest. *His head is hurting very badly. He feels . . . anger mounting to rage and is not used to such an emotion. He is fighting against it. It flared bright and hot when the healer suggested there was a problem here. He is very strong and does not like the idea that he cannot control his emotions.*

Can you soothe him without touching his mind?

Elisabeta tilted her head and suddenly Ferro found himself looking down into his lifemate's dark eyes. His heart stuttered at what he saw there. Amusement. Warmth. She looked at him as if he might not be quite as bright as she first thought. He was concentrating on her safety, not paying as much attention to the details of his woman's abilities. Of course she could soothe Tariq from a distance. She had that gift from when she was a child. As she had grown, so had that talent and that need in her to bring peace when those around her were agitated or lost. Tariq seemed both.

Ferro had never forbidden her to use her talent. If anything, he had encouraged her. He had told her he was proud of her for it. He should have known she was already sending those waves of peaceful energy into the room, encompassing everyone, not just Tariq. Every ancient felt the way her gift penetrated straight to the soul and healed the centuries of shredding, of that gray void of emptiness.

Scents of Italian bergamot and rare camellias mixed with extract of orange, lime, vetiver and sandalwood, drifting across the room in just a hint of a blended fragrance. Ferro knew it was all Elisabeta. It was impossible for any negative emotion to persist under the onslaught of that gentle persuasion.

I realize now that you will always have the upper hand between us, piŋe sarnanak. How will I ever stay annoyed with you when I inhale and you smell like the breeze that takes all cares away? He ran his hand down the back of her head, making certain she knew he wouldn't ever mind that she would have the upper hand between them.

Elisabeta had found her way into his heart with her quiet stillness. With her gentle compassion and this—that need to bring peace to his brothers, the other hunters weary from holding on to honor over so long. Not just those in the monastery, but all Carpathian hunters. It was his lifemate's nature and he loved her all the more for it.

Why would you become annoyed with me? Do I do anything that already makes you believe I will upset you?

The anxiety in her made him want to groan. She was very literal with him. She was programmed to want to please him. Naturally, she would take him seriously in spite of the fact that he was all but petting her hair in an effort to show her he was teasing her, trying to keep a balance when he didn't know what they were going to find and what the others were going to expect from his lifemate.

"Perhaps everyone should be examined again," Ferro said. "Starting with me. Starting with all of us from the monastery. Is it possible, Tariq, that we carried an unknown shadow with us that Xavier or another mage cast upon the gates without our knowledge? I do not want to take chances with the women and children here in the compound. If there is the slightest possibility that you believe we are putting them at risk, we will be examined or we will plan our escape. We can get past Sergey and his spics and cross back to the Carpathian Mountains. Once there, he cannot get to us." He poured confidence into his voice. All the while he kept his gaze fixed on the leader's eyes, needing to see what was going on with him.

Tariq once again rubbed hard at his temples and once again the flare of his rage filled the conference room. They all heard his elevated heartbeat. Gary glanced at Ferro as if he knew the ancient was doing his best to get Tariq to suggest that all warriors in the compound be examined. Clearly that wasn't going to happen. Before Tariq could speak, Gary did.

"We need every warrior here, Ferro. Had there been a taint on those of you from the monastery, we would have known. Valentin and Dragomir have been here for some time, as has Siv. All have the code of honor scarred into their skin as brethren."

Maksim nodded. "That is so. I agree, though, Ferro, that we should all be scanned again. First young Josef and then the rest of us, starting with Gary so we clear him to look at the rest of us. Tariq and I can go next."

He is aware something is wrong with Tariq, Ferro said to Elisabeta.

You have not told me what I have done to upset you.

She sounded on the verge of tears, although none glittered in her eyes. He still felt them in her mind. She kept her face turned away from the others, buried in his rib cage, pressed deep.

I was teasing you, letting you know that you will always be my greatest treasure. I should not tease you when we are in the middle of serious business.

Her fingers crept up his belly to fist in his shirt. *I do not mind. I am learning.*

Josef strode in, deliberately slamming the door behind him. He had piercings in his lip and eyebrow and a bar in his nose. "I can't imagine what you want from me now," he snapped. "It isn't like you aren't already working me like a dog. You said your computer system was the latest and yet I've been updating it for hours. You said your people could learn and they all have the IQ of a peahen." He put his hands on his hips and glared at Tariq.

Tariq surged to his feet, the chair falling over backward. Maksim and Gary stood as well, Gary gliding to put his body between Tariq and the young Carpathian boy. Ferro calmly rose, taking Elisabeta to the other end of the room out of harm's way. All the while, he kept his gaze fixed on Tariq. He didn't know Josef, but he was somewhat familiar with the leader of the Carpathian people here in the United States. He was acting very far out of character.

There are flashes of red around him, also around the boy, Elisabeta informed him.

Do you see it in anyone else in this room? Concentrate on the healer. Really look at him. Do you see anything at all off about him? Ferro hadn't detected anything, but Elisabeta was very sensitive. She picked up the slightest nuance when he didn't.

Elisabeta took her time, studying Gary while he was preoccupied, doing his best to keep Tariq from ripping Josef's head off.

I do not detect anything at all different about him. He gives off a powerful energy, but not a violent one. He is capable of great violence, but so are you. No one else in the room has those flashes of red that I can see.

Gary, Elisabeta is seeing red flashes around both Tariq and Josef. Whatever infected Sandu and Dragomir has also gotten to the two of them, Ferro reported, allowing Sandu and Benedek to hear as well.

Gary waved his hand at Josef, stopping the young Carpathian in his tracks as he aggressively took several steps toward Tariq. The boy froze, his expression one of belligerence. He would have been a lot more hostile if he could have seen that the healer had removed his piercings in an effort to help calm Tariq.

Allow Elisabeta to flow with you into Tariq's mind, Ferro instructed Gary.

The healer hesitated. He was second-in-command to Tariq, sworn to protect him. Ferro was an extremely dangerous man, one few—if any— could best in a fight. Opening Tariq up to him, even through Elisabeta, could be construed as betrayal. On the other hand, Gary's soul was tied to Ferro's. Ferro could always use that entry to anyone Gary had a blood-bond with.

Tariq didn't seem to care that Josef was frozen in place. He let out another roar and threw the chair toward the boy. Gary blocked it in mid-air. That only served to make Tariq angrier. Gary opened his mind to Elisabeta.

Immediately she flowed into the healer, Ferro merged with her. He wasn't about to allow her to go anywhere without him. She was that same light breeze, moving toward the bright red streaks that were slashed across the front of Tariq's brain like a canvas of rage. Ferro could see that Gary was doing his best to study the streaks, to find their origin. Ferro did as well. They seemed to be burned across Tariq's amygdala, the part of his brain that handled emotions. The red slashes reached to the prefrontal cortex, the part of the brain responsible for judgment. Tariq had that in abundance and the burns were hindering his ability to control the rage, although he was fighting it with his natural character.

Elisabeta's soft breeze moved through Tariq's mind, a gentle stream that carried just a hint of her scent, that natural fragrance that brought such peace. She was a soothing balm impossible to ignore. Like in Sandu and Dragomir, the burns began to thin and then dissipate. There were so many more of the angry slashes than had been in either of the other two ancients, and instinctively she seemed to know to take the one away from Tariq's prefrontal cortex to aid him in fighting the rage. Once he was able to get his judgment back, Tariq's leadership would come to the forefront. He would aid them in his recovery. Ferro had every faith in him.

Ferro could see the burns were etched a little deeper into Tariq's brain, as if they'd had more time to take hold. He stayed quiet, watching the healer examine the burns closely in the amygdala area of Tariq's brain while Elisabeta continued to slowly and gently dissolve the angry red slashes as if they were mere paint marks that could be erased from a canvas. Her presence was calming enough that even the brilliant red dulled in color over the amygdala.

Ferro called up the images of Dragomir's brain. The burns hadn't been nearly as deep or as numerous as in Sandu's brain. None had been on the prefrontal cortex. All the slashes of red had been concentrated on the region that controlled emotion. In Sandu, there had been quite a few more burns and much deeper scoring across the amygdala, but again, none on the prefrontal cortex.

That is not so, Ferro, Elisabeta corrected. *When I first entered, there were several surface burns I erased before moving to the worst burns.*

Ferro was a little shocked at the ease she displayed communicating with him only. There was no elevation in energy at all. No one would know she was talking to him. He doubted that Gary, who was sharing a mind merge with them, would know she was that adept.

You found burns on the prefrontal cortex of Sandu's brain but not on Dragomir's?

On both, but Dragomir had barely any and not at all deep. Sandu had surface burns, but more than Dragomir, she explained.

Ferro turned her clarification over in his mind, trying to figure out what it meant. The entire time she had had that very calm discussion with him she had never stopped that sweet, soothing breeze that swept gently through Tariq's mind, pushing at the deep scores of red slashes across his brain. The deeper burns were stubborn, but she kept at them, just filling him with her gentle presence and restful, relaxing aura so that it was impossible to feel anything but composed and tranquil. Sharing Tariq's mind as he was with her, Ferro felt that same serenity.

Elisabeta might not think of herself as powerful, but her gift was astounding. Carpathians healed by shedding their egos and bodies to become only spirit. Elisabeta was selfless by nature. She didn't need to shed her physical body. She didn't have an ego when she was helping others. That was when she was completely confident in herself. She gave without thought of what she would get back or the consequences to herself. She simply gave.

She was also adept at reading others. She had to be. She had been a prisoner for centuries and she had to know exactly what her captor was thinking or feeling at any given moment to stay ahead of him. She relied on emotions and subtle feelings, unlike Carpathian hunters. Ferro considered that. He had a huge asset in his lifemate. Whatever was happening to his fellow Carpathians, she had a better chance of picking up the nuances that might lead to the discovery of its origins. Gary was already indicating that he could find no shadow, no blemish that might signal a vampire had planted a threat against them.

The last of the red slashes was gone and still Elisabeta continued to fill Tariq's mind with her healing fragrance and that gentle breeze. Ferro moved closer to see what she was doing. When he did, Gary did as well. It was difficult to stay apart from one's body for so long and give unconditionally. It took a toll. Both would have left the leader and moved back into their own bodies believing Tariq healed.

On closer inspection of Tariq's brain, Ferro could see the scoring from the burns was deeper than he'd thought. There were no longer the angry red slashes, but the pitting was deep and worrisome.

Can she heal scars like that? Gary asked Ferro.

Ferro had no idea. *You will have to ask her.* He found his lifemate fascinating. Alluring. Her spirit was so pure and beautiful to him.

Gary didn't interrupt her with questions, he simply stayed in the background like Ferro, watching her flood that deep scoring with cool, fresh, pure energy. By turns, scents of Italian bergamot and rare camellias vied with sandalwood and vetiver. Next it would be orange or lime, the fragrance so subtle it was barely there, but carried on that faint breeze that was ever present.

Ferro was a little shocked when he saw the deep burn marks slowly disappearing as if they had never been. It didn't make sense. What had she done? Just willed the scarring away? No one healed that way. She was patient, taking her time until there was no evidence of any damage at all on Tariq's brain. Then she was gone, and Ferro went with her, slipping back into the room.

Elisabeta felt light and insubstantial, as if she might slip away from him at any moment. Sandu was there instantly, holding out his wrist to her. Even in her need, she tipped her head up, her dark eyes meeting Ferro's as if asking for permission or needing him to command her to take sustenance from another male.

Take his blood, piŋe sarnanak. You are so pale you look as if you might disappear.

She did as he instructed, politely taking what Sandu offered. Benedek gave Ferro blood while Maksim offered Gary his wrist. Tariq sat quietly at the table, his eyes on the young Carpathian boy still standing frozen in place by the healer's command. There was a look of belligerence on Josef's face.

Tariq waited until the three finished feeding before he spoke. "Clearly, whatever infected Sandu and Dragomir infected Josef and me as well. Have you any idea what it is, or how it is getting to us?" He looked across the table to Elisabeta. "Thank you, Elisabeta. I owe you a great deal. All three of you, but clearly, you seem to be able to deal with the violence this infection is causing."

Elisabeta attempted a small smile but Ferro could feel how uncomfortable she was with the spotlight on her.

"Gary might be better at explaining what is happening than I am," Ferro said, more to shift the attention away from Elisabeta than for any other reason. "Elisabeta, when you feel ready, you and I will do our best to aid young Josef."

"Before you do, I'd like to see just how deep the burns are and where they are on him as well," Gary said. "Tariq, did you train with Josef? Use his tablet?"

Tariq shook his head. "No, I've been using these programs from the time they were first developed. Josef actually wrote some of the software programs a year or so ago, and I trained myself to use them by the tutorials."

Show-off, Sandu whispered into Ferro and Elisabeta's shared merge.

Elisabeta's expression didn't change, but Ferro felt the amusement flare briefly in her mind and he was grateful to Sandu. Elisabeta really was uncomfortable in the presence of the others, even when they were saying things complimentary. He knew she just wanted to go back to their home and be alone with him. He was grateful. He felt the same way.

"Sandu, you and Dragomir both used the tablet and trained on the same program?"

Sandu nodded. "We compared notes. It really was not as difficult as it seemed at the time. We pulled the knowledge out of Josef's mind and then went over it several times. It seemed easy enough. Neither one of us could figure out why we had problems with it."

"This evening, Tariq," Gary continued. "How did the trouble start between you and Josef?"

Tariq frowned, tapping the table. "I barely remember, only that I had a major headache, but truthfully, I'd had one for several risings. Charlotte had tried to get rid of it for me. This rising, Josef stormed in very angry because he didn't want to work with any of the ancients tonight. I told him to get out. He did, but he was muttering under his breath. He had those piercings, and for some reason I felt like he was being deliberately disrespectful to me by wearing them. I yelled after him to get rid of them before he came back around. Then I sent someone to him to train. I don't even remember who right now, but I do remember I wasn't going to let some kid tell me what to do in my own home."

"All of that is completely out of character for you," Maksim pointed out. "Were you aware that it was?"

Tariq nodded. "I couldn't stop myself. I kept feeling this intense rage, so much so that I told Charlotte to keep the kids away from me and not to come around, either. I didn't tell her why. I tried to have the house quiet and just get work done."

"Work?" Gary prompted.

Tariq nodded. "I've been neglectful of the nightclubs and needed to oversee them. I try to be hands-on as much as I can, but lately, with everything going on, I've left them in the hands of the managers. I thought I could go over the books, the orders, that kind of thing. My head hurt so much, it was nearly impossible."

"Has anyone new come to work here at the compound? For the security team? Sergey has recruited human male psychics," Ferro said. "Could he have planted someone?"

"The humans working here are scanned on a nightly basis," Maksim explained. "Even if Sergey shielded them, we would find the shield."

Gary sighed. "Ferro, Elisabeta, let's help young Josef. It will be interesting to see how deep the burns are in him."

Elisabeta didn't wait, and Ferro realized it had been difficult for her to remain still when she knew the boy needed her help. He'd attributed her discomfort to being in the room with all the Carpathians, but it had been so much more than that. Someone had need of her. That was what mattered to her. Elisabeta's entire concentration was centered on Josef. Still, as much as he found himself loving her all the more for her compassion, he was going to have to caution her to wait for him to ensure her safety. For him, making certain his lifemate was safe took precedence over everything else.

The red in Josef's brain was dark and angry, even more so than in any of the ancients. The scoring seemed much deeper and there was much more of it, as if he had been exposed to the infection for a longer time than any of the ancients. He had been at the compound for only two risings, so did that mean he had been exposed prior to coming? Had he brought the infection with him? Ferro hoped Gary had more of an idea than he did, because he was at a complete loss. Nothing made sense. Now, for certain, they would have to inspect Traian and Joie, as well as everyone Josef had come into contact with. It was going to be a long night and he doubted the things he had planned for his lifemate would come about.

I do not like you feeling as if you have failed me yet again, Ferro. You have never failed me. I do not mind helping these people.

He knew she didn't. But in helping them, she wasn't able to have the time to learn the things necessary to help herself. *Minan piŋe sarnanak, there is so much for you to know of this world to make you comfortable. I do not want you to ever feel as if you are less than anyone else. You are more. You are beautiful and kind and powerful. As your lifemate, I wish to show you the things that will help you to realize this about yourself, but each rising you are called on to sacrifice what is best for you for the good of others.*

She was silent while she concentrated on sending her fresh, soothing breeze to a stubborn slash of deep, violent red that didn't want to dissipate. When, at last, the scoring thinned, tattered in places and finally beginning to slowly pull apart, she surrounded Ferro with her signature fragrance.

I have you. Each rising, kont o sívanak, I have you, and you give to me everything I need to learn to be confident. I am learning to trust. That is the most difficult of all things to learn. I am beginning to feel safe where for centuries I did not know what that was. Now, that word means you. You are my safety. While you and the healer inspect the others for the burns, I will do my best to be brave and stay with Lorraine and Julija as you wish.

Ferro knew just how difficult that was for her to say to him, and how much trust in him it required. He could feel her trepidation, and yet at no time did it change the sweet, soft breeze moving through Josef's mind as she worked at removing the terrible burns marring his amazing brain.

10

The waves among the rocks, music of the sea,
Thunderous harmonies carry you to me.

E lisabeta tried not to fidget. She dropped one hand to the skirt of her dress, her fingers folding the material in between nervously. Her mouth felt dry. She knew the other women would never know she was in a state of panic because she had become adept at hiding all physical symptoms from Sergey over the centuries.

She studied the other three women discreetly. Lorraine and Julija both wore soft blue jeans and T-shirts. She couldn't imagine that such clothes could possibly be comfortable, but both women seemed very at home in them. Emeline was dressed in a long, ruffled, very feminine skirt and a formfitting camisole top with silken ties that wove back and forth across her breasts. It was far more daring than Elisabeta's formfitting dress, and yet Emeline wore the outfit with ease and grace. She had kicked off her shoes, so Elisabeta, with great relief, followed suit, the hated sandals on the floor beside her chair.

Ferro wasn't present physically, but he was merged with her, not leaving her alone when she might summon Sergey. She was terrified the vampire would find a way inside the compound, desperate to get to her when she called him. She doubted she would be able to stop herself even knowing she was doing it. Emotions versus intellect was something she was going to have to learn about.

Emeline's home was cozy, not nearly as big as the house Ferro had. She wondered if he could split the room in half, making it approximately the size of Emeline and Dragomir's living room. She might do better handling that volume.

We could do that, sívamet, but it will take you more time to acclimate to the outside world. You are having a difficult time looking at the scope of land between the homes in Tariq's compound, let alone if we traveled and you had to see the open mountains, valleys and skies.

She hadn't thought of that. Naturally, there would be a reason Ferro had chosen a large room to introduce her to in their home. He always had a reason, and that was where trust needed to come into play. She was immediately ashamed that she had second-guessed him.

Elisabeta, you are doing just fine. There is no reason for you to be upset. I had time while you were in the ground healing to think about what would best aid you in your recovery. You have only had time to react to the many problems facing not only you but all the Carpathians. The world is much changed.

Ferro's voice was reassuring. Not only his voice. He was in her mind. Calm. Steady. A rock. Her rock. No matter what he was doing—and it was important—he took the time to reassure her.

I will be fine with these women. Stay with me, Ferro, but you do not need to speak with me. Her heart reacted, accelerating like crazy as she let him off the hook.

Julija was a true friend. Her very first. She sat across from Elisabeta in a very comfortable armchair holding Emeline's daughter, Carisma, in her lap.

She sent Elisabeta a quick grin. "Are you finished talking to that man of yours?"

"Yes. I think so. He is working with the healer to check everyone who might have been infected. Poor young Josef was mortified at the things he said to Tariq."

"What exactly is happening?" Julija asked.

Elisabeta frowned. She was uncertain how much she should say. *Am I allowed to tell them everything? You did not say.*

Yes, of course. This is no secret. The more of us aware, the more we have looking out for the danger.

"There seems to be something causing a burn across the brain in two different areas, one controlling emotions and the other, judgment."

"On the ancients," Emeline said, making it half question, half statement.

Elisabeta shook her head. "Josef was also infected. In fact, his burns were worse even than Tariq's."

The women looked at one another. Emeline tapped the arm of her chair and then seemed to make up her mind. "Is it possible that this could affect children as well? Or older people? Would they necessarily have to be Carpathian? Can anyone be infected?"

"Yes, I believe we all are at risk," Elisabeta replied. "I do not know what it is, or where it is coming from, but yes, everyone is at risk, including the children. Most likely those humans in the compound as well. Until we figure out the cause, all of us need to watch one another." She kept her gaze on the other woman's face, sending out her soothing energy.

Ferro, I think Emeline suspects a child, or maybe some of the children, are at risk of the infection. She also mentioned older people in passing. Specifically humans. I do not know if it is anything, but she is giving off some very heavy waves of distress.

Lorraine leaned toward Emeline. "Are you worried about the children, Emme? One in particular? Is someone showing signs of temper?"

Emeline tucked a strand of hair behind her ear. Elisabeta noted that her hand trembled just a little.

"Genevieve told me they all seemed out of sorts lately." She looked at Elisabeta. "Genevieve is their nanny. She's human, the sweetest woman ever, a good friend to all of us. She and Charlotte were best friends long before Charlotte found Tariq. Genevieve told me Danny shoved her. Danny is the most polite boy on the planet. He really is. And Amelia yelled at Lourdes and Bella and made them cry. Liv kicked her stone dragon and chipped out a piece of the rock, and then when she couldn't repair it herself, threw a temper tantrum. Genevieve said all the children have been out of sorts over the last few days."

"Last few days?" Elisabeta echoed. *Did you hear that, Ferro? Not just since Josef has been here. Do you want me to offer to look at them?*

Absolutely not. Ferro was adamant. He definitely sounded commanding whether he wanted to or not.

She kept the soothing energy moving through the room, making certain that Julija and the baby she carried in her body as well as the child in her lap would only feel happiness and peace. "You mentioned older people, Emeline? Do you feel they are upset as well?"

"Yes, Donald and Mary Walton. They live in the converted boathouse next to the lake. They're the sweetest couple and they never fight. The last few nights they've barely spoken to one another and Mary's been crying a lot. It just seems like everyone is going a little nutty. I talked to Dragomir about it and we both thought maybe it was from everyone being cooped up for so long. No one has been able to leave the compound in a while."

Elisabeta couldn't help but feel guilt. Maybe, had she not been there, the occupants wouldn't be so trapped.

Emeline gave a sigh. "I feel so bad that everyone's been here since the children and I were rescued. Vadim found a way to impregnate me, and if it wasn't for Dragomir, I would be dead and so would our daughter. Dragomir was able to change her blood and make her his." Her eyes met Elisabeta's. "I was one of his experiments."

Elisabeta had often been down in the labyrinth of tunnels the vampires had taken over beneath the city and seen the horrors visited upon women and children. She'd been helpless to do anything but watch. So many times she'd been taken to places of torture and no one had ever known she was there other than Sergey. If it hadn't been for Julija, no one would have even known she existed. Even when the hunters came and the vampires fled, Sergey would have been able to come back and retrieve her, but Julija had managed to allow Elisabeta to be seen, and the Carpathians had taken her with them back to the compound.

It had never occurred to her that Emeline might feel as responsible as she did for the others occupying the compound feeling so trapped. "Your daughter is beautiful, Emeline," Elisabeta said. "You and Dragomir have a gift beyond any price." There was suddenly longing in her heart for what she thought could never be. She had so much already and she would be forever happy and grateful that the universe had given her Ferro.

Emeline's face lit up. "Thank you, Elisabeta. I worried so much that Carisma wouldn't be accepted, but Dragomir was positive that she would be loved by the Carpathian people, and she has been. We use this house sometimes, but we have our own now, very close to the one your lifemate has for you. The property borders the woods like yours does. Dragomir wants to fill our home with children. He even gave me my own golden dragon with gorgeous emerald eyes right in the middle of our courtyard because he knows I love the stone dragons the triplets made for the children here. He constructed a beautiful little lavender one for Carisma for when she gets a little older. He's so thoughtful."

"I do not know about the stone dragons you speak of."

Instantly Ferro sent her an image of stone dragons in various colors: red, blue, orange, green and brown. *Lojos, Matias and Tomas made these dragons for the children. They come to life for them, whispering to them and flying them when they want to play. They are protective of the children. Dragomir has made one for Emeline and Carisma. Liv has asked Valentin to make one for Genevieve. He is considering doing so.*

The instant Ferro flooded her mind with the information, Elisabeta felt safe and warm. She hadn't realized, even with him merged with her, staying somewhere in the background while he worked with the healer examining the others in the compound, that she was uneasy without him. Not just uneasy, bordering on panic. Her heart pounded, although she automatically kept the sound from being heard. She'd learned to do that always, keeping her breathing and pulse from Sergey when she was especially agitated. She'd actually dug her fingernails into her forearm, deep, to concentrate on the bite of pain in order to keep her mind from panicking.

Emeline explained about the dragons and how the triplets had made them for the children to keep them from being afraid when they were fleeing the vampires. "The dragons represent freedom to them and also the friendship of the Carpathians when the hunters can seem so frightening at times."

"I can understand that," Elisabeta agreed. She rubbed at her eyes. The lighting in the room was dim. Ferro had made it clear to the women that she couldn't be exposed to too much light or space, but in spite of the room being smaller than the one in their home, she still felt sick if she looked too long at one thing.

She wanted to succeed in her friendship with these women. She was very adept at reading others; she'd learned to be. Sergey would bring her with him and secret her from his brothers. He would want her to tell him every detail of the meetings they held, what was said and what she thought their real intentions were. Reading others, their minds, their expressions and body language, even when their flesh was rotting, allowed her to keep her own brain functioning. These women were good and genuinely wanted to become her friends and help her integrate into her new life.

She knew all of them worried about Ferro being too domineering with her. To them, he appeared arrogant and controlling. They couldn't know she asked for him to shield her and sometimes even command her. She needed those clear lines because it was the only way she had lived for centuries and it made her comfortable when she was terrified.

Ferro, there really seems to be a problem with the children and the older couple. If Emeline invites one of them to the house, I could tell immediately if they have been infected. They cannot possibly hurt me. We could start with one of the children or the older woman.

O jelä peje teräd emni, absolutely not, I will be there soon. You will not take chances with your life. We have no idea how this thing is passed from one person to the next. You are already dealing with enough. I am not willing to take chances with you. Is that understood?

She wanted to hug herself. That was her lifemate, cursing at her in their ancient language. Sun scorch you, woman. She hid her amusement even from him, but somehow his reaction made her feel cherished, not oppressed as she knew the other women in the room would feel. They would take his instant response as a sign of his controlling behavior. She saw it as a sign of caring. In spite of her trying to hide her agitation at their physical separation, he knew.

Elisabeta, he prompted. *I require an answer.*

I understand. I wished only to help, Ferro.

"Are you going to spend what little time we have to visit talking to your lifemate?" Lorraine demanded. "Because he doesn't let you out of his sight."

Julija laughed. "You're one to talk, Lorraine. I'm surprised Andor isn't standing outside with his ear pressed to the door." She nuzzled Carisma and kissed the side of her neck before blowing raspberries to make her laugh.

"That would most likely be Dragomir," Lorraine redirected.

Emeline shrugged, not in the least offended. "That's true, and I'm totally fine with it. Unlike the two of you crazy women, I don't want to go off and fight some monster." A shudder went through her. "I've seen enough of vampires to last me a lifetime. Dragomir is the most amazing man and I love the way he likes to stay close to me."

Elisabeta liked her answer. Emeline was matter-of-fact and unapologetic. All three women were very different and she realized they must have very different relationships with their lifemates. Ferro was correct when he'd told her they would find their own way together and what was right for them.

"Are you really worried that the children might be infected, Emeline?" Julija asked, gently rocking back and forth to soothe the baby.

Elisabeta thought she looked natural with the child even though Julija had confessed she was worried about having a baby, since she'd never really been around one. She could tell Emeline was keeping a close watch but was generously giving time to Julija in order to help her overcome her fears of handling a baby. Elisabeta found herself liking and admiring Emeline even more for her compassionate nature.

Emeline nodded. "The children have been through so much already. I hate to think that whatever this is, they have, but their behavior is just so out of character."

"Ferro and the others are checking the hunters in the compound," Lorraine said. "I'm certain they'll check the children if we ask them."

"I don't want them frightened. Amelia, in particular, has been accused of all kinds of things. She was used as a spy and still feels that deeply," Emeline continued.

The worry in Emeline had Elisabeta sending a breeze of pure soothing energy around the room. She couldn't help herself. She had to reassure the other woman. "Ferro will find a way for the children to be checked without them even knowing." Ignoring the look Julija and Lorraine exchanged, she poured confidence into her voice because she had absolute conviction in her lifemate. He would find the perfect way to examine the children without upsetting them.

You know I can tell, päläfertiilam, and I would not get close to them. If I identify a problem, you and the healer can decide how best to handle it.

Masculine amusement filled her mind. *I see how you survived the centuries, minan piŋe sarnanak. You keep after what you believe is right.*

He was back to calling her his little songbird. That boded well and gave her even more confidence that when she was persistent, he wouldn't get angry with her or dismiss what she thought was important. *I would wait for you, but wish to reassure Emeline that you will look into this for her and take it seriously, even if they are children and the older couple are human.*

Ask her about Genevieve. Are there signs of her being infected? Is she out of sorts?

"Emeline, have you been around Genevieve? Do you feel that she might be infected as well?" Elisabeta kept her voice as soothing as the gentle breeze moving through the room. Already the baby had responded to the peaceful atmosphere and the faint blend of lavender, lime, orange and bergamot. The fragrance was so subtle it was barely there, but helped lift anxiety as she sent a wave of healing energy toward Emeline.

"Genevieve is one of the most calm, steady women I've ever met in my life," Emeline said. "I've never seen her angry. If she is infected, she certainly has an abundance of control to keep it in check, and I would find it hard to believe that she could do so better than Dragomir."

Julija nodded. "I have to agree with that statement. The ancients have checked their emotions for centuries. It doesn't make sense that they are having trouble not losing their tempers, especially someone like Sandu, who can't even feel his emotions."

Elisabeta frowned. "Ancient hunters without lifemates may not feel emotion, but they have feelings the same as everyone else. I can feel them when I'm near them. Sometimes even when I am not close but they are broadcasting because they are grief-stricken. Whatever this infection is bypasses the block that prevents them from feeling and goes straight to the core of where emotion and judgment are."

"Humans get illnesses, like the flu," Lorraine said. "I know Carpathians don't, but is it possible, with the composition of the soil changed so much, that the answer is that simple? It's a new illness sweeping through the compound?"

"That's an interesting theory," Emeline said. "One I wouldn't have considered and I doubt if the others have, although perhaps the healer has. He seems to give thought to everything. What do you think, Elisabeta? You've seen the results of it up close."

Elisabeta wasn't used to anyone asking her opinion. She went back and forth on enjoying the discussion with the women and then panicking a little at the completely unfamiliar need to actually give her own response.

It is okay to tell them what you are thinking, sívamet. They are simply speculating, as you would be. I have no answer. Gary and I are throwing out ideas in the hopes that we hit on something. I repeated Lorraine's theory of a flu of some sort to Gary, but he does not think it could be that.

She took a deep breath, taking the scents that helped with anxiety deep into her lungs. She'd sent the fragrances around the room to aid Emeline and now hoped they helped her. Not only did she have to talk—something she found difficult—and give an opinion—which was even worse—but even in the small space, without the bars between her eyes and the rest of the world, she found it difficult to look around her without feeling disoriented.

"I do not know what is causing this infection, but the burns can be very deep in some and not in others. It does not appear to be a sickness to me." Her heart beat so hard in her chest she pressed her fist there to help mask the sound. She thought she might faint. She bit down very hard on her lower lip and once again pressed her nails into her forearm. Her distress level was rising the longer she was there alone and the more that was required of her.

They wish only to be your friend, Elisabeta. Nothing is required of you. Lean on Julija. She will get you through any difficulty.

Merged as she was with Ferro, something alerted her to his state of mind when directing her to lean on her friend. It wasn't an inflection in his voice, or any hint of emotion, but still, her connection with him was extremely strong. She knew there was a cost to him when he gave her that advice. He wanted to be the one she leaned on, and yet he generously pushed her toward the three women, certain it would be good for her to have female friends.

You will get me through all difficulties, kont o sívanak. Deliberately she called him "strong heart." He was that to her. *I like them, but it is you I have placed my trust in. It is you I have given my allegiance to. I will learn, over time, to trust in my friendships with them, but it is you I have need of, Ferro, unless I am too much trouble.* She may have been reading him wrong. It was possible he was trying to pass her off to someone else because he was tired of her clingy ways.

Amusement flooded her mind. *You are certainly trouble, but never too much. I enjoy our little skirmishes. Isai comes for Julija. She is with child and we cannot take a chance that she becomes infected. He is not at this time and until we figure out what is happening, he will keep her away as much as possible,* Ferro warned.

Elisabeta could see that all three women had already been contacted by their respective lifemates.

Julija was up and handing the sleeping child to Emeline. "Isai comes to collect me. Thank you for allowing me to spend time with Carisma. She's beautiful."

"Dragomir is also on his way," Emeline said. "I'm going to talk to him about the children and Genevieve. She might be in real danger."

"No worries, Emeline," Elisabeta said. "I promise I will see to them without them realizing anyone is checking for trouble. You have a little one to protect."

"You've been through hell," Emeline protested.

"It helps me to concentrate on others." Elisabeta told the strict truth. "I do not have to think about all the little details I am expected to learn about this new life."

Dragomir's broad shoulders filled the doorway, his golden eyes moving over his lifemate, seeing everything. He gave a courtly bow to the other women as he stepped inside and took Carisma from Emeline, his mouth brushing a gentle kiss on his lifemate's temple. He took her hand and tugged until he brought her under the protection of his shoulder.

"Ferro and the healer will be careful with the children, Emeline. Elisabeta will keep them in line." He smiled at Elisabeta and then he was gone, taking his family with him.

Isai came in next, Andor right behind him. Elisabeta folded her hands in her lap, uncertain of what to do. This wasn't her home. Apparently, it wasn't Emeline's home, either. Isai saluted her and Julija waved as he all but carried her out.

It was good to see you out with just the girls, Elisabeta, Julija said. *I'm so proud of your progress. Isai is railroading me back to our home. Will you be okay until Ferro gets there?*

Would she? Elisabeta didn't move, frozen in the comfortable chair. *Of course, I will be fine. He is bound to turn up soon.* She wasn't going to ask him where he was. He would come for her. He knew the others had come for their women.

"Do you want us to stay with you until Ferro gets here, Elisabeta?" Lorraine asked.

Andor shook his head before Elisabeta could answer. "Ferro gave very strict instructions. He wants Elisabeta to sit in here. When we leave, we will leave the door open behind us. Amelia will come in at Genevieve's request to check the house and, Elisabeta, you introduce yourself and tell her you are waiting for Ferro to come. He will be here, unseen but close, should there be trouble."

Elisabeta nodded, hurt that Ferro hadn't given her the instructions himself. It felt strange to her to have Lorraine's lifemate speaking directly to her. Did that mean she needed to answer him? Her fingers twisted in the skirt of her dress. She couldn't look up at Andor or Lorraine.

He does not expect you to answer, pine sarnanak. I am Ferro, after all, and I do not share my lifemate. Just sit there and look demure. Lorraine will lose her mind again and call me a caveman. The night air will be cooling to you when they leave the door open.

"That horrid Ferro has commanded you not to answer Andor, hasn't he?" Lorraine demanded.

Before she could shake her head, Ferro laughed. *You are not to answer Andor, Elisabeta.*

You said that on purpose. She was relieved all the same. She gave the tiniest of nods to Lorraine.

Yes, Ferro admitted to her, making her want to laugh.

"I am going to *strangle* that man," Lorraine proclaimed. She went out the door. *Ferro, you had better not bully that girl. I thought we cleared this up.*

Elisabeta heard Lorraine's voice in her merged mind with Ferro. He didn't respond until Lorraine and Andor were gone completely.

You really like to get her riled up.

She has a bit of a temper. Andor finds her very appealing when she gets fired up and passionate. I like to give her an outlet to vent.

Someone is coming up the stairs. I can hear them. It is definitely the younger girl.

Amelia. Gary and I are in the house with you. Do you feel me close, sívamet? You will have to talk to her.

Elisabeta felt his hand sweep down the back of her head in a long caress.

She is fifteen now, but has had vampires assault her and use her as a spy. Her life has been turned upside down. She needs and wants to be converted but not without her brother, Danny. She does not want him to be alone. Her little sister and Lourdes can both be converted, but she refuses to allow at least Bella to be converted until Danny is safe.

Elisabeta knew Ferro wanted her to feel compassion for the teenager to make it easier to speak with her. A young girl stalked right into the room without hesitation. She was very slim and had thick, dark hair and vivid green eyes.

"Who are you? What are you doing in here?"

Elisabeta studied the teenager. Her fists were clenched. There was belligerence stamped on her face. There was no doubt, even without checking further, that Amelia had been infected. Elisabeta sent a sweet breeze to surround the girl, a soothing peace. "I am Elisabeta. I was visiting with Emeline, Lorraine and Julija, but their lifemates came for them and mine is late."

The peaceful calm settling over Amelia seemed to drain some of her anger, or at least minimize it. Ferro stepped up behind Amelia, materializing and waving his hand toward her as he did so. The teen froze just as Josef had done.

Josef knew what was happening to him. Does she? Elisabeta didn't want the child to suffer any more than she already had.

"Josef is Carpathian, and Gary wanted him to know what was happening, so he shared with him all information. Once you removed the burns, he could understand and was not angry. There is no need for her to know anything is wrong." Ferro spoke aloud, indicating to Elisabeta that they could do so.

As pure light, Gary entered the child first, allowing Ferro to follow through their bond. Merged as she was with her lifemate, Elisabeta moved straight to the damaged areas. She was prepared to see burns, but not to the extent that they were in Amelia's brain. The scoring was far worse in the teenager than it had been in anyone else she'd encountered so far.

This is horrible. This has been done over a period of time, longer than a couple of days. Perhaps a week? Two? She didn't want to think longer, the same amount of time she had been at the compound in the healing grounds. *Did you find burns in anyone else?*

No other hunter. Gary and I checked Lorraine, Emeline and Julija. They show no signs of burns.

Why the children and Tariq? Sandu? Dragomir? What of Traian and Joie? Elisabeta felt a little anxious over her birth brother and his lifemate.

No trace of burns. Neither were infected. I wish I had an answer for you, piŋe sarnanak, but I do not, and neither does Gary. We can only try to fit the pieces of the puzzle together. Can you rid her of these burns?

Elisabeta studied the terrible, angry dark red slashes. They were deep, and so many it looked as if they were one continuous mass coloring over the areas of the brain affecting Amelia's abilities of judgment and rational thinking. She was shocked that the teenager hadn't had far more outbursts.

She has more damage even than Josef, yet Emeline was not certain if Amelia was infected.

Gary answered her. *This child is extremely strong. She fought a master vampire's hold on her. She did her best against him, although eventually he did wear her down, and she still feels guilty over it. She most likely has restrained herself in order to keep from lashing out, knowing instinctively something is wrong.*

Elisabeta immediately felt kinship with the girl. She began to flood the teenager's brain with a cool, healing breeze, this one much stronger than she had ever used on the others. It was going to be a very difficult and long process to remove the deep scoring in her brain, but Elisabeta was determined.

Someone must examine Danny. If Amelia is this bad and Danny actually pushed Genevieve, then he could be worse. Can Sandu inspect him? Tariq or Maksim must be able to lead him into the boy's brain, Ferro suggested to Gary.

Elisabeta could tell Ferro was worried for her, not for the unknown boy. He didn't know the children, but she was expending a great amount of energy on Amelia. If Amelia's brother was as bad or worse, to clear out the burns and rid him of the infection, Elisabeta would be exhausted beyond measure. She wanted to surround Ferro with soothing peace but she knew she couldn't waste even a small amount of energy to reassure him. The task before her was too great.

I am worried for the boy. And what of the little ones? She kept working as she addressed both Carpathians.

Tariq would prefer either Dragomir or Andor go with him into Danny's mind. Gary addressed Ferro's concern. *They have lifemates to anchor them.*

That made no difference to this infection, Ferro pointed out.

That is true, Gary agreed, in no way perturbed. *But Sandu is still with-*

out his lifemate and, this infection aside, would be a threat to Tariq's children. He has adopted these children, human or not. He loves them.

Elisabeta stayed silent through the exchange, hoping the healer would address her concerns and allow Ferro to understand what Gary had said about Tariq and the children. Ferro had been sequestered in the monastery while the world around him changed. He had little to do with humans before that. He might have caught up with knowledge simply by extracting it from those around him, but that didn't give him the emotional understanding needed in these circumstances.

I will ask Tariq to inspect the little ones, with one of the ancients to guard him, Gary assured Elisabeta.

You have seen Elisabeta work, Ferro said. *Can you rid them of this infection?*

She knew the answer even before she felt the healer's negative reaction.

I wish I could say that I could, Ferro. I have the memories of my ancestors and all the many situations and experiences they encountered. None have ever run across this before. What Elisabeta does seems unique to her. This is not a poison or injury, although it appears as a burn.

Elisabeta felt Ferro's frustration and knew what he was going to say before he actually said it, and her heart sank.

She cannot possibly erase these destructive burns from everyone, especially if they are as deep and as massive as this girl's are. Elisabeta is still weak from long years without proper sustenance. If these children are infected—and you know they are—that is three more right there. That is without the older couple, who most likely are as well.

I am sorry, Ferro, Gary replied. *As a healer, I feel my failure even more than you. I am merged with you. We are tied together. I already know the exhaustion she is feeling.*

Elisabeta despised that she could not comfort either of them. It wasn't their fault that some mysterious infestation was creeping through the compound. She didn't want to think that she may have brought it with her, but looking at the violent scorching in Amelia's brain, she knew the damage had happened over the last few weeks, not just since Josef had arrived. She was almost certain if they measured the injury, they could pinpoint the exact night of her arrival.

I am an ancient, Gary, Ferro replied. *This is my failure as well. I am her lifemate and I have always been able to heal every wound, no matter how bad, yet this eludes my skills.*

Elisabeta couldn't stand it. *Neither of you has failed me. Please just find out about the children and the older couple. I will work as long as possible. If Sandu and the other ancients are willing to give me blood, I will be able to continue. It just takes time.*

Minan piŋe sarnanak, we do not know what is causing this. You may remove all traces of the infection only to have it back this next rising, Ferro said.

Elisabeta knew he was right, but she couldn't help the need in her to help. That trait overrode all else, the centuries of conditioning, the strange reaction to large spaces, her fear of giving her opinion, everything.

Perhaps we do not know what is causing this infection, Gary said, *but we might be one step closer to identifying it if someone who previously had it gets it back. We need to find something they all have in common.*

Because the scoring was so thick, it took much longer to heal, and a concentrated breeze centered on the heavy swath of red, but in the end, the burns gave way, first thinning and then floating in tatters before simply dissolving completely. Elisabeta took her time with the deep scoring, working on healing those crevices the burns had created before she was finally able to withdraw from the teenager.

She found herself dizzy and disoriented. At once, Ferro pressed her head to his chest and she blindly drank from him. Strength poured into her, along with the very essence of her lifemate. He filled every one of her senses. She became aware, after a few minutes, that he was completely supporting her, his arms hiding her from several others in the room. Someone, and she vaguely realized it was Sandu, was giving Ferro blood. Benedek was there, along with a couple of others she didn't really recognize.

Once she was back up to strength, Tariq strode in with two little girls on either hip. His lifemate, Charlotte, was with him. Lourdes was her niece and now adopted daughter. Bella was Amelia's little sister. All of the siblings had been adopted by Tariq and Charlotte. The little girls were four. They were beautiful and looked remarkably alike.

They have faint scorching on their brains, Tariq greeted. He sank into one of the chairs opposite Elisabeta and Ferro.

Charlotte sat in the chair beside him and took Lourdes from him to hold on her lap. Charlotte had very curly, thick auburn hair and was on the smaller side, with generous curves. The moment she had secured Lourdes, Tariq waved his hand and both little girls, who had been squirming to get down, immediately froze.

"I don't believe they were exposed to this infection very long," Tariq said grimly. "It is strange that neither Charlotte nor Genevieve have it when I did and the children all do."

"We'll figure it out," Gary assured.

With both Tariq and Charlotte looking so anxious and staring at her, Elisabeta felt the familiar recoiling, the need to bury her face and retreat from all those around her. Immediately, Ferro shielded her. "Elisabeta will be very gentle with the girls."

She took that as her cue to follow the healer into Lourdes first. It was Charlotte who led them, not Tariq. She wasn't surprised. Had she been the child's mother, she would have insisted she be there as well. Charlotte didn't know her at all and had no reason to trust her.

The red streaks were so faint on the developing brain that they were actually more pink than red. It gave Elisabeta, Ferro and Gary the chance to study the faint layers and how they lay over the frontal lobe. The burn hadn't settled into the brain itself yet, nor had it covered it. Elisabeta was able to simply blow the easiest of breezes to remove it. She did the same with Bella's. It took no real effort, as both girls had the same faint streaking.

"Do you have any idea what is causing this?" Tariq asked Elisabeta directly, rocking Bella gently. It was clear he expected an answer.

Elisabeta's stomach churned. She pushed her hand tight against the gathering knots and pressed closer to Ferro.

"The three of us were just discussing that," Ferro said, coming to her rescue. "We don't know. Send in Mary and Donald Walton. Andor found very few burns on them. Less so on Mary than Donald. We will lose the night if we don't hurry, and Elisabeta will grow too tired. She still has Liv and Danny to heal after the Waltons."

Charlotte rose. "Thank you, Elisabeta, we're in your debt. I hope to get to know you better when you have had the time to adjust to being with your lifemate. I know that is important. And now the entire compound is counting on you. This must be so difficult for you. I just want to say how much we all appreciate you."

II

Hand in hand we are strong;
Sing with me, it's to you I belong.

Ferro called to Elisabeta with the rain first. Their song. The drops played through the rich soil, reaching to tease her body, to wake her gently. It had been a very long night and she had been so exhausted after tending to Liv, the older couple and lastly Danny, who had very violent burns, that even after Ferro had given her blood along with Andor and Dragomir, he had to carry her to the healing soil beneath their home and place her in it. She had been pale. Ethereal-looking. Entirely unaware of her surroundings.

Ferro vowed this rising was going to be very different for his lifemate. It was going to be about the two of them. He would give her as many wonderful experiences as possible without the continual interruptions from those living within the fortress Tariq and the others had formed. He needed time with his lifemate, just as Charlotte had suggested. It was important to form those close bonds outside the merging of their minds.

The one good thing coming out of the continual need the Carpathian community had of her was that Elisabeta was growing more confident, understanding that her gift was unique and of great value. He wanted her to have the same confidence in herself with him. He had always thought there was an equal balance of power between Carpathian couples no matter how dominant the male might be simply because it was the male's duty to always see to his lifemate's happiness. It was impossible to set up a dictatorship if his partner wasn't happy.

Come to me, minan piŋe sarnanak. Rise and come to me. You have no need of clothes. Practice opening the soil above you and freshening your body and hair.

He gave her the command and waited, his body already anticipating her and what lessons they would learn this rising. What they would practice from the rising before. He had risen before her and gone hunting for blood. He had closed the earth over her so that she would have the experience of opening the soil for herself. On his return, he had deliberately woven strong safeguards around the property to keep everyone out, including other Carpathians, in the hopes that he could have his lifemate to himself.

Intertwined with notes of their song and in the drops of the rain, he threaded the deep passion he felt for her. Elisabeta. His world. His center. He needed her to realize how much she meant to him. How much he wanted her, both physically and emotionally. If she knew, she would have all the confidence in the world.

Ferro felt her then, that first moment when she awakened, hearing the raindrops beating in a rhythm with his heart. He scanned her carefully and noted immediately that she was different this rising, more anticipating than fearful, although trepidation was still there. In spite of all the energy she had expended ridding so many of the mysterious burns, she seemed healthier, most likely due to ancient blood given to her freely in large amounts.

I want to be selfish this rising, sívamet. I have safeguarded our home from the rest of the world. It will be just the two of us. He poured seduction into her mind.

Immediately, there was a reaction, both in her body and mind, but there was also a very strong hesitation. Fear. He had hoped they had dispensed with that emotion between the two of them, but he was making new demands of her each rising. She wanted to please him, to meet his every expectation, and even looked forward to his "lessons," but she was terrified of letting him down, especially when it came to anything physical between them. Elisabeta had a talent for soothing everyone around her. He had to be the one person who could soothe her.

I have a surprise for you, piŋe sarnanak. He used a coaxing tone. Still sensual. He wanted her to feel the sexual pull between lifemates. Anticipation. But no pressure. *Once you have fed, we will go together into the forest. It is so beautiful there, and I have made certain no one is around, nor can they disturb us. I have a long cape for you to wear while you practice your walking to get there.*

He would have to forgo seeing her feminine form, but she would feel too vulnerable naked. He wanted to build her confidence, not make her feel helpless. *Once there, we will practice shifting into any form you wish. If it pleases you, you can truly become a little songbird and fly. You do not have to go high into the sky, but go from branch to branch, if seeing through the eyes of a bird is still too difficult.*

Her heart rate accelerated as she opened the earth above her. He was extremely proud of how smoothly she was able to move the dirt. He doubted she even noticed because she was concentrating on floating out of the soil and freshening her body at the same time. He noted that she paid particular attention to her hair. That required even more concentration. He had been coming up out of the soil clean and fully clothed for so long the action was automatic, but Elisabeta hadn't been allowed to do the simplest task for herself.

Ferro noted that she had no problem floating, or removing the fine particles of soil from her body, but was extremely frustrated with freshening and braiding her hair. He was tempted to help her, especially as she tried several times without success. Still, she had achieved two of the three tasks easily, and he didn't want to take those accomplishments from her. She didn't look to him for aid so he stayed quietly merged with her, aching to do her hair but knowing she needed to feel as if she could be independent when she wanted to be. He found that watching her struggle was one of the most difficult things he'd ever done—and he'd fought countless battles with master vampires.

Feminine triumph burst through his mind when she managed the thick braid on her own. Elisabeta's joy was worth the agony of stepping back and witnessing her battle for so small a victory, and yet it wasn't small. For Elisabeta, it was an enormous accomplishment. He let his pride in her swamp both of them.

My amazing lifemate. Believe me, I wake each rising knowing what a miracle I have been given. Come to me, sívamet.

This was another hard chore, and he had struggled with whether or not to push her out of her comfort zone so quickly on these smaller tasks. Every Carpathian child was taught as a toddler to open the soil, float, clean and clothe themselves, as well as get from one place to the other easily. He knew Elisabeta felt inferior to others because she didn't know how to do the things she regarded as simple—things she knew children could do. The knowledge that a child could do more than she could made her feel ashamed. He detested that. She was a brilliant woman and just needed a little time to catch up.

How do I find you?

Fear swamped her, but she didn't falter or refuse. He felt her determination. The woman could bring him to his knees.

Do you feel me close? We share a mind merge yet you do not seek my knowledge. Reach for my location. I will shield you from the battles that would distress you, Elisabeta. I know a woman as compassionate as you would have difficulties viewing the things I have seen and done over the centuries. Unlike the vampire, I do not wish to expose you. He was cruel and enjoyed watching you suffer. I do not. Trust me. Share my mind the way I share yours.

He knew he was asking for a huge leap of faith. He was centuries old and Elisabeta had already heard the rumors of Ferro from the Malinov brothers, the relentless Carpathian hunter feared even by other Carpathians for his renowned skills. He felt her hesitation, heard her pulse jump and then begin to race. His woman had serious trust issues and yet she still wrapped herself in him.

He simply waited, giving her the choice, knowing that more than anything else this was difficult for her. Elisabeta preferred Ferro to make the choice for her. She wanted him to command her to look into his mind rather than leave it up to her.

Ferro. Her voice shook. *Is this what you desire of me?*

He was silent, turning over and over in his mind the various reactions to her trembling query. He wanted her to start making her own choices for her sake and know they were her own.

Minan piŋe sarnanak, only you can decide whether you feel you are able to trust me enough to shield you. If you cannot, I will not be angry or disappointed in you. We will simply try it another day. You have only to look into my mind, see where I am and come to me, or call to me and I will come to you. There is no wrong decision. He kept his tone as gentle as possible, giving her the sensation of his palm stroking caresses down the back of her head to soothe her.

Elisabeta paced back and forth on the grounds beneath the house, wrapping her arms around herself, unaware she was walking better and better. On the uneven ground she didn't stumble. Already, when she wasn't thinking about it, she automatically cushioned the soles of her feet so she didn't hurt herself on the rocks. He would point these things out to her later, just not now when she was desperately trying to force herself to make a choice.

Ferro found it agony to feel her mounting terror. He knew he wasn't going to be able to stop himself from taking the decision from her hands. He felt like he was torturing her rather than helping her. He was feeling his way with her, trying to guide her without pushing her too fast, but perhaps he was guilty of the very thing he had warned her female friends against doing. It was just that she was so confident when she came to the aid of those in need. Just as she was cushioning her feet automatically while she paced because she wasn't giving it thought, while she was using her gift to help others, she made decisions and gave her opinion with conviction.

Then suddenly, before Ferro had made up his mind, he felt that first tentative touch, a seeking. She was so timid, her fear filling him, and then she found the images of his location, of him quietly waiting for her. He knew the moment she felt his overwhelming pride in her and his feelings that had fast gone from affection to love and passion intertwined so strong and tight, the feeling would only keep growing for her.

He felt her gasp. She went still. At first afraid to trust what she saw. The emotions he felt for her. He couldn't blame her. Sergey had tricked her repeatedly over the centuries. The vampire enjoyed playing elaborate, cruel jokes on her. Ferro felt her move in his mind, daring to search further. Looking for truth. Needing to believe but terrified to do so. He held himself equally as still as she had, silently willing her to take the next step, but aware she might not quite get there this rising. She had already come so far. His Elisabeta, so courageous.

She found his location. She merely had to cross the ground that led out from under the house where he waited to give her blood. The building was situated so that one entire length of the house had views of the thick groves of trees. A pathway led through gardens of flowers straight into the cooler forest. Already, his lifemate had taken so many new steps that he was grateful he had thought to change his ideas of what they would share this rising. His body wasn't as happy with him, but for him, everything he did was about Elisabeta and her needs.

I am coming to you? She tried to pour confidence into her voice, but it still came out a question, as if she feared she had made the wrong choice.

Ferro wrapped her in love. *You are so brave, minan piŋe sarnanak. I do not know a single Carpathian hunter more courageous than you.*

He watched over her as she walked slowly, hesitantly, bolstered by his confidence in her as well as his admiration. He kept her attention on him, not on what she was doing.

I have explored the forest, and although it is much different than what we are used to, it is beautiful. I believe you will find it a place of serenity, as I have. I did not have as much time to investigate as I would have liked, but now I am glad. That gives us places to find together. It will be an adventure. I do know there are streams and mini waterfalls.

His breath caught in his lungs, stayed trapped there as she came physically into his sight. She was tall, like the women of his people, but because of his stature, he still dwarfed her in size. She was still on the thinner side but beginning to fill out nicely, losing the starved look he detested so much. Her skin glowed now. Her bone structure was beautiful. She had faint white scars from Sergey's careless treatment of her.

Scars were very rare on Carpathians unless wounds had been mortal. The master vampire had a lot to answer for—far too much for Ferro to dwell on when his beloved woman was coming to him of her own free will.

You are the most beautiful woman on the face of the earth. He meant it. To him, she was and always would be.

Her dark eyes met his a little shyly. Her smile was slow in coming, but when it did, her face lit up and then her eyes. It was as if the moon had risen in all her beauty, glowing bright for those on earth, shining down, spilling her silvery beams everywhere. Ferro held out his hand to her as she neared him.

She placed her hand in his without hesitation and his heart stuttered. More and more she was giving him her trust. A priceless gift, one he would forever treasure and guard carefully.

"*Hän sívamak.* My beloved. You must know how fast you have learned to do so many things. I will confess"—he bent to brush a kiss along her high cheekbone and down to the corner of her mouth—"that I will miss fixing your hair for you. It is a task I greatly enjoyed doing."

Although he knew it was self-indulgent of him, he couldn't stop his hands from drifting gently from her throat to the curve of her breast.

"I like you fixing my hair," she conceded shyly. "It was . . . difficult."

"And yet you were so persistent and accomplished the task. I found that very sexy." His palm slipped to the back of her head and urged her face into his chest.

Her tongue stroked a caress over his skin, tasting him. He closed his eyes, savoring the feeling. Already she was sensual in her every touch on his body. Her hand skimmed down his chest over his abdomen, lingering on the muscles there, feeling the way they came alive for her, rippling under her palm. She sank her teeth into him and he threw back his head, letting the bite of ecstasy carry him away.

You said I am to practice the things you teach me each rising, is that not correct?

He could barely think straight with her mouth on him. Who knew the simple act of feeding could be so sensual?

Yes, he managed to get out. *If you so desire.*

In the ritual binding words, it says that my body is in your keeping and your body is in mine.

He heard that loud and clear. He became very aware of her palm, hot now, very low on his belly. His entire being centered there. *Yes. My body is yours.*

Her hand slipped lower to find the hard, thick girth of him. She smeared the leaking drops of his essence over the broad head and then down his shaft, fisting him in the way he had shown her the rising before. When her fingers tightened around him, pumping in a slow, lazy slide, and her lips and teeth moved, drinking from him, he felt the burn of flames along his spine and the roiling in his belly settle deep in his groin.

When she slid her teeth from his skin and licked at the wound, she kissed the twin holes before she began to kiss and lick her way down his chest and over the hard muscles of his abdomen. Ferro caught at her thick braid, wrapping the length around his fist, widening his stance to give himself a strong platform when she was already threatening his self-control. Just knowing his woman had enough trust in him to take what she wanted was sexy to him, let alone seeing or feeling her do it.

She was naturally sensual with great instincts. She kissed her way to his groin, but instead of going straight for his cock, she dropped slowly and very gracefully to her knees and slid her hands up his inner thighs, ratcheting up his anticipation until he couldn't think straight. Her hands moved over his skin possessively, stroking caresses up toward his groin, her mouth following the path her hands blazed. She placed tiny, barely there kisses up his inner thigh to his heavy sac, her silky hair sliding along his left leg, teasing the nerve endings almost as savagely as her mouth and fingers were.

Nothing he had ever seen, read about or imagined had prepared him for the pure sensuality of that moment. He thought passion would be uppermost as his body reacted, the flames licking up his legs and dancing along his thighs, but as he looked down at his woman—the complete concentration, that loving expression—passion combined with overwhelming love for her shook him. The two emotions were so strong and couldn't be separated.

Ferro knew he would have this time etched in his memories for all eternity. This one moment looking down at her. Those long lashes, the softness of love and ache of tenderness she didn't try to hide from him. This was all for him. That was her secret. She had a growing awareness of sexual hunger, but what she was giving him had nothing to do with her. He was merged in her mind and he felt her joy at giving him pleasure. To her this was a gift, and in giving, she felt pleasure as well.

Elisabeta could bring him to his knees every time. She kissed and licked her way up his thighs to his heavy sac and then so gently breathed warm air over him before rolling and jiggling in between kissing, licking and sucking with exquisite tenderness. His breath hissed out of him and his hands tightened in her hair. He wanted desperately to pull her head over his cock but he knew the anticipation led to a mind-blowing orgasm. More, she needed to explore and know she had equal rights in their sexual world together. She needed this confidence in herself as his woman. He wasn't going to take the power from her, no matter if he thought the top of his head might blow off from sheer pleasure.

Her tongue moved up his shaft in a long, slow lick that sent heat rushing through his veins. She did that several times, getting him very wet until he thought he would have to command her to take him into her mouth. There was no choice. He might die if she didn't. Then her mouth settled over the crown, her lips stretching wide, the sight of her like that making his heart beat wildly. He wanted her eyes on his, looking into his as she took his cock deeper.

Immediately, her lashes lifted and Ferro found himself looking into the dark well of tenderness as her hot mouth drew him in. Her tongue curled around him, dancing and teasing, stroking the vee under the crown, flicking there, and all the while she practically purred, creating a vibration that raced up his cock.

Everything about that moment came together in a mad combination. The sight of her, the sensations pouring into him, her hot mouth surrounding him, the fireball burning out of control until his hips were thrusting almost helplessly into that impossible wet heat. That tight suction that threatened to carry him somewhere he'd never been. Stars burst behind his eyes. His entire being was focused on his cock. On the sensation her mouth and hands created. That vibration shaking his balls and running up his shaft.

No matter what he needed, the slightest little thought in his mind—*tighter—deeper—don't stop—swallow—keep swallowing*—she did it. She gave that to him. His cock erupted with a fury, jet after jet of relentless hot seed pouring into her. He couldn't release her, couldn't leave that exquisite perfect haven she offered him so selflessly.

When his body calmed and relaxed, sated beyond imagining, slipping out of her mouth, she sank back on her heels, looking up at him with that same look of pure tenderness. "Thank you, Ferro. I really wanted to be able to give you that pleasure. I needed to."

He framed her face with both hands, his heart beating out of control. That was his lifemate. His Elisabeta. That was the treasure he had. "You gave me a gift priceless beyond words, *sívamet*."

He could read in her mind that, although her body ached for his, she really didn't want to pursue sexual satisfaction for herself. He held his hand out to her and when she took it, he pulled her to her feet, in close to his body.

"Are you afraid of me, Elisabeta? Of the intimacy between a man and a woman?"

She didn't look at him but pushed her face into his chest. He could hear her heart accelerate. Her arms crept around his waist and she leaned her weight into him as if seeking solace.

"There is no wrong answer, *minan piŋe sarnanak*. We are having a necessary discussion. Simply that. You have become braver every day. We are getting to know one another. Still exploring. We can enjoy the journey along the way. There is no hurry." His hand came up to massage her scalp and ease the tension from the nape of her neck. "I do not want to take information from my lifemate. I prefer that she freely gives it to me."

Purposely, he didn't couch his words in a command. When others were close and she was afraid, he would do that for her, but now, when they were alone, he wanted her to be able to get to a place where she wasn't afraid of talking to him. He wanted her to have confidence in giving him her opinion. Voicing her fears. Even simply teasing him. He needed those things from her, but more, he knew she needed to give them to him in order to begin a healing process.

It wasn't until they were all the way past the first grove of trees and the darker shades of the forest surrounded them that he felt that first intake of breath that told him she was going to answer him.

"I thought so much about what we did together. Your mouth on me. I loved it so much, Ferro."

Her voice shook. Her body trembled. He felt her nipples grow hard and scented her arousal at just the mere remembrance. She'd been aroused when she was attending to his body, yet she definitely didn't want him to give back to her. He continued massaging her scalp and neck, staying silent, letting her work out what she wanted to say even though his own body responded to hers. He didn't try to hide his reaction from her. He refused to. He wanted only truth between them, even if that truth might frighten her.

"I want more. I do. But I want to go slow and know I can handle what we do. It was so frightening and exhilarating at the same time. I did not have any control at all. I could have done something wrong. I did not know what I was supposed to do, and I do not want to make a mistake. I thought I might study books, or perhaps take the information out of your mind?" The very last was a question delivered very timidly.

He should have known she was worried about not pleasing him in some way. He bent his head and dropped a kiss on top of her thick silky hair. "Sex isn't about control, *sívamet*. When I have my mouth between your legs, I want you to let yourself fly. To just feel. You do not have to think, only feel the sensations I am giving to you."

She tilted her head to look up at him, a small frown on her face. "You had control. When you were in my mouth, I felt you holding back."

He nodded, proud of her for daring to say what she had observed. "That is true, but only because I could hurt you. I could damage your throat if I go too deep. I could frighten you. You are new to these things and I want to be cautious until you know what to expect, what you like and do not like. I want you to enjoy everything you do to me when you are doing it, not fear it. As we grow used to one another, I will hold back less and less. It was difficult. Your mouth, the way you are, the things you do to me, make it difficult to keep control, but I want always to make certain that you are safe."

"I love to give you pleasure, Ferro."

He tightened his arm around her. "I know you do, Elisabeta. I love to give you pleasure as well. We are lifemates, so bringing pleasure to one another is a mutual need. I want to be the one to teach you these things, not have you learn from a book or an instruction manual. It gives me enormous pleasure to have you follow my instructions."

Just the thought made his cock hard, the blood running hot and pulsing with desire. He let her feel that response where his erection lay so tight against her body. All the while he continued to massage her scalp and nape, keeping that soothing pressure with his fingers, wanting her to realize he was proud of her for having the courage to discuss her fears and needs with him. He always wanted truth from her, just as he was willing to give it to her.

"We have many risings to learn these things together, Elisabeta, and I am looking forward to every one of them. Just as you learned today that anticipation can make the end result so much better, if we do not rush, if we wait until you are fully ready, then when we do come together, the wait will have been worth it."

"I never want to disappoint you." She pressed her face back to his chest, first kissing him with her soft lips and then touching the tip of her tongue to his skin, tasting him.

Just the small sensation nearly drove him mad all over again. He wanted to bury his mouth between her legs, but she was still concerned—turning what he'd said over and over in her mind. He could scent her arousal as she did this, so he needed a distraction. He took a step toward the interior of the forest, her hand in his, signaling they were going to work on other things.

"It would be impossible for you to disappoint me, *pi*ɲe *sarnanak*, most assuredly when it comes to matters of sex. When we return home after practicing flight, we can revisit this conversation. I have not had my fill of your delicious taste, but that is for later. I will let you think on that. Anticipation, after all, is good for you."

She squirmed. "I think you said that on purpose."

"Most assuredly I did. You made me wait."

She gave him a small, enigmatic smile that sent a heat wave rippling down his spine. Ferro brought her hand to his chest, right over his beating heart, as they walked deeper into the forest. He didn't want her to think about how uncomfortable shoes felt on her feet, or how awkward walking might be. And he desperately needed a respite from all thoughts sexual.

"You are truly magic, *sívamet*. You have wrapped me around your little finger. I assure you, that is very difficult to do. Before you, I made everyone I came into contact with uneasy. Now, I think they regard me as a cub instead of a wolf."

She flashed him a smile, a genuine one that lit her eyes. He felt the amusement in his mind as well. "I do not think that is quite true. Even I do not think of you that way. You can be quite intimidating when you choose."

He brought her hand up to his mouth, keeping his strides slower and even, an exact match for hers. Kissing her knuckles, he returned her hand to his chest. "Perhaps, but that is just to make certain you know I am in charge."

Elisabeta laughed. Aloud. The sound was melodious. Beautiful. He half expected to see birds flocking around them. She had a way of touching him inside with her lyrical notes. Stroking nerve endings so gently. He didn't know how she did it, but she was always so in tune with him. He would have to be careful if he ever was hunting the vampire. He would become a danger to her if he was injured in any way.

"I believe you will never have to worry that I will forget you are in charge, Ferro," she assured him, her tone soft and loving.

His heart turned over. She didn't seem to mind in the least his dominant personality. "*Piŋe sarnanak*, do you have any ideas at all about how the others are getting this infection? The children? The older couple? Young Josef? And our ancients? I have thought of this endlessly and turned every possibility over and over in my mind. There does not seem to be a connection between them. Sandu has never been near the older couple. I asked him. Liv was infected but not Valentin, her lifemate, and he stays close when he can stand it."

Elisabeta, as was her way, didn't answer immediately. They were close to the coolness of the deeper trees. Already, Ferro could hear the welcome of the creatures as they approached. He had managed to distract her from the unfamiliar weight of shoes on her feet and the awkwardness of walking. She hadn't stumbled once. Now, instead of panicking when asked for her opinion, she was giving it thought, trying to fit pieces together as he had done.

"There is a connection, Ferro," she said, a small hesitation in her voice. "We just have not seen it yet. We will. We have to. I found it interesting that Danny and Amelia had extremely heavy burns in comparison to everyone else. I expected that the little ones would not have much, and they did not. Tariq had more than Sandu. Josef more than both of them. If we figure out the why of that, we will figure out how they are being infected."

His woman had been working on the puzzle as well, and she was quick and intelligent. Gary, he knew, was looking into the memories of each of those who had the burns, but none had been touched by a vampire. None had encountered a creature of any kind, psychic or otherwise, who might have infected them.

"I do not like that you are the only one who can resolve the situation. It forces you to be called every time there is a problem. If it is one with one of the ancients, the potential for danger is enormous. It is dangerous enough even with the children. I know Charlotte and Tariq are fearful for Genevieve. They cannot protect her from them during the day. They will check the children to ensure they are free of this infection before they retire, in the hopes that if they are re-exposed, the burns will be far less and she will not be so much at risk."

"I presume she was checked as well."

"She was. There was not even the slightest scoring on her."

"Genevieve is very brave."

He stopped walking once they were on the edge of a small clearing. It was very small, surrounded by trees and bushes. A narrow stream ran off to their left, moving over rocks, winding through the trees, making its way through the groves of trees toward the lake. He kept her in the trees, conscious of her battle with open space.

"No one is around, *piŋe sarnanak*. It is just the two of us. We are going to practice shifting. For me, you will always be my little songbird. Your voice is magical. You have music in every note. I hear you when I sing to you each rising. When I call to you to come to me, I know you. That part of me, the only part that is not hard and battle-worn, feels the melody in you. I thought teaching you first to fly would give you a sense of freedom you have never known and that a bird would come the easiest. You have lived life in a cage, as some birds have done. I want to open that door for you. I also thought perhaps seeing through the eyes of a bird rather than the human eye, you would not have the same trouble looking at the world around you."

Once again he wrapped his arm around her waist and locked her to him while his other hand moved to the back of her head to soothingly run his palm down her braid. "There are no expectations, Elisabeta. If you find you cannot do this, we will try another rising." He poured truth into his tone so she would hear he meant it.

She leaned into him and daringly ran her palm from his belly to his chest. There was a hint of possession in her touch he doubted she knew was there. Already the threads between lifemates were adding to the building confidence she had in him.

"I want to do this, Ferro, so much. I thought about it all the time when I was in that cage. I knew I had been taught, but when I tried to remember, I felt such pain. My head would explode and sometimes there would be blood everywhere and I would wake up in the cage with the vampire over me and I could see he was worried and angry with me. I wanted to disappear. Fly away. Fade away. But it never happened."

"Gary and I have taken down the barrier that he constructed to stop you from accessing your memories without pain, *sívamet*, but Sergey erased most of your memories, and what he couldn't, he scarred over and distorted so you would not know truth from lie or be without fear. That was why you were so afraid of meeting your birth brother."

"He really took everything from me."

Her sorrow made him want to weep. Again, there were no tears on her face, but deep inside she wept for her lost relationship with her brother, especially after knowing he had spent centuries looking for her.

"The vampire tried to take everything from you, Elisabeta, but his success is up to you. You can establish a relationship with Traian and his lifemate if you choose. Traian is not only willing, but he wants it. He will follow your lead. The vampire did not steal my soul from you in all the centuries he had you. Your trust in me is growing faster than even I thought possible. He cannot take our bond from us. You are intelligent and an asset to not only me but our people as well, and he cannot take that. I could go on and on, but we do not want to lose one more moment of the night to him, do we?"

Elisabeta tilted her head up to him and his heart stuttered for just a moment at what he saw there. She looked at him with reverence, with a kind of worship he didn't deserve. "No, *minan hän sívamak*, we do not. Please teach me to shift into a bird and learn to fly."

She'd called him her beloved. She had not done so before. Strong heart, yes, because he was her warrior, but this was different. So very different. It was the way she said it in their language. That tenderness in her voice. She couldn't hide the way she felt about him or the love creeping into her heart for him. For the first time he had real hope that she might love him as he was and they would really find their way together so in the end, when she became strong and confident, she would choose him, choose to stay with him.

"Just like when you open the earth above your head or you are dressing yourself, you must pay attention to detail. I will have an image in my head. I want you to take that image and study it from every angle. Put it in your head and make certain you see it all. You are good with details, Elisabeta, meticulous about them, but anyone, when they are eager to try something, can get overexcited. Take your time. Eventually, even shifting will become automatic to you, but this is the foundation and it must be solid."

Ferro waved his hand, covering the ground with a soft, furred mat, and sank down, drawing her with him. She faced him, closing her eyes, concentrating. He felt her moving in his mind, finding the small Western

Screech Owl. The owls mated for life and almost always used tree cavities to nest in. During courtship, the male called to the female with a song, and when a lady accepted him, they sang back and forth in a duet, getting closer and closer until they found each other. Throughout the various seasons of the years, the male continued to sing to his chosen lady, as he intended to sing to Elisabeta.

The Western Screech Owl was particularly fierce when it came to protecting its nest and young, as he was certain his Elisabeta would be in spite of the fact that she thought herself timid. He didn't want her fighting vampires at his side. He would definitely forbid such a thing, but he wouldn't want her to be so terrified that the creatures could easily kill her and their children should he be away. Knowing her, he doubted if that would be the case. She was beginning to see her power, and although her voice might bring peace, he knew he could teach her to use it as a weapon.

"Look at the facial disk. Note every feather. The colors. Pale brownish gray. The lines are subtly dappled and darker in waves. The rim is very dark, not protruding much, with pale speckles along the edge. Because the eyebrows are slightly paler than the surrounding plumage, they do not show as well, but you cannot forget they are there. Take a good look at the eyes, Elisabeta. They are round, wide, bright yellow. You will be amazed at what they can see. The smallest rodent on the forest floor."

She wrinkled her nose. "You are not going to make this so real that I am going to have to eat a mouse, are you?" There was a hint of laughter in her voice.

In spite of the fact that he was feeling a little anxiety over her first time at attempting to shift—it could be dangerous—he shared the moment of happiness with her. She'd had so few, and they were both learning.

"You will have to learn to hunt, but fortunately, it isn't unusual for owls to miss prey, so that looks natural."

"That's a relief."

There was such vehemence in her voice, he found actual laughter rumbling in his chest. She joined him before they both sobered, and he went over the details of the Western Screech Owl with her several times, just to make certain she had all the features stored in her mind.

12

I'll be the bright star, in the dark hour of night;
When you're feeling lost, I will be your light.

F erro was the most exacting taskmaster in the world. Elisabeta had successfully shifted into the female owl dozens of times, spread her wings, hopped around and shifted back without one mistake, only to be told to do it again.

Is there a part where the owl actually uses her wings? She never would have dared to ask him had she been in human form. The little owl hopped more and more into the open, stretching her wings, getting used to the new shape, the feel and size of the bird.

The male owl called to her with his song. He sounded mellow and calm, just the way Ferro always sounded. Elisabeta felt the female owl's immediate response, the pull toward the male. She wasn't in the least annoyed with the male. She wanted to be with him. She hopped closer, singing back to him.

He spread his wings and took to the air, not high, just flying in a low circle along the ground, calling to the female to follow him. The female hopped several times, wings spread wide. Nothing happened.

Let her fly, Elisabeta. Be the owl. Let her fly.

Elisabeta turned what her lifemate said over and over in her mind.

She was making the actual act of shifting and flying far too complicated. Ferro was telling her that in the form of the Western Screech Owl, she was the owl. She became the owl, and she had to be that female with all the instincts of the bird. She had to let go of Elisabeta just as she did when she entered another Carpathian who was in need in order to heal them.

The male owl sang to her again. She loved that he called the female with song, just the way Ferro called to her every rising. Her lifemate had chosen well for her first shifting. She identified with her owl. The song resonated with her. She let it carry her closer to the male. The female fluttered her wings and sang back, calling out to her mate. She spread her wings and lifted into the air.

Triumph nearly had her tumbling to the ground, but she steadied herself and followed the male in a low, sweeping, very tight circle in the clearing, right next to the tree line. The owl flew in absolute silence, the wingbeats soft, steady and rapid. The strokes were fast at five beats per second. The wind ruffled the feathers, adding to the feeling of absolute freedom.

Are you good? Do you want to go higher?

Elisabeta had been concentrating on how it felt to fly. She let herself look at the world through the eyes of the owl. Her hearing was excellent, so much so that she heard the cry of a mouse at least half a mile away. But it was her vision that shocked her. Turning her head, she could see everything in the owl's world so clearly. She expected to feel sick and disoriented, but she was the owl, that beautiful little female flying for the first time in a whole new world, experiencing true freedom.

I am good. So good, Ferro, thank you for this.

We are going to go just a few feet higher, circle once and go back down.

His voice was very firm and held a hint of command she dared not disobey. She didn't mind in the least. She knew he was determined that nothing go wrong this first time, and he wanted to assess her to make certain she was fine. She was. She knew she was and she would continue to be. She hoped he would allow her to practice more, but if he thought she was going too fast, she would be disappointed, but she would accept his decision.

The male rose higher into the air, and she followed, rising several more feet off the ground so they were a good fifteen feet up. She took in the blades of grass, the beetles and cicadas, a small frog that sat on a rock a few feet from one of the trees. She was beginning to distinguish creatures now, prey the female owl would hunt. All too soon they had completed the circle and returned to the starting point. The male glided easily to the ground. Her landing wasn't quite as smooth, but she managed not to tip over and fall on her beak.

Shift back to your form, Elisabeta. That was definitely a command.

She obeyed without thinking. She hadn't been wearing clothes so she didn't have to worry about what she needed to put on, she simply took her normal form, fitting back into her own body easily.

Ferro caught her to him, hugging her tight. "You shifted and flew for the first time, Elisabeta. You did amazing." He sounded as happy as she felt. "I'm so proud of you."

He caught her chin between his thumb and finger to tip her head up to his as he brought his down so he could kiss her. Once his lips touched hers, it felt as though he'd lit a match and she'd caught fire. Flames licked over her skin, poured down her throat to rush through her veins, spread to her breasts and gather low. The burn deep inside her was hot, wild and out of control that fast.

She ran her palms up his chest and dared to link her fingers behind his neck so she could lean fully into him. Suddenly, she wanted his mouth between her legs where she was hot and damp and that burn was so terrible it bordered on brutal. She felt the slickness growing as she kissed Ferro back, giving him everything she was, promising him whatever he wanted with just her mouth, with her body, the aching in her breasts and the tight, hard nipples pressing into the hard, defined muscles of his chest.

He lifted his head, his eyes that beautiful silvery-blue she loved so much, his hand sweeping down her back to shape her buttocks, possession in the way he touched her. His gaze drifted over her face for some time as if waiting. His expression didn't change. He looked at her as if she were the most wonderful, beautiful woman in the world and he adored her. One hand cupped the side of her face, the pad of his thumb sliding over her lower lip.

"Are you tired? Do you think you can try again? This time in the forest? It is different there. In the trees you have to maneuver through the limbs."

It was all Elisabeta could do not to pull his thumb into her mouth or slide one hand down his belly to caress his very hard cock as it lay against her body, thick and hot. She wanted to fly, but she wanted to be with him intimately. He hadn't taken his thumb from her lower lip but continued to brush little caresses back and forth, mesmerizing her.

Ferro had told her to ask for what she wanted or needed. The burning inside her increased with every stroke of his thumb. She opened her mouth and drew his thumb deep. His cock jerked against her stomach. Immediately she brought her hand under his heavy sac to cup the weight and fondle the velvet balls with her fingers.

I am not in the least tired, päläfertiilam, she said softly, her mind to his. An invitation. She drew his thumb deep, sucked hard, curled her tongue around the heavy digit. *I do want to continue the lesson, but there is a much more burning need you must attend to.*

What would that be, sívamet?

Elisabeta had known all along what he had been waiting for. His eyes were more silvery than blue now, almost liquid silver, burning into hers, robbing her of her ability to breathe. The need between her legs had grown until she felt wild with it, unable to keep still, her hips rocking subtly, thighs rubbing together in an effort to alleviate the near-brutal ache.

I need your mouth between my legs, Ferro. Please. I burn and need you to make it better. I can barely think and it grows worse with each passing moment.

Ferro's eyes grew warm. Then hot. Her stomach fluttered. Then her sex. Very gently he removed his thumb and waved his hand toward the ground to cover it with a soft mat. There was a large rise that went across the mat.

"We will try something different this time. Just a little different, to see if you like it. Lie on your stomach with your hips over the mound."

Elisabeta immediately went to the mat, positioning herself as he had requested. She found that when her hips were over the mound, her buttocks were pushed high.

"Spread your legs very wide for me."

Her heart beat wildly. He stood behind her where she couldn't see him, but she could tell by his voice exactly where he was. From his position, he would be able to see how slick she was, that she was telling him the truth about her very urgent needs. She obeyed him, eagerly, opening her legs wide. At once the cool night air slid over her hot entrance, adding to the stimulation.

"You're so beautiful, Elisabeta."

He was much closer. On the mat with her. He'd moved so silently she hadn't heard him. His hand went to the nape of her neck, making her jump. Very gently he ran his palm down her spine to the curve of her buttocks. She felt his breath at her entrance and her entire body shook. Then something sharp, like the tiny points of needles, rolled lightly along the inside of her thigh, bringing every nerve ending leaping to the surface. She started to turn her head to see what he was doing.

"Stay facing forward. Take a breath and relax your body. Turn yourself over to me."

That was a direct command. Elisabeta did exactly what he said. Already his fingers brushed over her hungry clit. Her wet lips and slick entrance. Just little touches. His breath, so warm. His hand massaging her left cheek. The feeling of the rolling pinpricks just a little harder over the left cheek and then his hand came down in a gentle swat that sent every nerve ending spiraling out of control. His hand was back, rubbing and massaging, spreading heat, his tongue lapping at her entrance as she spilled hot liquid into his mouth, crying out, hips bucking so that he had to hold her down.

He lifted his head. "Hold still for me, Elisabeta."

"It is very difficult." She tried to lie quietly, afraid he would stop.

"Your body tells me you like what I am doing."

"Yes, it feels shocking, but so good I can barely keep still. I will try, Ferro. I promise."

He went back to rubbing her cheeks, his shoulders wedged between her legs. "You are being very good for me. I love to see you like this. Dripping for me. Needy. Hungry for my body. For what I can give to you. I love to make you feel good, just as I know you enjoy making me feel good."

She closed her eyes, gasping as his mouth closed over her, tongue stabbing deep, curling inside her, drawing out hot liquid and then retreating to circle her clit. Blood pounded. Hammered. She was acutely aware of sharp little needles rolling gently over her wet lips and then her clit, making her cry out and buck her hips. His mouth covered her clit, sucked strongly, his tongue flicking, and then his finger penetrated so that her sheath closed around it, dragging at him, desperate to have him inside her.

"Ferro." She breathed his name.

"This is where I belong, *piŋe sarnanak*, right here, deep inside your body. Right now I am craving the taste of you, so hungry. As much as I want to show you all the different ways I can draw out your pleasure, I need to devour you."

Ferro held her body and simply turned her over, catching her bottom in his hands so that her legs went over his shoulders. He lifted her soaked entrance to his mouth and proceeded to eat her as if she were the finest meal he'd ever had and he was starving.

She couldn't stop the cries escaping. It seemed impossible to drag enough air into her lungs. The assault on her senses was massive, coming from every direction, until her entire body was in a full-blown raging firestorm. She writhed under his relentless mouth, his tongue and teeth, the flick of his fingers and the brush of his thumb. Flames licked at her body, roared through her mind. It was beautiful and savage, merciless and perfect.

His palm went to her belly, fingers splayed wide to press deep, holding her in place while his mouth ravaged her. Deep inside, the coiling wound tighter and tighter until she thought she might die if the spring didn't release. He didn't let up, devouring her more. The growling, hungry sounds he made were sexy, adding to the sensual experience, feeding her own urgent need of him. The desperation for him was growing in her. She wasn't certain what "more" she wanted of him, but she wanted a great deal more.

The burning inside her grew hotter. His mouth was an instrument of the most exquisite torture. She didn't know if she could stand much more.

She whispered his name, her hands finding his shoulders, digging her fingernails deep to anchor herself in the real world when she felt she might be in danger of flying apart, flying too high. It felt too good and she was afraid of losing herself. Of losing him. Of this. Things could be too perfect. She hadn't had good or perfect.

Let go, sívamet. Let yourself fly. That is what this rising is all about. We are flying in all sorts of wonderful ways. Relax and I will catch you.

She was learning that Ferro's word was golden. He would catch her. He would be there for her. Her rock. Her sword. Her shield. Whatever she needed him to be. The inferno burned wild and she had no choice, it was either have complete belief in him or go insane. She let go and let the fire-storm take her. The blaze raced through her, out of control, sweeping through her body, an ever-widening conflagration that shook her to her core.

She felt as if she spiraled completely out of control, ripples building into wild waves of pleasure, taking hold of her body, burning through to leave her in ashes only to start all over again. She was dimly aware of Ferro lifting his head, wiping his face on her thighs and then pulling her shivering body into his arms, holding her until she calmed.

She buried her face in his neck, stunned that she could feel so wonderful and yet so completely out of control. Little aftershocks rocked her, over and over, until gradually her body quieted, leaving her feeling somewhat sated and yet still feeling as if she might be missing out on something big.

She lifted her head to look at him. "Thank you, Ferro."

"I am very proud of you for asking me for what you wanted, Elisabeta. It gives me great pleasure to see you like that. There is so much more, but we will save those lessons for another rising. The anticipation always makes the reward greater, as we both have discovered."

She smiled up at him. "I am willing to do whatever you wish." She secretly thought continuing along the lines they had just gone might be perfect.

"We are working on flying, and shifting is very important for a number of reasons." He brushed kisses over her eyes and along her nose and then released her.

Elisabeta rolled over onto her stomach again and laid her head on her hands, closing her eyes to savor the feeling of belonging to such a man. He gave her so many new experiences, all of them good. Every time he touched her, he brought her pleasure. Even now, he rubbed her bottom gently, massaging her, keeping the heat moving so exquisitely through her body.

"I feel so lucky to have you for my lifemate, Ferro," she said. "All those centuries I felt lost and alone, guarding your soul, but it truly was worth every single moment because you are worth everything the vampire put me through and much more."

Beside her, he went utterly still. His hand ceased moving. He was in her mind and she was aware he would know she meant what she said. Guarding Ferro's soul had not been easy, and she didn't want Ferro to know the terrible tolls Sergey had forced her to pay time and again throughout the centuries, but she had held out against him. She would never give up her lifemate's soul. Never. That had been her line in the sand, so to speak. If Sergey wanted her alive, he would have to come to terms with that. There were times her defiance drove the vampire mad, and he had made her pay dearly.

She should have known Ferro wouldn't leave it alone. He had been careful not to search too far into her memories, as she hadn't into his. Now, however, she felt him move through her mind. She shook her head, starting to sit up, but he placed his palm very gently between her shoulder blades and held her down on the mat.

"Please do not. It is not necessary for you to see." She spoke in a low tone. He would see so much—too much. So many times she had traded lives for what she would not give the vampire. Several times she had taken her own life, only to have the vampire bring her back. He would see that. Ferro had been so strong, refusing to meet the dawn even when he had gone past the point of hearing whispers of temptation—when there was nothing left but being a danger to the very people he had protected.

"What the entire cost to you was? I think it is more than necessary, *hän ku vigyáz sielamet.*" His voice was very gentle. He kept his hand on her back, a connection between them as he moved through her mind.

He'd called her the guardian of his soul. She had been that. She had fiercely guarded his soul because that was all she had. It was the one thing Sergey couldn't take from her. Not even the memory of having to protect it and what it meant to a Carpathian woman.

"Ferro." She whispered her protest again, tears burning behind her eyes. She didn't want him to see her cowardice. Her failures. Her many humiliations. After the perfection of the rising with him, for him to see her in such a terrible light, she couldn't bear it. She wanted to run and hide herself away.

His hand moved up her back very gently to the nape of her neck, where his fingers began the familiar slow, gentle massage. It felt good and she wanted to press herself into those strong fingers like a cat, but she also wanted to bury her face on the furred mat and cry her heart out.

Elisabeta. Be calm. You always think the worst of yourself in spite of me telling you how I feel about you. You saved my life and the lives of so many. Had I turned vampire, which I would have if Sergey had gotten to my soul, I would have killed many before I would have been destroyed, if indeed I could have been destroyed.

As always, his voice was steady and calm. Ferro started at the beginning of her captivity, not at the end. He knew Sergey would try when she was young and terrified to get what he wanted from her. She could barely remember those days, yet she could vividly recall the horrific punishments he meted out when she refused to hand over her lifemate's soul.

Elisabeta, there is no need for you to experience these memories again. I want you to lie still and think of flying. Re-create the female owl in your mind. Every feather. Her ears. Her beak. Her tail. I especially want you to hear the notes of her song so you can sing the duet with her male. Any vampire listening must believe the female is truly a bird. That is a command. Do you understand me?

She closed her eyes, tears leaking out. His voice was so gentle, as only Ferro's could be. He would spare her those ugly memories. She hadn't looked at them in centuries. The earliest ones were the worst—before Sergey had learned to fear she would really kill herself and he couldn't bring her back. She had chosen that option only out of sheer desperation, unable to think of any other choice when the vampire threatened the lives of children or entire villages to get to her lifemate's soul.

She had endured the torment all those centuries for Ferro—her life-mate. He had been the reason she had continued. She'd feared for him. Feared what it would do to him if she was gone from the world. She'd sensed him somewhere, still alive, still hunting, still holding on. As long as he could, she had vowed she would. And yet there had been so many moments of weakness . . . She was so ashamed.

Ferro surrounded her with warmth. Wrapped her in the intensity of the emotion she had come to realize was love for her. His love for her.

You will feel such shame of me if you persist in looking into my memories.

I will love and admire you more. Do as I command of you, little songbird. Give me time to look upon the crimes this vampire committed against my be-loved. It is necessary for a man such as me. I have waited for you to tell me, but realized it would be impossible for you to do so. I am not asking you, sívamet; I am telling you. This is something I need and must have.

It was impossible for Elisabeta not to obey. She had been conditioned by centuries of obedience, but he had called her his heart in that voice that could turn her inside out. She kept her eyes closed and turned her mind to studying the little female screech owl, focusing her attention on the small details she might miss if she ever became distracted.

She hadn't thought about how a vampire might hear her calling back to her mate and realize her notes weren't exact. It would be a small detail, such as a single wrong note, that would give her away and, in doing so, her lifemate. The things he was teaching her weren't just for fun; they could well be the difference between life and death.

Ferro's owl's call was beautiful. He showed her the muted trill of the male's *hoo, hoo, hoo* that sped up at the end but always maintained a con-tinuous pitch. Sometimes he sang to his female a different song, one of double trills, a much more rapid burst. He had a soft croon when greeting and an excited bark. During mating season, their duet included a trem-bling note, a rapid tremolo call from the male, answered by a short trem-olo from the female. The two owls sang a duet together and she practiced her part in her mind over and over for every season.

Ferro had a beautiful voice and often sang to her when she was upset. She loved their song. He added verses to it each rising, soothing her when she was so afraid. Now, his male owl sang to her female with that beautiful wild call, soothing and calm to his lady the way Ferro was to her. He was such a rock, an anchor in the worst storm. He didn't make her feel as if it was only that she belonged to him; he made her feel as if he belonged to her, that it was mutual.

The male owl was that same rock to his female. They protected each other and their nest fiercely, even against humans, creatures much larger than they. She studied every aspect of the owl's life that she could find in Ferro's mind. She had been in the female owl and she drew on what she had found there as well.

Elisabeta had no real idea how much time had passed when Ferro suddenly yanked her into his arms, startling her with his aggression. He held her to him, nearly crushing her, his palm pressing the back of her head tight into him, so her ear was over his wildly beating heart.

"Elisabeta. Beloved. What you suffered to protect me."

She tilted her face up to look at him. Bloodred tears dripped from his eyes and her heart nearly stopped. She couldn't take his sorrow. At once she swamped him with soothing harmony, surrounded him with love, with everything she was, giving him all that she knew how to give. She wrapped her arms around him and held him just as tightly, closing her eyes and breathing for both of them, willing his heart to find the slower, steady beat of hers.

Ferro held her for a long time, rocking them both gently, while Elisabeta continued to keep them entwined together in a cocoon of peace. She didn't speak, not knowing what to say. In her wildest imaginings she never would have expected her legendary warrior to care enough to shed the bloodred tears of their kind for her. That kind of sorrow and respect was reserved for greatness.

She didn't know how to react. This was Ferro. Her lifemate. She felt panic-stricken. She had no one to tell her what to do, only her instincts. His hands stroked caresses in her hair, and every now and then she felt his lips brush kisses on top of her head. There was such an intimacy that had nothing at all to do with sex, straddling him, her body crushed against him, rocking with him, their hearts beating together.

Elisabeta felt such a part of him. She'd been terrified for him to see her past, the terrible choices the vampire had forced on her, and yet now she felt closer to him than ever before. Each time she feared Ferro's reaction, he always came through, teaching her to trust. Not everyone was cruel like Sergey, certainly not her lifemate.

"I know I do not say it to you, Elisabeta, and you most likely need the words, but they are in my song to you. When I tell you a world of love awaits you, vaster than the ocean, I am not merely singing a lyric to you. These words are yours. For you alone. What I feel for you is incomprehensible to me. Unimaginable. I hunted centuries for you. I carved the vow to you into my body, yet even then I did not know what I would feel for you. How could I? Until I merged my mind with yours and learned to know you, found out the tremendous gift I was given, there was no way of knowing how the love in my heart for you would grow."

He couldn't say such things to her. She would fall apart. Already she was weeping, pressing her face into his chest and weeping like a babe. They held each other for comfort, still rocking gently, her soothing, peaceful cocoon surrounding them like his shield.

You do not have to give me the words, Ferro. I hear them in your song to me. I feel them in the things you do for me. I especially feel them in your touch. She couldn't tell him aloud because she would be sobbing if she tried to speak.

"Never think, for one moment, that I am ashamed of you. Any sacrifice you think I made pales in comparison to what you made for me. I could not feel. I had no emotions. You felt everything. Every lash of torture that evil creature thought up, the emotions of those he forced you to witness being tortured, you endured all of that—for me."

Ferro suddenly caught her chin and tugged until she was forced to look up at him. His eyes glittered down at her, more rust than iron. He looked like what he was, a violent, dangerous predator, the legendary hunter the Carpathian people spoke of in whispers.

"I am privileged to be your lifemate, and you are more than worthy to walk beside me." He sounded fierce. "Understand me, *hän ku vigyáz sívamet és sielamet*, you would always be my choice."

He called her "keeper of his heart and soul." Not his soul. His heart and soul. She felt her lips tremble before her smile broke through. Happiness blossomed.

"You are my choice, Ferro. You will always be my choice."

Something moved through his eyes, something she couldn't quite catch, but she wished she had because it was important, and then he bent his head to hers, his mouth brushing hers with that exquisite gentleness he had that turned her heart over. She parted her lips to let him inside and he kissed her. Really kissed her, going from gentle to possessive instantly.

The moment his tongue swept inside her mouth, he poured love into her. She felt his emotion in her throat, in her veins, rushing through her bloodstream until it spread to every part of her body. He was pure fire, flames licking at her skin and settling deep in her core all over again. Just when she squirmed restlessly, he lifted his head, those eyes of his glittering down at her, all liquid, silvery-blue, making her shiver with need.

"All right, *minan piŋe sarnanak*, we have more work to do. I want you to learn to fly in the woods. The more you practice shifting into the owl, the faster you will be at it and the more comfortable. I trust you studied her from every angle so you know exactly what she looks like down to the smallest detail." He sounded steady.

She took a deep breath, trying to match his calm demeanor when she was a bundle of sexual nerves.

"Yes." She was grateful she had honed her ability to pay attention to detail over the centuries. It had been necessary to keep her mind active, and Sergey insisted that she aid him in his fight against his brothers.

"Good. Go ahead and change for me."

Elisabeta shifted into the form of the little female Western Screech Owl. Ferro had her shift dozens of times, just as he had the first time. He wanted faster. He wanted smoother. She didn't protest, knowing he wanted her to be absolutely comfortable, to have the details so ingrained in her mind it would be second nature to her.

It is rather nice that she is larger than the male. She felt very daring pointing that out to him since he was an extremely large man. Carpathian women were tall, and she was no exception. The males were taller as a rule, but she noticed that the brethren seemed to all be extraordinarily tall and broad shouldered.

Male amusement filled her mind. *I should have given you a few extra swats on your beautiful bottom while I had the chance. Fortunately for me, my ego is not fragile and the size difference does not matter in the least.*

The female owl spread her wings and fluttered them as she hopped along the ground. *I do believe you are protesting a bit too much. It is okay. I know you are used to being much larger and probably have trouble being so small.*

Only attempting to squash certain body parts down.

That made her laugh hard enough that she had to shift back to her normal form. She landed abruptly on the ground with her arms out for balance, glaring at him. "That was not fair."

You have to stay focused no matter what. He sounded very self-righteous. *Shift back.*

Elisabeta shifted immediately. *I think that was cheating but it was funny all the same.* Her little female turned her head this way and that, taking advantage of the ability to rotate her head about 270 degrees in order to see around her.

It is much different flying in the woods than in a clearing, piŋe sarnanak. You have to be certain to keep your head tucked in tight as you were doing, but do not allow it to come up at all. We will not hover or glide, but move more like a bat might, flying erratically through the trees and branches. At first, we are going to practice flying low through the trees and land back here. When I feel you have the hang of it, we will learn to land on the limb of a tree.

Even within the form of an owl, Elisabeta felt her heart quicken. It was exciting to learn to fly this way, to really be able to shift and have Ferro teach her to do something so freeing and exhilarating as flying through the woods and landing in trees, even if it was really just in the very edge of the woods.

You will do exactly as I tell you. When I say to land, you are to do so immediately.

Of course, Ferro.

She was not going to fail him, or herself. He had given her so much this rising. Too much. She knew no matter what happened in their future, she would always look on this rising as the one that made her feel as if she could eventually find her way back to her birth brother—because of Ferro. She could eventually grow confident and have friends—because of her lifemate. He had given her a belief in herself.

You tell me if your eyes are giving you problems, piŋe sarnanak, or if you begin to tire.

I will. She gave him her assurance, trying not to hop in her owl form, but she desperately wanted to fly in the forest. The woods beckoned her.

Always remember that the danger of shifting to another form is that there is simplicity in taking an animal form. The longer you are in it, the more you might wish to remain. You cannot do so, Elisabeta, no matter the temptation. Your life has been difficult and the vampire knew that if you were aware of how to shift, he would lose you. I do not want to lose you to temptation.

For the first time she caught real fear from him. Not in his voice, that was as steady and as calm as ever. Not in his owl. The little male was a completely wild creature. Ferro was merged deep within her, and it was there she felt his trepidation, that very real worry that had been there all along and she hadn't seen. In spite of his fear of losing her to shifting, Ferro had still chosen to teach her, to give her that gift. His present meant all the more to her.

I do not want to be apart from you, Ferro. No temptation would be that great.

Elisabeta had no other way of reassuring him. She wasn't used to speaking directly to him yet, and she didn't know how to put together words of affection, or of love. She wanted to express how much she cared for him, as he had done for her, but she didn't write songs and she didn't know how to express the things in her heart properly.

For one moment, Ferro, the man, moved through her mind, as if seeking reassurance, and then he was back to being her instructor.

When we hunt, it is normal to hunt from a perch at the edge of the woods such as this. We can make short forays into the open fields to capture flying insects.

She couldn't help her natural reaction to his suggestion, pulling back and shaking the owl's head back and forth in repugnance.

There may come a time when you have no choice. If you are under a vampire's scrutiny, you have to follow through. Your owl must keep the need to hunt uppermost in her mind. Small prey is normally swallowed whole on the spot. It is your owl consuming the prey, not you, and you must allow it. You have to let go of yourself so not the slightest hint of you remains for our enemy to detect.

Deep inside the owl's body, Elisabeta made the commitment. She let go of all ego, of all sense of self, when she needed to bring peace to the ancients, and she could do so when tricking an enemy. If that was what was required of her, then she would do it with no squeamishness. She felt Ferro's instant approval and it warmed her.

Larger prey such as a vole will be carried in your beak to a perch just inside the woods and torn apart. He gave her a list of the various types of prey the Western Screech Owl hunted.

Now that she understood why she had to accept that she might have to hunt insects and deer mice and even devour them, she became very dedicated to learning that art as well. She was well versed in shedding her ego, that was never her problem. She needed to know the mechanics of being an owl, so she wanted to be at the forefront while she was learning. She needed to be. Now, more than ever, she paid rapt attention to every detail.

Her little female made it into the air with no problem when Ferro finally gave her the go-ahead, and then was able to fly in ever-widening circles, higher and higher, around the clearing. She didn't allow the soaring elation to distract her.

Is your eyesight good?

She realized that as the owl, not only was she able to focus her eyesight much more clearly and for longer distances, but when she had taken back her own form, she hadn't once even noticed that she was looking at the clearing or woods without seeing through the bars of a cage when peering around her.

Ferro, I did not have to put bars in front of my eyes.

I noticed, Elisabeta. And now?

Of course he would notice. Nothing about her seemed to escape her lifemate. *My owl sees perfectly.*

Good. Let her follow me into the woods. Stay right with me, sívamet. You do not want to hit a branch and knock yourself out.

She definitely didn't want to do that and end the fun. She loved the woods. Flying was great excitement, but the forest called to her. The trees and brush, all the various animals, even the insects, made her feel as if she belonged with them.

We are Carpathian, a part of the earth, Elisabeta. You bring peace to those around you. I have noticed that even the creatures are drawn to you, so it stands to reason that you would be drawn to them.

She felt his amusement welling up.

It seems I will always have rivals for your attention. Not only the ancients but the children and now the creatures of the woods. Perhaps even the insects.

He took an extra turn around the clearing. She knew he did it on purpose so she was able to share his laughter with him. He didn't want her distracted before she began learning to fly through the forest where the trees were close together and the branches could be high or low.

The lessons continued for some time, landing on various sizes and shapes of branches, listening and identifying prey, and, finally, hunting and trying to actually capture their quarry. By the time Ferro called a halt it was close to dawn and she was ready to return to their home and the welcoming soil beneath it. She'd never been so exhausted but happy in her life.

13

I am by your side with every step you take;
Fighting every demon, your love I won't forsake.

Ferro knew this rising was going to be a difficult one for his lady. Outside the compound, there were signs of their enemy everywhere. He glanced at Benedek, the ancient closest to him. His brethren had gone out in force, all seeking blood, as they did every rising. Benedek shook his head in response. There was no answer for this newest threat. They couldn't fail to see the signs of Sergey's anger and impatience at not being able to get his most prized possession back. This evening, there were three humans staked to the gates of Tariq's compound.

Fortunately, the children hadn't seen the victims, barely alive, dripping blood, straight out of a horror film. Sergey sent a polite note addressed to Elisabeta, stating that at each rising she would have more to greet her at the gate. He would add to the number until the gates would groan under the weight of her refusal. The ancients had mercifully killed Sergey's victims, as there was no way to save them.

Tariq had the bodies gently taken down and had all evidence removed. He heaved a sigh as he turned to Ferro. "I do not envy you talking to Elisabeta. She is far too sensitive and this vampire knows it. These deaths will weigh heavy on her, as will his threat."

"Sergey knows it is not safe for him to come near this place and yet his stench is everywhere. He cannot resist her. This was done by his human servants so that we would see it upon rising. He hoped Elisabeta would be with me when I rose." He crumpled the note in his fist. "He could not conceive of leaving her in the soil safe while he went about his business. I hunt for the two of us. When I return to her, I will awaken and feed her."

"Malinov has long ago forgotten what it was like to be Carpathian."

"Sun scorch him, Tariq. I must hunt him now. I had hoped for more time to allow her to get to know her birth brother. Her friends and you. There is this infection that no one knows the source of, yet I cannot have him threatening her with bodies hanging on your gate each rising."

"Gary says no one else can deal with the infection other than Elisabeta, and she cannot do so without you," Tariq said.

"I am aware of that."

"You are not the only one capable of hunting the vampire," Benedek pointed out. "We are simply sitting around doing nothing, and time is weighing on us. Already, several of us have discussed picking up his trail or having your lifemate summon him out into the open."

Ferro's first reaction to the suggestion was an instant and irrevocable no. He didn't voice it, not when his brethren were ready to hunt the master vampire that it was his duty to dispatch. They wouldn't see it that way. They were vampire hunters and had been so for centuries. Like him, they always would be.

Sergey Malinov had wronged Elisabeta, Ferro's lifemate. Hunting vampires was never personal. Emotions could never be brought into their battles. Fortunately, even for those who eventually found their lifemates, they had gone so long without emotion that when hunting the vampire, it was easy to slip back into hunting mode where emotions were completely suppressed. Ferro hoped, even with the things he knew Sergey had subjected Elisabeta to, he could still deliver justice in the way the Carpathian hunters were taught to do. Just his reaction to having his brethren hunt rather than him told him he wasn't as in control as he should be.

The ancients had gathered around Tariq and Ferro, right at the front gate of the compound, consulting together. Already the sound of children laughing could be heard. Genevieve's soft voice replied to something Charlotte said, and the children laughed again. Charlotte was aware, through Tariq, of the carnage outside their gate, but she played her part, making her children and their nanny comfortable, acting as though this evening was like any other. The children could laugh and have fun before their studies began.

"We will hunt together," Ferro decided. "While Sergey's trail is fresh. There are enough of us that one of us should be able to find his latest lair. If we do, we can send word to the others and go after him together. No doubt he will have surrounded himself with an army." They could never forget that the moment Sergey's life was threatened, the slivers of his brothers and Xavier would abandon him to seek other hosts. They would need preparation for that. It would not just be a simple matter of destroying the vampire, as much as Ferro wanted it to be. He would need a plan.

Tariq turned to Gary. "Did you have time to examine those of us who were exposed to the infection earlier?" He turned to the others to explain. "We are keeping a log of everyone who had the burns. What they did prior to receiving them, and what they did after. Eventually, we should find a connection."

"I examined you, Tariq, and there is evidence, as I told you, of light scorching. Josef has much heavier burns and is showing signs of becoming belligerent again. Traian and Joie are watching over him and he's aware that the burns are back. He's doing his best to keep his temper under control until Elisabeta rises and can free him of the scoring. Sandu and Dragomir show no signs of any burns."

"Have you any idea why you are unable to heal these burns when our healers have always been able to learn to heal anything very quickly?" Tariq asked.

Gary shook his head. "The infection is spread differently than an actual disease. I do not yet know what it is."

Tariq sighed. "What of the children?"

Gary answered him. "Lourdes and Bella are both without burns. None at all. Liv has light scorching, much like you, Tariq. The scorching is heavier in Danny and Amelia but not nearly as bad as in Josef. Charlotte is aware of this and has conveyed the danger to Genevieve. Maksim and Tomas are watching over the children. Neither shows signs of scorching, yet Lojos did this morning, and that is new. He had no such injury before when I checked him."

"So it is spreading," Tariq said. "Are there any others?"

"I didn't have time to check beyond those," Gary admitted. "The three victims were found at the gate and I came here to see if I could help them. They were beyond all aid. I agree with Ferro, we should hunt Sergey while his trail is fresh. He expects us, and will have planned an ambush, but all of us here should be far too savvy to fall for his tricks. He has forgotten what it is like to go up against very experienced hunters."

"I don't like leaving the compound with too few to protect the women and children," Tariq admitted. "His calling card could very well be to lure us away so he can attack."

Ferro considered Tariq's concern. There was merit to it. More than merit. It would be just like Sergey to think to pull the ancients out of the compound in order to get to Elisabeta. She was the vampire's ultimate goal.

"Let me speak with Elisabeta." He didn't want her to ever think he would betray her in any way, but this threat to her and those around her had to be stopped.

Taking a deep breath, he summoned his woman. *I have need to consult with you, minan hän sívamak.* She would be forever and always his beloved. *Wake for me. Hear my song to you. A song of hope, of love, Elisabeta. I have great need of you.*

I hear you, kont o sívanak. You have only to ask and I will do my best to aid you.

She came into his mind slowly, a gentle presence, filling every lonely crack and space, those terrible scars left from too many battles, the killing of old childhood friends. Hunting took a toll on one's soul, and Elisabeta's nature was the opposite of his, gentle and compassionate. She filled him with those tender, caring traits, bathed him with them, soaked him in them until he felt as if her gentle soul mended the terrible tears in his own blackened soul.

She called him "strong heart." He felt she had the strongest heart, the most caring, and he hoped it was true. She would need it for this rising. He detested this and suddenly found he was reluctant to continue.

What has happened?

He had no intention of telling her until he was with her and could hold her in his arms.

If Sergey made his presence known, left his stench all around the outside of the compound where we could find it, even though he deliberately masks it as he leaves, do you believe he has some treachery planned, such as drawing the ancients away from the compound in order to attack it? Would this be his strategy? You know him better than any other. He wants you back. Would he make a mistake like this?

As always, Elisabeta took her time, thinking his question through thoroughly before she answered. She looked at everything he showed her from every angle. He was careful not to give her any information on what Sergey had been doing at the compound, or what he had left, but she knew the vampire too well.

He would not have just come here and sniffed around leaving tracks. What has he done?

I prefer to talk to you about that later. One has no bearing on the other. We need to know whether to go after him immediately, before his trail fades and he has more time to prepare for an ambush, or set up our own ambush here. He poured authority into his voice and mind to keep her from questioning him further.

He is planning on attacking the compound. I wish to rise, Ferro.

I will call to you as soon as I have hunted for blood for the two of us. He broke their connection and turned to the others.

"No doubt, it is his plan to attack this compound," Ferro announced to the others. "Elisabeta was absolutely certain, and she knows him better than any other. I need blood to get to full strength, as do all the rest of the brethren. We must make it look as if we are falling for Sergey's plan."

"My security force is human," Tariq said. "We have used them before to feed. Some are aware of who we are and volunteer. They serve us as the families in South America have served the De La Cruz family for hundreds of years. They will provide what we need. I ask that you treat them with respect and care as I consider them family and they are under my protection."

"What of Elisabeta?" Gary asked. "Will she be able to aid us with the spreading infection?"

Ferro's eyes met his, two slashes of silver watching the other man carefully. Ferro had to tell his lifemate what Sergey had left behind at the gate and the threats he'd made—threats that she would know were all too real. Ferro had chosen to look into her memories and he knew that on many occasions the vampire had killed others in front of her to get her to give up her lifemate's soul. She was an empath and Sergey knew that would hurt her far more than physical torture ever could, although he had resorted to that as well at times.

"I do not know, healer." Deliberately, Ferro chose not to call the ancient by his name. He refused to allow anyone—not even Gary, who shared ties to his soul and therefore knew the agony Elisabeta had suffered—to push him into forcing his woman to help when she would be devastated.

"We cannot allow this infection to spread further or get out of hand, no matter what else is happening," Gary insisted, his voice mild but his eyes deepening to a liquid silver that contained a hint of a threat.

Ferro felt the threat in his mind. Something more was going on than he knew. He saw Sandu, Andor and Dragomir all spin around and then move in close. They felt that same vague threat to Elisabeta as he did, but were as uncertain as he was as to why there would be one coming from the healer. Gary would be a difficult threat to vanquish, but fighting all four ancients would make it impossibile to win, and Tariq's second-in-command had to know that.

Ferro frowned and rubbed at the bridge of his nose. "We know this burn is spreading, Gary. Sandu and Dragomir were both infected. I need to be inspected. No one has scanned me, or you, for that matter."

Tariq took his cue instantly. "We should go back inside, feed, and scan while we do so, all those who haven't been looked at. Then the ancients can lay down false trails as if they are searching for Sergey once we have a plan." He was already moving, as if expecting everyone to do as he said. He was their leader. Gary his second-in-command.

Gary took a deep breath, clearly fighting for control, and then he fell into step with Tariq. The four brethren tied to him created a loose semicircle close enough to contain him. He politely pretended not to notice. The other ancients created a second circle, a little wider, flaring out around them.

Once inside, the safeguards were woven even stronger. "How does Sergey expect to get past the safeguards?" Tariq asked. "Even if all warriors were gone from the compound, he could not find a way to break that weave. Julija, a powerful mage, has added her elements in. The ancients from the monastery who stopped using Xavier's spells long ago and came up with their own unique spells intertwined with each other's strands. The safeguards are woven above, below and on all sides of the compound."

He had called the trusted members of his security force to the secluded area. Matt Bennet, Tariq's head of security, immediately told the others that only those comfortable with giving blood needed to do so, but there was an immediate threat to the compound and the warriors needed to be at full strength.

Ferro was a little surprised at the human response. The De La Cruzes were a legendary family of Carpathian vampire hunters, and he had been skeptical of their choice to interact with humans. It forced the brothers to protect their servants and made them more vulnerable to their enemies, and yet, in the end, the loyalty of the humans had proven undeniable. They had fought with the De La Cruz brothers against the vampires, knowing some of them would die. The De Le Cruz family had placed shields in their human brains, which over the centuries the families had begun to be born with. The De La Cruz brothers had further strengthened those.

Every man immediately consented to giving his blood freely to the Carpathians. Ferro noticed that Tariq stayed close to Gary, watching him as he fed, ensuring that the healer was careful with the security team.

You believe I have been infected. Gary spoke directly to Ferro, allowing Sandu, Andor and Dragomir to hear him as well.

Yes. You are . . . not yourself.

Gary sighed as he carefully and respectfully closed the small holes on the wrist of the volunteer, healing the wounds as if they had never been. *I feared that might happen eventually. I know you do not want to tell Elisabeta that Sergey has threatened her with the murder of more humans, and then on the heels of that, ask her to work on those of us infected, but if she does not and these burns worsen, the results could be disastrous. There is a chance that ancients would turn on ancients. The compound would be destroyed from within.*

Ferro went very still. All of those connected through Andor's soul did, too. Ferro let his breath out as he carefully closed the wounds on one wrist and took another. He had to have enough blood for his lifemate as well. *Repeat what you just said, Gary. I think you found the motive behind this infection.*

Sandu, Dragomir and Andor clearly agreed with Ferro. Gary waited for Tariq to give orders to Matt and then hurried him across the compound, back toward the main gate where they knew Sergey's spies would be wondering what they were up to.

"We believe that this infection is to turn us against one another. It attacks the judgment center in the brain. It doesn't matter if you have a lifemate, if you're male or female or a child," Gary explained as the hunters gathered in a tight circle around him.

Andor nodded. "Once the scorching is bad enough, the victim reacts with violence. The person he's angry with has no choice but to protect himself. This infection has the potential to destroy lifemates and turn our ancients into vampires right here in the compound."

Without looking at Ferro, Gary continued. "We are very lucky we have Elisabeta here. Without her, this would most likely have worked. There is no one else capable of stopping it. We still have not tracked down the source. We know some of us are infected to varying degrees. We also know Sergey has set a trap, hoping to lead the warriors away from the compound, which means he believes he has a way in. We have to figure out how he believes he can bring down the safeguards."

"We don't have much time to figure this out," Tariq said. "If we wait too long to go after him, Sergey will know we're onto him."

Ferro wanted to curse at Gary for forcing him into the position of bringing Elisabeta to the surface immediately. He dissolved into mist and streamed away from the others, back toward his house, where his lifemate waited for him. He had looked forward to every rising with her. Now, he dreaded calling her to him.

He opened the earth above her as he woke her, singing their song softly promising to always be at her side, swearing with every breath he drew that he loved her more than life itself. He didn't have her exert energy but brought her to him, right into his waiting arms, freshening her, dressing her, holding her close to him, caring for her in the loving way he wanted and needed to do. For her. For himself.

He took them into the woods, the place where she felt the most sense of peace and belonging with him. She cuddled into his lap, looking up at him, and though he could see far too much knowledge in her eyes, she didn't ask him questions, and he was grateful. He opened his shirt for her. Right before she bent her head, she touched his face, sliding her fingers along his jaw so gently it turned his heart over.

She knew he was upset and she sought, as always, to comfort him. He felt her familiar soothing grace settle around him, cocooning them in her world of tranquility. She nuzzled his chest. Her tongue slid over his skin and his body reacted in spite of the gravity of the situation. Elisabeta would always bring him both serenity and an impossible erotic rush that spread through his body like a fireball when she sank her teeth into him.

Tell me what he has done. Now, while we are one.

He stroked her hair back from her forehead, looking down on her beautiful face. Her eyes were closed. Long lashes—two thick crescents, dark and beautiful fans—lay against her pale skin. She was still recovering from centuries of starvation. Her cheekbones were high and prominent, her mouth generous and her lips such a perfect bow.

We are always one. He can never separate us. I just need these few minutes for me, piŋe sarnanak, holding you close to me. You bring me joy and allow me to feel peace when sometimes I feel there is no longer harmony in the world.

She slid one hand up his chest to his shoulder and then curled her slender arm around his neck. The gesture felt intimate, causing his belly muscles to tighten in reaction. She was quiet while she fed, giving him exactly what he asked for without hesitation.

Around him, the forest creatures moved, going about their business, when they never would have had he been alone. He was a predator and they would have recognized him as one. Elisabeta masked that trait in him with her tranquility. She was extraordinary and he was humbled that she was his. Such a gift. Such a miracle.

All too soon, her tongue swept across the twin holes, closing them and healing the small openings. She lay in his arms, waiting. There wasn't a single sign of impatience. Not in her body language, and not in her mind.

"Sergey left a message for you—us. Three bodies." Ferro dropped his head over hers to comfort her, to comfort both of them. He said it fast, no preamble, needing to get it over with. There was no use dragging it out any further when it had to be said.

She made a single sound of such pain, such agony, not aloud, not in her throat, but in her mind, as if she didn't dare let that sound loose in the world where Sergey might hear and rejoice.

I was so afraid he would resort to his old method of controlling me. He threatened to continue until I returned to him. She made it a statement.

It was a measure of her terror of the vampire that she didn't speak aloud to Ferro but had crawled into his mind and stayed there, whispering to him as if Sergey would hear.

"Yes. We are going to lay a trap for him. We will allow him to believe the ancient hunters have taken the bait to follow his trail, leaving the compound with few to guard it. We hope to draw him close. Elisabeta, several within the compound have the infection back. We believe that it has been introduced in order to destroy us from within. If ancients turn vampire and/or begin fighting one another, it would not be difficult to do such a thing. Could Sergey be behind this infection?"

She sat up, her eyes meeting his. As her confidence in herself had grown, so had her clarity in the way she saw her time with Sergey. She was no longer starved and in terrible pain. She wasn't terrorized. She could think very clearly. She took her time again, and now, very slowly, she nodded her head. Ferro could feel her struggling to remember something. Merged as he was with her, he could feel her frustration when she couldn't grasp the fragments she needed to put the pieces together.

"You will remember. We are coming closer to figuring this out," he assured her. If he knew what to look for he would have searched her memories himself. "You are needed again, Elisabeta. Gary and Tariq are both infected. Josef as well and some of the others. The hunters must be cleared first so we can leave. While I take you to them, would you consider a way Sergey might think he could bring down the safeguards we have woven? He must believe he can get past them, yet so many of us added to the weaves, including Julija, and she is a mage of the highest order. It makes little sense."

He couldn't just take his woman and go out of this country, far from a place that was painful to her. He didn't want to bring her to the others and have her work on removing the infection from them, especially when he knew Sergey was planning on attacking and she knew it as well. He felt as if he wasn't protecting her the way he should be, that she was being attacked on every front.

Elisabeta framed his face with both hands. "You always think of me, Ferro. It humbles me the way you do that, the way you think you should shield me from the harshness of what is happening around us. I always knew Sergey would come for me. When the Carpathians rescued me, they knew it as well. I had been his prisoner for centuries. You saw the way he controlled me, the deaths he put on my soul."

"*Never. Minan piŋe sarnanak*, never on your soul. Every death is on him. Completely on him. You cannot take that on your shoulders. That is what evil wishes, to convince the innocent that what evil does is the fault of the innocent. You took no life. You would never do so. You would never conceive of taking a life. Sergey is evil and cruel and he enjoyed seeing not only you suffer, but those he tortured and killed suffer as well. Had you complied with him, do you honestly believe he would have spared them?"

She shook her head. "Even when I was very young, I could read him. That was his greatest downfall and one of my worst and greatest gifts. After he took my blood and forced me to take his, before he turned vampire, it allowed me to see into him much more clearly than he realized. Being in that cage, with only limited space and so much time, I could only do physical and mental exercises to keep myself sane. One of the best was observation. He was with me a great deal of the time, even if he wasn't interacting with me. I knew he wouldn't have spared any of the victims."

There was so much sorrow in her that, again, he felt her unshed tears. He gathered her close to him. "I cannot take away the scars he left on you, Elisabeta, the ones unseen on flesh. He deliberately cut as deep into your soul as possible. But I can be your refuge. I want always to be that for you." He bent his head to hers and brushed his lips gently across hers. "Yet I always seem to be asking such sacrifices of you."

"It is no sacrifice to aid others. Just as you are compelled to hunt the vampire, Ferro, I am compelled to help others in need."

"Then we must go. Time is slipping away." Ferro didn't want to lose one moment of their time together, but already he was aware of Sandu, Gary, Andor and Dragomir pushing at him to hurry. Sergey would be expecting the warriors to rush out to the hunt. "Slide your arms around my neck, beloved. I need to hold you close while I take you to the others. When you remove each of the burns, let us know how deep they are and if you can get any hint of when they were created or how."

Ferro took her to the group that had gathered there in the courtyard. Tariq had brought them all together, warriors, humans and children, any found with the infection and those that would be the first line of defense against the vampire and his army.

"Good eve, Elisabeta," Tariq greeted. "Thank you for once again coming to our aid." He gave her a courtly bow.

Ferro was a bit surprised that the other ancients and even Josef followed his example of respect and did the same. Elisabeta kept her eyes downcast but she gave a dip of her head and a small smile to the others while her fingers spasmed in his hands. She took a step back into his body, as if for protection. He knew he shouldn't like that—he wanted her to be confident—but there was a small part of him that liked that he was the person she turned to when she had need of someone to anchor her.

"Elisabeta, it would be best if you would start with me," Gary said.

"As we scan each rising, it is best to be safe and remove the scorching from the ancients. If the idea is to turn us against one another, we can't take chances that an ancient with fighting skills and no anchor becomes enraged."

"We also want our fighters to look as if they are exiting in order to hunt Sergey, so we need them fit. If his spies are watching and the crows are surrounding the compound," Tariq added, "we want them to return to the vampire and say we were planning some strategy."

She inclined her head again and immediately moved with extreme confidence, flowing into Gary's mind. Ferro had to move quickly to keep up with her. Sandu also joined them to protect her should there be anything built into the infection allowing it to fight back. So far, that hadn't happened, but it didn't mean it couldn't.

While you went to get Elisabeta, we scanned as many as possible. None of the ancients other than Tariq and Lojos has any scorching, but it was found in several of the human security force. Charlotte has light burns as well. Maksim checked his lifemate, Blaze. She was over with Charlotte last rising, but she showed no signs at all, Gary informed them.

What did Charlotte and Tariq do last night? If both have the burns, they must have been exposed at the same time, Ferro speculated.

The two of them are writing down everything they did in order for us to compare, although at the moment, preparing for war is a far more important task, Gary said.

I think this is a huge part of the war. Ferro was certain he was correct.

Elisabeta made short work of removing the burns in Gary's mind and immediately went to Tariq. His scoring was extremely light in comparison, certainly nothing like it had been, as if his exposure had been very brief. The slash marks weren't even a vivid red, and they blew apart in front of her gentle breeze easily the first time she sent the steady draft toward the marks.

Ferro was surprised that when his lifemate returned to her body—a little pale, but still very strong—she didn't go straight to the next ancient. Lojos stood beside Tariq waiting for her to remove the burns, and Ferro felt the hesitation in her mind.

What is it, sívamet? He locked his arm around her waist, holding her to his side beneath his shoulder.

He is uncertain. I do not want to intrude.

"Lojos, Elisabeta is very sensitive. She feels your hesitation. If you wish to live with the infection, there are others for her to work on. Gary knows better than I how bad it is in you and whether you can be trusted or whether you must be sent from the compound."

Lojos shrugged. "I do not yet know if I can trust that Sergey did not somehow figure a way to use her to introduce this infection into our midst."

Ferro took a deep breath and pushed down the strange swirling rage that wanted to erupt like a volcano. He was unused to feeling such overwhelming emotions, much less such dark ones. His lifemate had worked nearly from the moment she had risen to try to stop the spread of the infection, and yet, as an ancient, it was a fair reasoning and one he might have had himself. He worked at keeping his voice dismissive.

"We do not have time for you to make up your mind whether or not my lifemate is working with a master vampire. Tariq, I believe all the warriors necessary are free of the infection. You and Gary can decide what you wish to do with Lojos. Elisabeta can start on your security force. She will need blood soon."

At once he felt Elisabeta's soothing tranquility wrapping him up as if she had enfolded him in her arms.

He knew the Malinov family very well, Ferro. What they did felt very personal to him, to all three of the brothers. I can feel the sorrow beating at him. The sense of deep betrayal. He does not feel it, yet I do.

Although I understand it, I do not like that he regards you with such suspicion. You must use Tariq for entrance into the security guards, Elisabeta.

You are always calm, Ferro. Always. My steady rock.

He felt a brief flash of amusement. It might be true that he was calm and steady, but only until it came to her. He found he didn't like anyone slighting her or implying that she was in league with her captor—even if it was something he might have done—just because it was an explanation that fit when, so far, there had been no other.

"Tariq, you will have to guide us into your human force," Ferro said. "We will work as fast as we can here to be ready in order to protect the compound from the attack."

I have been considering what you asked me, Ferro, about how Sergey will bring down the safeguards to enter. He cannot, and he knows that.

Ferro started to reply to her but then stopped himself. There was speculation in her voice. He felt the stillness in Gary and the other ancients tied together. Like Ferro, they knew she was on the brink of a discovery. She turned the pieces of the puzzle over and over in her mind along with her knowledge of the vampire, a master strategist.

He will open the gates from within. She said it with absolute certainty.

Tariq, not tied to the others, was already leading the way to the first of the humans infected with the burns, and Elisabeta and Ferro followed into the man's mind. The burns were not nearly as severe as Josef's had been, but they were moderate, with more scorching than Tariq had. It would take a little more effort on Elisabeta's part.

How will Sergey possibly open the gates from within, piŋe sarnanak? Ferro asked, watching her work. She was so efficient at what she did now, soothing the man and removing all trace of the burn, that she didn't have to pay that close attention.

Tariq was with them now and Ferro felt him startle, but he said nothing.

It would be easy to be wrong. Very easy. There was hesitation in her voice now.

Ferro knew she wasn't used to giving her opinion on any subject. He sent an entreaty to the others, keeping his command on the pathway for them alone. *Do not say anything. She was never allowed to voice her view. This is extremely difficult for her. Gary, make certain Tariq knows not to speak. Let her take her time. Do not be impatient with her.*

If any of them spoke or showed impatience, she would instantly clam up and they wouldn't get anything further from her. As it was, he would have to coax the information from her. Her first thought was always that she might say the wrong thing.

I am simply looking for your input, Elisabeta. You know him better than anyone. You have studied his ways. What would he do, based on what you know of him?

Elisabeta carefully removed the scorch marks from the human brain. *I believe he somehow was able to introduce this infection into the compound. If that is so, it is very possible that I missed something. These burns were extremely deep in some. Light in others. It occurred to me that it is possible that a suggestion was planted into the burn, branding it into the brain, the behavior part of the brain, so that even if the brain was healed, the suggestion sank so deep, the healer, in this case me, would miss it.*

Ferro felt Gary's instant reaction to her reflections. His heart sank. Gary thought she was onto something. If that were so, it was one more thing his woman was going to blame herself for. At once, Gary's healing spirit entered the human. He was so bright and hot that it took a few moments to adjust to his being close.

Show me where you think this suggestion could have been branded into the brain, Elisabeta, Gary demanded.

Ferro moved closer to protect her. Tariq moved closer to see. Elisabeta again sent her soothing breeze moving around them all, as her healing spirit shone against one tiny spot she was concerned with.

I noticed this little speck, like a hook right here in the same place. It was so tiny and not really black at all. It looks like part of the brain, but . . . Elisabeta trailed off.

Please continue, Gary said. *I'm looking at it and I see nothing that would alert me to danger of any kind.*

I am most likely wrong.

Ferro felt her instant retreat. Elisabeta was uncomfortable. She didn't want to continue to speak to the ancient healer. He could feel her begin to withdraw out of the human. She'd removed the red scorching from his brain. She was tired and needed more blood to sustain her.

Elisabeta, please, Tariq pleaded with her. *I don't know how to ask you or explain to you how important this is. I am aware this is difficult for you. You have already put so much effort into saving all of us, and I know we can't repay you, but I'm asking you to continue to help Ferro and Gary try to figure this puzzle out.*

Each time he heard Tariq reach out to someone, Ferro knew why he was the prince's chosen leader there in the United States. He had a gift. Elisabeta was ready to run and yet he had stopped her, made her feel as if she was needed, appealing to her on the exact level that would make her respond.

Perhaps I phrased that incorrectly, Elisabeta, Gary tried again. *I, too, have examined every patient you have examined, so if you missed something, I have as well. What have you noticed that is now raising some concern?*

Ferro knew the other ancients tied to him felt the terrible struggle in her. She had gone back to that place of insecurity, yet she braced herself, sliding her spirit up against his in an attempt to find strength and recoup.

I am with you, sívamet, he assured.

It is silly, really. The hook is so tiny, a barb, turning toward the brain and eventually driving into it. Not at once. I have seen it in the lighter scoring with the hook upright, then in more medium stages to one side, but in those that are dark and angry, such as Josef's, it is buried. It was the difference that caught my attention when everything else looked the same. I suppose my conclusions are simply fanciful.

Elisabeta sounded somewhat disparaging, and Ferro found himself tightening his arms around her, wishing he could just take her back to their woods where she laughed in a carefree way, with no worries about what others thought of her. He went very still, realizing she wasn't concerned with how others viewed her for herself. She was his lifemate. He was a legendary warrior of the Carpathian people. She didn't want them to think less of him because of her.

He had to suppress a groan. Of course she would think that way. Elisabeta put him first. She always would. He would always have to take great care to do the same for her.

Can you show me the images in your mind, Elisabeta? Gary asked and then hastily retracted his query as she retreated even more. *Show them to Ferro and he can share them with us.*

Elisabeta, Ferro and the others left the human, Elisabeta pale and weak. Ferro immediately turned her face to his bare chest, away from the others, sheltering her so she wouldn't have to look at them while she fed.

*Give me the various images of this strange little hook, pi*ɲ*e sarnanak.* He kept his voice very gentle. Very loving.

She did so, and he immediately shared with the others the tiny speck that seemed as if it were part of the brain and looked no different to Ferro.

14

When evil seeks a place, deep within your mind;
I will be your shield, protecting what's inside.

Tariq and the ancients immediately carried out their supposed exodus from the compound. Ferro noted that Lojos didn't go with them. He remained a short distance from Ferro and Elisabeta while Ferro fed his lifemate. Charlotte, Blaze, Lorraine and Julija had come to join the tight circle of those waiting to be rid of the infection.

Julija wove a spell, her voice murmuring softly in the night as her hands moved gracefully, creating illusions—Ferro, striding purposefully with the other warriors, taking to the air once outside the gates. Gary and Maksim close to Tariq as they took to the air following a different scent Sergey had laid down. Lorraine and Blaze clearly were there to guard the group while the others waited for Elisabeta to clear them of infection.

Elisabeta worked fast, trying to get through as many of the security guards as possible in the shortest amount of time. Gary tried to help her, but the burns didn't react at all to the Carpathian way of healing. The lighter scoring showed the strange little speck with the hook upward, and he could deal with removing that. The medium scoring had the hook sideways and, taking his time, he could get the speck to move to him, but no manner of work could get the one embedded into the brain to release itself.

Elisabeta has to be right, Ferro. The infection is to turn all of us against one another, but it is also for introducing this little tiny suggestion into whoever it comes into contact with. Big or little. Old or young. It does not matter the sex. The more implanted with the suggestion, the better his chances that one will succeed, and all Sergey needs is for one person to open a way into the compound for him and his army, Gary said. *Someone will have to check my brain for this nasty hooked speck. Josef, for certain, will have this branded into him. Tariq, to keep the gates from being opened from the inside, what do you propose?*

It mattered little that Elisabeta had worked so hard to stop the infection and clear the brains of the terrible burns. She may have kept the ancients from turning on one another, but every single person who had been touched by the infection could potentially betray the entire compound. Maybe all of them at once—including their leader. If there were any they had missed and weren't watching, it would be easy enough for the gates anywhere around the massive compound to be opened from the inside and the vampires invited in. It was far too big of an acreage to be kept safe if those inside were determined to open it to their enemies.

They could try to safeguard the gates from the inside, but every entrance and exit would have to be safeguarded, and Sergey would know what they were doing. Ferro was proud of his lifemate. Around her, the discussion raged on, but she simply went about her work, taking care of Charlotte and then Amelia and Danny. She was swaying with weariness as she replenished her blood, refusing to take it from Ferro, thanking Lorraine when she volunteered to give it to her.

You need to be one hundred percent for the coming battle, Ferro. If I take small amounts from others, it will not be so draining on any one person.

His woman. The voice of reason whether he liked it or not. Josef was going to be next, and both of them knew by the way Gary had described him that the burns were going to be bad. The boy looked in a bad way. His skin was drained of color, his eyes bloodred. He clearly knew exactly what was going on and fought his need to explode into rage. Tiny beads of blood seeped out of his pores, indicating his tremendous inward fight. His two guardians, Traian and Joie, appeared quite anxious.

"Elisabeta," Traian said softly. "This boy is a good being, amazing and selfless. He has already done things at his age that few can say they have done. I fear this infection is taking a great toll on him. He just got to this place. I want to stay here and get to know you, but I feel a great responsibility to our people, who need him, and also to his family. If he is being targeted and you feel it is unsafe for him, we will escort him home."

Ferro would never have allowed Traian to put such undue pressure on Elisabeta had he had any inkling that her birth brother planned to appeal to her. Already she took on far too many sins and guilt that didn't belong to her. Guilt rode hard on her slender shoulders, guilt that didn't belong there. Traian didn't understand just how difficult things were for his sister, and Ferro knew the Carpathian tried. He wanted her to be fine. Healed already. Carpathians could heal bodies so easily and they were used to doing so. One couldn't do the same when the damage was done over centuries to a mind.

Elisabeta's gaze flicked up to Ferro's eyes as if asking for guidance. He realized she did that often when she felt helpless and at a loss for how to respond. "We will do our best to assess the situation," Ferro answered for her.

Gary led the way into Josef's mind. Ferro's breath hissed out of his lungs. The burns were much worse than Gary had led them to believe. Elisabeta didn't falter.

You should have warned her, Ferro told the healer with a hiss of displeasure.

I wanted to see what her reaction was. How she decides on the best way to handle this and what her conclusions are. This makes no sense at all to me, Gary admitted. *Had I warned her, I could have tainted her response.*

Ferro couldn't feel a difference in Elisabeta. There was only kindness and compassion. Her genuine need and willingness to help Josef. She sent the boy waves of reassurance and that gentle caring breeze that tugged at the horrendous vivid slashes of what looked to Ferro like a solid wall of crimson, bloodred paint.

He is not alone in this battle, Ferro. There are two others, an ancient warrior and a young woman belonging to Mother Earth. I feel them in him. They are a great distance away, but they have forged their strength to his.

The moment Ferro heard his woman say Josef was not alone in his fight to keep from exploding into violence, he and the other ancients moved to surround Elisabeta with their protection.

Gary, is it possible Sergey set a trap for her?

Give me a minute. Josef has powerful friends. They cross oceans for one another. I will feel them if I get close enough.

Ferro had a moment of near anxiety while he watched as the thick wall of vicious red, woven so tightly together, refused to even thin in the least. Elisabeta didn't seem to notice. That slight breeze never changed but continued to flow gently toward the violent painting, changing angle occasionally to come in at one corner and then another, all the while providing Josef with her calming serenity. It was impossible to feel anger and hatred in the face of very real compassion.

The ancient is Dimitri and his lifemate, Skyler. Josef and Skyler are childhood friends. Josef helped Skyler save Dimitri's life and then when all was lost, he helped Dimitri save Skyler's life.

Even a hunter who cared nothing for rumors, legends and the outside world had heard the story of the three young ones who had defied all odds and had gone into the very heart of werewolf country to save Dimitri from death by silver, a sentence passed on him unfairly to start a war between Carpathians and Werewolves. Josef, Skyler and Paul, the human nephew of the De La Cruz brothers, had prevented that war.

Elisabeta, can you remove such a deep scorching? Gary asked.

Yes, of course. There was complete confidence in her voice. *It will take time. Sergey will attack before I am finished.*

Ferro felt her hesitation. She turned to him alone. *We will need to be under some kind of shelter where we cannot get out. Josef will try to reach a gate or entryway just the way all of those that have been infected will try. Gary included. I have no way of knowing how hard any of them will fight to reach their goal. I can only surmise that the deeper the hook in the brain, the more they will try to open the compound for the vampire and his army to enter. You can put him to sleep, but there are so many others, and we may not know all of them.*

She gave Ferro the information as if she knew he would know exactly what to do. He relayed the supposition to Tariq. *We need to set up our warriors at every entrance to stop anyone who might try to open those accesses to the vampire,* he concluded. *Anyone with deep burns, like Danny, Amelia and Josef, needs to be locked away or put to sleep until we can see if they need to be controlled. That includes any of the humans in the security force that Gary feels were particularly heavily burned.*

Take Elisabeta and Josef to the house Dragomir and Emeline shared. We can safeguard it so Josef can't leave. Hurry, though, Ferro. The illusion Julija wrought was extremely good. Already I can feel an unease in the night creatures. The stone dragons in the courtyard are beginning to rumble, their bellies glowing with fiery coals in preparation to fight the vampire. That only happens when the vampire draws close, Tariq said.

It wasn't difficult to scoop Elisabeta's body into his arms while Traian took Josef. They hurried with their charges across the courtyard to the house Dragomir and Emeline had lived in until their daughter had been born. To Ferro's surprise, Lojos paced along behind them. Trailing after him was Joie, Traian's lifemate. She looked very small, someone others might overlook, but there was something about her, and Ferro had been too long in the world to be fooled. The woman was lethal, and if Lojos was a threat to any of them, there was no doubt in his mind that the Carpathian hunter would be dead before he could carry out that threat.

Tariq and Charlotte went with Danny and Amelia to the safe room, where they were locked in. Genevieve took Lourdes and Bella to a second safe room and again, they were locked in. The older couple, Mary and Donald, followed suit.

Tariq was the ultimate general sending his best warriors to the gates to prevent anyone from opening them from within. Isai and Julija stayed at the main gates to defend them. Together they held extreme power. Warriors spread out. Security guards were placed in defensible positions.

He is coming, Elisabeta announced. Her calm was gone. She pulled abruptly out of Josef's mind. She staggered and threw back her hand to catch herself before she went down. Ferro caught her around the waist, holding her upright.

I am sorry, Ferro, I cannot do this while he is close. I cannot concentrate. I am leaving this poor boy in a terrible state and it is not right, but I cannot . . .

Terror was building beyond anything he had ever experienced with her. It filled the room so there was no way to shield the others from what she was feeling. Her body shivered continuously, her hands rubbing up and down her arms as if trying to peel the skin from her body. Ferro very gently stopped the movement with his hands.

Josef will feel nothing. I have made certain of that. He is frozen until the time you are able to heal him.

Aloud, to steady her, he spoke matter-of-factly. "We knew he would come, beloved. This was the hope. We wanted to draw him to us. I know it is frightening, but all those with the scorching will be watched so that they do not betray us."

They are programmed. You know he has succeeded in doing this.

Ferro nodded, his hand moving up to the nape of her neck, a gentle, soothing massage. "Yes, Elisabeta. He has programmed even our ancients to betray us, to open our gates from the inside, but we are aware of this, thanks to you. Tariq has given orders and all who carry the burn marks will be contained." Deliberately his eyes met Lojos's.

The ancient immediately understood what Ferro meant and the repercussions. "I have the scorching," he admitted.

Ferro inclined his head. "That is so. Even had Elisabeta removed the burns, we believe the programming would still be there. That is speculation only. We do not know for certain."

Lojos turned his attention to Elisabeta. He bowed from the waist, a courtly, elegant gesture from centuries earlier. "Forgive my continued suspicion, Elisabeta. I am from another time, when one questioned everyone and everything. Ferro's word should have been good enough." He raised his gaze to the warrior. "What would you have me do?"

"We are weaving a safeguard to hold Josef inside, but we may need your fighting skills," Ferro admitted. "The healer said the burns were light, so although you are showing signs of having to fight against the tendency for violence, you are winning that battle. You know what you are up against. The warriors at the gate will prevent you from opening them should you try."

Traian and Joie stood to one side as Ferro walked with a very reluctant

Elisabeta out of the house and onto the porch. The safeguards were woven so that Josef, should he manage to break free of the frozen state he was in, could not escape the house.

Ferro, he is so close now. He whispers to me. I hear him.

Ferro could hear him as well. A dark, ugly voice, like nails on a chalkboard, a high-pitched note that scraped at the walls of Elisabeta's mind, trying to force its way inside. When Sergey could not break through the barrier Ferro had constructed, the vampire became enraged and began throwing himself at the shield, battering at it, desperate to bore his way through. He was so determined that Ferro had a clear image of the vampire's surroundings and was nearly able to pinpoint his exact location before the creature realized he was throwing such a tantrum he was putting his life in jeopardy and pulled back.

"He is about six miles away," Ferro reported. "His pawns are close to the gates. We should know if we were right about the programming. At any moment we should see if those with the small specks Elisabeta found will try to walk to the gates to open them."

As he spoke, Tariq, who had joined Gary after helping Charlotte put his children in a safe room, peeled off from their circle and both began to walk briskly toward the front gates, striding with great purpose. He neither looked left or right. Maksim called out to Tariq but he didn't look up or miss a step. Ferro waved his hand toward both men, sending out a command to stop them both in their tracks.

Elisabeta, how long do you think the command to open the gates will last? Sergey is directing them to obey him. He had to stop trying to get to you in order to give the command to those with the branding in their brains. Is it a lasting command or a temporary one?

It was an impossible question to answer. How would she know the answer? Still, he asked her for two reasons. She needed to concentrate on something other than the terror that was reducing her into a ball of nothing but sheer nerves. She wanted to curl up in the fetal position and disappear. The other was, Elisabeta really did know Sergey better than anyone else, probably better than he knew himself. If anyone could anticipate his every move, she could. She might actually guess the right answer.

Her moan was her only response. He caught her thick braid at the nape of her neck. *Elisabeta. I need you to stand with me. Now is the time we must fight against this madness. I need an answer.*

He poured command into his voice. She understood and responded to absolute authority, and he gave that to her. He felt her stiffen. Snap to attention. Her mind, chaotic and fearful, cleared. Became once more sharper thinking. Intelligent.

It will be momentary. He rules by fear. He believes all will obey him once he gives the order. No one will dare disobey his given command. They will continue to try until it is done.

Thank you, piŋe sarnanak. It is important we do this together. Stand with me.

Once again, to give her courage, he swept his hand down her braided hair as he walked the two of them closer to the gates. She straightened her shoulders, wrapped one arm around his waist and kept pace with him. Only he knew the cost to her. Her body shook terribly with each step, but she kept her head up and she didn't falter.

Around them, his brethren gathered, fanning out in a semicircle to take in a wide area behind them. Tariq and Gary stood frozen, while Sandu joined them at the forefront, waiting for the first wave of Sergey's pawns. These would be the lesser vampires. They had learned his "cannon fodder" were newly made vampires in the form of human psychic males, eager to be turned so they could have the same power as the vampires they chose to serve. They would expect the gates to be wide open because Sergey had said they would be.

The human security force had weapons designed specifically to kill the vampires, and they were stationed along the top of the fence in safeguarded positions where they could defend the compound yet not get taken prisoner by the enemy. With the safeguards woven so tightly, it was nearly impossible for even a stray arrow or bullet to slip through to injure or kill one of them, yet they could fire their unique weapons at the vampires at will.

Ferro released Gary and Tariq so they could participate in the upcoming battle after Julija had woven safeguards to prevent anyone from inviting vampires into the compound.

Hold fire, Tariq ordered Matt, head of his security team, as the first wave of vampires approached the gates. *Hold your men steady.*

He clearly was still fighting the compulsion to open the gate. Julija countered the impulse in Tariq and Gary with a spell, helping to ease the need to obey that vicious hook in their brains.

It was always unnerving to see newly made and starving vampires coming all at once. They were hideous creatures with twisted faces, once handsome, some still partially so, but most decomposed and rotting in places, as they weren't experienced enough to hold illusion through the desperate starvation they'd awakened with. Hair fell out of scabbed scalps, so only a few long stringy strands hung oily and loose. Teeth were pointed and jagged, the thin lips drawn back from shrunken gums. Maggots crawled on them, wiggling over the rotting flesh as they rushed forward, eager for blood promised to them—the rich satisfying blood of an ancient.

The newly made vampires were so frantic they would take any blood. Sergey had kept them in the ground for a longer period of time so they would wake starving. He wanted this killing frenzy, this madness, a desperation that would ensure they would kill and devour every living creature they came into contact with.

Sergey needed a bloodbath, the insanity of a chaotic seige, so he could slip in and reclaim Elisabeta. Once in the compound, he knew he could find her unerringly. He had lived with her scent, her soft, soothing presence, and he would never be able to live without it. She had been the one to give him the small details that allowed him to defeat his brothers. They had intelligence, but he had Elisabeta, his secret weapon, and he needed her back. He couldn't continue without her. He had relied on her for all those long centuries and he didn't know how to move forward without her.

He is furious. Do you feel him, minan päläfertiilam? Ferro asked Elisabeta to keep her grounded with him. *Do you feel his fear that he has already lost you? You are too important to him. Do you know why? He cannot continue without you. He needs you. You are powerful. That is why he kept you starved and under his control. That is why he made you so weak and unable to care for yourself, made you so dependent on him for everything. You are much more powerful than he is, and he knows it.*

"Hold steady," Tariq ordered both aloud and then again telepathically to his security force protected on the walls. "Let them come close and think the gates will open for them. Stay sharp that those of us pro-grammed will not obey the order to allow them inside."

You plan on going out there to hunt him. Elisabeta made it a statement.

Ferro could not deny it. *As long as he is alive, hän sívamak, he will con-tinue to come after you. He cannot help himself. You are a necessity to him, just as blood is.*

Ferro could feel her turning over the things he said to her, trying to absorb them, trying to believe them when her mind held such terror for the master vampire.

The terrible growls and snarls of the lesser vampires could be heard as they approached the compound, groups of them coming at the various entrances, some on the ground, some in the air, some clones, others very real. All had the same intent. The hunters were used to seeing those hol-low, starved faces, nearly caved in, with sockets for eyes, but Ferro was a little surprised at Tariq's human security force. They were stoic, waiting for the signal before they began to fire their specially designed weapons at the vampires.

The moment they did, the ancients dissolved into mist, taking to the air, while Julija wrapped her arm around Elisabeta, taking Ferro's place as he streaked into the sky toward the wooded area by the lake where Sergey had stayed while his army had prepared to take the compound.

Tell me where he is, Elisabeta, Ferro ordered, staying merged with her, making it an order so that she didn't have time to dissolve into terror because he was no longer physically with her. *We do this together.* He kept his voice calm and matter-of-fact.

Straight ahead. Can you feel his anger growing? He is concentrating on opening the gates of the compound again. He cannot understand why he was not obeyed.

Ferro went very still. At the same time, the other hunters tied to his soul—Andor, Gary, Dragomir and Sandu—did as well.

Piŋe sarnanak. Ferro strove to keep his voice extremely calm. He didn't allow any emotion into his mind. Deliberately, he used his nickname for her so she would feel at ease, as though any question was not one of great importance. *How do you know he is trying to open the gates and that he does not understand why he was not obeyed?*

He moved toward the woods, taking the straight route over the lake. The fog helped to hide movement in the mist. Sandu and Gary were on his right, Dragomir and Isai on his left. Benedek and Petru circled to the east to try to get behind Sergey's position. He would have other, much more experienced vampires guarding him, most likely master vampires. He wouldn't be alone. His desperation wouldn't make him careless—yet.

Maksim, Siv, Nicu, Val and the triplets remained at the compound with Tariq, Traian and Joie to ensure no gate was opened and everyone there would remain safe while they hunted Sergey.

I just know. Elisabeta sounded puzzled. *Ferro? Do you not know this?*

He felt the tiniest bit of alarm spread into her mind, as if she were doing something wrong. It was the last reaction he wanted from her. If she had that great of a connection to Sergey, they could use it to destroy him.

I have long hunted vampires and little else, Elisabeta, he replied gently. It was no real answer, but he knew it would soothe her.

He was nearly across the lake and he could feel the threat emanating from the woods ahead. It was dark and still in the trees. There was no wind, no breeze whatsoever, no sound of any kind other than clacking that sounded like tree limbs rubbing against one another. Insects had ceased all noise, as if cowering away from the unnatural beings hidden near them. No mice or lizards scurried in the leaves or rotting foliage.

I do not have your empathy, nor can I, while hunting, move through your mind to find what I would need to tap into his actual thoughts.

Could she do that? Ferro didn't break away from her, but it took his centuries of discipline to keep away excitement.

There is no need, then, Ferro. I will tell you what he is going to do before he does it. He has abandoned his plan of storming the compound. He knows he cannot get inside and is leaving those he regards as his pawns to their fate. He realizes it must be a trap and that you are coming for him.

Ferro had Gary share that knowledge with the other hunters unable to hear Elisabeta.

He is directing those he has set up to guard him to remain, and he is fleeing with two other master vampires. He told those remaining that you are coming and will be there any moment. They are expecting you.

Anxiety was in her voice, in her mind. Ferro couldn't believe she was able to know exactly what Sergey was saying to his "soldiers." He couldn't hear the vampire and he was merged with Elisabeta.

Ferro, they know you are coming. They will ambush you. There was a catch in her voice.

Which direction is he fleeing?

He should have reassured her. She was worried about him. He had been hunting and fighting vampires for so many centuries without emotion, without thought for his safety. He hadn't considered that she would be concerned for him.

This is what we do, sívamet. Believe in my ability.

He is heading south, but do not go in that direction. He will circle to the west and head for the mountains. You can get ahead of him if you make for the . . . She broke off, trying to form an image in her mind and send it to him.

Gary shared the image with the other hunters of the mountain peaks of Cuyapaipe Mountain. He referenced the exact location he saw in Elisabeta's mind.

Do you know this place, Ferro? I do not. I see it in his mind. He has a lair there. I cannot yet see the exact location. Now there was frustration in her voice and mind, as if she were failing him.

This is more information than I counted on, Elisabeta, Ferro assured.

On the private path between brethren, Dragomir asked what all of the hunters were considering. *Are you certain we should do as she believes and go west rather than follow his trail to the south, Ferro? You are merged with her and yet you cannot read Sergey's thoughts. Not one of us, not even Gary, can do so. How is it she can?*

I will go west, Ferro declared. He believed Elisabeta could tap into the vampire's mind. He had no idea how, but he was certain she was actually able to. He didn't want to miss this opportunity to at least make a try for him. If he didn't succeed, he would at least disrupt him, make him all the more vulnerable so the vampire was even more likely to make mistakes.

I believe her as well, Gary said. *I will go with Ferro.*

I will go with Ferro, Sandu said.

Petru and I will join with Ferro, Benedek added. *Sergey will have more waiting to guard his lair.*

The rest of us will engage with those here in the woods and destroy as many of his army as possible, Isai decided after a brief discussion. *Then return to the compound. The more we take from Sergey, the better for all of us. Good hunting.*

Do you recognize the image of the mountain peaks? Ferro asked Gary.

The healer had spent the most time in the region in comparison to the other ancients. All of them had been in the mountain range when they had rescued Andor, but most of that time had been spent fighting off vampires while trying to heal his mortal wounds enough to get their fallen brethren back to the compound.

It is very near the same area the human family camped and Sergey used them as bait to draw us in. All of us thought he wanted to use Lorraine as a substitute for Elisabeta.

Ferro turned that over in his mind, sharing the information with Elisabeta and his memories of Andor's injuries and the fight to keep him alive.

This was when we bound our souls together. The healer could not find Andor when he went to the tree of life to retrieve him. Lorraine wanted to go. She was human, not yet tied to him. It was the only way we could think of to give the necessary strength and yet keep her safe as she traveled in that world.

Ferro and the others streaked toward their destination, determined to get ahead of Sergey and the other master vampires traveling with him. He wanted to keep his lifemate calm and reassured that the other hunters and he were safe and not worried in the slightest about the coming battle. There was no reason to be. He had already slipped into that place where he could shed emotions quickly again when need be, which meant he would have to disconnect from Elisabeta when the battle started.

She is very brave, Elisabeta conceded.

You were in the healing grounds, sleeping, Elisabeta, when Sergey baited this trap for us. We had no idea that Lorraine was never going to be enough for him. His ultimate goal was always you. Did you have knowledge of this place by the lake where he set his trap or that he planned to use another woman to barter for you? Again, Ferro was casual about it.

There was a very long hesitation. Ferro stayed very quiet as he streaked across the night sky, hoping he wouldn't have to prompt his lifemate to answer him when she was so clearly reluctant.

I know of this place by the lake. He favors it. Many humans like to camp there. I have not seen the way to it, but I know of it.

There was guilt in her voice. Too much guilt. Ferro didn't like that, nor did it make sense to him. He broke the connection between Elisabeta and the others so that only he maintained a merge with her. Whatever was said was private between his lifemate and himself.

Did you know that he planned to use another woman to barter for you? A lifemate of a Carpathian, he added.

She stayed silent, retreating from him. That wasn't a good sign.

Elisabeta. I am asking you gently, and I do not wish to make this a command to answer, but it is important to me. We have trust between us. I want us to maintain that trust.

You will not like the answer.

There will be times you will not like my answers, but I will answer you when you ask me questions and I will do so truthfully. He wrapped her up in his arms from the distance, letting her know that whatever her answer, good or bad, he was her lifemate, her partner, and they would work through the answer.

There was great reluctance in her mind as she reached for him. *Before you slept in the healing grounds with me, protecting me from him, when they insisted I had to wake to feed, I would hear him. Now, I am aware, I summoned him. I swear, Ferro, I did not realize I called to him.*

I am well aware you did not, piŋe sarnanak, he assured gently. *No one blames you, least of all me.*

I see into his mind sometimes, especially when he is calling to me. He had planned to take this woman—Lorraine, as it turns out. He bragged about it. He told me how he had harassed all of you, wore down the ancient hunters until they were low on blood and one among them was so far gone he would most likely die. I saw every move he planned and I told him it would not work. He was very angry with me.

Ferro found her assessment of Sergey's battle plan interesting. She had been proven correct, but how had she known? She didn't know any of the ancients, and Sergey had shown her that most of the hunters were wounded or had given large amounts of blood in order to keep Andor alive. She was belowground most of the time, sleeping, kept that way in an attempt to heal her body and mind after her centuries-long ordeal.

Sergey's brothers were considered very intelligent by all accounts. I did not know them, but I had heard of them from Zacarias De La Cruz. Of all of them, the younger brother, Sergey, was not put in that same category of genius. He was considered of average intelligence by everyone, and his brothers, even while growing up, sometimes were cruel to him. At least, that was what Zacarias conveyed to the other hunters. Would you say that is a fair assessment?

There was a long silence as Elisabeta considered what Ferro had asked her. The longer the silence played out, the more he could almost feel her squirming. She didn't like the conclusions she was coming to at all. She wanted to withdraw totally from him and yet, at the same time, she didn't want to let go of the merge, afraid of losing him in the upcoming battle with the master vampire.

Below him, city lights were so bright it seemed impossible to see the stars as he circled around the tip of the city, making his way toward the mountain range and the lake to get in front of Sergey. He didn't understand the need for so many artificial lights. All the technology that humans relied on so much—it just seemed to him that they tied themselves to it, and now, Tariq and the prince were asking all Carpathian people to do the same. Was that a good thing or a bad thing? He thought there should be more of a balance. Clearly, the Malinovs had learned to use technology while the Carpathian people hadn't done so as quickly, and that had allowed the vampires to pull forward in the war between them.

Elisabeta. I require an answer.

He felt her sigh. *Sergey's brothers were very cruel to him, as often as possible. Throughout the centuries, from the first of my captivity, they would say ugly, demeaning things to him. He was pushed aside and treated as less than the others always. He had a place in their planning, but was not allowed to speak. If they did ask his opinion, they laughed at him when he gave it.*

He knew she had deliberately skewed what he'd asked her. She'd jumped on Zacarias's assessment that Sergey's brothers were cruel to him, confirming that they had been. She knew that wasn't what he was asking.

Ferro remained patient. *Minan hän sívamak, is Sergey every bit as intelligent as his brothers? More so? Or far less so?*

If the Malinov brothers were as smart as everyone said they were, how could they be so deceived by Sergey? The De La Cruz brothers were considered geniuses, and yet none of them had considered Sergey anywhere near the threat of his older brothers.

Elisabeta's tears were unexpected, drowning him in sorrow. *Please do not ask me these things, Ferro. What does it matter?*

He stroked his hand down her hair the way he did to comfort her. Sang his song for her in their merged mind. *You know it matters. I need this information. You know him better than anyone. I think you know him better than he knows himself. He has a vision of who he is. He has made that illusion in his mind his reality, but it is falling apart because you are not there to keep it real for him. I need your honest assessment of him, sívamet.*

Again, there was a long silence. He had the impression of extreme anxiety. Of her chewing on her lower lip. Her fingernail. He heard Julija whispering softly to her. Elisabeta assuring her she was fine. He waited her out, knowing she was working up her courage.

Sergey's brothers were very good at thinking far into the future. They planned every battle in minute detail. He reacted to everything they said and did, and they knew it. The only memories I have from my childhood were memories of our friendship. I did not know if he planted them, but I doubt that he did. They followed too closely to the way his brothers treated him. He would come to the house and sit on the porch. I would talk to him and soothe him after they were particularly ugly to him. He was already approaching a point where he was losing his emotions, but their barbs still struck. I was very young, not more than sixteen. A child, but I could bring peace to him. I felt bad for him.

Ferro understood why Sergey had made his plan to take Elisabeta with him once he realized his brothers were going to voluntarily turn vampire. They would expect him to choose their way. If he didn't, they would kill him. In his mind, he had no choice, so he plotted to take the one person he knew could make him feel better and subject her to the life he was terrified to lead with the brothers he feared.

I had forgotten that Sergey did not always understand what they were doing. I was very afraid at first. He kept me away from them. One day, they came unexpectedly and he had to hide me. He was almost euphoric that they had no idea I was there. They talked openly in front of him—and me. He made me repeat everything they had said. I caught all of their inflections and hand movements, every nuance. Every detail. I could tell when any of them was misleading him or one of the others.

Ferro held himself very still at her innocent revelations. Sergey wasn't the genius. Elisabeta was. Sergey's brothers had laid out their plans and strategies far in advance and set things in motion. Those plans were most likely already in play, with or without Sergey, but Sergey wasn't going to plan the meticulous battles that his brothers were able to, not without a general like Elisabeta.

How is it that Sergey ended up with slivers of Xavier and his brother, Vadim, and yet he is nowhere near their intelligence? How did he become the last brother standing?

Ferro was in the mountains now, flanked by Sandu and Gary. Benedek and Petru had come in from the east, careful not to move against the wind or disturb any of the owls or insects in the trees, all most likely servants and watchers for Sergey.

He has slivers of all of his brothers, Elisabeta told him in a small voice. *He can access them for their ability to plan battles or use technology. He can use the ones of Xavier to call upon mage spells if he needs them.*

Ferro had to revise his thinking. *All of us believed that Sergey was the genius all along, that he devised the plan from the very beginning, but he was scared. He was more than scared, he was terrified. That was why he took you with him. You brought him not only peace but courage. You listened to the brothers, Elisabeta, their plans. You heard them, and you helped Sergey get through those centuries by coming up with ways for him to strike back at them.*

Yes, she admitted. *They were horrible. He was, too, but not like them. I knew he did not have the ability, even if he had the slivers of his brothers in his mind, to fully access and understand what they were talking about, not without me to explain, and I often misled him. When things did not go right, I took my punishment and acted innocent, as if I had no clue what went wrong.*

Ferro turned the information over and over in his mind. *Sívamet, were you going to tell this to me?*

I have only just begun to realize it. The vampire kept me in such a state of terror that I believed him to be completely invincible. In some ways, I still do. I can barely overcome that way of thinking. Sometimes I am very clear, and other times I feel like a child huddled in a ball of terror on the floor.

Ferro could understand that. The more she grew in confidence and strength, the more her mind cleared. *The infection and strange speck left behind in the brain to open the gates was most likely done by one of the others, and now Sergey just thinks it is one more thing he does not understand without you, is that safe to say?*

Yes. I have never heard or seen such a thing, though. Not even a whisper of it. If it was planned, it was never done around me. Sergey had to have known about it, but he did not share it with me, which was unusual.

You gave him the idea to talk his brothers into sharing a tiny piece of themselves to aid him in understanding their plans? Ferro wanted to make certain he was very clear on that.

Again, there was a hesitation. *Yes. It was long ago, Ferro. Centuries earlier. Xavier and the Malinovs were so treacherous. I thought I could at least manipulate Sergey a little bit.*

This is good news, not bad news, hän sívamak. Sergey will be unraveling the longer he is away from you. I am coming up to the lake and woods and do not want to put too much energy into the air. Stay quiet until I have need.

15

I can't heal your scars or take away the pain;
But I can be your shelter, a refuge all the same.

As Ferro dropped into the woods, he was surrounded by an oppressive feel of utter gloom. Airless, stifling, even suffocating, the farther he drifted into the interior, the heavier the oppressive force surrounded him. There was no doubt that Sergey as well as other vampires had invaded the forest to the point that nature could not fight back against such an abomination.

The vampire was unclean. Anything it touched withered. Blackened. No vegetation could remain alive and thriving near it. Everything about the vampire went against nature. As Ferro drifted through the trees, he noted that many of the trunks and branches were twisted into macabre shapes and already blackened in places.

Dark sap ran down the deadened bark, like rivers of blood, to pool at the exposed roots. Birds, tree frogs and lizards were caught, held and died slow, ugly deaths in the thick acid-filled sap. Ferro, like all Carpathians, was a keeper of woods, of nature. The sight of a once-beautiful forest with the animals and fowl reduced to such a state was difficult to witness.

Sandu, Benedek and Petru moved through the depressing woods as well, sizing up the dark, twisted trees, noting every position of the crows and owls that prowled the twisted branches with beady, shiny eyes, searching for any movement that would trigger their instantaneous response, a warning to their masters.

Ferro gave thought to what Elisabeta had revealed to him. The Malinovs wanted to take over leadership. Theirs had been a total power play. They were brilliant generals, ambitious and driven, and had the discipline and patience to carry out their schemes. Sergey did not have the genius of his brothers when it came to planning battles. The vampire knew if he was going to have a chance to defeat the prince of the Carpathians, he would need Elisabeta.

What had Sergey developed to cope with his brothers and their arrogance, even as a child? Sergey would have to be cunning. He would be crueler, because his brothers had been cruel to him. Merciless because his brothers had been merciless to him. He would want to dominate. He had shown those traits in his dealings with Elisabeta, in the way he treated her, even though she was the one to get him through those long centuries, and he needed her.

He had stolen her when she'd been a child and he had already been a fully grown male Carpathian hunter. He had known what he was doing. He had planned the abduction carefully. He couldn't possibly have known what Elisabeta was capable of—the defeat of his brothers. Did he give her credit for that? Or over the centuries did he convince himself that he was really the one with the genius? Of course he thought himself the genius.

Ferro circled back around, moving to the outer area of the woods, back toward the lake, keeping to a very slow, drifting pace. It took a great deal of patience to stay almost still when time was a factor and the vampire would be coming soon, but he had honed that trait in centuries of hunting and had it in abundance.

He doubted very much if Sergey gave Elisabeta any credit for defeating his brothers. The vampire was vain. He would believe that he was the true genius in the family. He had slivers of all of his brothers and the high mage. No one could defeat him. He was desperate to get to Elisabeta only because she kept his body from decomposing so rapidly and kept his emotions intact when she was around. She'd been his constant companion and he was used to her company.

Sergey would tell himself all kinds of things, but deep down, he would be panicking, because all the things he could access before, like those slivers of his brothers' genius, or the high mage's spells, he could no longer reach. He would know, on some level, that without Elisabeta, he would not have access to the things that would allow him to rule.

Yet even without any of those assets, Sergey was a cunning, cruel master vampire in his own right. He would be a vicious fighter. He had defeated more than one Carpathian hunter in battle. That had nothing to do with Elisabeta. Having skill in battle didn't necessarily take genius. Sergey was willing to fight when he believed he could win, or when he was fighting for his life. Simply because he wasn't what he appeared didn't mean he was going to be easy to defeat in a battle, and it would be foolhardy to dismiss him as so.

There was little moon, just a sliver, and the black clouds moving across the sky hid even that most of the time, so the lake's water mostly appeared dark and shiny. Out of the oppressive stillness of the woods, Ferro felt a breeze. The draft tugged at the surface of the lake, creating ripples across it so waves lapped at the shore. It looked and even sounded like an idyllic scene, until one felt that ominous decay creeping out of the forest and hovering so close.

The owls and crows made no sound, but continuously walked back and forth on the twisted limbs, peering toward the lake, their gazes suddenly focused in that direction, alerting Ferro and his brethren. Crows were day birds, but they were out in numbers, spies for their master. Shadows appeared darker, staining the surface, as several hideous creatures flew low just above the lake's waters.

Do not engage. Let us see where their lair is. They must have an entrance nearby, Ferro cautioned.

Ferro doubted if this location had been chosen by Sergey originally. It was more likely one of his brothers who had scouted the area and realized it was perfect to provide them with the hikers and campers for a steady blood supply. They were far enough away from the Carpathian compound that few hunters would stumble across them.

The four ancient hunters stayed a good distance apart, careful not to make any movement that would alert the watchers or the master vampires hurrying back to their lair. Ferro wanted to know how extensive Sergey's army really was. How many could he count on to throw at the compound? How many would he be willing to sacrifice in order to get Elisabeta back? Would the hunters be able to wipe out the threat in one major attack, or would they have to hit hard in several smaller ones?

More than anything, Ferro wanted to eliminate the threat to his lifemate, but first he needed to have answers to protect all of those in the compound. It was ingrained in him as a hunter that the protection of his people always came first, and no matter what it meant to him personally, the code of honor instilled in him had to be followed.

Three vampires dropped out of the sky near the shore of the lake and strode purposefully toward the forest. They weren't trying to impress anyone with their looks. They appeared in their real state of decay, rotting flesh stretched over bone, hair mostly gone or falling out in chunks, teeth pointed and stained. At the tree line they separated to about twelve feet apart and lifted their hands high into the air.

Ferro and the brethren watched closely as they wove a complicated pattern, opening an unseen entrance so very well hidden that not one of the ancients had detected its presence. They noted the positioning of the three advance guards. Ferro vaguely recognized the three vampires. They were much younger than he was, but he had run across each of them on more than one occasion while they were still hunters.

The one to his left was from a good lineage. He remembered the father. A great hunter, legendary even. He'd been killed by three master vampires. He'd taken one of them with him before he'd succumbed. His son went by Van Halen. Luther Van Halen.

Sedrick Overtower was in the middle. Ferro didn't know much about him or his family, but he seemed to be a decent enough hunter.

The one on the right had been sloppy as a hunter, too loud at times, and Ferro was a little surprised that he had managed to survive and battle his way to become a master vampire. It didn't seem likely given the fact that he should have been killed early on in his hunting career. He had called himself Edward Varga back then. Even now, when he was opening the gates of the lair inside the forest, Varga was a bit sloppy, his movements less precise than the others'. Ferro found it interesting that he had been chosen as one of Sergey's advance guards. He couldn't imagine any of the other Malinov brothers tolerating Varga's ways.

A veil appeared, like a thick spider's web, a dank, dingy gray color. It hung like Spanish moss might from the twisted branches of the trees, a macabre shawl dripping in poisonous venom. Little beads of darker gray oozed from the web, ran down the strands to trickle onto the ground where they hissed and steamed as they hit the rotting vegetation. The pools spread out into a thin stream, connecting until they formed a moat, a semicircle—a barrier around the opening the vampires had disclosed.

Once the moat was in place, the strands of the web drew back, hissing and moaning as if alive and reluctant to part, the threads reaching toward the vampires, down toward the ground, and up into the trees toward the sentries there. One tentacle managed to wrap itself around a crow and drag it back into the center of the web. The crow screamed horribly, beak opened wide, eyes rolling wildly as the hungry threads began to consume it alive.

The vampires paused what they were doing to watch, clearly amused by the spectacle, enjoying the bird's pain. Varga's thin lips stretched wide and he made a squawking sound, imitating the bird's distressed cry. The other two vampires laughed. Even as they did, the air around them suddenly grew so dense that they began to cough. Varga coughed up blood and spat maggots onto the ground. Some landed in the moat, where the acid fried them instantly.

The three master vampires looked cowed in spite of the fact that they had gone centuries battling and defeating Carpathian hunters, earning the title of master vampire. The three shuddered and turned toward the five vampires striding toward them. Sergey was in the middle, two master vampires on either side of him. Clearly, he wasn't taking any chances with his own safety. He had left with two master vampires, and somewhere another two had joined him. He had pawns at his disposal and no less than seven master vampires to fight for him. That was serious firepower.

There was fury in every step Sergey took. He had been thwarted in his goal of retrieving Elisabeta. He had no idea why the infection wasn't spreading or working. The healer wasn't supposed to be able to stop it. Many of those inside had to have the command in their brain to open the gate, yet no one had done so. By now the ancients should have been turning on one another. Chaos should have been reigning inside the compound. He didn't understand and he didn't have Elisabeta.

He had thought he could always contact Elisabeta, that she would be unable to resist coming to him, but she had. The few times they had connected he had felt her terror, but those times had been too few and hadn't lasted long. He would find a way to get to her, and when he did, she would suffer as she never had before. He was just getting started, pinning humans to the gates. He would surround the compound with the dead and dying in her name. He would stick the heads of children on spikes and put them on the fence facing her, to stare at her with accusing eyes, so she would see them and know she had forced him to go to such lengths.

Snarling, he looked for a target for his impotent rage. Any target. He wanted to kill and keep killing, but cruelly, mercilessly, painfully, the way he had as a boy when his brothers teased him and he felt powerless, just as he did now. He would go into the forest and spend hours ripping apart animals and watching them suffer, looking into their eyes, feeling such immense satisfaction while their blood spilled around him and they silently begged him for death. He wouldn't give it to them.

Later, he graduated to human children. That had been even more satisfying, especially when he had befriended them first, over time making them believe that he was their friend by bringing them little gifts and even doing chores occasionally. Knowing all the while that sooner or later his brothers would shove him around or make fun of him and he would come back and spend time enjoying torturing his victims. He welcomed the way they tormented him just so he could have the satisfaction of feeling omnipotent when he spent hours with his victims. It was one of the most delicious and powerful rushes in the world. Taking Elisabeta out from under the nose of her family and forcing her to his will each rising kept that feeling in him, especially knowing he hid her from his brothers.

He strode straight up to Luther Van Halen. The master vampire had always thought far too much of himself. He strutted around, his followers loyal to him rather than to Sergey. It wasn't to be tolerated. And laughing? At him? Because he couldn't get to Elisabeta? Luther had most likely conspired against him. Luther wanted to lead the others. He was just like Vadim, one of Sergey's older brothers. He'd been one of Vadim's trusted lieutenants, although Sergey had no idea what Vadim had seen in the vampire.

Luther stood there impassively as Sergey continued to come at him, no expression on his face. Sergey didn't slow down, but the fact that Luther stood his ground infuriated him even more. He should be cowering. The other two would have had the good sense to back away, but not Luther. He was always challenging for leadership. Sergey had every right to reprimand him. To let loose his fury on the conspirator.

Without warning he slashed across Luther's face with the talons of the harpy eagle, ripping through what flesh was left, tearing it from the bone and tossing it carelessly into that writhing, poisonous, starving web. The threads came alive, hissing and fighting for the morsel of flesh. The moment they had a taste, the web wanted more, sending out tentacles in every direction, greedy for even that rotting meat.

Sergey kept slashing, not giving Luther a chance to recover, stepping into him, ripping into his chest, tearing at his belly to get at entrails, slitting the vampire open so that black blood poured onto the ground. The tentacles acted like tubes, dangling from the trees, dipping into the thick gel of shiny black in a frenzied feeding.

The moment the vampire's blood was spilled, from inside the hole the three master vampires had opened, lesser vampires stumbled out, clearly starved, desperate for blood, any blood, even the acid blood of another vampire. There were ten of them, newly made and fresh from the ground. All had been human males, presumably the psychic males Sergey was using as the pawns he would throw in front of the Carpathian hunters.

The newly made vampires rushed for the pool of black blood the vampire had torn open, knocking into him and driving him into Sergey, who stumbled backward. Luther slammed his fist into Sergey's chest as the momentum from the starving, eager vampires shoved him forward. His fist buried deep, the long extended claws at least four inches long, he dug for the withered, blackened heart of the master vampire.

Sergey screamed out his fury, raking at Luther's eyes and neck as he pulled back, closing down his chest with razor-like blades in an effort to chop off his lieutenant's arm before it could grasp the heart and extract it. The lesser vampires threw themselves on the ground right under the feet of the two combatants, licking at the blood pool, heedless of the danger to them from the reaching tentacles.

The poisonous spider's web went crazy. It was stretched across several trees, a very effective guardian to the entrance to the underground lair beneath the forest. The long threads swayed and rocked, reaching in every direction, looking for anything unwary enough to get close so they could attach themselves to it and pull it into the center of the web where it could feast.

The tentacles had to be sticky or have suction cups on them because two of the crawling vampires licking frantically at the black blood were gripped, rolled fast and dragged up and into the web where hundreds of threads locked them in place. The feeder tubes jammed into their still-intact flesh and blood spurted, drawing the attention not only of the newly made vampires but of the master vampires as well. The scent of blood permeated the air.

Sergey and Luther narrowly escaped the thrashing threads. Ferro caught sight of Edward Varga backing far away from the fray, answering the puzzle as to how he had survived for so long. He was the same coward, looking after himself and disappearing when he thought he could get away with it. Sergey's four guards circled cautiously, trying to find a way to get to him without putting themselves in danger of being eaten by the protector of the lair.

Sedrick Overtower hooked one of the hapless newly made vampires, still with red blood in his veins, and pulled him away from the others, dragging him across the ground, heedless of the rocks and debris. He skirted around the combatants, continuing to tow the doomed vampire across the uneven ground and into the trees, away from the opening that led to the lair.

He crouched down, tore into the neck of the starving vampire and began to consume him. Immediately, crows made their way down from the higher branches to hop across the ground, pecking at the kicking, screaming vampire, tearing strips of flesh from the bones. Sedrick didn't seem to mind sharing the flesh, as long as he was able to drain the last of the blood from the veins.

"You will be still, Luther," Sergey commanded. "Remove your fist from my chest."

Ferro heard the gift in the Malinov voice. One of his older Malinov brothers was reputed to be able to command others to do whatever he ordered, not just human but Carpathians and humans alike. Ferro hadn't believed it. Now, hearing that beguiling note in Sergey's voice, he could almost believe it was true. Luther didn't obey, but he hesitated. That was enough to tip the battle in Sergey's favor and warn all the brethren that Sergey had a few tricks of his own up his sleeve.

Sergey struck hard, ripping Luther's heart from his chest and tossing it into the air. One of his guards called lightning down and incinerated it. Sergey stepped back and indicated Luther's falling body. The lightning forked and jumped to the body, burning it as well. Just like that, Sergey seemed in good spirits again, although, watching him, Ferro could see he was tense and not in the least bit at ease the way he wanted the others to think he was.

The moment lightning lit up the night sky, Sedrick was on his feet, abandoning the vampire in the forest to the crows. Varga made his way back quickly to press close, as if he'd been there all along. Sergey kicked at the remaining newly made vampires.

"Get up before I feed you to the puppets, or our guardian." The web seemed satisfied with the two men it was devouring. Their piercing cries seemed to make Sergey even happier. He did nothing to silence them, although the sound carried across the lake, far into the night.

He kicked viciously at the vampires on the ground and they crawled hastily out of his way before stumbling to their feet. Sergey stood in front of the web, his guards by his side, and waved aside the dangling strands of the web. One master vampire moved up in front of him and another dropped behind him. The other two flanked him on either side.

Ferro could see why the entrance was so large. It had been deliberately made that way so it was safer for the vampires to pass through when their guardian was in a feeding frenzy. He drifted closer, Sandu, Petru and Benedek closing ranks so they were in tight formation, almost on the very heels of the master vampires. They had to time their entry so the vampires wouldn't feel them, yet be close enough that the guardian wouldn't, either. They couldn't stir so much as a drop of air and had to move in perfect sync with the vampires as they entered the lair.

Nothing smelled as bad as a vampire's lair. When many vampires shared the same lair, the stench was overwhelming, even to the most hardened of Carpathian hunters. They might not feel emotion, but they had a heightened sense of smell. They were predators, and like any predator, their senses were acute, no matter what form they took.

The passage may have started out narrow, but over time it had been widened, and now three grown men could easily walk side by side down the steps hewn out of the dirt and root systems to the floor below. Someone knowledgeable in engineering had designed and fortified the underground fortress. There was a series of smaller rooms to the front that presumably housed victims the vampires kept alive to feed off of for long periods of time.

As they floated past the rooms with the open doors, the brethren could see evidence of captivity, the chains and smears of old blood left behind with echoes of screams still encased in the dirt of the walls and flooring. There were no prisoners, and hadn't been for some time. Either Sergey hadn't been using this lair for very long, or he had abandoned the practice of keeping his food alive and close while he worked at retrieving Elisabeta.

The hallway ended abruptly, spilling into a large circular room cut out beneath the forest. The vampires had made an effort to make it comfortable, even somewhat livable, with chairs for the master vampires on a raised dais and more scattered around for the lesser vampires following them. The pawns sat on the floor, not yet worthy of a chair.

Ferro and the others exchanged notes on the master vampires entering the room with Sergey. Two of them were cousins of the Malinov brothers. Cornel and Dorin were often seen with their five cousins when they were young, preferring to stay in the background. They were quiet but skilled hunters, a force to be reckoned with from early on when they hunted vampires. Still, it shouldn't have been a surprise when they followed their cousins and made the decision to turn. The members of the Malinov family were close and they believed themselves superior to the Dubrinsky family—those who ruled the Carpathian people.

The Astor family had always followed the Malinovs. As children, Georg, Fridrick and Addler had hung around them, and when they were first learning to hunt, they followed the direction of one of the older Malinov brothers. They had all been good hunters, although unlike Cornel and Dorin, the Astors were on the flamboyant side. At times they had gone so far as to act in theaters in various countries, choosing small stages where they could perform, be stars, and then when they had gotten enough accolades to pander to their vanity, they would stalk any critics and drain them of their blood, sometimes killing their families slowly in front of them first. They needed attention constantly, and following someone like Sergey had to be difficult for them. Georg and Fridrick had been killed recently by Tariq and the others in their fight against the vampires, but Addler had survived.

Addler was a smart, colorful vampire, very reminiscent of the man he had once been. Unlike the others, he kept himself looking fairly decent, even though there were no humans to fool. He wore a suit with a purple shirt and black stripes. Ferro could see that his once handsome face would appeal to modern women. He had always been a good hunter, even as a young man, a careful student of the Malinovs, and apparently, he still was.

The fourth master vampire was one who, again, didn't surprise Ferro all that much. He hadn't been related to the Astors or the Malinovs but he had grown up with them and, as children, it was reputed that where they were, he was. He was called Ambrus Balog. In Carpathian culture they took names suited to the times and whatever region they lived in. Often they kept their childhood name, given by a parent, for sentimental reasons, but even that could change if it wasn't suited for the country where they were residing. Ambrus liked his name and continued to use it.

He was a big man and liked intimidating his prey. He'd used his size against other children when he was a boy and still did so as a vampire. It was said he crushed children's heads in his hands in front of their parents just to hear the elevated heartbeat, the rush of blood in their veins, hoping the heart would explode in their chests. He played with his prey for a long time before finally giving them death. He was a vicious fighter and one to respect in battle.

Ferro, Sandu, Benedek, Petru and Gary exchanged everything they knew of the four men as far as every battle they'd ever heard of or observed them in. They did so without words, simply calling up memories to share in their merged minds. They weren't taking any chances that a flare of energy would give their presence away before they had the information they needed.

"Vadim's infection was not effective at all," Sergey greeted, his voice shaking with fury once again. He glared at Cornel. "Unless you set us up to be killed. They were waiting. An ambush. We were lucky to get away. As it was, we lost all of the idiot fawning pawns."

Cornel frowned and glanced at his brother. "That doesn't make any sense, Sergey. The infection had to have spread by now."

"Well, it didn't, so you tell me, Cornel, how is it that the infection *didn't* spread when you assured me that it would? When you told me the ancients would turn on one another and that the gates would be opened from the inside? How is it that none of that happened?" Sergey demanded and threw himself into a chair.

The few remaining newly made vampires crawled into the room, covered in black shiny blood, and prostrated themselves on the floor. They whined in high-pitched voices, although the sound was more of a whimpering, grating on Ferro's nerves with his acute hearing. He knew it grated on the other ancients as well. He didn't see how the master vampires could tolerate such a din in spite of how low the actual sound was. It felt like nails scratching over a chalkboard.

"I have no idea." Cornel sighed in frustration. "I can't work from here.

I need to be in a location where we have access to the internet. Eventually we'll be able to trace the hunters. We'll know their locations when they choose to move around. They have energy fields, and we've been working to perfect an algorithm for that."

Ferro had no idea what that meant, and he doubted if Sergey did, either, although the master vampire cocked his head to one side and nodded as if he did know.

"Who do we have developing that?" Sergey asked, frowning as if he were very interested.

"It was Fridrick, Addler's older brother, but he was killed when Vadim insisted he try to get those women pregnant," Dorin answered, his tone slightly disparaging. "He brought the hunters right to us before we were ready."

"Had you taken over sooner, Sergey," Addler added, "we would be in a much stronger position." He casually kicked one of the newly made vampires who had crawled too close. It was a hard kick, delivered with the strength of a master vampire. "Know your place, worm. You don't ever get near Sergey unless he chooses to acknowledge you."

The man fell back, shuddering and whining, crawling back to the other newly made vampires. Once human, they had been young college-aged males who had gone to the Morrison Center for psychic testing. The Malinov brothers had conceived a plan to use them as pawns, dangling immortality and the promise of power in front of them. They converted them and then sent them into battle with the experienced Carpathians, using the new vampires as diversions or to wear the hunters down before launching the main attack.

Ferro and the others felt no emotion as they watched them fawning, trying to win favors with the master vampires. The high-pitched whining increased in volume to the point Ferro found it strange he couldn't turn the sound down. Carpathians could always lower the volume when noises were too loud, yet that screech was persistent and growing louder until he thought he might go mad.

The large room seemed to shudder, the ground rippling as if something alive moved beneath the vampires' feet. For one moment, the walls in the circular room appeared to do the same, the dirt walls undulating in a slow, uneasy wave, alerting Ferro that there could be things hidden that could be equally as dangerous as the master vampires and the poisonous web they had guarding the front entrance.

Cornel impatiently waved his hand toward the newly made vampires to silence them, annoyed by their continuing noise. The whining broke off abruptly. When it did, the uneasy rippling in the floor and walls ceased as well.

Ferro experienced an unfamiliar sense of relief. A flutter of awareness touched his mind. The merest hint of fragrance pushing out the scent of decay and rot. Bergamot, orange, vetiver, camellias and sandalwood. It was there and then gone as if it had never been, but strangely, it was an alarm, triggering an unease over the rising sound of the newly made vampires. If they didn't always sound off like that to their masters, why had they continued to do so and increased their volume? There was no answer. He had to be watchful. There were secrets here, and the brethren had risked everything to learn them.

Cornel paced across the floor, his movements so smooth he appeared to glide. "If we had that kid Josef, we would have exactly what we need by now. That idiot prince, Mikhail, has no idea what he has in that kid. They'll never catch up with you, Sergey. Never. They don't have your foresight. You're working without their tools and yet you're still ahead of them."

Ferro had to admire Cornel. He didn't fawn on Sergey. He didn't apologize or back down even with the implied threat that Cornel might be trying to get Sergey killed. He simply spoke matter-of-factly, stating what he needed and then ending with praise, knowing that was really what Sergey would focus on the most. After centuries of being abused by his brothers, always looking like the buffoon, Sergey craved and demanded respect. He needed those around him to stroke his ego.

The conversation told Ferro a lot about Cornel. He might be content to stay in the background, but he had the streak of brilliance that ran in the Malinov family. He could be a huge threat to the Carpathians. Cornel hadn't mentioned Elisabeta. Ferro wondered if he was aware she was the real brains behind Sergey's genius and now that she was gone, Sergey was incapable of leadership without her. Perhaps it was too soon for any of them to have figured that out yet.

Ferro knew Josef was considered very special by Gary, and that was huge praise. At one time Gary had been in the human world and he was a genius with a quick, decisive mind. He knew the ways of modern technology. When he had been converted by Gregori Daratrazanoff, second-in-command to the prince and from a powerful family in the Carpathian lineage, Gary had been presented before the long-dead ancients to be judged worthy of becoming a Carpathian warrior. If accepted, he would be wholly of the Daratrazanoff lineage and all past warriors would pour their battle and healing experience into him, as well as all other knowledge. He would wake a Daratrazanoff but already ancient, without emotion or the ability to see in color.

It would take a man of great strength to handle the terrible burden of such a sudden difference in one's life. Carpathians lost color and emotion over time. Those things faded, allowing them to get used to it and giving them time to reinforce their desire to uphold honor at all costs. Gary was forced to deal with it almost immediately.

If he said Josef was needed by the Carpathian people, it didn't matter that the kid had blue spiked hair and piercings, which didn't offend Ferro in the least. The kid had to be protected. Knowing the vampires had their eyes on him made that even more imperative. Ancients were used to sharing knowledge by acquiring it and simply sending that information to the others. The internet and the use of it seemed useful but not imperative until just that moment when Cornel acted as if Josef was the most important person to focus on acquiring. The implication Ferro was getting was that he was more important even than Elisabeta.

"This Josef you speak of is the boy Traian and his lifemate brought with them to the fortress where they are holding Elisabeta," Sergey said. There was speculation in his voice. Too much interest.

Cornel nodded. "Yes. It would be good if we could lure them both out from under Tariq's nose. Or if we can give the infection more time to spread, place our spies so that the command works and the gates are open,

we can go in and retrieve both. That way, we can kill as many as possible."
Before Sergey could reply, Cornel turned toward his brother. "Dorin, what of the plan to use our pawns in Tariq's club? Are they in place? That could be just the thing to bring the hunters out into the open."

Sergey looked pleased. "A bloodbath in Tariq's precious nightclub. Feasting on his well-dressed patrons. A great idea."

"Beneath the main club is the underground club," Dorin said. "That one is for those who like to play at being creatures of the night. We fit in perfectly there. To test for safety, I have entered numerous times, picked up a lovely woman, left with her and dined deliciously in the lair beneath the city, feasting for days before she succumbed. I had others do the same. It will not be difficult to deal with the cameras and feast right there in the underground club and then go floor by floor. Fear is such a wonderful addiction."

Sergey sat up much straighter, definitely pleased with the direction of the conversation. He clearly wanted to get back at Tariq for stealing Elisabeta out from under him. "Perhaps this Josef could be lured to the underground club. He's young. Is there a female we can use? One who would want to sacrifice to save her family? Dorin, if you've been to the club, did you meet anyone this Josef might be intrigued with?"

Dorin shrugged, looking bored. "I don't pay attention to the dating habits of silly little Carpathian teens."

Cornel hissed his displeasure right before Sergey raised his hand and slammed it toward Dorin, pushing not only air but something unseen and violent that tore open the master vampire's chest, driving him backward and down off the dais, toward the group of newly made vampires. Lips pulled back to reveal sharp teeth, the vampires slithered forward fast on their bellies, extending claws toward Dorin as he staggered on the uneven surface. The master vampire caught himself and viciously kicked the closest newly made vampire in the head, smashing in his teeth. He whirled around to face Sergey, his chest repairing itself, fury in every line of his body.

Cornel glided between his brother and Sergey, the move smooth and practiced. "We should go to the lair in the city, Sergey, where I can access the computers. I am certain there will be a file on young Josef and his preferences for females. For several years he has been friends with two humans, a male and female."

"Find them," Sergey snapped.

Cornel shook his head. "The female has been converted. She is related to several powerful Carpathian families and is the wife of Dimitri. He is both wolf and Carpathian. The male friend is the nephew of Zacarias De La Cruz. He is in South America. It would be better to find his prefer-ences and provide him with the exact girl to meet here. She can lure him out for us." Cornel kept his voice soothing.

Dorin hesitated, kicked at the newly made vampire on the floor who was already hastily retreating, and then the master vampire made his way back up the dais, putting Ambrus Balog between him and Sergey. Through the entire encounter, Ambrus had been silent, watching for the most part, his red-rimmed eyes on Sergey and then darting around the room, dropping to the floor to find the agitated newly made vampires and then back to Sergey again.

"We need to get Elisabeta," Sergey snapped. "This boy can be taken anytime, but we need to get her back immediately. If we need to move back to the lair beneath the city in order for you to understand why the infection isn't working then we should go now, before we lose the night. I want her back next rising. I've waited long enough." There was a distinct threat in his voice.

The vampires on the floor were back to their whining again, the ob-noxious high-pitched sound that seemed to shred the insides of Ferro's ears. Evidently, he wasn't the only one the noise bothered. Cornel once again lifted a hand to silence them, but Ambrus shook his head.

"No. Wait."

The dirt floor rose and fell as something alive skittered beneath it. At the same time the walls undulated like a giant snake coiling and un-coiling.

Cornel stepped close to Sergey. "Dorin, lead the way. Sergey, follow him. I will be right behind you. Ambrus, guard the rear. Sedrick and Edward, you stay close behind Ambrus. The others can follow or not. We will be sealing the corridor, so keep up if you want to get out."

Ferro had no idea what had tipped the newly made vampires off to the ancients' presence, but whatever it was, the master vampires were fleeing, and if the hunters wanted to engage them in battle, they had to do so immediately.

Dorin didn't hesitate. He whirled around as Cornel swung his arms into the air and created an opening just behind Sergey's throne-like chair. Dorin dashed down the narrow corridor followed by Sergey, Cornel almost directly on his heels.

Ferro, Gary and the other ancients started after them, just as Sedrick and Edward leapt forward and the newly made vampires jumped to their feet, attempting to push each other out of the way as they had to go down the narrow hallway single file.

16

I'll teach you the words, and show you the way;
You're strong on your own but tell me you'll stay.

G*et out of there now. Do not follow them. It is what they want. Go up,
toward the ceiling.* Elisabeta's voice burst through Ferro's mind,
tormented. Frightened.

We are hunters, Elisabeta. We are here to kill the vampire. In contrast, he
remained steady and calm as he streaked with his brethren after the master vampires down the very narrow passageway.

*That way is a trap. An ambush. You will not get close to them. Please, kont
o sívanak, I would not deceive you in this. I have seen the preparations. You
would not escape. All of you must go back to the meeting room and go up to the
ceiling. They know you are following and they lead you into a trap.*

Ferro felt her heart as if it were that of the wild songbird he always
called her, beating out of control. Her warning had been heard by the
others merged with him. He believed in his lifemate. So far, she had never
steered him wrong. He doubted if her fears for his life would have allowed
her to suddenly overcome centuries of submission so that she made up her
warning just to force him away from his prey.

Immediately he halted his forward momentum and signaled the others to follow his lead, waiting for Ambrus, Sedrick, Edward and the newly

made vampires to pass below them. In their frenzy to run, he was certain whatever had tipped them off would most likely elude them just long enough for the five ancients to get out of the underground lair, if Elisabeta could show them a safe way out.

Do not get caught in the corridor. Once in the meeting room, be very still and do not speak. Hurry, they will close the doors and you will be trapped. There are so many poisonous guards in place at the entrances and exits and along the walls, ceilings and floors of the corridor. Her anxiety showed in the quaver in her voice, but she was very clear in her instructions.

They streaked down the corridor before the last vampire was through the opening, so that when the door slammed shut, they were on one side and the vampires on the other. Back in the circular room, they drifted toward the ceiling, careful not to touch anything. Behind the closed doors, an agonized shriek signaled one of the newly made vampires had been unwary, or not fast enough, and was caught in one of the traps made for anyone pursuing the master vampires.

On the ceiling, toward the left side from Sergey's chair looking toward the center of the room, there is a root. It looks like a small loop, almost pushed into the dirt. Do not talk to each other if you can help it. Do not expend any energy. There are terrible, vile creatures in that room, and any energy not known to them will now unleash them.

Ferro could still feel her anxiety. She wanted them out of there fast. He knew that once the master vampires realized that whoever had been secreted in their meeting room hadn't followed them, they would be returning. The ancients weren't opposed to being outnumbered in a battle, but going up against seven master vampires and a few starving pawns inside a small room fraught with poisonous traps was suicide. More, Ferro didn't believe that Sergey wouldn't have other vampires, the ones each master vampire would have to serve and protect them, close by.

The plan was to get information and then separate Sergey from the others and kill him. The last thing they wanted to do was have the slivers of his brothers and Xavier find homes in other master vampires. It might still be doable to kill him, but first they had to get out alive from the lair that had become a trap. Ferro's woman was going to ensure that happened. He had every faith in her.

The five Carpathian ancients searched the ceiling of the meeting room. It was a large room and there were numerous roots sticking out of the dirt. Some of the roots had fine hairs on them, and even getting close to them in the invisible form they were in sent chills through their molecules. Other roots were twisted and gnarled, graduating from smaller, elongated limbs to thicker ones. Some looped back into the ceiling to disappear out of sight, while others hung down. Looking for that small little loop almost pushed into the dirt was like looking for a needle in a haystack.

The five ancients quartered the area, each taking a section of the left side of the ceiling to search. Benedek found the very small root nearly buried in the dirt. It was a twisted loop of braided wood about two inches thick, marbled in color so that it blended in with the dirt. He stared at it from every angle, sharing the image with the others and with Elisabeta.

That is the correct one. You have to grasp it and pull straight down. Be certain to pull straight and be to one side. There will be a hole you can float through. Do not touch the sides or you will trigger the guardians. The webs are very hungry. Their tentacles are always looking for prey. Movement prompts an immediate response. Noises. Drift through very quietly. When you all have gotten through the door, let it fall back naturally into place.

Thank you, Elisabeta, Ferro said. There was a still fear in her, but she was sticking with him, refusing to give in to panic as she might have those first few risings.

You will be in the forest, Ferro, and the vampires have taken over that section of the forest. Many of the servants sleep beneath the trees. That is why so many of the trees have become diseased. The moment Sergey and the others know you have eluded them, they will send word to cut you off so they can trap you between them. They have alerted the guardians already.

Ferro indicated to Benedek to open the trap door so they could drift through. *Cornel will be the one to realize we have escaped their ambush in the corridor.*

Cornel or Ambrus. Ambrus is cunning, like a wild animal. Cornel is much like the older Malinov brothers. He develops strategy quickly and is fluid about it. He can change battle plans on the run, Elisabeta answered.

Elisabeta was a wealth of information on their greatest enemies. Ferro waited as first Gary, Petru, Sandu and then Benedek successfully floated through the square hole created for an escape into the forest. He streamed up slowly in mist form. As he passed into the forest, he again felt the oppressive weight of hopelessness settling on him. There seemed to be nothing to breathe but sorrow. Even in the form he had chosen—and it fit with the gray veil covering the trees—that bleak, depressing burden seeped into his pores and found blood and bones where there were none, making it nearly impossible to think.

At once Elisabeta's cool, soothing breeze was floating through their merged minds, carrying the familiar scent of orange and lime mixed with a hint of Italian bergamot, sandalwood and vetiver. Her presence gently blew the burden of sorrow away, sending it drifting through their minds, allowing it to dissipate so they could see the complicated weave of spells creating the overwhelming melancholy that was another trap to hold unwary victims for the vampires to feast on.

There was no doubt in the ancients' minds that they could have worked through the spell, but it would have taken time and the master vampires might have been on them, along with their army sleeping beneath the trees, before they had finished working it out.

That spell is the combined work of several master vampires that you feel. Both Dorin and Cornel wove the base of it and the others layered their weaves over the top.

Ferro took the time to study the spell, although he could feel Elisabeta's anxiety. She wanted them to leave the forest as quickly as possible. The ancient hunters knew that if they could identify the magic being used by each specific vampire, it would give them further insight into that creature and his fighting ability. Did he pay attention to detail? Was he sloppy? Precise? Was he old-school or modern? Did he use a combination of both? Did he find his own magic?

Will you be able to identify the creator of each strand?

Yes. Elisabeta practically hissed it. *Ferro, get out of there. He is coming.*

All five of the ancients went still. Ferro felt their silent question to him. How did she know that when they didn't? There was nothing yet in the forest to herald the arrival of the master vampires. No shuddering or even welcoming. Sergey's spies, the crows and owls, remained somewhat lethargic within the gloom of the gray mist. He didn't have an answer, but if she was right and the master vampires were already on their way, the ancients couldn't be caught in the middle of the forest surrounded by an army of vampires. They had to choose their own battleground.

Which way?

They will expect you to go out by the lake. It is closest, and that is the way you had to have come in. He has already alerted his servants to be waiting for you and to search that entire area for any signs of hunters. He does not want to alert his spies in the forest in case you are still inside. That is a break for us. Go north. Move as quickly as you dare without triggering the guardians. They hang from every tree branch. You cannot disturb them.

North meant deeper into the forest. *Can we go above the trees?*

No. Anxiety rippled through her voice. Sheer terror. *Ferro, please, do not try that way. It is cut off to you. All Carpathian hunters take to the sky or go to the ground.*

He had to soothe her before they lost her to a panic attack. The forest had become a labyrinth of traps for the unwary hunter. They would have to return with a large faction and remove all snares so any campers wouldn't be caught.

We are moving to the north, piŋe sarnanak. There is no need to be upset. It was simply a question. You know Sergey's traps better than any other, and we are grateful that you do. He kept his voice very steady and calm, soothing her as they made their way carefully, following the direction in her mind.

She was very precise, weaving her way through the trees, and the ancients saw immediately there was a pattern to the "back door" escape route set up by the Malinov brothers. Ferro had never really run across it before, but he still recognized it from Zacarias De La Cruz sharing information. The brothers favored a certain flow they could move quickly through when running from hunters. They wound through trees, moving forward ten feet, and then abruptly veered right two feet and backtracked another two before moving forward ten, veering left and backtracking two to move forward ten. They repeated the pattern for several yards and then changed it, varying the forward movement by six feet and one foot left and then one foot right.

Elisabeta guided the ancients through the forest, careful to keep her soothing fragrance moving gently through their minds so their brains were always sharp and clear, free of the heavy burden the master vampires' spell had woven over the forest. Long webs dangled like Spanish moss from the trees, looking innocent and even beautiful, when in fact, the deadly tentacles waited for any unsuspecting bird, insect, rodent or man to approach too close. Elisabeta showed them how the vampires moved beneath or through each of the webs without disturbing the deadly predators so they didn't have to slow down as they moved quickly.

Ferro kept their fast movement from displacing the air around them. He ensured the same with his energy, as did the other ancients. Knowing exactly what could trigger the ever-starving webs made it much easier to do the things necessary to speed through the trees. Elisabeta directing their way so they didn't have to worry about when the pattern was changing increased their ability and would give them an advantage if they made it out of the forest and could double back on those pursuing them. He was careful to keep that thought from his lifemate, knowing it would distress her unnecessarily.

You are at the very edge of the forest. This is where you go up, Ferro, but there is only one way out or in here, unless you can open the path through the webs. If you do that, Sergey will know immediately. There is a thin, scraggly tree between two much larger ones. The trunks of the larger ones are twisted and blackened. You must be extremely careful. Servants sleep beneath them. The roots are tangled and looped above the ground. Look to your right.

He saw the trees. All three were covered completely in the gray webs. The thick threads draped artfully over every branch, and stuck in the sticky centers were decomposing birds, squirrels and various other rodents. There were bones, feathers, leaves and twigs caught in the gray veils as well. Below, on the ground, the root system was blackened and formed cages. Human skulls and bones were strewn inside the twin cages.

I see them, minan pine sarnanak.

Without touching the web, go straight up the scrawny tree and out into the sky. Use it like you might go up a chimney. A guideline only. Do not touch a branch, a leaf, a twig. Nothing at all can brush against any of the three trees or those webs. The entrance at the top is small. She sent the image to the five of them, showing the vampires ascending to the sky from the forest floor, moving straight up in mist form, but no more than an arrow of molecules.

Elisabeta's anxiety was higher than ever in spite of him calling her his little songbird. Normally, the familiarity of his loving name for her kept her very connected and calm, but this last trap had to be very deadly for her to be so filled with terror when they were this close to being free of the forest.

We will take extra care, sívamet. Gary will lead the way out. Sandu, Petru and Benedek will follow. I will bring up the rear. Stay merged with all of us and allow us to see the images so we make no mistakes.

Ferro felt that as long as she was actively aiding them, Elisabeta would keep from succumbing to the mind-numbing panic. The fact that she seemed to know exactly where Sergey was at all times would be extremely helpful. He wanted to know *how* she knew. He turned that puzzle over and over in his mind. He was merged with her, and yet he hadn't found anything to signal an alarm, nor had any of the others.

The five ancients couldn't wait to be out in the open, where they could turn the tables on the master vampires, so smug in their belief that they were safe in their numbers and with their army of servants hidden beneath the forest. They might only be five, but they were ancient hunters, and they had more battle experience than any of the vampires could conceive.

The moment Ferro was in the clear sky, he turned back to streak toward the lake.

How is it we felt overwhelming sorrow when we are ancient hunters and have no emotion, Elisabeta? Sandu asked.

Ferro could almost see his lifemate wringing her hands anxiously. He surrounded her with warmth. *You can answer me and I will relay the information, or just answer all of us, pine sarnanak,* he said gently, more to remind the ancients that she was fighting centuries of submission to Sergey, of never speaking to any being other than the vampire.

He felt her sudden determination. He knew what kind of courage it took for her to answer them, to do what she was doing, defying her captor and leading them through his traps. Others would never know, but he saw into her, knew the horrific details, the cruelties Sergey had put her through over those long centuries.

You do have emotions; they are inside of you. That is why my gift works on you and I can bring you peace for a short while. You cannot tap into those emotions anymore. When you find your lifemate, she provides that pathway and it is once more open to you. That is the simplistic version.

Ferro glanced down at the trees below him. The canopy was covered in those same sticky webs, although these appeared much finer, more fragile, as if they were real spider webs. A Carpathian hunter would not realize they were a deadly, poisonous trap set by master vampires to ensnare him. If he survived the web itself, the vampires would feed on his rich, ancient blood for a long time before the hunter saw death.

How would they know this? They were Carpathian and they lost their emotions. They feel only the rush when they kill or when they hurt others. They can feed off others' pain, Benedek asked. *I know the Malinovs were intelligent, but that seems far too sophisticated for them to figure out. Do you know how they did it?*

Ferro already knew the answer. Elisabeta's compassion for Sergey in the early days had often had her giving him things to contribute that she thought wouldn't hurt anything or anyone. She was innocent. A child. She had no idea of the depravity or cruelty vampires could conceive.

You were a child, Elisabeta, he reminded. *A baby. You had no idea that anything you said to help Sergey when his brothers were shoving him around would result in a poisonous web to capture Carpathian hunters.*

And human campers, she added in a small voice. *Do not forget them.*

We will take this entire trap down, kislány sisar, Petru assured. *No one knew that the Malinovs were capable of such horrendous crimes. Their own sister was betrayed, chopped into pieces and strewn across a meadow for the wolves to devour. Instead of hunting the vampires, mage and the weasel of a*

Carpathian who had conspired against her, they betrayed her even further and turned vampire in some pact, as if that would honor her.

Petru had called Elisabeta "little sister." He'd struck exactly the right note. Matter-of-fact, not in the least accusing, and giving her a story she couldn't help but be interested in.

Their poor sister. That's so awful. I have only vague memories. I cannot hold on to them. She sounded frustrated.

Ferro took up the story. She hadn't yet realized the five ancients weren't on their way back to her. *Ivory was her name. Draven, the prince's eldest son, was to inherit the mantle of authority, but the rot of the bloodline was in him. The prince didn't order him destroyed as he should have. Draven wanted Ivory, although she wasn't his lifemate. He didn't care. The prince, thinking to protect her, sent her to Xavier, the high mage, to school. He wasn't aware that Xavier had his own agenda and was plotting to take down the Carpathian people. Draven, the prince's own son, entered into a conspiracy with the high mage. In exchange for a Dragonseeker woman, Draven would provide the mage, Xavier would turn over Ivory. Rhiannon had a lifemate. He was killed and she was taken prisoner. Ivory did survive the terrible things done to her. Mother Earth accepted her and, over time, centuries, healed her. She hunted the vampire with a wolf pack and eventually found her lifemate, Razvan. That is another story I will tell you some rising.*

Below was the lake, the surface shining a dark silver. The clouds drifted in a lazy pattern, allowing the sliver of a moon to peek out and reflect below on the surface. A slight breeze skipped across the top of the water, creating small waves that lapped gently at the shore, creating an idyllic, inviting scene.

What are you doing? Ferro. He is there. Right there. Waiting for you. The newly made vampires are there. He has leashed them. He knows they are his only warning system. You have to leave before they sense you.

Ferro and the other ancients stilled, not moving at all. They had no idea how close they were to Sergey's newest pawns.

How do they sense us?

A small sob escaped. *You have to come back. Just come back.*

He poured steel into his voice. *Elisabeta. I need you to help me. Tell us how they know when hunters are near. Answer me at once.*

There was a moment he didn't think she could overcome her terror, not even when he fell back on giving her a command. He resisted sending her waves of reassurance, which was what he found he needed to do more than anything else, but it wasn't what *she* needed. Gary, Sandu, Petru and Benedek were merged with them, and she would forever view a panic attack as cowardice if they saw.

The psychic males, when they are newly made, pool gifts when they are close to one another. It happens when they first emerge. That allows them to be far more sensitive to any other with energy such as yours. You are using a different form, and that form produces an altered power source no matter how dim. Together, they can feel it.

Are the master vampires aware of this phenomenon? Ferro asked before any of the others could. He used his gentlest voice to make certain she knew he was not accusing her of anything.

There was no way any of the vampires, no matter how intelligent, could have guessed that. Cornel hadn't known; he'd silenced the whining vampires. It had been Ambrus who had eventually paid attention to the continual moaning of the newly made pawns, and even he had taken time to work out that a possible threat was close. Elisabeta had said Ambrus was like a wild animal, and that went along with the way he had puzzled out the strange communication.

No, they have no idea.

Not even Ambrus?

He knew eventually something was in the room with them but not what, only that the newly made vampires were uncomfortable and feeling alarmed. He is animal enough that he acted on that warning.

So, they are uncertain that hunters have followed them.

Elisabeta was silent for a moment. Ferro was patient. He tried to follow her wherever she went, but as far as he could tell, she simply went blank, disappearing into her own mind, a refuge she'd retreated to over the centuries when Sergey's cruelties were too difficult to bear. As he attempted to follow her, he was aware that Gary silently attempted the same thing, even though he was on a different path. Elisabeta had shut him out, closing every pathway almost automatically, as she must have done when Sergey tried to get into her mind.

Cornel and Dorin urge caution. Sergey is angry that Ambrus disturbed him from his lair when clearly there was no threat. Cornel wants to wait before leaving to go to the lair beneath the city, and when they go, he wants their servants to go with them to protect Sergey.

Ferro sighed. She clearly hadn't retreated. She had a way of reaching Sergey and getting into his mind. He didn't understand how it was that he, as her lifemate, couldn't find that path and follow her.

Does Cornel believe Sergey can really lead them?

No. He does not care who leads as long as he can direct the leader, at least that is my impression of him. I cannot always read his thoughts.

That was a revelation. *Elisabeta, you never have said you can read thoughts.*

She was silent for a moment. *Did I do something wrong? You read thoughts. I did not realize I would be doing anything wrong.*

You did nothing wrong. If I scan someone's mind or take their blood and force them to take mine to tie us together, then I can read their mind. The way you do it appears to be something very different. His lifemate was truly extraordinary and she didn't even realize it.

I spent centuries watching these vampires. Every expression. The way they move. The things they say. Eventually, I knew the way they think. That allowed me more and more to read their minds, I suppose.

Ferro could feel the restless buildup of tension emanating from a small grove of trees independent of the forest about sixty yards from where the five ancients had stopped moving.

Sergey grows impatient, doesn't he? he asked Elisabeta.

Yes, he is insisting they leave to head for the lair in the city. He does not want to wait for the lesser vampires' servants. He does not like to wait, he never has. He feels it makes him look small. He says clearly there are no hunters close. He is insisting Sedrick and Edward go out in plain sight, walking beside the lake. They are to take to the air and see if that draws anyone out. If it does not, he will send the whining, simpering newly made vampires next. I am quoting him.

Elisabeta clearly didn't want the ancients to think she would refer to the victims in such an uncompassionate way. Ferro sometimes found himself swamped with love for her at the most unexpected times. She was incredible, guiding the hunters through the traps and now waiting with them to see what Sergey would do. At the compound, she had Julija and Lorraine with her, shielding her from so many curious eyes watching her.

You must be very careful that the newly made vampires do not come in your direction, Ferro. If they alert, Ambrus will know you are close whether or not Sergey believes it. He will call all the servants out, and it is an army of them. They will be hungry and the five of you are ancient. Your blood is the most prized of all.

They were all very aware of the truth of what she was saying. *We will go higher, into the clouds, drifting slowly so there will be nothing to trigger an alarm. Elisabeta, I am counting on you to let us know if there is the least concern. We will stop moving if you warn us.*

Ferro again wanted to give her a task so she wouldn't panic. He knew any movement near seven master vampires was extremely dangerous. Elisabeta had spent centuries around them. She would know that just as well as all five hunters. The five ancients began their ascent just as Sedrick and Edward emerged from the small grove of trees. Edward hung back a little on the pretense of adjusting his clothing to make certain he looked fresh and clean.

Sergey is very fed up with Edward. He wants Cornel to discipline him. He has noticed that Edward takes the lion's share of all victims' blood and runs from a fight. Cornel agrees with him and said he has waited for Sergey to give him the go-ahead. He has something special planned for Edward to learn his lesson.

The effort to keep Ferro and the others informed was taking a toll on Elisabeta. He could feel her worry that she might make a mistake and they would pay the price. She paid strict attention to the vampires now, staying more and more in the place of retreat in her mind where Ferro couldn't follow. The situation was suddenly very unsettling to him. He found he didn't like her being there. He wasn't certain if she was safe or not. He had no way of knowing, and there, in the middle of danger, he couldn't ask her.

Piŋe sarnanak, it is more important that you stay safe for me than for us to have this information. If you are not safe, retreat now and stay in the compound. We will do what we always do and I will come back to you when I am finished. That is a command. His heart ached. His soul ached. She had to obey him in this one thing. This could not be the time for his little songbird to decide it was time to fly from her cage and soar free.

Why would you think I am not safe? Julija and Lorraine are with me. I am merely getting information for you.

Does Sergey have a way of detecting your presence? If he had a heartbeat in his present form, it would be accelerating so fast it might burst in his chest.

Not unless I want him to know.

The relief was tremendous. *We definitely do not want him to know.* Ferro was adamant on the subject.

The two master vampires, Sedrick and Edward, took to the air and were gone without interference. Only the sound of the waves could be heard lapping at the shores of the lake.

They are sending out the newly made vampires. Are you high enough that they cannot detect you?

Ferro hoped so, but they had no way of knowing what the range was.

Do not move, Elisabeta warned, her voice tight. *None of you.*

Below them, coming out of the forest from various directions, looking like gray, shadowy wolves, the newly made vampires emerged, slinking apprehensively on hands and knees or bellies. There were only six left and they were quite a distance from one another, something Ferro hoped would help raise the odds in their favor. Each crawled or dragged itself to the lake and then stood, stumbling as if drunk. One raised his head a few times, looking skyward, but the clouds continued to drift and he shook his head as darkness engulfed him and twice he went to his knees.

They were more bait for the hunters, but Ferro thought it was a little insulting that Sergey and the other master vampires would think such easy victims would draw them out when Sedrick and Edward hadn't managed to do so. Now the newly made vampires were trying to take to the air, running and leaping, falling flat on their faces. They were human, not Carpathian, and they had no idea how to fly. No one had ever shown them. They'd woken starving, disoriented and mostly terrified, a condition the master vampires would enjoy to the fullest for as long as they could.

Ferro, Gary, Sandu, Petru and Benedek watched impassively the terrible spectacle below, but all of them could feel Elisabeta's silent weeping. Her compassionate nature couldn't stand the horror of what these once-human men were going through. It had been their choice, through greed, to join with Sergey, but she wouldn't think or care about that; she would only see their suffering. He felt the rise of her need to aid them, to soothe and comfort them, that giving nature, her gift that she sometimes felt was a curse—as it was at that moment.

Do not, Elisabeta. That is a command. If you must break our merge to hold back aid to them, then do so now. Ferro detested that he had to use what to him amounted to the same tactics that Sergey had for all those centuries, taking Elisabeta's free will from her.

He had always thought he would be the kind of lifemate who would want his woman under his command, but the more he saw what that kind of life of total submission had done to Elisabeta's true nature, the more he knew he didn't want that. Not for her. She was beautiful inside and out, whether she knew it or not. She was strong and powerful. She was gentle and compassionate. She was intelligent. She was a partner. He wanted that. Yes, he wanted, even needed, to stand in front of her and protect her—he would always be that kind of man—but he would never want to suppress her true nature.

An extremely large owl flew from the grove of trees, talons extended, digging into the back of one of the vampires as he fell over. The vampire was lifted into the air, kicking and screaming. The others, on the ground, lifted their heads to look as the owl took their companion over the lake and dropped him into the very center, where he sank beneath the murky waters like a stone. He might drown, but he wouldn't die. Vampires didn't die, not like that.

There was a distinct snicker coming from the grove of trees, and a rustle of leaves told Ferro one of the master vampires—it sounded like Addler Astor—was hidden in the trunk of the tree right on the very edge of the grove. The owl wheeled in the air and dove at another of the cowering vampires now desperately trying to take to the air, their only way to keep from being targeted for amusement by the master vampires.

Cornel is disgusted and wants Sergey to put a stop to this. He says it will prevent the hunters from coming in to take the bait.

Cornel knew no hunter would believe that, in chasing master vampires, they would accidentally stumble across such newly made vampires unable to fend for themselves.

He and Dorin insist they call some of their servants to escort Sergey and the rest of them to the lair beneath the city so Cornel can use the computers to see what went wrong. Sergey is ignoring him, but that is what he does when he gets stubborn. It is Addler who has one of his servants playing with the newly made vampires. He does things like that to incur favor with Sergey. Sergey can be very cruel, and he enjoys cruelty and even admires it in others. Addler knows that and feeds that vile streak in Sergey as often as he can.

The vampires scrambled in all directions, looking up at the sky, watching for the owl as it dropped out of the darkness, having already selected its next victim. Addler's high-pitched giggle gave his position away. He was definitely the master vampire hidden within the tree trunk at the very edge of the grove.

Do you know Sergey's exact location, Elisabeta? It suddenly occurred to Ferro to ask. She had known where he was going and pointed the ancients in the right direction.

There is a tree, a large one in the center between five others. Addler is directly in front of him, although Sergey is higher, so he has good visibility of the lake and the surrounding area. Cornel is to the right. Dorin to the left. Directly behind him is Ambrus. Do not ever make the mistake of discounting Ambrus.

Each time Elisabeta mentioned Ambrus, Ferro not only could hear but could feel her nervousness. That told him that, although she admired Cornel, and Dorin's intelligence, Ambrus had a cunning in battle that was frightening to her.

The owl approached again in attack formation; razor-sharp talons extended as it came straight at the vampire standing awkwardly frozen, motionless onshore. The mouth of the newly made vampire was open wide as he screamed, but he still didn't move. The other vampires dove for cover, although one did manage to make it into the air. He took off into the night, triumphant, presumably following the coordinates placed in his head by one of the master vampires.

The owl struck the frozen vampire hard, knocking him to the ground, ripping the flesh from the bone, shredding his face from eye to chin, removing it completely.

Elisabeta made a single sound of pain and sorrow. Before Ferro could order her to leave him so she would not continue to see the cruelty the vampires were displaying toward their newly made brethren, she began reporting the conversation between Sergey and Cornel. Her voice was tight and dripped with tears, but she held herself together.

Cornel is arguing for a compromise. He wants Sergey to allow each of the master vampires to bring seven to ten servants with them.

Seven to ten? There were seven master vampires if one counted Sedrick and Edward. If they weren't bringing all of their servants, that meant the Carpathians were outnumbered by far more than they had counted on. The Malinov brothers had planned their coup for centuries. They'd had a tremendous amount of time to find a way to get other vampires to follow them. No one had ever thought it possible.

They will call some to go with them, but not all, because they do not want a bloodbath in the city. That would draw too much unwanted attention. Cornel still wants to draw Josef to the underground club using a woman he would be attracted to. At that time, he would bring more servants to feast.

Ferro had wanted to kill Sergey. That had been his primary mission. Now, for the safety of the Carpathian people, as well as the humans who had thrown their lot in with Tariq and were helping to guard the children and even the Carpathians, the ancients had no real choice but to get the information back to the compound. With Sergey and the other master vampires traveling with such a large army, they wouldn't be able to attack without the vampires becoming aware that they had overheard their plans and even knew their numbers. It went against the ancient hunters' code to leave the master vampires without killing a single one of them. It was almost painful to let them go.

Ferro studied the exodus of vampires, the way each of the master vampires and his servants left the forest. Ambrus was the last to leave and he kept circling above the twisted trees with their dank, gray netting of poisonous webs. He showed the suspicion of a wild animal. At one point he even put his nose to the ground and sniffed and had his servants do the same. Eventually, he gave up and took to the air, heading in the same direction as the others.

He will come back. Do not move, Elisabeta warned.

Ambrus returned a few minutes later, swooping out of the sky and dropping low to examine the earth again. He quartered the area, using his heightened sense of smell. Finally, satisfied, he followed the others.

You cannot clean up the forest or clean out the lair yet, Elisabeta cautioned. *Not if you do not want them to know you have been there.*

That was also a blow to Ferro, but the safety of the compound had to come first.

17

A symphony of power rolling through the land;
You and I together, here we make our stand.

Ferro sang his song to wake his lifemate, to bring her to him. He had woken, his first thoughts of her, his woman, his true purpose now, where before his life had been consumed by hunting—and killing the vampire. Now, the first awareness was of Elisabeta. The joy of her. The compassion in her. The soft sweetness of her. Just . . . Elisabeta.

She had become his everything. His center. His world. He had always held such a misconception of lifemates. Maybe it was just him—or perhaps all males did. He had never thought to ask Isai or Andor what they had considered before they found Julija or Lorraine. Ferro had believed he would be Elisabeta's center and she would devote herself completely to him. He would carry out his work hunting the vampire and return to her when he was able. It had never occurred to him that the power of lifemates meant he would never want to be without her. Again, it was possible that it was Elisabeta's power over him.

The moment he was aware, even before he opened his eyes, he felt joy in just being. In the miracle of knowing she existed. He found her to be the most amazing, multifaceted creature on the face of the earth. She held so much talent, so many gifts, was so giving and yet was so selfless and thought so little of herself or for herself. She was a complex, wonderful puzzle he knew he would never completely understand in the time they had to share together.

He had hunted for fresh blood, taking enough for both of them, as he did each rising. There would come a time soon when he would have to teach her to be more self-sufficient, but there were so many other lessons, and she was pushed to her limit as it was. She never protested, but he could feel her struggling at times and he felt he walked that fine line of trying to shield her and letting her take those steps on her own.

Ferro opened the ground for her and met her there, his arms welcoming. The moment Elisabeta floated to him, her body tight against his, he took her to their forest, where he knew she was the happiest. Without the modern confines of a house and the pressures of trying to figure out furniture and entertaining, they could just be Ferro and Elisabeta, lifemates, learning about each other and enjoying the process. They had this one rising before they would have to once again serve their people. This time was theirs.

Elisabeta wrapped her arms around his neck and nuzzled him, the feel of her mouth against his skin exquisite. The softness of her breasts pressing tightly to him as she took his blood added to the sheer intimacy of the erotic feeding. He had taken blood over centuries and given it, but nothing had prepared him for taking from or giving to his lifemate. She made his blood rush hotly in his veins to pool wild and thick in his groin. He savored the feeling and always would, never taking it for granted after so many centuries without her.

He pushed back her dark hair, needing to see her beloved face, her high cheekbones, her large eyes and those lush lashes. He had memorized every detail of her, but each rising he marveled at her beauty. It seemed impossible to hold the exact feel of how soft she was, or how feminine her form truly felt against his no matter how many times he took those images into his mind and etched them there.

Ferro. You think these things and I do not know how to process them. The healing saliva closed the pinpricks, her tongue sliding over his neck in a velvet, sensual rasp. She slowly sat up, blinking up at him with a faint smile on her face.

His woman. She was still uncertain what she really meant to him. She had so long been made to believe that she was worthless. It was difficult for her to really understand his feelings even when she was merged with him.

He bent his head to take her mouth. Those lips of hers. So tempting. How could he possibly resist? *I think those things because they are true, minan pine sarnanak. It would be impossible for me to do without you. You really are my world.*

That mouth of hers. Hotter than hell. Igniting a firestorm in him—in her, in them—until it burned so out of control neither could think clearly. Kissing her took him to another realm, one he hadn't known existed. Fire burned through him, flames licking along his spine, dancing over his skin, over their skin. Little sparks of electricity arced between them.

They had to stop before he couldn't. He knew it was getting more difficult for him every rising, not claiming his woman. He didn't want her to come to him for the wrong reasons—and she would. That would be so like Elisabeta, putting his needs before her own. Throughout the centuries they would spend together, he would always have to check himself that he didn't take advantage of her giving nature.

He broke off the kiss reluctantly, clothing both of them as he stood, setting her on her feet, right on the narrow deer path just at the edge of the meadow.

"Ferro?" Elisabeta touched her lips with slightly trembling fingers. "Is something wrong?"

"Everything is right, *sívamet*. Too right. You are very difficult to resist." He took her hand and began to walk along the trail with her, deeper into the woods. "I want you to pay attention to every detail around you. You are very good at that. You have to have every image in your mind so that you can reproduce each detail when you need it. That will be essential when we lay our traps this next rising."

She moistened her lips, her gaze shifting up to his face. "Our traps?"

He nodded and pulled her closer, matching her shorter steps. "Cornel has devised a plan to attack the nightclub. He plans to let loose an army of their servants, all hungry for fresh blood, a diversion to acquire young Josef for them. And you for Sergey. We do not want to lose any humans to their army of servants. We have called our own army to combat them. You are our secret weapon against them, Elisabeta. And you are my secret weapon against Sergey."

She walked beside him in silence, her back and shoulders straight. His woman, up to the challenge. Thoughtful. "Sergey is very dangerous. Cunning. Never forget that he has slivers of each of his brothers residing in his brain. If that is not enough to beware of, he also has two of Xavier, the high mage."

"Does he know how to access their aid without you?" Ferro asked, keeping the inquiry gentle. It was always a sore subject whenever he brought up just how much Elisabeta had helped Sergey against his brothers over the years. She didn't really understand that her own nature had betrayed her. It was impossible for her to watch the victim of cruelty suffer, no matter if that person was good or bad themselves. She was compelled by her nature to help them.

"I have never seen him do so. He has a disconnect in his mind with certain things, especially anything to do with magic or psychic abilities beyond Carpathian skills. His safeguards were always the weakest of the brothers'. They were always extremely cruel to him over his safeguards."

"And you aided him?"

Elisabeta nodded. "I had to be careful when I was teaching him to weave more strands because he would get so angry when he couldn't do it. I felt bad that I made him feel less intelligent. I didn't mean to. I spent time studying how he learned things. Once I knew, it was so much easier to teach him things."

The entire time they walked along the narrow winding path in the deeper forest that moved around and between trees, he could see she was scanning both sides of the path and noting every tree and bush along the way. She didn't seem to miss anything even though the conversation they were having was obviously important.

"You taught him every one of his safeguards? He has never made up any of his own?"

"No. He is incapable of straying from utterly basic safeguards or the more intricate ones I taught him. He normally used those to keep his brothers and cousins away from his sleeping chambers. He was always paranoid, with good reason, that they might want him dead."

"Did they want him dead?"

"Yes, they thought him the weakest link."

"And without you, he was."

She nodded. "I made certain that he became an asset to them, without making them feel as if he was in any way a threat to them. It was a difficult balance and I made mistakes. His ego, especially when they made fun of him, could make him especially cruel. He had to believe he was the one outsmarting them. It is strange that over the centuries I lost sight of that. I began to believe he was the one who was so powerful on his own."

"Sergey had to know it was you."

"He knew, but that made him angrier and more resentful. I suppose that was why he set out to convince me I was worthless to him."

Ferro realized just what a terrible balancing act Elisabeta always had to have with Sergey. He would want to feel as powerful as his brothers. He had been a mean, cruel boy, killing animals in the forest and then, later, human children, preying on those weaker than himself in order to bolster his belief that he was every bit as formidable as his brothers. He was just cunning enough to hide his sickness from those adults around him in order to keep them from destroying him.

His father was off hunting vampires, preoccupied with his life. In those days, parents often paid little attention to the children as they reached the older ages. Other Carpathians took over training. A boy like Sergey could easily slip through the cracks. He would become a loner, going into the forest to carry out his ugliness while his much more intelligent brothers held the spotlight.

"He was close to his sister, Ivory. She protected him from much of the teasing from his older brothers. I think she softened it so it sounded less cruel and more affectionate. They were often together. When she disappeared, he was devastated. Even that was seen by his brothers as weakness. They wanted him to hate the prince, to turn on him as they had. To blame Vlad for her disappearance. Sergey blamed himself for not looking after her. The crueler his brothers were to him, the more that sickness in his mind came out and he started that ugly behavior, going into the forest and hurting animals and then children."

There was compassion in her mind for the lost soul of Sergey Malinov and for all those he tortured and destroyed over the long centuries he lived. She was incapable of feeling loathing for him or any other. There was no such thing as hatred in her makeup. She sought to prevent Sergey from feeling the need to hurt others. On some level she simply couldn't understand that driving compulsion in him and others like him to watch others suffer.

"You are certain Sergey will only use safeguards you have taught him to weave, then?" Ferro reiterated.

"I am very certain," Elisabeta said.

"I think we have gone far enough," Ferro decided. "Have you memorized the entire pathway?"

Elisabeta looked around her and nodded. "I believe so."

He framed her face and kissed her again, just because there was no resisting her, especially not there in their forest. "Of course you have. We need to put in a little time with shifting fast, *piŋe sarnanak*. I know you have no objections to that." She particularly loved shifting and flying and she'd become very adept at it.

"Right here?" There was a touch of eagerness in her voice.

They were in deep forest and he had always had her shift near the edge of the meadow. It was much more dangerous with trees close together and branches overlapping. They had practiced flying through the forest, but they'd stayed within the trees on the outskirts just ringing the meadow.

"Yes. I believe you are more than ready for shifting and flying through the interior of the woods. We will start out slow, Elisabeta." He couldn't help pouring caution and command into his voice. It was always dangerous in the smaller confines of the trees. One mistake and it would be easy to suffer an injury—or worse. He knew Elisabeta had the skills. She was too detail-oriented not to. She hadn't missed a single thing he'd shown or told her since he'd started with any of their lessons, and she loved flying.

"I want you to be able to move very fast through these woods, whether it be on foot, as an owl or in any other way you have to do it," he added. "We've gone through them. This is our home. Our haven. It is where both of us feel safest."

Dark suspicion crept into her mind and then her eyes but she refrained from voicing a single question, nor did she go into his head as she could have to read what his intentions were. Elisabeta's brain was sharp and moved fast, figuring out what he planned. He didn't want her to be afraid, not for herself or for him or anyone else. To distract her, he pointed to the upper branches of the shortest tree.

"We are both going to start at the bend in the path, running and shifting as we go. You will have to rid yourself of clothes, hold the image of the owl in your head, every detail, and lift yourself into the air all at the same time."

They had practiced running and shifting in the meadow over and over, so he knew she could easily shed her clothes and become the owl. They'd also practiced the owl rising into the air and moving through the trees at the edge of the woods. Those trees were farther apart, but some branches were still interlocking. She had been extremely successful at that as well. Now, he wanted all the pieces put together because this might be life or death.

Ferro would stay merged with her so there would be no mistakes. He kept his hand firmly wrapped in hers as they walked to the bend in the very narrow pathway. The trail was no more than a deer path cut through the brush and trees, not really allowing for both of them to walk side by side. He had led the way so when he stopped and turned, she was ahead of him. He allowed her hand to slip from his.

Go, Elisabeta. Run. Shift. Fly. He pushed the commands into her mind.

She didn't hesitate, taking off instantly. He was right behind her, stride for stride, his footsteps in hers, his breath on her neck. She was astonishingly fast. They had practiced repeatedly and he had noticed that she had improved every time, but she also went over and over the procedure in her mind until she was faster and better at it every time.

Her clothes were gone and she was already the small Western Screech Owl in the air, maneuvering through the low branches of the trees toward the one he had indicated he wanted her to come to rest on. She actually flew faster than he would have liked for their first time, but he didn't distract her by admonishing her to slow down. She landed on the exact branch he had designated, digging her talons into the limb, her wings out to steady herself, and then folding them neatly into her sides. Ferro landed beside her.

That was amazing, Elisabeta. I am very proud of you. Terrified, but proud. She might need that speed. *We will fly back to the bend at a much more leisurely pace and do it again.*

He didn't want to tire her out. She would need every ounce of strength when they went up against the army the Carpathians were certain they would be facing. This night was for them—perhaps the only one they would have. One never knew what the future would hold and he wanted time for them. It seemed they got very little for themselves.

He had her make the run two more times before he called a halt to her continuing lessons. She really didn't need them. They were more for his peace of mind.

We do not have a lot of time to be alone together, Elisabeta, and I wish to spend what we have enjoying every moment with you. I share you with so many out of necessity, but I do prefer to have you to myself. This night is for us.

I prefer that as well, she admitted.

There was a sensual quality in her voice he'd never heard before, one that played over his skin in spite of being deep within the owl's body. He was merged with her, mind to mind, and it was impossible not to feel the way she responded to him both physically and emotionally. He wanted her with every breath he drew, and it felt as if Elisabeta wanted him the same way.

They flew back to their favorite spot in the forest, just on the outer edge of the meadow but in the shadow of the trees. As they both shifted to their human forms, he waved his hand to provide them with the thickest of fur rugs. Nudity didn't bother him and he preferred to look at her feminine form. If she was at all uncomfortable, he would provide her with clothing. Both could regulate their temperature without a problem, and if the weather proved unpredictable—and already a small storm had moved in—he could provide a transparent roof overhead.

The clouds swirled overhead, moving to cover the small slice of moon and blot out the stars. They would need that gathering storm and the more natural, the better. The Carpathians coming in to aid them from all directions were already doing so, hopefully unseen by any of Sergey's spies. The breaking weather would definitely be helpful. A series of storms had been predicted over the next few risings, a good break for them. The Carpathians traveling their way would have adequate cover and hopefully, during the battle, they could utilize the storms as well.

Fingers of mist drifted across the meadow and through the trees. Ferro immediately provided a transparent roof so they could see the slow rolling clouds overhead and the first of the silvery drops as they began to fall from the sky. He laid back, stretching out, drawing Elisabeta with him, so both could look upward at the display. Her head rested on his shoulder, her body tucked in tight against his side. He was aware of her every curve. The softness of her form against the hardness of his.

"I never noticed how beautiful rain could be until this moment," he admitted. "Instead of individual beads falling, each looks like a thin silver streak dropping out of the darkness. Each rising I find something new and amazing you have gifted me with."

She turned her head to look up at him. "Ferro. You are the true gift. I have spent each rising for hundreds of years living in terror. Now, each is a joy, whether or not there is fear, because there is you."

Elisabeta turned completely, her body sliding over his boldly so that she was blanketing him. Her hands framed his face. "*Hän sívamak*, you have my heart. Always, you have my heart." She brushed kisses across his eyes and then down his face to the corner of his mouth.

Ferro's body reacted with a hot rush of blood pounding through his veins, thundering in his ears, to center in his groin. She moved her hips subtly, rubbing against him, inflaming him further. She began to move down his body, kissing his chin and then his throat.

Ferro closed his eyes, his hands moving in her hair, stroking and massaging. He needed to be satisfied with what they had together already. She had come so far so fast. Asking any more of her was selfish, and she took him to heaven with that perfect mouth of hers every single rising.

Elisabeta lifted her head. "Ferro? What more? I catch needs in you that are fleeting, but those needs are very strong. I am your lifemate. I provide for you."

He suppressed a groan. "You are providing for me. The things you do to me are beautiful, Elisabeta. What we do to one another is an expression of love."

She studied his face for a long moment. "*One* expression of love. I see that in your mind. I also see other things as well. Intriguing things. I want to do those things with you, Ferro, not just one. *All* of them."

His fist bunched in her hair. She could drive him right to the very edge of his control, and he had always thought himself extremely disciplined. He wanted everything he gave her, everything they did together, to be perfect for her. To be beautiful for her. "When you are ready, *sívamet*, we will do them."

She pressed a kiss to his chest and then looked up again, her dark gaze colliding with his. "How do we know if I am ready if we do not ever try?"

Ferro's heart stuttered. She was killing him. How was he going to protect her if she was going to lie on top of him, give him those innocent, seductress eyes and move her silken body over his already inflamed nerve endings, threatening to drive him past all sanity?

"Ferro?" She pressed kisses to his throat and chin. "I am asking you to show me. To teach me. I want everything with you. Everything there is."

He stared up at her beloved face, love for her nearly overwhelming him. "*Minan piŋe sarnanak*, no woman will ever be as loved or as treasured as you."

Very gently he rolled her over so that she was beneath him. He sat up slowly as he laid her out before him there on the softest of thick furs, not wanting anything to mar her pleasure, not a single twig, pebble, or even the swell of the ground. The feel of the fur as it rubbed against her sensitized skin would heighten her pleasure, not detract from it. He took his time looking down at her body, that perfect feminine form that was so outrageously different from his and yet fit so perfectly with his.

Elisabeta's gaze clung to his, trust in her dark eyes. Love for her welled up, a tidal wave of emotion, shaking him as nothing in his long life ever had. He had never considered that he could ever feel such strong emotions, but the strength and depth of his love for her was almost beyond his comprehension. There were no real words to express that to her, so he simply opened his mind more fully to her to allow her to see what she meant to him.

He had been so careful to protect her from the emptiness of his past, from the disturbing battles and kills. She was too sensitive an empath, and there was no need for her to have to share his violent past, but she needed to see what she truly meant to him. She deserved that much. If she caught glimpses of other things, he hoped that didn't diminish what he wanted to give her in this moment.

Tet vigyázam. He whispered the truth into her mind. Saying he loved her in their language. It was not enough, would never be enough, but it was all he had.

He stroked his hand lovingly from her throat, over her collarbone, down the soft swell of her breasts to her rib cage and belly, lower still to her mound and the dark curls covering treasure beyond any price, that secret haven meant for him. All the while he let himself drown in her dark eyes. Let her see how vulnerable he felt when they were alone together and he could show her how much she meant to him.

"Can you feel me, Elisabeta? Inside your mind? Merged with you? Loving you?"

She nodded, her gaze soft, melting. He felt the way she poured love into his mind. It was impossible not to feel her there, filling him, giving him everything she was, because that was her way. Elisabeta never held anything back when she made up her mind to give. For the first time, he had given her the same, letting her see she was his world.

"I want you to feel me inside you. In your body. Moving in you. Filling you with love. With me. I want our bodies to be one, just the way our minds are."

He watched her eyes. Those eyes of hers that said so much, that were so poignant. If she was too afraid, he would see it there almost before he would know it in her mind. Her fear might be in her mind, but admittedly, when she didn't know what to expect, she was often afraid but willing to try. But her eyes . . . They shared the same soul, and it would be there in her eyes that he would see the truth.

"If you are not ready, we will wait." He would find the patience because she was worth the wait. "If it takes years, we will wait." He let her see that he meant it. "Being with you is a gift I never really expected to have and it is greater than I ever thought possible. You bring me such joy, Elisabeta. *Minan piṅe sarnanak*, you truly hold my heart and soul in your hands."

Elisabeta reached up and framed his face with her hands. "You are what I hold dear, Ferro. You are what I believe in. I wake with joy and look forward to each rising, wondering what new journey we will have together. You have taught me so many things already and I am always eager for each lesson. Sometimes I am afraid, that is true, but I trust you. Each time I have put my faith in you, you have come through for me, so my trust runs very deep. More than anything, I want to be wholly yours in every way."

He could hear the ring of truth in her voice. Feel it in her mind. See it in her eyes. For Elisabeta to be able to trust anyone, let alone a Carpathian male, especially one as dominant and frightening as he knew he appeared, was a miracle in itself. The fact that she gave that trust to him each rising, each time he called her from her slumber and brought her from the healing earth to once more face new lessons that had to terrify her, humbled him beyond imagining.

Ferro bent his head to brush a kiss gently over her eyes and then her lips. His teeth bit down gently on her lower lip and then slipped over her chin to her throat. His hands were more possessive than he had ever allowed himself to be with her, sliding over her skin, claiming her body, gentle in his touch, but making it clear that she was his.

He kissed his way to the curve of her breast, found her left nipple and suckled there, drawing her soft flesh into the heat of his mouth and then using the edge of his teeth, making her gasp as he tugged and rolled her right nipple with his hand. He kissed his way down her ribs to her belly button, feeling the delicate little shudder of anticipation that went through her body before lifting his head, knowing his eyes were blazing at her. Possessively. He felt that way.

"You are wholly mine, Elisabeta, in every way. I'm wholly yours. I want you to be very sure. I am not trying to rush you." He gave her a rueful smile. "Or perhaps I am." He settled his fist around the girth of his cock. "Perhaps I am. My body is impatient for yours, there is no hiding that fact from you."

His smeared the leaking pearly drops of liquid over the aching, sensitive crown with his thumb and then slid it between her lips. Her eyes darkened with passion and her tongue curled around his thumb and then lapped at the pad, making his cock jerk. Her hungry gaze dropped to his heavy erection. He knew exactly what it felt like when she took him into the heat of her mouth. She was so naturally sensual, and yet she had no idea.

He bent his head once more to hers and kissed her. There was fire there. Pure flames. They burned through him until he could barely breathe or think rationally. He wanted to eat her up. Devour her. He might have started out kissing her gently, but that went away fast when she responded with her fingers bunching in his hair and the other hand digging nails into his buttocks, pulling him closer to her, pulling his weight right over her. He lifted his head and once more started down her body with kisses and nips.

"Ferro." There was an ache in her voice.

"Your body has to be ready to take mine. Have patience." His little songbird. Nearly as impatient as he was. That was a good omen.

Her skin was exquisite. The taste every bit as addicting as her blood, as the nectar between her legs. He was making his way in that direction, and already the need to devour her was there, filling his mind until he felt nearly feral, the wild craving driving him to lift her legs over his arms, opening her to him as he settled between her thighs and took that first long, slow lick of the perfect aphrodisiac.

Elisabeta cried out. Her hips bucked. That mixture of citrus and sandalwood spilled onto his tongue, threatening to drive him insane. He clamped down on her legs, holding her in place, one hand splayed wide on her belly.

I am only getting started. You have felt my mouth on you before. His tongue circled her clit and then flicked. Her entire body shuddered in reaction. *Look up at the rain. Relax and let your body feel the pleasure I am giving to you.*

There was always pleasure, but never like this. This burns. Coils deeper. Burns deeper and hotter as if you are branding me deep inside.

I want to eat you alive, piye sarnanak, not worry that you will be afraid of the things I do with my mouth and teeth to get your body ready for mine. Will you trust me? You will feel pleasure, I promise.

I will always trust you.

That was all the consent he needed. He had held himself in check with her since the moment he had first discovered she was his lifemate. He had been careful to suppress his wild nature in order to be whatever his lifemate needed. Now, he let himself feast on her, an aggressive assault on her senses using his lips, tongue, his fingers, flicking and tapping and then raking with the edge of his teeth only to soothe with licks. He suckled gently and then stabbed deep, switching from gentle to rough until she was writhing and sobbing his name, her nails biting deep into his shoulders or, alternately, her fingers fisting in his hair.

He took her over the edge twice before he was satisfied that she was slick with heat, mindless with need, and ready for the girth of his body. The relentless pounding of his blood through his cock was nearly terrifying as he knelt up between her legs. Her gaze clung to his, her teeth biting down on her lower lip. She looked radiant, disheveled, sensual, and so completely his.

Ferro pressed the broad crown of his cock into the scalding heat of her slick entrance, feeling the flames licking up his spine with a ferocious burn that spread over his body, a wildfire out of control. He had to breathe deep to keep from slamming into that tight, scorching sheath. Instead, he fought for control and pressed into her with measured care, inch by slow inch.

Her tight silken muscles resisted but gave way reluctantly in the face of his persistent invasion. Her breath exploded out of her lungs in a long rush. His did the same. She was a pure white-hot silken fist grasping his cock tight, massaging and milking, a thousand fiery tongues licking and stroking, wet and so scorching hot he was nearly out of his mind with the need to move fast and hard in her.

Elisabeta's hips bucked. She squirmed. Pushed herself onto him. Caught at him. *Ferro.* His name was a plea. For more. For everything he could give her.

"Almost there, *piŋe sarnanak.* Another minute. We have to be careful." His voice was nearly hoarse with the effort to hold back.

I do not want to be careful.

It was the first time his little songbird sounded out of control, impatient and just a little bossy. He loved that. Loved that he could give that to her. He pushed deeper, found her barrier, gripped her hips hard with his hands and took the pain from her mind as he surged forward, letting her only feel the explosive pleasure as his cock ground over her most sensitive spot. She cried out as he buried himself deep, fully planting himself in her, so they were not only sharing minds but sharing bodies.

He paused for a moment, savoring the feeling of Elisabeta's feminine sheath surrounding his cock, gripping him so tightly, so ferociously, as if she would never let him go, feeling her heartbeat right through the walls of her silken sheath, treasuring the intimacy of the moment between them. It was the most exquisite, perfect, amazing moment of his life.

For me, too. You have given me so much, Ferro, and then you give this to me. Her eyes were dark with passion and liquid with emotion. Silver drops tipped her lashes, just like the dazzling ones falling from the sky above their heads. *If I have not yet told you, tet vigyázam, beloved.*

His heart clenched hard in his chest. Turned over. *Have no doubt, Elisabeta, that you are in my heart and soul for eternity.*

Then he began to move, withdrawing slowly, savoring the drag of her muscles as they reluctantly released him, stimulating every nerve ending. He surged forward hard and fast, driving through her folds so that lightning seemed to streak through his body, through hers. She cried out following the direction of his hands, lifting her hips to meet his every thrust.

Her instincts, as always, were right with him, a sensual feast he could never get enough of. Her eyes, her body, the way her breasts swayed and jolted with every surge of his hips as he drove his body into the paradise of hers. Her soft little moans began to rise in urgency. The pleasure in her mind expanding to surround him the way her silken tunnel surrounded his cock. He could feel her heart beating hard and fast right through his thick shaft in time with his, that was how tight she was, squeezing down on him like a vise.

His breath came in harsh, ragged gasps, accompanying her soft moans, a different music, a different song, but one that resonated with their bodies. The rain hit the roof above their heads, a counterpoint to the building crescendo, the wild explosive music tearing up from every cell in his body, every cell in hers, to come together in a fiery climax to their ever-building symphony.

Ferro. Breathless. Fearful.

Let go, sívamet. Fall with me. Trust me.

Elisabeta's body was coiled tight, and just like that she relaxed, giving herself to him, putting her mind and body into his hands. Her tight silken sheath clamped down around his shaft, strangling him, milking him, biting down with scorching fire. He couldn't take his gaze from hers, watching her go there with him, as the two of them were taken some place neither had ever been before. Her gaze clung to his, a little dazed, but soft with love, passion darkening her eyes.

He gripped her hips harder as he emptied himself into her, the wild, helpless jerking of his cock a fiery, volatile reaction to the continuous grip of her silken muscles working him, eager for every drop of his seed. The more he gave her, the hotter the walls of her sheath, until one orgasm rolled into the next and wrung them both out. Until even the little aftershocks were enough to send perfect shuddering through his body as he shared them with her, as he collapsed over the top of her.

Ferro let himself absorb her soft feminine form, the rightness of loving her, his body still in hers, his mind merged with hers, while their hearts pounded together. He didn't try to think, he just let himself feel love for her. Feel euphoria. Feel one hand in his hair and the other gliding down his back. Hear the rain and their heartbeats.

He had no idea how long he lay there but it took effort to slide his body from hers and roll off of her, to lie beside her. Elisabeta lay sprawled out beside him on the fur, staring up at the silvery streaks of rain and the lightly rolling clouds. He threaded his fingers through hers and brought her hand to his chest over his wildly pounding heart.

Are you all right? He wasn't certain he could get enough air to breathe, so it seemed much more prudent to use their telepathic form of communication.

I am not certain if I am alive. In any case, if I am not, I am good where I am. Do not send a rescue party.

He laughed, mostly in his mind, sharing her amusement. Sharing his joy in her—in them. He brought her hand up to his mouth and brushed a kiss to her palm before pressing her fingers to his lips. *I think I might still be right there with you in outer space somewhere, riding the tail of a comet.* He scraped his teeth back and forth over the pads of her fingers.

I think you should have started with that lesson, Ferro. Perhaps we could have dispensed with all the rest.

Elisabeta sounded very serious and thoughtful, but her mind, merged with his, mellow and serene, held that amusement he found so incredibly wonderful, mostly because it was so different from those first risings when he had sung to call her to him.

He drew his thumb back and forth across her knuckles. *No doubt you are right, minan piŋe sarnanak.* She was about most things. Who was he to say, especially on such an important subject, anything different?

Her soft laughter poured over and into him. When she did that, it always felt like a cleansing, like she filled every crack and tear in his mind that all the centuries of hunting and killing, all the centuries of living in a gray void, had caused. She filled him with love.

18

Once blinded by the wicked, now your eyes are clear;
Look inside yourself, there's nothing left to fear.

Elisabeta can't keep doing this every rising," Ferro objected. "Gary, you see the toll it's taking on her."

Gary nodded. "There's no doubt it's hard on her. I still don't know what's causing the infection. I can heal the deep scoring to the brain, the one that results after the infection, as can some of the more skilled ancients, but none of us can actually take away the infection the way she can. I don't know any other word to call it, although technically, it isn't an infection. It isn't bacterial or viral. If it was, I could heal it. I've tried to mimic her actions. She has a gift, Ferro. She's unique."

Ferro didn't need to be told that his lifemate was unique or special or gifted. He already knew those things about her. He didn't want to take out the frustration he was feeling at his failure to protect Elisabeta on Gary at every turn. He had hoped to give her female friends and a home, where she could slowly learn the things that would make her comfortable in their world, but instead, every rising she was called on to repeat the same duties, clearing up repeated infections.

Josef, Danny and Amelia were infected nightly, Tariq nearly nightly, the ancients the least. The numbers were increasing, although because everyone was scanned nightly, the scorching was much lighter and easier for Elisabeta to remove. Still, the number of people she had to help tired her, although she never complained. Sandu, Andor, Dragomir and Gary stayed closer, as concerned as Ferro about her health.

"We've been keeping track of what everyone has been doing throughout their days and nights," Gary said. "Trying to find a pattern, something everyone has in common. Keep in mind, these are human, Carpathian, men, women and children. A huge mix."

The door to Tariq's large meeting room crashed open and Josef bounded in. Ferro tightened his arms around Elisabeta and swung her away from the entrance, shielding her with his larger body. Startled, the action took her out of Tariq's brain, bringing her back into the mix with the various ancients who had come together to try to puzzle out what was spreading the infection.

Josef didn't seem to notice the frowns or glares of the older Carpathians or the amused looks of the women. "I found it. I know what's causing the infection. They were so clever. I can't believe I didn't figure this out sooner." There was admiration in his voice. "Seriously. And by the way, Ferro, Cornel saying they were working on some new algorithm to track the hunters was a bunch a bullshit. He knew Sergey wasn't going to understand whether he could or couldn't do what he said. He wanted access to the computers. Although they do have a program that they started working on that senses energy if a hunter is moving in the air . . ."

"Josef." Tariq sounded patient. "What is causing the infection?"

"Oh, yeah. It was a really simple idea actually, and I should have realized it. We all use computers now. Even the kids. They just needed to get someone to bring their program into the main computer and let the virus spread to all the programs. One of the kids downloaded a game that carried the virus and it spread slowly at first and then took off, moving from program to program. You don't have to have the original game. Danny and Amelia both have the game. At first I couldn't figure out how the scorching was happening in the brain, but then I had to think outside the box when nothing else added up. So eventually I came up with the idea that they were able to embed magic into the code through the process of elimination, and asked Julija to take a look."

"Is that even possible?" Maksim asked.

Ferro kept his eyes locked on the kid. He settled back in his chair, Elisabeta beside him. It was no wonder Cornel had his sights on Josef. The boy really was a true genius. It would be such a relief to finally have the mystery solved.

"Not only possible, but they also programmed everyone who was infected to open the gates to the compound on command," Josef continued. "That way, if one was stopped, a number of others would obey the vampires. The infection would cause chaos, hopefully turning the ancients against one another. It really is a stroke of genius. The code is simple but extremely effective. They covered all the bases."

"Are you able to get rid of it?" Tariq asked.

Josef shrugged. "It's eaten through most or all of your programs. Everyone's personal computers have to be wiped as well. It's going to take a while to fix this. Your security people, all the kids. It's a process. I'm going to have to check your computers at the club as well. If you used any of the same programs, you could have infected those computers."

Ferro winced inwardly. They had to tell the kid that he was being targeted by Cornel and Dorin. Sergey couldn't think past getting Elisabeta back, but his two cousins were set on bringing Josef into their fold any way they could.

Tariq waved Josef toward a chair. "We have some things we have to go over with you, Josef. As you know, the Morrison Center for psychic research has become a front for the vampires to track possible lifemates for Carpathian males. They wanted to get to them before we could. They also found psychic males. They're recruiting and using them as pawns. Some of the males have been hired to work in my club. Others are being turned into vampires and used as the first wave of their army against us, as you saw when they attacked the other night."

Josef sat quietly, a feat Ferro hadn't thought possible for the kid.

His brain is always assessing every possibility, Gary said. *It never stops.*

Elisabeta agreed. *I do not think it is possible for him to slow his brain down. He tries to. When I was working on him, he tried not to think too much about what was happening to him or to the others, but he could not stop himself. He was especially upset with that first time, when he said things to Tariq. They were very unlike him. He went over and over the things he said in his mind to try to puzzle out why he had said them.*

Ferro was gifted at reading others, and a young Carpathian should have been easy, but Josef held himself aloof, away from the others. Ferro could guess why. The boy was different and had been his entire life. He hadn't lost his ability to feel emotions, and the opinions of others had to be hurtful. He often was the smartest one in the room but was overlooked because of his youth. He had to have been frustrated that no one listened to him. He'd learned to school his features into an expressionless mask when he was in the room with ancient hunters who most likely would look down on him. He wore his spiked colored hair and piercings as armor. All the while, he fought for his people in his own way.

The boy has courage. It was a high compliment coming from Sandu.

Ferro nodded his head. *I agree. I do not want him walking into the lion's den. No doubt he will volunteer to go to the club the moment Tariq informs him that Cornel hopes to lure him there with a woman and acquire him.*

Gary, merged with the other ancients, gave the mental equivalent of shaking his head. *We can't take chances with him. He's far too valuable to the Carpathian people. I gave my word to Mikhail that he would be safe. He gave his word to his adopted parents. They nearly lost him once before, and the prince doesn't want to have to tell them again that Josef is in danger.*

Ferro could well imagine that Josef was in a perpetual state of being in danger. The boy was slender but appearances were deceptive. A rod of steel ran through him. His devotion to the Carpathian people ran as deep as every warrior's.

"Based on the intelligence Elisabeta has provided for us, we don't believe Sergey is necessarily the mastermind behind the plot to bring Mikhail down. With his older brothers dead, we think Sergey's cousins, Cornel and Dorin, are working behind the scenes to carry out the original plans. Both are gifted, as were the older Malinov brothers." Tariq paused, his gaze sweeping around at the men and women sitting at the table in the room.

Josef followed his gaze and then came back to rest thoughtfully on the leader. "They're planning a major bloodbath, aren't they?" There was resignation in his voice. "It has to be a diversion. What are they really after?"

The boy was really too smart.

"Sergey hopes to lure Elisabeta there, and Cornel hopes to lure you." Tariq was honest.

Traian shook his head. "Josef can't go near that place."

Josef frowned. "Excuse me, Tariq, but that doesn't make sense. We have to break this down. If those psychic males were planted at the club over time and not just since Sergey took over, then there was no way of knowing that he would lose Elisabeta. Cornel would have no way of knowing I would make a trip from the Carpathian Mountains to the United States. If a plan was made by the Malinov brothers for the vampires to create a diversion, then it was for another reason altogether. Elisabeta and I are merely additional reasons now."

That kid is worth his weight in gold, Petru said. *He is right.*

There was a stunned silence. Traian inclined his head in a show of respect toward Josef. "You never cease to astound me. Tariq, what do you have that the Malinov brothers would want that they would risk exposure to the world for? Not only exposure to the world, but the retaliation of every Carpathian hunter coming after them?"

"I can't imagine."

"You have lived here for a very long time. You have been in the States longer than any other Carpathian and lived among humans the longest," Traian reminded.

Tariq shook his head. "I'm sorry. That's all true, but it doesn't mean anything to me. I have no idea why they would target me, other than I represent the prince here, and that's recent."

"Elisabeta?" Traian turned to her. "Do you have any idea what the Malinov brothers were after?"

As usual, when asked a direct question in front of so many people, she shut down, withdrawing into the safety of her mind merge with Ferro.

Ferro mentally bared his teeth at her birth brother. He knew better than to put Elisabeta on the spot like that. There were too many people in the room, too many eyes on her. Too many ways for her to be wrong.

There is no wrong answer, piŋe sarnanak. Traian may be your brother, but he is a thoughtless lout and his lifemate will spend centuries teaching him how to be kind before she ever allows him in her bed again.

Not only did he allow his beloved woman to hear him, but Sandu, Andor and Dragomir heard as well. All three of the ancients looked at Traian and Joie. Red flames flickered in the deep black of Sandu's eyes.

Strangely, Tariq and Gary had gone silent, and once again Ferro got the very uneasy feeling he'd had almost from the moment he'd brought his lifemate from the rich healing soil that first rising when he'd claimed her. He flicked them a quick gaze. There was nothing to be seen on either face, but he hadn't expected there to be.

I apologize, Elisabeta, Traian said immediately. *It was thoughtless of me. I was thinking only of solving the mystery. I know you're tired and probably frightened by all of us. I have to ask you again, though, do you have any idea what the Malinovs may have wanted from Tariq? Did you overhear them talking? It would have to be something extremely important for them to risk so much. Sergey might not even know or understand what they were talking about.*

I do not . . . She trailed off.

Cornel and Dorin would know. Sergey is fixed only on getting you back. That is all he thinks of. Cornel and Dorin would know what their cousins were after. They would know the importance of it and would seek it as well.

Ferro.

Ferro knew his lifemate deliberately addressed him alone.

I need time to think about this. There were so many conversations. So many things said, and this is important, so I have to really give myself time to sort it all out.

"Elisabeta will need time to think about this, Tariq. She does not want to rush an answer. In the meantime, we can discuss the fact that the danger to Elisabeta and Josef is very real and we need to keep a close watch on them. Josef, will you be able to work on the club's computers remotely?" Ferro asked.

Deliberately, Ferro engaged with Tariq, pushing just a little to see if the leader really wanted answers to the question Traian had proposed.

Josef was slow in answering. He shrugged casually. "I'm not certain. I have to go over the programs here first and wipe everything clean and reinstall them. Julija needs to work with me just to make certain the magic isn't lingering behind in the computers. In the meantime, everyone, including your security people, has to stay off their computers. If they took laptops or tablets home, they need to wipe them clean and start over. If they have families, they should make certain they do the same with those computers, and someone should check their children or spouses to make certain no one is infected."

Ferro had the feeling the boy was hedging a bit. He was leaving himself an opening to go to the club. He didn't think it was because Josef was foolhardy, it was more he thought he needed to serve the Carpathian people in whatever capacity he could.

He does not believe he will ever be a decent hunter of the vampire, does he? he asked Gary, deliberately engaging with him, trying to feel his way. That threat to Elisabeta was definitely back, yet Gary was still the same, still felt calm and matter-of-fact.

No. I've seen that in his mind many times. His genius lies with technology, although he is skilled in healing and he does have many skills in fighting already. He's been in battles with werewolves and vampires and done very well.

He is alive, that is saying a lot about him if he managed to remain so after a fight with either. Ferro regarded the boy, trying to think ahead of him.

Elisabeta's gentle essence filled his mind, her soothing nature creating that sense of peace she always brought with her. He glanced down at her and found she was looking up at him with her dark, beautiful eyes. His heart clenched hard in his chest. He tightened his fingers around hers and brought their clasped hands over his heart. He loved her with every part of his being. More than he thought possible. More than he knew love existed in the world.

He has been told often that he will never make a great hunter of the vampire. That he is too slow. Too thin. His body type too wrong. There is another who is close to him, one he admires, who says vicious, cutting things to him to make him feel less, and he believes it because he feels different and apart from others. He has been made to feel that way for many years.

Ferro felt a sense of protection well up for the boy. *Where are those who should be caring for this boy?*

His parents are dead. He did not believe his adopted parents wanted him until they came for him when he went with Skyler to find her lifemate and took him back from the werewolves. Elisabeta had found that information in Josef's mind.

Why would he think his adopted parents did not want him? Ferro had no idea why he was pursuing the matter. It wasn't like he was in the market for taking on a boy like Josef. He didn't know the first thing about young kids—especially modern ones, and Josef was definitely modern. Ferro considered himself a throwback to the old days.

They have a son. He was or is very jealous of Josef—at least it feels that way to me when he says the things to Josef that he does. I have no real way of reading him unless he was here. I feel sad for him as well. The misunderstanding of youth when parents are not paying close attention can be brutal.

Ferro didn't know about that. His parents were long gone from the world and it was difficult to access any real memory of his childhood. He did know they had instilled a sense of duty and honor in him.

"We have to go to the club and identify those males working for the Malinovs," Maksim said. "The club is quite large. We'll need several of our most sensitive to move through the floors as quickly as possible and scan."

"The Malinov brothers will have provided them with some kind of shield to prevent us from reading them," Tariq pointed out. "If it was going to be that easy, we would have discovered them already."

Ferro knew that was true. *Elisabeta, these male psychics working in the club, if we go there and are in another form, moving unseen, as we were in the forest, would they be able to detect our presence the way the newly made vampires were able to do?*

If they are close together, I think they will, although they will not know you are there for the specific purpose of finding them.

"When we were hunting Sergey and the other master vampires, the newly made vampires could detect us when they were together," Ferro told the other hunters. "It has something to do with the psychics being close to one another and their gifts specifically blending together. However it works, they can detect our presence, even when we're unseen. Elisabeta thinks it will occur the same way in the club if the males are close to one another, although they will not know the reason we are there."

"You have their names, right?" Josef asked.

"Naturally. They applied for the job, interviewed and got it," Maksim said.

Josef put his laptop on the table and opened it. "This is clean, you don't have to worry. If you have the names, I can check them against the ones in the database of the Morrison Center. They tried to wipe some of them, but I have all the original data and receive it as it comes in. I might not get all of them, but we can get most of them. That should cut down on a big part of the search."

Ferro liked the kid more and more. He was also beginning to think there was more to technology than he'd given it credit for.

Tariq pulled up his laptop. "This isn't clean," he said. "But I've got our secret weapon, Elisabeta, if she doesn't mind once more helping me out, so I can send these names to you."

"Just lend me your laptop," Josef objected. "I can do the work on yours and then wipe it, and if Elisabeta doesn't mind, she can work on me instead. She's getting used to the mess inside my brain." He sent Elisabeta a small smile.

Elisabeta smiled back at him and nodded her head. "There's no mess, Josef."

Ferro was shocked that she spoke aloud in the room filled with so many others. Apparently she shocked all of them as well, but no one reacted or brought attention to the fact.

Tariq pushed his laptop across the table to Josef and they all watched as his fingers flashed across the keyboard. Ferro hadn't thought it possible for anyone to type that fast.

Ferro, what is it that the Malinovs wanted more than anything else? Elisabeta asked.

Ferro frowned. What was it the Malinovs wanted? They were reputed to have had many fiery debates all night and close to the dawn with the De La Cruz brothers, Astors, their cousins and so many others before they turned vampire. They were always riling against the prince and discussing how he didn't deserve to rule the Carpathian people. They felt they could do a better job. That others could do a better job. They claimed the Dubrinsky lineage had a defect that ran deep and would bring disaster to the Carpathians if they didn't do something soon. They achieved quite a following with their persuasive arguments and fiery rhetoric.

Power? To rule? They wanted to become the prince. To have what the Dubrinskys had.

Elisabeta was silent. They could all hear the keys clicking as Josef sat hunched in his chair, his fingers flying madly over the keyboard. Ferro had eyes only for his lifemate as her mind turned over the puzzle set before her.

Ferro suddenly felt the stillness in the other ancients so connected to him—to Elisabeta. They were aware she was putting the pieces together. Like Ferro, they knew how astute she was.

The prince of the Carpathian people cannot want power, Ferro. He has to be selfless. He has to be a vessel for his people.

That is true, Elisabeta, but not everyone understands that concept. Many rulers, in fact most rulers, are just the opposite. They do not serve their people; they expect their people to serve them.

Again, there was silence. This time, Ferro realized even Tariq was aware, through Gary, that Elisabeta was considering what the Malinov brothers were after. He didn't want to influence her thinking one way or the other, and he hoped the others wouldn't make the mistake of asking her questions. Elisabeta had her own way of getting to the right conclusions. She had spent centuries observing the brothers, more time than anyone else. They hadn't known she was there, so they hadn't been guarded.

Was Tariq born around the same time? Or was he older than them?

It was nearly impossible to tell any Carpathian's age. *Tariq was born after we were, but before the Malinov brothers. He knew them. He knew Vlad's oldest son. He knew many of the Carpathian people. He came to the monastery once.*

Again, Elisabeta fell silent. This time, Tariq flicked a quick glance at Gary, and Ferro knew immediately the two men were communicating telepathically and no one else was privy to what they were saying, not even Maksim, Tariq's partner. Another prickle of unease slid down Ferro's spine, and this one was fierce. Often it was that first acting on the awareness of danger that saved one's life.

There was no real reason to think that Elisabeta could be in any kind of jeopardy, but he wasn't about to take risks with her. All along he had had a vague impression of danger toward her, and now it was definitely defined and emanating from Tariq's second-in-command. Gary. A man Ferro trusted.

He stood up, all flowing muscle, his arm around Elisabeta's waist, bringing her up with him and sweeping her casually behind him so he was shielding her body from those at the table but making it seem as if it was an automatic gesture.

"We will return when Josef has finished with his work. It is a little close in here. Elisabeta needs to feed after removing the infection from so many, and she'll have to work on Josef."

He took two steps toward the door when Tariq and Gary both rose as well. At once those in the room went on alert.

"I believe Elisabeta still has to work on Tariq," Gary said smoothly. "She was interrupted. We can follow you outside."

Tariq shook his head when his guards rose. "You stay." There was complete authority in the leader's voice. "I wish to have a quiet word with Ferro and Elisabeta." He gestured toward the door.

Ferro couldn't think of a good reason to keep from going out in front of him. He pulled his lifemate around his body. *Stay directly in front of me and walk straight out the door and down the hallway to the outside door. Open it and go outside. Don't stop moving for any reason.*

Elisabeta didn't question him. Alarms were shrieking at him. On their private path he felt the stirring in his mind—his brethren as uneasy as he. *Ferro? What is it?* Petru asked the question all the brethren wondered.

I have no idea. Has Tariq alerted his guards against you?

No, they are as uneasy as we are. They do not know what he is up to, but they do not like him unprotected. Isai gave the answer.

Ferro made a sound of disbelief in his mind. *He has the healer with him. Gary has the knowledge of every battle fought by every Daratrazanoff in the entire lineage. I hardly think Tariq is unprotected.*

If you have need, we will come to your aid. That was Sandu, always ready to stand with him. *Is Elisabeta in danger?*

That was the worst of it. Ferro felt danger, but why would Tariq, or even Gary for that matter, threaten Elisabeta, who had gone out of her way to aid them? That made little sense. All along, from the moment of her first rising, there had been something Gary, at least, had known that Ferro didn't.

His lifemate followed his instructions to the letter. She walked briskly down the hallway, straight to the door leading to the courtyard.

"I would prefer to talk inside," Tariq said from behind them.

Ferro didn't slow down. "Elisabeta is uncomfortable inside. I told you, she needs to be out in the fresh air." He pushed air at her back, urging her to open the door before either Gary or Tariq held it shut on them and he was trapped in the narrow hallway with little room to fight their way out.

She yanked the door open and stepped outside. Ferro was right on her heels and he whirled around the moment he had room to face the two men emerging from the house. *Elisabeta, stay behind me. If necessary, trust only the brethren. I do not know what goes on here, but I feel a threat to you. I am uncertain why. You should be safe here with both these men, but I do not feel as if you are. Can you read either of them without their knowledge?*

They would know the moment Ferro touched their minds. He wasn't going to risk an all-out battle with two experienced ancients like Gary and Tariq when Elisabeta was in such close proximity.

Perhaps. I would have to be very careful. Gary is . . . difficult. He is closed off. Tariq is more open but right now he is watchful and much more like the brethren than I have ever seen him. He is very dangerous right now, Ferro. I do not know why he is upset, but he is very upset.

"Elisabeta is asking you questions. Private questions, Ferro, and those questions are about me." Tariq made it a statement. "Specifically, about the prince, the past and about me."

"We asked her whether she could figure out what the Malinov brothers might want from you—want enough that they would be willing to expose themselves and the Carpathian people to the humans in order to get it. Now, because she needs to ask questions to get information pertinent to solving the puzzle, you are all but threatening her." Ferro pushed back at both of them, daring them to deny it.

Gary and Tariq exchanged another long look and clearly another brief telepathic consultation.

Elisabeta assessed the two Carpathians carefully. *They are both very unhappy. Uneasy. They are uncertain whether they can trust you, Ferro, because you have never sworn allegiance to the prince.*

You are reading their actual thoughts?

No, more like their body language and the nuances of their eye movements along with the glimpses of images I'm picking up from their minds. I am more familiar with Gary through you and the others than Tariq, but Gary is very closed off and I cannot penetrate too deep without risk of detection. I hesitate with Tariq because it feels like invasion. Prying. He is a good man. A decent one. He has the good of the people placed before all else. Even confronting us is difficult when he knows we came to their aid.

"Why have you never sworn allegiance to Mikhail?" Tariq asked. "Few of the brethren have done so."

"It has never been required of us," Ferro said.

"That is so, but some have done so. Is there a reason you have not?"

"I have never met Mikhail Dubrinsky. I do not blindly follow anyone. His father ultimately betrayed us in order to satisfy his lifemate. She could not stand the idea of losing her firstborn son, even though he was sick with the taint of the bad blood. Vlad had enough precog that he saw the downfall of the Carpathian people. He knew what we would suffer. He knew what his younger son would face, the near extinction of all of us, and yet, to please his woman, he refused to have his second destroy his son."

"And yet you continued to serve our people with honor."

"Vlad continued to try to serve our people with honor. He was weak when it came to his family, with the people he loved. I did not have a lifemate. I had no way of judging what I would do if I was in his shoes. Perhaps the fault lay with his second-in-command. I have no idea how that pairing works or if Roman Daratrazanoff could have killed Draven without destroying the bond between the prince and him."

Gary and Tariq again looked at each other before Tariq nodded his head. That feeling of imminent danger was beginning to fade just a little from Tariq, but Ferro wasn't any less alert. He still felt Gary was the main threat.

Tariq feels he should share information that he believes I will eventually figure out. Gary is resistant and says it is dangerous to trust anyone with the information, especially one not sworn to follow the prince.

In spite of the seriousness of the situation, Ferro couldn't help but feel amused. His woman was just a little too intelligent and perceptive for men in powerful positions. She had learned her observation skills out of necessity and honed them over centuries. Like Tariq, he had no doubt that she would eventually uncover whatever secret Tariq was hiding. Somewhere in the past, one of the Malinovs had to have mentioned it, probably more than once in front of her without realizing she was in the same room with them. Something would trigger that memory.

Tariq insists that I already know but just have to remember, and Gary says that would mean the Malinov brothers knew, and it was an impossibility that they knew.

Do you know what they mean? What is it that you might know, Elisabeta? Ferro knew he was pushing her when she really needed time, but Gary was clearly in charge of protecting Tariq as well as something huge, something very few in the Carpathian world knew of. Maybe a secret that could mean the downfall of the prince and therefore the extinction of the Carpathian people.

Tariq says not if their father was one of the members of the council.

The moment she repeated the word *council* to him she went silent, and Ferro felt her once again withdrawing to the past, searching for more information through those centuries of conversations she'd overheard.

He needed her to sort through those conversations fast. If Ferro and Elisabeta weren't lifemates, Gary would be able to catch portions of their private communications. He already knew they were speaking telepathically to each other as Tariq and he were. As Tariq's appointed second-in-command and guardian, he would fulfill those duties with honor whether he wanted to or not. He was uneasy and watchful. He knew engaging in battle with Ferro would start an all-out war with every ancient in the compound, and they would have to take sides.

Elisabeta, I need to know what Gary and Tariq are saying to one another. He detested pulling her away from her memories, but he had to be warned if Gary was going to attack. He had to get his lifemate to safety. Killing her would be the fastest way for Gary to defeat him. He should have had Sandu or one of the other brethren accompany him whether Tariq wanted it or not.

Tariq says the Malinov brothers may have overheard their father talking to Roman. That is always a possibility. Or he broke the rules and talked directly to them, which Tariq doubts. He believes their father was a man of honor, and he would be appalled if he knew what his sons had chosen to do.

Ferro edged back, away from the two men, forcing his lifemate to step back as well. *Keep moving very slowly toward the house Dragomir and Emeline used when they lived here. Inch back, piŋe sarnanak.*

You believe Gary will attack us.

It is a possibility.

Because I know something they do not want me to reveal to the others. Tariq really does have something the Malinovs want, and it is that important.

I believe so, yes. Keep moving, sívamet. I need fighting room. The brethren will come to our aid. He said it with conviction. He knew he could count on most of them. Others had made a home with Tariq and he was no longer certain if their allegiance held to those sharing centuries in the monastery or had switched to the prince's representative there in the

States. There was irony in the fact that the infection hadn't divided the compound and turned ancients against one another, but the unknown item the Malinov brothers searched for was close to doing so.

"Ferro." Tariq sighed. "The Daratrazanoff family have been the guardians of the Dubrinskys for as long as the Carpathian people have existed. The Dubrinskys are the vessels for the collective power of the people. You are aware of that. We exist because they exist. Gary was sent to advise and guard me here at Mikhail's request. We don't always agree on everything, but we do try to listen to one another."

Elisabeta laid her hand very lightly against the small of Ferro's back, connecting them physically as well as mentally. She was merged with him, that delicate, compassionate mind, quiet within his, waiting to hear Tariq out. Like Ferro, she was patient, waiting for Tariq to find the right words to express himself. Both felt Gary's disapproval. He didn't agree with Tariq's decision to share with the couple.

"You are also aware that when there is power such as the Dubrinskys wield, there can also be weakness. The taint of bad blood."

Ferro inclined his head. That streak, unfortunately, didn't just run in the Dubrinsky family. It was in many of the very powerful lineages. Sadly, the Dubrinsky family had been hit the hardest.

"I must have your word of honor that anything I tell the two of you will be held in absolute secrecy no matter what." Tariq looked Ferro in the eyes. Man to man. Warrior to warrior. "You must close off your mind to all your brethren, including those soul-tied to you."

Elisabeta? Ferro was not going to commit both of them to something without asking her first. She had to agree. She was intelligent and she had a way of reading others far better than he did. *I know you do not like making decisions.* They paralyzed her. *I am not asking for that. Rather, I value your input. I will make our decision based on what we both think jointly.* Hopefully she understood what he meant.

Tariq is a man of absolute honor. He cares deeply for those he leads. Not only the Carpathian people but the humans around him as well. I believe him to be a good man. He is very torn because in telling us, he must break his vow of secrecy, but he believes I will discover the truth anyway.

Do you already know it?

She hesitated.

Elisabeta?

I believe so.

"It is possible Elisabeta already knows what you are going to tell us," Ferro admitted. He ignored the way Gary stiffened, although he did move subtly to indicate to Elisabeta to step back from him. "We do not want to put you in a position of forcing you to break a vow you have held for centuries if you do not have to."

"If she knows, it would be best for me to tell you up front about it so there are no misconceptions. No one is going to harm either of you. I am making that perfectly clear," Tariq decreed. He glanced at Gary. "You have my word of honor on that. I still need your word, Ferro. From both of you."

I am willing, Elisabeta said without hesitation.

"We both give you our word of honor that whatever you say to us goes no further."

Tariq walked over to the bench placed in the garden, the one Genevieve loved to sit on while she watched the children play on the playground. He sank down, suddenly looking as if the weight of the world was on his shoulders. Ferro waited until Gary had followed and placed himself in a watchful position at Tariq's right side. Ferro made certain he kept Elisabeta in a position where he could defend her. He believed Tariq meant his decree, that both were safe, but he was taking no chances with his lifemate's safety. Tariq had given his word, Gary had not.

"It was decided, long before Vlad became prince, that no one could have that much power without someone watching over them, especially when a strain of bad blood could mar the ruling family. A secret board was set up, a council to oversee the prince if there ever is a question of leadership or his state of mind. The council members are not known to one another. It is for their protection. If their identity is known to the prince, or to anyone else for that matter, they could be hunted down and killed for any number of reasons."

Ferro frowned. He had been alive for more centuries than most and he had never heard the slightest rumor of such a thing. Not one whisper.

"It is my understanding that there are five council members. If the prince's actions come under question, each member is contacted separately and asked to visit the prince on some pretense. One speaks with him and eventually discusses the matter. Individually, the council member must determine whether they believe there is cause for concern and give an opinion on whether the prince needs to be removed and his heir put in place or a different solution made. Some way to resolve whatever the situation is."

"Five council members, so if three weigh in the same way, the matter is decisive," Ferro said. "That makes sense."

Tariq nodded. "We do not know who the other council members are and we've taken a vow of honor never to speak of this so we can't consult with one another and persuade each other over to one side or the other."

"What do you have that the Malinov brothers think would allow them to take over the leadership of the Carpathian people? Is there some actual tool that could take the power from the Dubrinsky line?" Ferro asked.

Tariq glanced at Gary and then shook his head. "There is a misconception perhaps. The Dubrinskys are vessels that hold the power of the Carpathian people. The Malinovs do not have that in their lineage."

That said nothing at all. It was avoiding the question.

Elisabeta?

He is very concerned. There is something he guards. Each member of the council has something. He is worried that the Malinov brothers found their father's when he died. It should have returned on its own to the Daratrazanoff line but it didn't.

Ferro flicked his gaze to Gary's impassive features. "It is impossible to hide things from Elisabeta. You know they have what should have returned when Malinov died. You have known this for some time."

Tariq's head jerked up and he glared at his second-in-command.

Gary shrugged unemotionally. "We suspected, but we had no way of knowing until now. We couldn't do anything about it and there was no reason for anyone to know."

Tariq stared at him for another long moment, clearly disagreeing. He turned back to Ferro and Elisabeta. "Each council member is given . . ."

"Tariq, this is going beyond what they need to know," Gary cautioned.

"Is it?" Tariq asked. "If Cornel and Dorin are going to allow Sergey to use Elisabeta as their excuse to turn my club into a bloodbath, Ferro and Elisabeta should know what they are fighting for." He smiled at Elisabeta. He looked tired. For the first time, the centuries—and his duties—seemed to really weigh heavily on his shoulders. "In any case, no doubt our Elisabeta will be able to find that piece of the puzzle somewhere in her memories as well, won't you?"

To Ferro's utter astonishment, she gave Tariq a tentative smile, surrounding him with her fragrance of soothing peace. "Yes."

A small breeze rustled the leaves on the ground and blew them in small eddies around their feet, bringing with them a sense of comforting atmosphere. It was impossible not to relax in the wake of Elisabeta's serenity. Ferro could see the darkness in Gary lifting, just being close to her, in spite of the heavy burdens centuries of warriors had instilled in him.

"There are five extremely small pieces of what is believed to be made from a single larger stone from the earliest history of the Carpathian Mountains. The flysch band is the only interconnecting band that runs throughout the entire mountain range. These five pieces should be fragile, as they are from what is essentially shale carved into interlocking pieces. They are of the earth, of the mountains. The piece I have is extraordinarily strong. Still, I have kept it safe and free from harm for centuries. I would imagine that Malinov did his piece as well, if, indeed, he was a member of the council."

Elisabeta nodded her head. "He was. At least his sons talked as if he was."

"Do you know where that piece is? Who has it now?" Gary asked.

I would have to think about it. It is not easy to remember all the conversations, but at least I know what I am looking for now.

"Elisabeta will try to remember," Ferro relayed. He found it interesting that Elisabeta elected not to talk to Gary when she was willing to speak with Tariq.

Gary contemplated starting the war by killing me in order to get you to turn vampire. That would give him ample reason to kill you and force the other ancients to aid him in defeating you.

She wasn't upset with Gary for considering killing her—that was acceptable because he was protecting the interests of the Carpathian people—but it wasn't acceptable to her that the healer was putting Ferro at risk to lose his honor after so many centuries of holding on.

"She is not happy with you, Gary," Ferro couldn't help but add. "Looking into your mind and seeing your plan did not sit well with her. She didn't mind that you would kill her, but she did mind that you wanted me to lose my honor and become vampire."

"Had he carried out his plan, Elisabeta, which would have been despicable, we would have lost the potential to know where the Malinov piece was," Tariq pointed out. "A little short-sighted."

"That is why I am not the leader of our people," Gary said.

"Cornel and Dorin believe that you hold this piece at the night club. Tell me you do not," Ferro said. "I do not wish to know where it is, only that it is not there."

"It is not. It is nowhere they could ever get their hands on it."

19

The cage has collapsed, the prisoner stands tall;
The battle is ours to end, once and for all.

Ferro didn't know if he sang their song or if Elisabeta did when he first woke that next rising to find them blood. He only knew that much later, when she came to him in the sanctuary of their forest, she surrounded him with love. He felt so much emotion he was drowning, threatening to a centuries-old warrior who fought without a single sentiment for so long. It was beautiful. She made the colors of the forest, already so vibrant now that he could see them, even more vivid.

He had doubts for so long that she would never be able to live with him as he was, but the way she looked into his eyes, holding his body close, her hands pressing into his back, fingers digging into his shoulders and then down to his hips, told him she would stay for eternity. She made the earth move under them while the moon and stars seemed to spin overhead. Sounds of the ocean roared in his ears, a symphony of the greatest music the world could give them.

He threaded his fingers through hers, there in the forest, their favorite place of complete harmony, his body deep in hers, surrounded by fire, by her tight, silken sheath, knowing what he had been given and yet already her body was claiming his, driving out every sane thought until it was only the two of them going up in flames. Her breathy moans, the way she chanted his name, as if he were her only focus in the world. She made him feel that way.

He loved her with every stroke of his body. Every movement of his surging hips. Of his fingers clamping down so tightly on her hips, urging her to meet his thrusts. He had wanted to be her shelter, and yet she had become his. He found himself lost in her. The way she came so gently into his mind and memories, filling all those tears and cracks that had formed over the centuries from the battles and kills, the wounds he'd sustained. She managed, with her compassion and soothing nature, to find a way to repair every tattered rend in his heart, those terrible black holes that had stripped his humanity from him.

Ferro framed her beloved face with both hands and looked down into her eyes. "I love you, *sívamet*. You are *hän ku vigyáz sívamet és sielamet*, keeper of my heart and soul, and you have done so in ways I could never imagine. I am so in love with you, Elisabeta. I will make mistakes, and I will forget to tell you how truly beautiful you are, both inside and out, and if that happens, please remind me that there are very necessary things to say to you each rising."

He bent his head and brushed kisses over each eye, her nose, the corners of her mouth and then her lips. He loved her mouth. The curve. The definition. The way she tasted when she parted her lips for him. The fire there. The love he found there. The true meaning of *lifemate* when she gave him everything that she was.

"We could just stay right here, *piŋe sarnanak*. You could practice your flying, although you have gotten quite good. So much so that I believe that last time you were showing off a bit."

She laughed. He loved when she genuinely laughed. He knew that was so rare for her, and when he could actually give that to her, those moments of joy, he found those were the times he valued the most.

"I would like that, *kont o sívanak*, but somehow I do not think they will allow us the freedom to do so. No doubt one of the brethren will be calling you soon, wondering where we are. We have this battle plan, and you and I are an integral part of it."

"The more I think about it, the less I like this idea," Ferro said with a sigh, rubbing his face on the curves of her breast, leaving red marks from the short stubble he knew she liked when he was extremely attentive between her legs. "Why is it that no matter what I do, you always seem to be in some kind of danger?"

"Tariq put the call out for more Carpathians and I thought many came. Am I wrong?"

Elisabeta was always that voice of calm—of sweet reason when there was none—when it came to putting her in danger.

He growled at her to show his disapproval. She laughed again, not in the least impressed with his very lethal imitation of a wolf. He bent his head to her bare breast and nipped. She jumped and settled when he lapped soothingly at the little mark with the healing saliva of his tongue. Her fingers fisted in his hair.

"Josef will be in more danger than I will. I do not like that he will put himself in the open like that in order to draw the Malinov cousins in. I honestly do not think it will work. Sergey I can call in. He will not be able to refuse my call, but they will send servants to collect Josef. They will be counting on the diversion to search the place they believe the object they seek is."

"Have you remembered where that is?" He stroked his hand down her body, a bit possessively, from her throat to her waist.

Ferro knew they were running out of time. He detested giving up their brief moments together. It was never enough. No matter if they spent a day, a week, a year alone, for him it wouldn't be enough. He wanted more time to just take her in. Revel in her. Please her. Find ways to make her laugh and enjoy life. Show her the wonders of the world. Learn things together. Have firsts. Just be.

"I have no way of knowing where Tariq put his piece of the object. But I am trying to find the Malinov piece. I think I am getting closer. It is a lot of centuries and conversations to go through in order to find that one thing we are looking for. Ruslan was the one who referred to it once. I think he was the brother who thought he knew where his father had hidden it. He did not want to tell anyone else, so they would consider him too important to conspire against. In the beginning, when they first turned, they all had major issues with vanity and the need to be the one in charge. All of them were quite cruel and violent. They had to overcome those traits to get back to working smoothly with one another."

Elisabeta gave a delicate little shudder and Ferro immediately wrapped his arms around her and sat up, pulling her with him so she was sitting in his lap. He wanted to assure her that she was safe, but it seemed each time he said that, she was attacked in some way. He drew in a deep breath.

"We are powerful together, you know that, right, Elisabeta?" He rubbed his chin over the top of her head, back and forth, allowing her hair to catch in the stubble along his jaw. "I have always been a force against the vampire. They fear my name. We are twice that force when we are together. You may be gentle and kind but you have learned to bend with the wind, not break. We are forged together in a way few will ever understand, certainly not our enemies."

"I no longer fear Sergey," she whispered, tilting her head back to rest it against his chest. "I have learned so much from you. I realized that all this time I gave him power over me. He kept me starved and afraid. He kept me from knowing even the smallest thing so that I would feel completely dependent on him. You opened my cage and set me free."

Ferro tightened his arms around her. "You were so terrified of being out of that cage at times I felt as if I was torturing you."

"This journey has been frightening," she acknowledged. "But in a good way, Ferro. I found myself learning faster and faster, taking in everything you showed me. Lorraine and Julija showed me many things. Even Emeline shared with me. So many people were around me, willing to give me knowledge. I was afraid of them, and if I'm honest, still am, but I can feel myself getting stronger, growing in courage with each rising, thanks to you. You give me courage, Ferro. You make me believe in myself."

"You are going to need all that courage today, *minan piŋe sarnanak*." Ferro knew he was going to need it as well.

He stood up reluctantly, taking her with him, setting her on her feet. With a wave of his hand he clothed both of them, dressing her in the longer dress she preferred.

"I heard you extend an offer to Josef to help train him in the ways of a hunter, you and your brethren. That was very sweet of you, Ferro." Elisabeta turned into him, sliding her slender arms up his chest and around his neck to link her fingers together there.

He winced a little at the word *sweet*. He had never been considered sweet in his life. The kid needed confidence that he would make a good hunter of the vampire. Ferro was certain Josef would have no problem. He paid attention to detail. He had the desire and drive. Body type didn't matter as much as stamina did. At the end of the day, sometimes it came down to who was in the best shape.

Josef didn't back down from a fight. Ferro had studied him. It didn't matter who confronted him; if he believed in what he said, he argued his position passionately. All of the brethren had respect for the kid. Like Ferro, they wanted to train him so that he had the best of chances when he was old enough to hunt the vampire. There would come a time when he would lose his emotions and his ability to see in color, and all that he would have left to him was his honor. It was then that he had to believe in himself. The foundation they gave him was important. He couldn't be adrift, thinking he was never good enough. He had to believe he was an honorable Carpathian male and an asset to his people as a hunter.

"All the brethren are going to work with him," Ferro told her.

"Because you asked them to," Elisabeta pointed out.

He wrapped his arm around her waist. "*Sívamet*, do me a favor and never use the word *sweet* in front of any of the others. I would never hear the end of it. Especially in front of Sandu. Or Lorraine."

"Lorraine thinks you are sweet."

"No, she doesn't. She thinks I'm a caveman and I like that she thinks that. It makes for fun evenings when she visits with you. Julija, on the other hand, can think I am sweet. You can share that with her as often as possible, just not when the brethren are around. I have no wish to be turned into a toad, or suddenly have a tail or donkey ears, no matter how temporary. She's mage and can be vengeful."

Elisabeta's joyous laughter spilled out, filling the air, lighting Ferro's world. The forest took on a distinctly festive atmosphere, a phenomenon he found happened quite often whenever he was in Elisabeta's presence.

"You deliberately keep the others from knowing you have a sense of humor."

That was true. He wasn't the kind of man who would ever be that comfortable being too close with his neighbors.

Elisabeta rubbed her face against his chest like a little cat. "You persist in thinking that once I come into my own power, growing as modern as Lorraine or Julija, that I would not choose you because you are a dominant, overbearing tyrant. That is completely absurd. First, you are not any of those things. And second, I am your lifemate. As you need to please me, I need to please you. That is the way lifemates work. And you lived with the brethren for centuries. All of you follow one another. You are a family. You fight for one another. You are already setting up homes here in this compound together, so that negates what you were just thinking about yourself."

Ferro closed his eyes and held her to him, savoring her. Her scent. The feel of her feminine form up against his. "We are going to do this together. If nothing else, *minan piŋe sarnanak*, we will end Sergey's reign of terror once and for all."

She tilted her head. He saw trepidation, but there was also belief in him. In her. In them together. She nodded her head slowly. "We will, Ferro. And we will keep Josef safe as well."

He took his time kissing her because he found he needed to. There was so much courage in Elisabeta. So much steel. She had thought herself small and insignificant, and all along she held so much power in her slender, womanly body and that quick, intelligent mind. He was fiercely proud that the universe had partnered him with such an unbelievable treasure.

Music blared, the lights spinning dark purple and blue as Josef sauntered into the underground nightclub, his gaze arrogantly scanning the crowd. Women turned to look as he passed them. Like all Carpathians, there was a magnetism to him that was blatant in the fluid way he moved. He was dressed in black leather pants, a black shirt with cord laces going up the front. He appeared confident, sexy, charming and very modern as he walked briskly through the first bar straight toward the second one.

Behind him, two couples had also entered, talking together, their faces obscured by their costumes, the men taller, holding hands with their partners as they cut through the crowd going toward the second bar. Barack and Syndil, two members of the Dark Troubadour band, legends in the Carpathian community, were dressed in black, taking in everything and conveying the information to the other Carpathians as they followed Josef. Dayan, another band member, and Corrine, his lifemate, also followed, dressed in black, their makeup impeccable, impossible to be recognized as Carpathian as they moved through the crowd, picking up the strains of thoughts as well as conversations.

The underground club was designed to appeal to the goth crowd. It was very popular with both the goth and goth-vampire cultures. The full basement beneath the large nightclub had been renovated into three bars, each looking like a series of caves, one leading into the next. All had well-marked exits, but the interiors were dark and lit mostly with wall sconces that looked like old-fashioned candles so that flames flickered on the walls of the caves.

Each bar was quite large and shaped like a cave, the sides appearing as if carved from the inside of the bowels of a mountain. The walls seemed so real, glittering with rock that had strains of minerals and even gems running through them. In a few places water appeared to leak in steady trickles that created dark curved streaks playing through the "dirt" of the walls. Rocks jutted out here and there, giving more dimension and realism to the feeling of a cavern.

Colors pulsed through the bars, dark purple and blue, a bruising heartbeat that vibrated the floor and walls and bodies of those inside, connecting them together. It became a singular experience to attend the club, one to be repeated, almost an addiction, a need to return again and again to find others accepting of differences so many felt.

The feel in the club was quite different than Ferro expected. It wasn't the men drooling over the women, looking for a quick lay. It wasn't even a bunch of depressed crazies coming together to hang out, staring into their glasses of alcohol. These were people of all ages, dancing to different types of music, dressing the way they wanted, accepting one another the way they were no matter age, gender or preference for partners.

Ferro was with a contingent of Carpathian hunters scattered around the underground club, unseen, a part of the walls, impossible to detect by the human psychic males that had been placed in the nightclub systematically over the last few years. Tariq had been shocked that so many had been. Seventeen of his servers had been identified by Josef as actually working for the enemy.

Tariq had looked at the work schedule and discovered that all were working this rising, that they had traded shifts with others to be certain to be on, which only proved Josef was correct. One other had also traded shifts, making him appear suspicious, so they added his name to the roster, bringing the number to eighteen.

They couldn't have any of the human psychics working close together and take a chance that their combined gifts would give away the fact that many of the Carpathians were in the club. Fortunately, the building was four stories high with a club on each floor. Each floor had a different type of dance music playing, creating a different atmosphere. The center of each floor was open so one could look down and see onto the dance floors of the clubs below it—all but the underground cave, which was kept extremely private.

The underground club added an additional working environment that had to be covered. Not only was the nightclub enormously popular, crowded and always busy, but Tariq employed quite a number of workers for each separate club. Tariq simply shifted the workers around.

Woman is approaching me, Josef announced. *Definitely human. Her mind is protected. She has to be Sergey's.*

Ferro and each of the other Carpathians reached out very gently in an attempt to try to scan the redheaded woman walking boldly up to Josef. She was short, with large brown eyes and a generous mouth.

She looks a little bit like Skyler did when she was younger, Josef said. He nearly groaned. *I think of Skyler as a little sister. How am I supposed to flirt with this girl?*

It's called acting, Dayan said. *We all know you're good at that. Anytime you're around the prince you put on a good show.*

Ferro would have given anything to ask questions about the kinds of things the kid did when he was around Mikhail. Any of the Carpathians could have broken through the shield erected in the woman's mind, but Sergey would have known and immediately been alerted.

Elisabeta, can you tell if Sergey was the one to place the barrier in the girl's brain, and if so, can you push past it without his knowledge? Ferro asked.

Elisabeta was hidden, Julija and Lorraine close to her, along with Blaze, Maksim's lifemate. Ferro had an aversion to the women being any-where near action that could be as intense as this battle might prove to be, but they needed Elisabeta close and they wanted to keep the humans safe. Cornel and Dorin intended to start a bloodbath right there at the night-club for a diversion no matter what. To save lives, they had to take the risk.

Yes, her name is Linda. She was protected by him, but it was easy enough to move past it. Her orders are very simple. She is to get him to take her to the third bar and go to a specific table in the far back near the exit. They are waiting to take him there. Linda will distract him while they come up on him.

Does she know about the plans for the vampires to hunt in this bar or the ones upstairs?

No. She has no idea. They did not warn her to leave.

Of course they hadn't. Ferro wasn't surprised. Once she did her job, she would be of no more use to them. More than likely they would throw her in the van, or whatever means they used to transport Josef, and take her as well for her blood. They wanted to feast this rising. The vampires were looking forward to it.

I can call Sergey to me, Elisabeta offered.

Not yet. I have to know where Cornel and Dorin are. Where their servants are. The hunters have to stop them, Elisabeta. Then we will go after Sergey. He is the least of our worries for now. We protect Josef and the humans.

She was silent a moment. *This is not the best place for me to be, Ferro. If I were higher up and not so closed in, I could give exact locations for you, just as I did when I could tell you where Sergey was. You want me safe. I understand that,* she added before he could protest. *But you also need all these people safe. That is our true purpose as Carpathians. You just stated what we were to do. Let me move locations. You, Sandu and Gary can escort Lorraine and the others with me. Every Carpathian warrior can stand by if need be, but I am telling you I will be far more valuable to you if I am where I can be useful.*

Ferro tasted fear in his mouth. He had known all along it would come to this. When he had first woken, that moment even as his heart had taken its first beat, he had known Elisabeta would be in terrible danger. There was Josef, his arm slung around Linda's neck, sauntering slowly through the third bar toward that back table where he knew a trap waited for him. An ambush.

Josef. A kid with more courage than he should have. Elisabeta. His woman, terrifying him with her bravery, knowing she was facing the Malinov brother who dared to deceive her centuries earlier, kidnapping and keeping her in a cage, mentally and physically torturing her. Ferro had to have that same courage. If they could do this, then he could as well.

Josef, delay reaching that table until I let you know it is safe to do so.

Josef whispered in Linda's ear. She shook her head, but he just laughed and turned them, heading toward the actual bar where people were lined up to get drinks. Ferro waited until Josef was at the bar, engaging with others around him. Dayan and Corinne had come up behind him. Barack and Syndil had hemmed Linda in on the other side, making it just a little difficult for them to move. Syndil immediately began talking with Linda. Her voice was very mesmerizing, enthralling Linda so that she barely realized minutes were slipping away as Josef waited patiently for his turn instead of calling for a drink as he could have.

Ferro immediately hurried to the second cave and the middle of the wall where the women waited unseen and impossible to detect, protected by not only the Carpathian warriors but Julija's mage magic. Julija alone would have been a force to be reckoned with, but the combination with the Carpathian ancients should have put Ferro's mind at ease. It should have, but Elisabeta was his world, so it didn't.

"Where do you need to be?" He knew exactly what she was going to say before she even said it.

"The rooftop."

Out in the open. Exposed. Of course it would have to be the rooftop. He looked in despair, first at Lorraine and then to Andor, Lorraine's lifemate. Andor knew. Isai, Julija's lifemate, understood the danger as well. The rooftop was where the vampires could strike easily with just about any weapon. The two ancients had joined him to escort the women to their new location and then weave safeguards around them.

"Is there a second choice?" Isai asked.

Elisabeta looked at Ferro. For the first time, he silently willed her not to answer. If she couldn't do it on her own, as she normally couldn't, then maybe he would have every reason to justify keeping her safe—but he knew better. He knew he wouldn't.

For finding the army of vampires and directing our hunters to them, it has to be the roof. There are so many of them, and so many different directions you need me to find them in. From there, I can find the master vampires as well. Elisabeta gave her answer to Ferro alone. *There are safer places, but those places will limit me. I do not wish you to be so uneasy, beloved. I will do whatever is your preference.*

Her courage astounded him, as did her audacity. Sun scorch the woman; she was manipulating him and it was working. He couldn't very well be a coward when she was a shining example of female daring.

"I will take Elisabeta to the roof. Lorraine and Julija do not need to be with her there. In fact, they might be of more use in the club."

Lorraine rolled her eyes. "You are not in the least good at telling lies, Ferro."

"I said *might*," he pointed out.

He took his lifemate in his arms. She could fly. She might even want to fly, but he needed to hold her as he took her out of the cavern and into the night air. His brethren could deal with their lifemates, decide one way or the other what they were going to do, but right now, he was going to let himself just feel the soothing comfort of his woman's gift.

Elisabeta surrounded him with her serenity, heightening the night's deceptive illusion of peace with her familiar and haunting fragrance, the one that now stayed with him even when he was away from her. Above them the moon had begun to slip into its next phase. Clouds drifted lazily across the deep midnight-blue-colored sky so that a slightly wider sliver of a silver curve peered down at them. A sea of stars, each trying to outshine the next, surrounded the moon as the gray clouds floated almost languidly. The clouds were deceptive; already the predicted storm was moving toward them.

Her breath caught in her throat and she pressed her face into his shoulder. *The vampire servants are spread out, Ferro, moving through the city, all heading this way.*

Numbers? At once he was all business, a full Carpathian hunter, setting his lifemate on the rooftop, his two brethren joining him with their women.

They began to weave their safeguards over the top of the building, an intricate web with Julija adding in her strand of magic and binding it tight every few strands over and over as they shared information with the others as quickly as possible. They couldn't leave Josef waiting too long or Sergey would become suspicious.

Each of the master vampires has ten servant vampires. That is all they can seem to sustain at any one time without things beginning to go very wrong. There are seven master vampires somewhere close, so you are looking at seventy of them coming to you. Do not forget those unfortunate newly made vampires. They will be the most aggressive, the bloodiest and the first they will send in.

Where are the ones looking to acquire Josef? Are they servants? Do you know who they are? Ferro asked.

He was already on the move, taking one side of the building while Isai, Andor and Julija each took a different side, all four continuing to weave the safeguards as they hurried to the underground cavern. Once there, Julija broke off and returned to the rooftop, slipping through the magic loop she'd left for herself and then pulling it tight behind her to enclose herself inside.

Edward Varga waits at the exit with two of Cornel's highest-ranking servants. Varga knows if he shirks his duty in any way, he will be punished in a hideous way. Cornel has stressed to all of them that Josef cannot be harmed. He is to be alive and in good condition.

Ferro was grateful that Cornel had no idea that Elisabeta could tap into Sergey's mind. Everything was shared with Sergey. Leaving him alive was difficult but necessary. Elisabeta could feel where the others were, but she would know exactly what was being said or what orders had been given as long as Sergey lived.

Josef, let her take you to the table. Move slowly. Stop and start. Keep talking to others around you. We are going to move on their army as they head toward the nightclub and begin to take them out one by one, coming up on the ones in the rear, Tariq ordered. *Dragomir, you take your men and start the hunt to the west.*

Fane and Aleksi, two brethren from the monastery, had answered the call, bringing their lifemates as well. Both ancients were hunting with Dragomir. They were fast and deadly, and few could best them in any battle. They needed that kind of firepower this rising.

Maksim, you take your men and hunt to the east. Get in behind them. Elisabeta has established a grid for us. Take the last man on the grid and move up. The clouds are thickening slowly so they seem natural. I don't want Cornel to worry too early and make a run for it.

Andre, a Carpathian male who had come and gone from the monastery bringing the brethren news and blood, joining them when he needed to be away from hunting and killing, was a brilliant addition to the hunt. He was the equivalent of an entire wolf pack. He'd brought his lifemate with him, the granddaughter of Fane's lifemate. Both fierce women were in the compound, helping to protect the children there if need be. He was very close to the triplets.

Julian Savage, one of the legendary Carpathian twins, lifemate to Desari, singer of the Dark Troubadour band, was known for centuries for his skills in battle against vampires. Just his name alone would send vampires scuttling out of a region if they knew he had entered it. Both men had joined with Maksim to clear out as many of the servants of the master vampires as possible.

Valentin, your men must hunt to the south. All of you will have at least seven to try to destroy before they reach the nightclub. That does not give you a lot of time, Tariq added.

Darius Daratrazanoff was a force to be reckoned with, like all those in his lineage. He was by turns a healer or a master hunter. He had been cut off from all Carpathians as a very young child with the responsibility of several young children, and he had risen to the occasion, keeping them safe and raising them as best he could, without the knowledge of their culture. He had finally met his lifemate. Tempest was at the compound with their twins, Aniko and Andor, under heavy safeguards while the Carpathians hoped to strike a huge blow at the vampires.

Afanasiv Balan spent more than a century in the monastery with the others before he had to leave, unable to keep from battle hunting after so long doing so. He wore the vows carved into his skin as they all did and came back often to ensure he stayed strong for a lifemate he had yet to meet. He was a fierce hunter, very skilled and fast.

Petru, take your men to the north. All of you be aware of the five newly made vampires that will be turning up somewhere. If Cornel or Sergey is so lax as to allow them to come through the city, they will be unable to resist preying on anyone, man, woman or child, they come across. The servants each of the master vampires has will be anywhere from close-to-master-vampire status to centuries-old vampire, so battle experienced. They would not have one serve them with less skill.

Ferro knew Petru had wanted to remain with those at the nightclub, not head a team of warriors going after lesser vampires. Still, there were at least ten for each team to kill, and they had only spared three men to hunt them down. Lojos, the last of the triplets, and Nicu Dalca, another ancient who wore the vows of the brethren on his back, had preferred to stay and protect the nightclub and the number of people inside it. Nicu was deceptively slender but all muscle, and moved like lightning in a fight. The teams were formidable, there was no doubt about that.

Ferro couldn't monitor them. That wasn't his job. Ensuring Josef's safety was. He watched the woman carefully. She was all over Josef, touching him, laughing, whispering into his ear. Trying to sit in his lap. Kissing him repeatedly. Ferro narrowed his eyes. He had excellent vision, but the table was low and he wasn't at the right angle to see when she kept squirming around.

Linda is up to something, Josef. Be very careful. Watch her hands. Can any of you see what she is up to? Elisabeta? Can you delve a little further into her mind without Sergey becoming aware of your presence?

Ferro didn't like to take his lifemate's attention away from aiding those in the streets. An army of vampires moving through a city where there were innocent humans, blood running in their veins, hearts beating a terrible temptation continuously. Still, unease was growing in him. He suddenly had the desire to come out of the wall, straight at Linda, and tear her away from Josef.

Is it possible that Josef is a distraction? That Cornel knows about your connection with Sergey and has prepared for it?

As always Elisabeta took her time deliberating before answering him. Any other time he wouldn't mind, but right at that moment, when the redheaded Linda was clearly using her every move to seduce Josef, squirming on his lap, kissing him passionately, running her hands through his hair, down his back, and all over his body, his alarms were screaming at him.

Barack, Syndil, can you stop by Josef and Linda's table with a drink for them and interrupt? Or at least see what she's up to? I do not have a good angle from here. The waiter closest to that table is one of those working for Sergey. He is watching the couple very closely. In fact, he's paying more attention to them than he is to his customers.

We can deal with him, Dayan offered.

Corrine suddenly appeared directly in the waiter's path while his head was turned toward Josef and Linda's table. The waiter ran right into her, the collision much harder than expected, throwing her to the floor and sending him sailing over the top of her. He somersaulted, smashing both legs into the edge of the wall. He screamed, as did Corrine. Heads turned toward them. Josef stood, nearly dumping Linda off his lap, hurrying across the short distance to crouch down beside Corrine and run his hands lightly over her legs and arms looking for injuries. Linda tapped her foot, one hand on her hip, looking annoyed. The waiter continued to scream, writhing in pain.

Both legs broken. They'll have to delay whatever plan they have for a few minutes while he's taken out of here, Dayan said, satisfaction in his voice. *That should give our teams in the city time to do some thorough hunting.*

Linda is very frustrated. She wants to go home. Her head is hurting but she cannot leave without accomplishing her task. She does not even remember why it is so important, only that she must get Josef to be so enamored with her that she can inject him with a syringe filled with a chemical the vampire gave her. The vampire was an Astor, not Addler but a different Astor, so it has to be the cousin that came and went upon occasion. He was younger. He did not like to be around the Malinov brothers and refused to give them the kind of allegiance they desired.

I need his name, Elisabeta. He tried not to push her, but Carpathians such as Tariq, Gary and the triplets, the ones who spent time in the Carpathian Mountains or around humans, might recall the names better than any of the ancients who had been locked away in the monastery.

Again, there was that slight retreat.

Minan piŋe sarnanak, I thank you for the information and the infinite patience you have with all the demands we keep putting on you. I know you must be tired.

She was aiding the four teams in the city, helping them hunt, showing them where the enemy was as best she could, giving them locations on a grid while they were moving.

Cornel cannot know what I can or cannot do, Ferro. He is not aware of me even when I touch on him. I can always tell when someone is becoming aware of my presence. There is a slight change in their energy. It is much like an automatic reflex. We can control our heartbeats, our breathing, but even with all those things, those gifts, there is always that one moment when a change takes place in the body. When we become aware.

Ferro could tell she was choosing her words carefully.

I am not talking about the outside tells that I read, although they give people away easily as well, but these are very subtle in the mind. You are extremely good at reading them, you just do not always recognize that you are reading something you do not like. When you called to me with your song that first rising, drawing me from the earth, you already knew something was wrong. You already felt it and you were wary. You are tied to Gary and you read his unease over me. Instinctively, you moved to protect me without fully knowing what caused you to begin to separate yourself from those who lived here in the compound.

How could he know that you can do the things that you do when you were not fully aware of your gifts?

I knew I could read others, Ferro, I just never shared those things. Gary is an ancient from a powerful bloodline. His ancestors poured themselves into him, all of them. They reside in him, both a blessing and a curse. By tying his soul to yours, when you recognized me as your lifemate, little by little he began to recognize traits in me.

Before you even came to the surface as my lifemate.

Ferro didn't know why, but it bothered him that Gary would recognize her brilliance and perhaps want to crush it before she could even find her power. Or before Ferro had the chance to recognize she was truly in danger from someone he considered a friend and ally. Did that make him the worst lifemate ever born?

Hän sívamak. She whispered "beloved" in his mind, surrounding him with her loving serenity that only Elisabeta could provide. His woman. She made him feel as if he was her only focus when she was providing information through Lorraine and Julija to Tariq so his teams could wipe out the servants of the master vampires.

Ferro, his name is Robi Astor. He is a second- or third-generation cousin. There was triumph in her mind in the remembering. Excitement and confidence. *I did not see him often. He did not like being around any of the Malinovs. He did consult with Cornel because Addler would report to Sergey or Cornel would. He was intelligent, and much less flamboyant than the other Astors. I thought he was very smart to keep his distance from the Malinovs. They would have considered him a rival. Anyone with a true brain was considered an opponent and either had to be shown to be less than them in a very decisive way or killed.*

Ferro was so proud of her sharing her thoughts with him. She pulled up memories from so long ago, analyzed them and gave him the results.

She'd come such a long way in only a few risings, already believing in herself. It was there all along, she just needed an environment to thrive. He was going to ensure that was never taken from her. Never.

Too many of the servants are beginning to disappear, Ferro, and the master vampires are noticing. Cornel is becoming concerned. They are discussing launching their attack on the nightclub right now. Elisabeta went from triumph to fear in moments.

20

Now tell me this and tell me true;
Say you'll choose me, as I chose you.

Ferro wasn't about to wait for Cornel to decide to launch an all-out war on Tariq's popular nightclub. The paramedics had already taken the waiter from the underground bar, and the music was once again pounding a bruising heartbeat through the club, signaling to everyone to start up the fun. Josef slung his arm around Linda's neck and started to walk her toward the dance floor.

She halted and stamped her foot, the syringe hidden in her clenched fist at her hip as she posed, pouting. "I just want to be alone with you. Is that too much to ask?"

Josef leaned into her, one hand wrapped around her wrist, controlling the fist clutching the syringe. He put his lips next to her ear. "Yeah, babe, especially when you plan to drug me and let your friends cart me off in their waiting chariot."

Linda's eyes widened and she opened her mouth to scream. Josef smiled, holding one finger up, shaking his head and drawing the finger across her lips. Abruptly all sound was cut off. She looked panic-stricken as she attempted over and over to cry out. Nothing emerged from her throat, not even a simple croaking noise. Josef grinned at her and escorted her to the table, sitting down and pulling her onto his lap.

What is the signal that Linda has Josef ready for transport? Ferro asked Elisabeta.

She is to open the exit door herself.

Ferro had been certain she would be taken or killed right there. There would be no advantage to the vampires in sparing her. She was a pawn, nothing more, a pretty girl they had picked up and programmed, thinking she was Josef's preference when it came to women.

Josef's amusement moved through his mind. *I will switch places with Linda. She will sit here docilely like the good Carpathian boy under the influence of the drug that shouldn't work. I really want to see what they put in that drug. It should be interesting. I can open the door. When they come at me, I hope all those moves you've been teaching me work. In the meantime, you can maneuver around and get the master vampire.*

Ferro didn't think Edward Varga was much of a master vampire. He was planning on leaving the pathetic monster to Josef's guardians. Somewhere, hidden out of sight just on the other side of the exit, were Traian and Joie. Traian wasn't in the least bit happy that vampires had tried to kidnap his charge right out from under his nose.

Dayan and Barack will aid Traian, destroying Varga and his servants when Varga attacks you, Josef. You let them handle the master vampire. You can hone your skills on a lesser servant or perhaps a newly made vampire at a later time when I am with you, but not a master vampire. There is no need to prove anything to anyone, least of all to yourself. You are too valuable to our people to lose in a battle where we have many warriors available. Do you give me your word of honor that you will do as I have said?

I have no intentions of losing my life to a vampire, Josef said immediately, shedding his appearance even as Linda became Josef sitting at the table, slightly slumped in his chair, looking a bit drunk. Josef, now looking the part of a redheaded woman, stood, leaned down and brushed a kiss on the forehead of the man, glanced toward the wall and gave Ferro a cocky wink.

He is very clever, Elisabeta observed.

Ferro sighed. *I am centuries old, Josef, not born yesterday. You take one more step toward the door without giving me your word and you will not take another.*

Josef halted abruptly. *I'm not stupid, Ferro. I have no intention of fighting anything. I'll open the door and let Dayan, Barack and Traian do all the work.*

Ferro caught the faint trail of shame in the boy's mind. *You are not being relegated back to being a child. I do not think of you that way. There are women in that club. Our women. Human women. O jelä peje terád, Josef.* He swore in his native language. *You are a valuable asset Cornel has already devised a plan to kidnap. Why am I even bothering to explain this to you?*

He caught a glimpse of a smile in his lifemate's mind, and at once all annoyance was gone. He understood now why Josef's reputation had preceded him, although he didn't think it was truly deserved. The boy was a good kid; he just needed a little guidance. And a firm hand. A much firmer hand than anyone had ever given him, probably because he managed to squirm out from under it too fast.

Josef sauntered over to the door, took a firm grip on the bar and shoved down to open it. The door was heavy and he had to step outside. The moment he did, a man with stained teeth exposed through loose, salivating lips caught at his long red hair and dragged Josef to him, spinning him as he did so, exposing his neck. Ferro recognized Varga trying to feed off the woman he thought he controlled. Two others came close but the master vampire paused long enough to kick at them and indicate for them to get inside and collect their intended victim.

Before Varga could sink his teeth into Josef's neck, Josef shocked Ferro by slamming his fist deep into Edward Varga's chest and wrenching his head to one side, avoiding the long teeth seeking his blood. That small split second allowed Traian to come in behind the vampire so that when Josef drove his fist into the front of the chest wall, the force of the blow helped send the vampire straight back into Traian's fist.

They know. They are here, Elisabeta warned.

Ferro didn't wait to see the outcome of the battle between Varga and Traian. He had to believe that the Carpathians stationed in the underground caverns could protect those there. He had to find the master vampires and destroy them. Once they were gone, any lesser vampire breaking through into the nightclub would no longer have direction and would be easier to kill.

We need the location of the master vampires, Elisabeta. Let the hunters do their jobs now. Drop everything else. You cannot be distracted. He wished he was with her to shield her from what they all knew they couldn't completely prevent.

On the private path between brethren, he reached for Isai. *Let Julija know she will have to do her best to keep Elisabeta from feeling the full effects of the vampires tearing into the humans. Once Cornel or any of them are aware she is aiding us, they will know she is too sensitive and they will order their servants to be as cruel and as messy as possible.*

Ferro was grateful to be out of the underground and into the night. He could smell the ominous threat in the air. Overhead, the clouds churned a dark twisting mass of gray and black threads, blotting out the moon and stars as if they'd never been. When he inhaled, he smelled rotting flesh. Grating noises hurt his ears. Shrieks and talons scraping at windows told him vampires were trying to get into the nightclub.

The waiters in service to the Malinovs had been contained by the Carpathians the moment the notice was given. They couldn't open doors or invite the vampires in. That didn't mean any number of the guests inside couldn't do it. Sooner or later, someone would. The moment that happened, the vampires would begin to feast. After the first blood spilled, it would turn into a frenzy for the servants of the master vampires they'd deliberately kept so hungry.

Elisabeta? We need direction, he prompted.

She hissed at him—actually hissed at him. His beloved, sweet, docile Elisabeta was definitely coming into her own. He would have smiled but she would have known.

This is not easy. They have to move in their minds. They are hidden, buried deep in their disguises. I have to discover them, see them through those disguises. It takes patience and attention to detail.

He did smile. He had used words very similar when he was giving her lessons in shifting or flying. He'd made her practice hundreds of times. She was taking not just him but many centuries-old ancients to school. She might pretend she thought it was just her lifemate she was talking to, but she knew those he was connected to were listening and he was sharing with others.

Forgive my impatience, piŋe sarnanak.

At once he felt her instant horror that she had come close to rebuking him. She *hadn't* considered that any others might hear them. *No, Ferro, please forgive me. I feel stretched in so many directions, trying to reach out to find them, and I was not thinking.*

He gentled his voice, cursing the entire situation, wishing he was a gentler man. *You are doing fine, sívamet.*

He was moving with the wind, letting his body drift toward the heaviest cover. There was a massive parking garage. There would be plenty of victims for the vampires to prey on there, but he doubted if any of the master vampires would want to be caught with concrete and stone hanging over their heads. They would want to be very close to the nightclub itself. Cornel in particular was certain the piece that he thought would aid him to rule the Carpathian people, or destroy them, was hidden somewhere in the building. Where? Where would he think Tariq would keep such a valuable item? His office? That just seemed too easy.

In the landscaping at the back entrance where the patios are on the ground level. There are heavy bushes there. Elisabeta seemed tentative, as if she'd lost her confidence.

Ferro couldn't pour himself more fully into her mind without risking giving her away to Sergey or one of the others. He detested using her. The ancients were used to hunting their way. They shouldn't need his woman to spotlight their quarry for them.

Sandu, Benedek and Isai had spread out, drifting like Ferro with the wind, looking to spot a single sign of the master vampires hidden in the city structures, the cars and parking garages, rather than the forests and mountains that were their normal hunting grounds.

Sedrick is in the patio itself. He has made himself part of the roof. Ivy grows along the overhang and hangs down the supports. Are any of you close enough to see if the leaves have withered? Elisabeta sought confirmation that she was correct.

Benedek answered immediately. *I will work my way around to the patio, little sisar.*

Ambrus has concealed himself just to the left of the underground club exit door, closest to the trees. He is working to bring down the safeguards over the door of the nightclub, not the underground club. While he works, he is in communication with someone inside. She was silent for a moment.

Ferro, as did all the others, felt the brush of pain, as if an electrical charge passed through their minds. He went very still. *Elisabeta? Is Ambrus aware of you? Does he know that you are tracking him?*

He is very powerful, and each time I touch his mind, he is wary. I told you, his instincts are more animal than human. He senses a presence, but has no idea who or what that presence is. He sent out a probe. I was slow in shielding all of you from his investigation. It can sometimes be painful. I am used to it and forgot you would not be. I apologize.

Elisabeta's admission set Ferro's teeth on edge. That sweet, gentle voice admitting that she knew Ambrus's probe would be painful meant she had often reached for his mind and felt him trying to find if an enemy really might be close. Could he trust his senses? She didn't flinch from the pain because that would give her away. Sun scorch the woman, she was going to be the death of him, not some master vampire. She was going to tear out his heart.

Ambrus, yes, Elisabeta, I see him now. He is very busy, Sandu said. *He has two servants with him, guarding his back.*

His servants are like him. Elisabeta was quick to give out the information. *Instinctive, like animals. Fierce in battle. They always go for the belly and genitals. If you have spotted two, there will be three others concealed nearby. Ambrus hunts with a pack. He is the one I would consider the most dangerous in battle. Cornel is the strategist. He can plan a war, but Ambrus is the fighter. His servants are close to having the skills of a master vampire without being one.*

Ferro didn't like the sound of that. Sandu wouldn't hesitate to take on Ambrus and his pack of servants. He was an ancient and they did one thing—they destroyed vampires. He had no lifemate and no reason to continue his existence. Ferro chose to make his stand with Sandu. Sergey was not going to escape him again, not unless he was dying or dead, but he had to make certain Sandu had a fighting chance to survive.

Ferro. Her soft little protest trembled, but Elisabeta pulled it together for him. *Addler is sending two of the newly made vampires to the door of the nightclub. He is watching to see what happens. A couple just drove up in a car. He wants to use them as bait. The vampires will tear them to pieces.*

He heard the trepidation in her voice. *How many servants does he have left?* He knew the master vampires had counted on their servants coming through the city, but the hunters had quietly wiped out most of them.

Only two. He is very upset. He has two servants but also two of the newly made vampires with him as well.

That meant that the Carpathian numbers were growing as the hunters were tracking the last of the servants of the master vampires to the nightclub. That was a plus.

I have Addler in my sight as well as the vampires and the couple. Have stopped the couple from getting out of their car. They are driving away, Petru reported.

All of them felt the buildup of energy in the air as Addler attempted to force the couple to turn around. Both newly made vampires took to the air to fling themselves at the windshield. Petru waved his hand and both dropped from the sky, feathers bursting from their shrunken bodies so that they appeared to be nothing more than two owls. As he did so, lightning forked across the sky and thunder crashed.

Lightning had been lashing the city for what seemed nearly a quarter of an hour as the storm stalled, bringing heavy roiling dark clouds, thunder and an endless electrical show that kept everyone off the streets. A series of lethal sizzling bolts hit dead center on the roof of the extremely popular Asenguard Nightclub. Sparks flew in every direction, rising into the air, a colorful display rivaling that of fireworks.

Over and over the jagged lightning bolts continued to hit in exactly the same spot. Each hit was precise, as if directed by laser beam.

Elisabeta tried not to wince each time a bolt struck. The weaves of protection held, but that didn't stop the shaking of the building from the strength of the blow. Each time the rocking was so strong it nearly knocked the three women off their feet.

"That is Cornel, knocking politely," she announced solemnly as they clung together.

Lorraine and Julija burst out laughing with her. Elisabeta found herself amazed that she could be sharing laughter when the night was lit up with bolts of lightning aimed specifically at the rooftop where the three of them were standing.

"How very polite of him," Julija said. "I suppose we should be just as eloquent in our response to him."

Lorraine and Elisabeta automatically stepped back to give Julija room. She was from a powerful Carpathian lineage, but she was also a direct descendant of one of the most powerful mages in the world. She lifted her hands and began to weave her spell, concentrating on that small pinpoint where the tip of the bolt was directed with each strike.

Julija timed her response so that when Cornel slammed his next attack onto that weave of protection in order to penetrate it, her spell countered his. A blue ring whirled around the tip for one brief flash and then rushed up the jagged electrical bolt, seeking the sender.

The strikes abruptly broke off and black smoke trailed through the sky. A thick, noxious vapor poured into the air, smelling of rotting and decomposing flesh.

"Cornel," Elisabeta said, a little shocked. "Julija, you not only incapacitated him for the moment, but you brought him out into the open."

"As I meant to do." Julija spread her arms wide to encompass the sky, taking in as much of the dark, spinning clouds as possible. "I reversed his intentions. It won't last long but it should give you enough time to find his heart."

Elisabeta closed her eyes and sent her mind seeking Cornel's while Julija began to move her hands gracefully, murmuring her powerful spell as she did so. Cornel was stunned almost beyond comprehension. He had no idea what had happened to him and he was incapable of protecting himself. His heart, a black, withered organ he protected by moving it continually around his body, was still for the first time in many centuries while he was awake. She found it near his belly, a shriveled lump. Immediately she directed Julija to the target.

Lorraine held the whip of lightning, ready for Julija's magic to penetrate the inevitable shields the master vampire would have around him while Elisabeta pinpointed the target with absolute precision. Julija struck at the shields and Lorraine simultaneously sent the bolt of lightning straight at the master vampire's heart.

The white-hot sword hit an impenetrable shimmering barrier, sending a tower of sparks high into the air, thunder crashing, roaring so loud it threw all three women to the ground. Fireballs rained from the sky, a meteor shower of bright, hot spinning orbs pounding down on the roof, aimed directly at the heads of the three women. A dark shadow swept back and forth over them, wings spread wide, mouth open wide spouting a long, steady stream of fire at them.

"Dorin," Elisabeta said, trying to get her hands under her to get to her feet. The building kept rocking, as if an earthquake had seized the ground and was desperate to split it in two. "He threw that shield up to protect Cornel at the last second."

She subsided onto the roof, letting her exhausted body have a reprieve. They weren't going to get a second chance at Cornel and all three women knew it. He was too intelligent to stay around when his servants had been attacked, the nightclub was protected and he had been injured. He could leave, regroup and fight another day.

Cornel is injured and is near the trees just north of the parking garage. She passed the information on to the hunters. *He is trying to escape. Dorin is protecting him along with their combined servants. They have called to Sergey and Ambrus and the other master vampires to leave with them.*

The three women sat together, heads back, looking up at the dark, malevolent clouds, linking their minds together, using the pathway through Elisabeta to follow the various battles.

"Ambrus, I see that you desire to dance with the devil this rising," Ferro greeted as he strode up the intricate paved walkway leading to the door the master vampire was attempting to open. "I must confess, I thought you had a liking for the forest, as I do. This city is too closed in for my taste, and these buildings feel as if they are nothing but heavy weights hanging over my head where I cannot breathe." He kept his voice friendly.

Ferro had removed all traces of Elisabeta's scent from his body. He kept her from his mind on the off-chance that Ambrus had found a way to read Carpathian hunters. He ignored the two servants who pressed close, inhaling deeply, drawing the scent of rich, ancient blood into their lungs as he passed them by. It was very necessary to keep Ambrus and his servants' attention completely centered on him. He wanted the master vampire confident that he could take him at any time. The vampire had three more servants in hiding, waiting to spring his trap. He would want to kill Ferro before he joined Cornel in what he saw as defeat.

"Ferro," Ambrus greeted in return. "It is good that it is you. Someone worthy at last. So many with no skills have challenged me in the last half of the century that I thought maybe there were none left."

Ferro shrugged. "A few. We were in the monastery, but the call came upon us and we had to answer. You know how it is."

"The call?" Ambrus prompted, gliding a step closer. His eyes had taken on a red glow. His arms dropped low, giving him the appearance of harmlessness, his fingers spread wide, but his nails had lengthened just a tiny bit and sharpened to lethal points. He tapped his index finger on his thigh, a subtle sign few would catch.

"Two women came to the monastery. Both had gifts and were able to tell the brethren that our lifemates were alive in this century. Naturally, we once more set out looking."

Ambrus lifted one hand to his angular jaw and scratched. "You still believe in such a myth, Ferro? That is how the prince keeps you tied to him. You should know better. I always thought you smarter than that." The finger tapped again.

Behind Ferro and to his right, a leaf whispered as something brushed against it. Ambrus slid his foot an imperceptible quarter of an inch forward, much like the stalk of a leopard.

"I believe because I did find her, Ambrus. It is no myth. You know Andor found his lifemate. I have found mine."

Ambrus froze. He shook his head slowly. "This is impossible. Not for one such as you. They say Zacarias De La Cruz also found a lifemate. We all know this to be impossible. It is simply a trick to make us believe the Malinov brothers lied to us."

"What would I gain by telling you I have found my lifemate?"

A look of absolute cunning crept over Ambrus's heavy features, giving him that animalistic look that further warned Ferro that this man thought and fought with the skills of both hunter and animal. "It matters little your intention, Ferro. You walked into an ambush and I bid you good luck surviving, although you seem to have proven your skills in battle time after time these long centuries. It will be interesting to see how you fare against my pack of very hungry dogs. I like to keep them on edge so they fight all the harder for their reward."

Ferro smiled, started to give a small courteous bow, and Ambrus attacked, rushing him. Simultaneously, the master vampire's two servants converged from either side, talons like the harpy eagle reaching for his belly and eyes to rip and gouge. Three more of the pack leapt down from above, straight at his back and head, their intention to drive him forward onto their master's fist so he could wrench the beating heart out of Ferro's chest and be done with the fight before it ever truly began.

Ferro, the bait to draw out the entire pack, dissolved into mist and went down, not up, going low between the legs of the master vampire and coming up behind him. Sandu, Petru, Fane, Aleksi and Dragomir surrounded the master vampire and his pack. The last three ancients, all brethren from the monastery, had arrived to join in the hunt against the master vampires.

Ferro slammed his fist straight through Ambrus's back. Ferro was a big man and enormously strong. The blow shattered bones and drove through muscle, half turning the vampire toward him. Ambrus tried to reach him with his arms, curling back toward his opponent while all around him his servants fought for their lives against battle-experienced Carpathian hunters.

These were not men concerned with ego or whether or not anyone noticed how many individual kills they made, or even if they fought the most difficult of the vampires. They simply sought to remove the vampire from the world. That was the sole purpose of the Carpathian hunters.

Plants erupted beneath Ferro's feet, long, hungry, eel-like tubes with teeth, latching on to his legs, attempting to drag him beneath the ground, wrenching at his body so hard the creatures yanked him away from Ambrus, allowing the master vampire to stagger free. Black acid coated Ferro's arm and hand, eating at his flesh, while the hungry creatures sawed at his legs, continually trying to pull him back toward their wormhole.

Ferro reached toward the sky with his uninjured hand and lightning responded, slamming into the creatures' bodies right where they emerged from the hole, slicing them cleanly in two. At the same time, he bathed his injured arm in the spray of white-hot energy, cleaning the acid from it, removing the vampire's blood to prevent it from eating its way to the bone.

As the creatures dropped away from his legs, Ferro snapped the lightning whip at Ambrus's head, dropping loops of sizzling-hot energy around his neck, leashing him to prevent him from shifting and getting away. With a snarl, Ambrus turned back to face him, the coils of lightning slipping around his entire body, spinning, holding him in place, exposing him as he truly was, not as he preferred to appear.

Rotted flesh hung off skeleton bones. What seemed a fit body was no more than an illusion perfected over centuries. Ambrus might not appear to be as vain as any other vampire, but clearly he wanted to appear to the others as a mountain of a man with a muscular, battle-scarred body. That was worth noting—that Ambrus had included scarring when forging an appearance. He hadn't made himself as the Astors had, flawless and handsome.

Instead of the long hair of the traditional Carpathian warrior that Ambrus favored, his skull had great scaly patches of some gooey substance that oozed from inside his brain to dribble in a steady stream down his head and trickle out of holes where his ears should be. His eyes were sockets of flaming red. He had no nose, only twin sunken holes, and his mouth was filled with jagged, pointed teeth so stained with blood they appeared black.

Elisabeta, in all the centuries Ambrus has appeared to the Malinovs, has he always appeared as you have seen him? With this image? He showed her the copy of a very fit Ambrus, trying to spare her the true rotted soul of the vampire.

Within the coils of the lightning whip, Ambrus began to sway back and forth, murmuring to himself, his long, bony fingers tapping a rhythm on his thin, emaciated leg.

Always.

As the coils dropped from Ambrus, Ferro flicked his hands casually toward the vampire, surrounding him with mirrors, above him, below and completely circling him. There was nowhere the vampire looked that he didn't see himself reflected back in his true, hideous state. He stretched his thin lips in a wide protest, screaming in horror, throwing up his arms to cover his eyes while maggots and a wealth of parasites tumbled from his mouth and throat to spew against the reflective glass.

Ferro slammed his fist deep into the chest wall, breaking through the brittle bones without the armor of Ambrus's woven muscle and dense bone he most likely threaded with other things to make it much more difficult for a Carpathian hunter to get to his heart. His fingers sought the withered organ, but it wasn't where it should have been.

He has moved it lower, to the base of his spine.

Ferro didn't hesitate. He withdrew his fist and slammed into him a second time, searching for the heart, fighting to get to it. Ambrus was already recovering from the momentary shock of seeing his true image after centuries of convincing himself of what he looked like. The master vampire leaned forward and bit down viciously into Ferro's shoulder, tearing great chunks of his flesh from his body, and gulped at them, gulped at the rich, ancient blood that would give him a burst of strength.

The vampire tried to turn his head so he could sink his teeth into Ferro's neck and get at the jugular. Ferro continuously whirled in a circle, driving Ambrus backward into the mirrors so the glass shattered, driving the shards into the bones, keeping the master vampire from being able to shift or get his bearings. Ferro was too fast and too strong, holding off the vampire's teeth as his fist dug for the heart against his spine.

Ambrus retaliated, turning his hands into knifelike weapons, plunging them over and over deep into Ferro's chest, driving straight for the Carpathian's heart. Ferro heard Elisabeta's gasp and cut off all contact with her immediately, stoically accepting the pain. It was a battle. Hunters expected to be wounded. They had to be close to extract the heart, and that meant the vampire would be able to rend and tear at their bodies. That was drilled into them from the time they were young boys. It was one of the reasons he didn't want Josef hunting the undead too soon. The boy might have the courage and the knowledge, but he didn't yet have the body to be torn into pieces and survive the experience.

The moment Ferro had the heart in his palm he closed his fingers around it and ripped it from the master vampire's body, turned and flung it high into the air. *Lorraine!*

It would be the last thing any vampire would expect. Ambrus would try to steal the lightning from him, and he raised his hand as if wielding the whip as it blazed through the dark sky. Lorraine targeted the tiny wizened organ, impossible to see because Ferro had thrown it so high, but tied to him through their soul bond, she tracked that blackened target.

Ambrus triumphantly reached for the sky, hands wide in an effort to snatch the lightning bolt from Ferro, but the sizzling, white-hot whip danced through the air, crackling ominously, heading with unerring accuracy right to that tiny object. Ferro dropped his hands to his sides and regarded the master vampire who shook his head in denial, unable to believe what he was seeing. The tip of the whip hit the heart, incinerating it, so that black, noxious smoke billowed up for a moment and then was cleaned in the bright hot burn of the electrical current. Ambrus stood swaying, head tilted toward the sky. He was still standing that exact way when the whip of lightning hit him and he turned to that same black ash, burning until there was nothing at all left behind.

Something heavy hit his body, nearly knocking Ferro down, and he reacted, spinning, catching at one of Ambrus's servants as he tried to dive into the air to get away from Petru. Ferro blocked the snarling beast of a vampire from the air by throwing his body fully in front of him. The vampire immediately attacked, raking at him with claws and snapping viciously with teeth while hurling dozens of poisonous arrows behind him in an effort to keep Sandu from approaching from that direction.

Most of the lesser vampires were trying to follow Cornel and Dorin in their orders to retreat, taking to the air, but there were too many hunters pulling them out of the sky or tracking them on the ground. There was nowhere to hide. The few that had nearly made it into one of the clubs because a door had been opened had been immediately stopped by one of the hunters inside. The Carpathians had too many experienced warriors waiting for them, an impossibility to fight against. Retreat was the only reasonable solution, and when the vampires tried to flee, they were set upon immediately.

Ferro managed to slide out from under the raking claws as if giving the vampire a way out, and then as the creature redoubled his speed, it impaled itself right on Sandu's outstretched fist.

"Traian and Josef killed Edward Varga," Tariq reported. "Benedek disposed of Sedrick. Petru killed Addler, and Ferro destroyed Ambrus. Cornel and Dorin Malinov managed to slip away, but that doesn't surprise me." He looked around him at the Carpathian warriors with various wounds as they aided one another, giving blood and helping one another to heal. "While some of us are making certain there are no traces of the vampires at the clubs and the male psychics are either free of all influences or they met with very sad accidents, we are not yet finished. Ferro says Elisabeta can call Sergey back to her. If she can do this, we can destroy five of the seven master vampires and most of their army in one decisive blow this night. Sergey is very dangerous with the knowledge he carries in his head from his brothers and the high mage. Can Elisabeta really call him to her, Ferro?"

Ferro nodded his head decisively. "Yes, absolutely she can. He will be unable to resist answering her. He will come." Gary was working on healing him. Three of the ancients had replenished his blood. All of them would need to be in their best shape of the night. Even better than they had been if they were going to win this next battle.

"Call to him, Elisabeta. Bring him to you. Sergey is unable to resist your call." They stood together, Ferro and Elisabeta, at the very edge of the meadow. Before them was a long expanse of grass and flowers. The flowers looked asleep, petals closed, while the clouds moved across the sky overhead.

Her long lashes lifted, her dark eyes liquid with tears. She gave a small shake of her head, resisting his command for the first time. "You are injured, Ferro. He may not be the most intelligent of the Malinov brothers, but he makes up for it in both cunning and cruelty. He will smell your blood and crave it. That will spur him to greater heights of viciousness."

"Call to him, *minan piŋe sarnanak*." He was implacable.

"He has a sliver of all of his brothers in him. He has not one but *two* of Xavier, the high mage, within him. If you defeat him, the moment you extract his heart, all of those slivers will desert him and seek a host. They will scatter, tiny, very dangerous shadows impossible to track. They will find human hosts, possibly children. Each sliver is evil and will corrupt their host and lead them back to the nearest mage or vampire."

The plea in her voice shook him. The liquid in her eyes spilled over and tears tracked down her face. Ferro wrapped his arm around her and pulled her beneath his shoulder.

"You should know me by now, *sívamet*. Would I go into battle without knowing what I face? I saved Sergey for last because I know what he holds. He cannot live. He will never stop trying to find a way to get to you. Bodies of innocent men, women and children will be nailed to the gates of the compound each rising. We cannot have that. Eventually, your kind heart will break and you will go to find him. Where is your faith in me? Your trust? More importantly, *minan päläfertiilam*, where is your belief in us?"

Elisabeta's dark eyes drifted over his face. "You look so worn, beloved." She sighed. "If you wish to do this, then we do this."

He waited, letting her feel their combined strength. Their power. It rolled over the meadow, filling the air, impossible to contain. She had to feel it the way he did. It wasn't his power alone, it was hers as well—the two of them together.

She straightened her shoulders and nodded. "You have a plan. I know that you do. Tell me what you want me to do once he arrives."

She knew Sergey would come. Like Ferro, she had no doubt. Ferro smiled down at his little songbird who had finally escaped her cage and yet, with the cage door wide open, she had chosen him, chosen to stay with her centuries-old lifemate.

"You know the plan, *piŋe sarnanak*, we have practiced it a thousand times."

Master. Elisabeta whispered the call in her mind, keeping her voice thin and fearful. *Can you hear me? I have little time. He is not aware.*

At once there was a stirring. A black malevolent presence poured into Elisabeta's mind, thick like an oil, clogging every pore. Over the centuries she had developed false walls so that the master vampire believed he could search her mind and know what she had been up to. With the exception of having access to her lifemate's soul, he believed he controlled her completely, when she had slowly built compartment after compartment, pushing him further and further out.

Now he saw only what Elisabeta wanted him to see. Terror. Fear of her lifemate. Of the Carpathian people. Of their demands on her. She understood nothing of their lives and they made fun of her behind her back because she didn't know how to do anything for herself. Her lifemate was ashamed of her.

Why do you bother me? Sergey sounded disdainful.

Elisabeta hesitated. Retreated. The old Elisabeta would never have answered him or begged him to take her back. She would have been too terrified of the consequences of speaking to him.

He is drawing closer, she cautioned Ferro.

In the meadow she stood, appearing shaky, one hand half covering her face, taking several steps back into the deeper concealment of the trees, bending forward as if to peer out, looking up at the sky hopefully.

Why would he be unaware of what you are saying to me? Sergey demanded.

He was gone for a long time this rising. When he returned, he was wounded very badly. They called for the healer and several of the ancients to give him blood.

Does he come alone? Ferro asked. That would be so arrogant but so like Sergey, thinking he could secret Elisabeta away once again. Cornel and Dorin wouldn't know she was back with him and he would forever have the advantage over them.

He has two very minor vampires with him. They are circling around the meadow to ensure that I am alone. His intention is to slay them both after he takes me back with him.

Sergey made a show of sighing heavily. *Very well, then. I will take you back, but you will be punished. Walk out into the middle of the meadow. My servants will collect you and bring you back.*

Elisabeta froze. Retreated further into her mind. Shook like the little mouse she was.

I command you to do this. Walk out into the meadow now or I will leave you to those people. I have no time for your stubbornness.

She didn't move. She didn't speak. She simply shivered, a small ball of absolute terror as only Elisabeta could be. She was so magnificent, Ferro wanted to kiss her senseless. Sergey would never leave her there. As a lure, she was absolute perfection, too scared to move. The master vampire was too close to his obsession. He needed her with every breath he drew, and there was no way he was going to allow her to slip through his fingers.

The two servants of the undead flew toward the forest where Elisabeta had entered. She immediately shifted, just out of sight, rising to the branches, a small female owl, while a young woman in a flowing cape seemed to be running into deeper forest, away from the meadow. She was barefoot, and her dark hair tangled on brush, slowing her down so that the servants caught glimpses of her, just enough to keep them following.

Elisabeta, stop this game at once. Come to me.

Where are you? Her voice was very tentative. *I do not want to speak to those men or have them touch me. You never allowed it. Never. How do I know it is you?*

Ferro found himself smiling. That was a good point. Sergey couldn't dispute that. Elisabeta was very clever.

I am waiting in the meadow, just as you asked. Hurry. Dawn is approaching and I tire of your tantrums.

Elisabeta allowed her first real, although tentative, excitement to spill into her mind, that Sergey might really be coming for her. Deliberately the leaves rustled by the entrance and she froze. *Where are those men?* She let fear spill into her voice and mind all over again.

They cannot get to you. Hurry, Elisabeta. Sergey came into view, hovering just above the ground, building safeguards to surround the entire meadow with just a small path for her to travel. *They cannot enter. Only you. Step inside and I will close the safeguards behind you. Once I have you, we will leave this place. The one who claimed you will not be able to follow, either.*

Sergey's servants following the elusive shadow of Elisabeta were being tracked by Carpathian hunters. The moment Ferro gave the word, they would be taken down.

Appearing almost small in her cape, although she was tall, like all Carpathian women, Elisabeta looked all around her before she stepped from the shadow of the forest and set foot into the meadow, allowing Sergey to weave the safeguards behind her to lock her there with him.

He beckoned to her impatiently with one long finger. At the end was a wicked-looking nail. "Come to me now, Elisabeta." He snapped his fingers. "We have to leave this place."

Ferro shifted as he approached within a few feet of Sergey. Ferro's appearance revealed the wicked wounds from his battle with Ambrus. His clothes were torn and showed bloodstains.

"I see she called you. She fears a new life, but she will get used to it in time."

"What have you done with her?" Sergey demanded.

Elisabeta let out a small moan and presented an image of rocking herself back and forth, of being very small, curling into herself as if terrified. Ferro glided a little closer, covering the smallest of limps, one arm tight against his ribs.

Sergey flung up his hand, weaving replicas of himself and sending them spinning in a wide circle around Ferro. The ground shifted and rolled, sending the Carpathian tumbling to his knees. Above their heads, within the safeguards, thunder roared and the swirling black clouds opened up to dump acid rain on them. Sergey moved in fast to kick at Ferro's chin, determined to knock him on his back so he could more easily extract the heart. He also wanted as much of the Carpathian male's body exposed to the painful acid as possible.

Ferro caught his ankle, twisted and took him down with his enormous strength, caught the stake Sandu threw to him and slammed it straight through Sergey's heart, pinning him to the consecrated spot in the meadow. Smoke rose as the vampire's skin burned. He screamed horribly. Ferro waved his hand to stop the rain.

Elisabeta, take down his safeguards above. We will need the lightning. Strengthen the ones we wove in the ground so the slivers cannot burrow.

The ground is both hallowed and safeguarded, Ferro, Elisabeta assured. *I am removing the safeguards above you now.*

The grasses disappeared as if they'd never been to reveal the wide expanse of bare dirt, all of which had been sanctified. Ringing the entire prepared circle were the ancients, waiting, all eyes on the writhing, fighting master vampire as Ferro held him down with the sacrosanct wooden stake. He had to use both hands. Black blood bubbled up around the wood. Benedek held the legs of the vampire as Sergey kicked and drummed his heels into the dirt.

The master vampire spit his hatred at Ferro. His red inflamed eyes promised retaliation, flames burning in their depths. At times they glowed silver or brown or green, malevolent, promising torturous, painful death. He tried to dig claws into Ferro, to tear skin off his ribs and arms, anything to get him to remove the stake.

Minutes passed while they waited. The ancients wore the expressionless, stoic masks of the hunters. They didn't pass judgment on the creatures they were forced to hunt and destroy. They rid the world of their presence because they had no other choice. They waited now in silence, all eyes on the writhing master vampire.

Maggots and parasites oozed from his pores, abandoning the undead's body. More and more he appeared a rotting, decomposed corpse. The moment the parasites or maggots hit the soil, they burned into white ash so that soon, the vampire's shape was drawn with a pile of ash much like a chalk outline surrounding him.

Each of Sergey's four older brothers had placed a sliver of themselves in their younger brother. He also had two slivers of Xavier, the high mage. Those slivers would abandon him when it became apparent their host was not going to survive. The ancients simply waited while Sergey hissed and screamed his hatred. While the hallowed ground under his body burned and seared his back and skull. While the sanctified stake spread purity through his insides, forcing out every corruption.

Without warning, six tiny shadows emerged from Sergey's ears, rushing in all directions, each seeking the safety of the darkness and the higher grass several yards away. The slivers were so tiny they were nearly impossible to see, even with Carpathian vision, but for the plume of smoke rising from each as the hallowed soil burned them, marking each abomination as it made its desperate run.

Lightning forked across the sky in a dazzling display, seven whips arcing above their heads. Six jagged spears slammed to earth with deadly accuracy, each striking one of the fleeing slivers. Hideous shrieks tore through the night, a frightful cacophony that rose in strength. Faceless skulls with wide yawning empty holes for mouths appeared in sheets of rising black smoke. Venomous silver eyes glared for a brief moment and then flames consumed them, burning them to ash.

Ferro jerked the stake free in one swift movement and the remaining white-hot lightning whip hit Sergey's heart with deadly accuracy. The master vampire stared up at him with unrelenting hatred until there was nothing but the rotted corpse left, and then that, too, was gone. The ancients stood for a brief moment, heads bowed, before they cleared the land of all traces of the vampires and made their way back to the compound, just beating dawn.

21

What once was a blaze, grows stronger than before;
A metal in the forge, turns a sword for the war.
A life of hope sings to you, melodies of devotion;
A world of love awaits, vaster than the ocean.

Ferro woke Elisabeta gently, singing their song to her, one of deep love and commitment, of devotion and hope. She was truly free, his little songbird. No longer in her cage, free to choose her life, and she had made it abundantly clear that her choice was Ferro. He found that humbling. A miracle. He knew he would never take her for granted.

They'd gone to ground together, wrapped in each other's arms, his body protectively curled around hers. He was grateful for the freedom to be able to do so without frightening her. He never wanted her to think he was caging her in, but he found he needed to be close to her. Skin to skin. Touching her even in their slumber.

Before, he had slept above her to protect her, to give her a sense of safety, but now she welcomed him in the ground with her, his body in the same resting place. He woke before her to hunt for blood for them both, but then he had the privilege of waking her with their song. He was able to feel that first awareness in her mind, the joy in her when she recognized the notes of their music together. Her long lashes lifting so her eyes met his. The moment that happened, his heart clenched and his stomach did a slow roll of acknowledgment.

Ferro opened his arms to her and Elisabeta floated from the earth, clean and refreshed, all on her own. He closed his arms, cradling her to him, rubbed his jaw along the curve of her breast, her pulse calling to him as he took her to their favorite place deep in their forest. Neither would ever be entirely comfortable in a house. He supposed someday, when they had children, they would have to be used to a roof over their heads, but they preferred the canopy of trees.

Elisabeta slid her arms around his neck, offering herself to him. "I love the way you smell, Ferro. Wild and elusive like the forest itself. I would know you anywhere."

He would know her by scent alone as well. She came into his mind slowly, drifting in like a soothing breeze, her fragrance so subtle but distinct, rare camellias, Italian bergamot, that hint of orange and lime, sandalwood and vetiver, the mixture almost elusive and yet lingering. Her skin held that same faint scent. Even her taste had hints of those flavors.

"When you would merge with others to rid them of the infection and I would be with you in their minds, I could feel you cleanse them with that soothing serenity, that peace and compassion that is so much a part of you, but also there was always your fragrance. Your scent clings to your skin. It is in your mind, Elisabeta, so deep in you that when you are in my mind or in another's I can catch your scent. I think that is a good part of the way you soothe the ancients."

He rubbed his chin over the top of her head, not wanting her to look into his eyes and see that he might not like sharing that part of her with anyone. In ancient times, many Carpathians didn't allow others near their lifemates because it could be dangerous if those warriors turned vampire. He understood that concept. He would have been one of those men. Now, he wanted to carry her off somewhere they would be alone without interruption from all the demands the Carpathian world seemed to put on them.

"I prefer always to be with just you, Ferro," she admitted.

The notes of truth in her voice slipped into his mind and lodged there, reassuring him. When she had first awoken, he had worked to be her light in the darkness; now she was his bright star. He tipped her face up to his and kissed her. The moment he did, he tasted passion. Love. A mixture of both.

The burn came slow, easy, a decadent lazy heat that swept through his veins, sped through hers, picking up speed as kisses grew passionate and hotter. Until the fire became a storm of emotion.

Ferro took his time worshipping her. Showing her how much she meant to him. Elisabeta was meticulous in answering him back, her hands and mouth moving over his body with equal loving. Whispers and laughter, the sound of bodies coming together and soft cries of passion rose long into the night.

With Elisabeta snuggled in his arms, looking up at the stars through the gently swaying canopy of trees, Ferro reminded her that there was a big celebration going on and it was expected that they make an appearance. It didn't have to be a long one, but they should go.

"You have gotten so good at flying and clothing yourself, I thought you could fly to the compound from here and dress yourself in that beautiful green gown you know I love. I put it in your mind a couple of times." Deliberately, he enticed her with flying. She was feeling very sated and loving, her hands sliding over his chest and hip very possessively.

"The scandalous one?" She tilted her head to look up at him, a hint of laughter in her dark eyes.

He couldn't help his answering grin. The dress could be scandalous if they were alone. Only if they were alone and his fingers were busy on the corset, pulling the laces free so her breasts spilled into his hands. "Yes, that is the one I think would be perfect for a celebration. The material is soft and drapes well on your body. You will look beautiful."

She laughed, rolled over and nipped at his chin with her teeth. "You will be thinking about those laces the entire time we are at this celebration."

That might be true, but he hoped she would be distracted enough to get her through when she saw the number of Carpathians concentrated in a small area. Already she was shifting, a little screech owl, wings outspread, flying into the night. He was after her, the male owl smaller, lighter and much faster. He kept pace, alert for any danger to her as they covered the distance to the compound.

The two owls circled above the party below them before slowly beginning a spiraling descent into the shadows of the garden just beside the healing grounds. When Elisabeta emerged in her true form, wearing the long forest-green dress with the tight corset of crisscross cords over her breasts, she turned and gave him a look of pure reprimand.

"You knew what this would be like."

He couldn't deny it. He took her hand and walked her to the very edge of the garden and then wrapped his arms around her waist, pulling her back against his body to shelter her. "We had our time this rising together, and I knew I could not be so selfish as to keep you from seeing the celebration the others are having."

The music was beautiful, rising to the night sky, the band playing instruments and couples dancing. Others talked and laughed together while children ran around, sometimes dancing and other times pretending to fight an enemy. The little girls somehow had gotten hold of sparkles and glitter and were generously dousing the ground, flowers, people and everything in sight.

Josef came into view, several older children following him, each armed with buckets of glitter on their belts and some kind of weapon they had tied to their backs in easy reach. It wasn't hard to see that he was the instigator.

I do love to see the children playing like this, Ferro, but sooner or later, someone will insist I talk to them, and I just can't do it yet. She spoke on their much more intimate pathway. *When so many are around I feel too exposed.*

Ferro kept his arms around Elisabeta's waist, holding her tight. "You are doing just fine, *minan piŋe sarnanak.* As you can see, most of the Carpathians are coming together either for the first time or getting reacquainted. No one is going to notice or be upset if I do the talking for us. I do wonder what Josef is up to with all this colored glitter. It looks as if these children are up to something." Now the children were all gathered around the stone dragons in the middle of the courtyard.

He was just a little too pleased that she still preferred him to talk for her in a crowd. He wasn't certain he liked that trait in himself, the one that wanted her a little reliant on him.

I will always like to have you close to me, Ferro. It is my nature. That does not make me less empowered.

Her voice brushed gently through his mind, her soothing fragrance surrounding him, there in the midst of so many other scents. He heard the sound of children laughing and watched as Tariq's oldest boy, Danny, bent to lift Darius and Tempest's son, Andor, in front of him onto his brown stone dragon's back. The boy slipped up behind him and waited while Amelia put Andor's twin sister, Aniko, on her orange dragon. The two teenagers whispered to the twins and then to their dragons.

"I want you to continue to grow in confidence, Elisabeta," Ferro said. "Do you see Danny and Amelia? The way they are with those children? Darius and Tempest are part of the Dark Troubadours. Whenever I watch the children in any village, they are like these, ready to teach, to entertain, to always share what they have with the little ones. They help with their confidence and self-esteem. They give them knowledge, even in play."

The way you share your knowledge with Josef to help him feel as if he can become a great hunter of the vampire when his time comes.

She wasn't understanding what he was trying to say. She wouldn't, because she was so caring and compassionate and it wouldn't occur to her that he was in any way holding her back.

"Elisabeta, I am sometimes pulled in two directions," he confessed reluctantly. "You have a giving, loving nature. I do not want to take unfair advantage of you. If I do so, I do it without realizing that I'm doing so. I confess I like you to rely on me, but by encouraging that behavior rather than insisting you speak with others I am only hampering your independence. I do not want that for you." That was both true and not. He closed his eyes briefly, trying to find the right way to express his feelings honestly.

He wanted to be her anchor. He liked the intimacy of their merged minds when it was only the two of them speaking together, when she looked just to him. On the other hand, he wanted the world for her. The world meant she needed to come wholly into herself as a woman capable of standing on her own feet.

"I want you to always feel as if you are a fully confident woman. Fully capable in your own right of doing anything you feel you wish to do. You will never reach that if I keep you dependent on me as Sergey did."

That was one of the most difficult, painful confessions he had to make to her. It hurt. He was grateful he was standing behind her, not looking into her eyes. He didn't like to feel as if he were letting her down in any way, or that he was falling short of what a true partner should be. He was feeling his way with her, still trying to find a balance of letting go and holding her close when she needed it.

Love swamped him, slipped gently into his mind, a warmth beyond anything he'd known, filling him up until there was only Elisabeta and her sweet serenity. Her fragrance was in his mind, that soothing tranquility she projected when she merged with him, when they simply talked intimately. He never wanted to give that up.

You have always encouraged me, Ferro. You opened the door to my cage that very first rising and since have been giving me the tools I needed to learn to fly on my own. I appreciate you so much. I do.

He nuzzled the top of her head, his heart hurting. Pounding with love for her. Swelling with pride. He was a warrior, a skilled hunter, and he couldn't conceive of the courage it took to face the challenges she faced each rising.

I will always be me, she continued. *I will always have the kind of nature I have. It is possible, even probable, the centuries as a prisoner added to my natural sensitivity. I developed certain skills, honed them much more than I might have had I not been locked up. I feel things very deeply and sometimes cannot turn that off. You shield me when I cannot do so. You are my shelter. My refuge. I count on you and retreat when I know I cannot take any more bruising.*

"Any more bruising?" He didn't like the sound of that. He went very still inside. Had he pushed her too hard? Was he guilty of listening to the voices around him instead of being in tune with his lifemate's needs? "What do you mean, Elisabeta? Am I not taking proper care of you? You promised me you would always tell me if you were upset with anything."

I do push myself, Ferro. I do because I want to be strong and always stand with you as your partner. It does not upset me to do that, but it does feel as if sometimes I am battered and cannot even look at my surroundings one more moment.

"Elisabeta." He breathed her name. With reverence. With regret. How could he not see her struggle? He was merged with her, yet he had not known.

He stood in the shadows of the courtyard while around them the music of the Dark Troubadours played, the hauntingly beautiful voice of their singer, Desari, floating into the air, touching all within hearing distance. She had a gift, and yet in that moment, Ferro could hear only what his woman had admitted to him. How had he not known?

He was used to the wild country. The mountains and forests, not the cities with houses and so many people. His instincts were honed beyond even the majority of the Carpathians' greatest hunters, yet his own life-mate, a gentle, compassionate woman, suffered because he hadn't been able to see her pain. That was unconscionable. Unacceptable.

He had gone to the monastery when he had proven to be too danger-ous even to his own kind. The mists had surrounded him when he was in those thick walls, behind the heavy gates, but that protection had en-hanced his instincts, not diminished them.

"How could I not know you were struggling, *sívamet?* How could you not share this with me? You had to have found a way to hide this from your lifemate."

He found himself hurt—and that was a rare and unfamiliar emotion, as was the anger that mixed with it. "Omission is dishonesty, Elisabeta. By your omitting what was happening to you, I was unable to take proper care of you. How did you hide this from me?" He poured demand into his voice, and for the first time he truly didn't care if he sounded too much like a dominant, demanding male.

She was silent for a long moment while he worked at breathing in and out of his lungs in a deep, natural pattern. He kept his heartbeat steady. He didn't tighten his hands or his arms on her when he wanted to crush her to him. She needed him to be calm for her. Fine tremors went through her body, all too reminiscent of when she first had risen to his beckoning song.

She had come a long way in a short time, but truthfully, he had expected too much from her. Everyone had. She had risen to the occasion because he had asked it of her. Ferro nearly groaned aloud. Desari's voice, so hauntingly beautiful, filled the night sky. The sound of the children's delighted laughter added to the beauty of the evening. His woman stood at the edge of the courtyard with a virtual crowd moving around her. Men and women dancing, dragons in the air, wheeling and dipping as their riders gave the young children a thrill. This was all new to his woman and yet she was expected to participate.

He waited, knowing Elisabeta took her time when she answered anything that she felt was very important to him, choosing her words carefully. He would have stopped her, told her he was the one in the wrong, but he had to know how she hid things from him. It couldn't continue. He had to have access to all parts of her mind. He never wanted her to suffer, or feel bruised and battered. If they were going too fast in her lessons, or she didn't want to learn to be so modern, they had centuries to learn. He had to know when to stop her. She clearly wasn't going to tell him.

I am very sorry, Ferro. I have been alone for so long and had to be so careful of my thoughts that it is automatic for me to compartmentalize. I think of my mind like a beehive and place different thoughts in these little cells. I do not hide things from you on purpose. I would not do that. I turn to you when I know I cannot take any more.

"I do not understand, Elisabeta. I have full access to your mind, yet I do not see these cells you have hidden. Why?" He was careful to keep a neutral tone. He wasn't angry with her and didn't want her to think that he was. This misunderstanding was on him. That didn't negate the fact that he had to see these hidden compartments and always have access to them in case she was "bruised and battered" again.

I had to keep Sergey from seeing into the places of my mind I didn't want him to see. The same with any of his brothers or cousins, just in case one found out about me. I hid the tiny cells in the walls so they appeared perfectly normal, as if they were part of the structure of my mind. I had centuries to perfect the images and to keep them from ever being given away. Even the healer did not discover them when he repeatedly inspected my mind. There was a hint of satisfaction in her voice.

"Elisabeta." He swept his hand gently down the long, thick braid of her hair. "Just the fact that you deliberately kept this part of you safe from the healer meant you not only remembered these compartments hidden from anyone looking, but you wanted them to remain hidden. I understand you hiding them from Gary and even the other ancients. But your lifemate? From me? What is your reasoning?" He kept all reprimand from his voice. He feared he already knew the answer.

She turned her head to look up at him over her shoulder, her dark eyes wide. There was overwhelming emotion in her eyes and his belly did a weird roll. His heart clenched hard in his chest. He was looking at love. Drowning in it. Swamped in it. He felt it surround him. She was both wonderful and terrifying to him. For a moment he was looking into her soul. She was so unbelievably compassionate she was beyond his comprehension. She'd been given to him. Somehow, the universe had entrusted her into his care.

Her long lashes fluttered. She turned her head to stare back at the laughing, joyful men and women, at the children celebrating a hard-won victory she'd been such a big part of.

"You didn't want me to know." He said it for her. "You pushed yourself as hard as you could until you were so uncomfortable you could barely take it, and you didn't want me to know."

Elisabeta ducked her head. *You hurt inside, Ferro. When you think you are not shielding me enough, you hurt inside. When you do shield me, you compare yourself to the vampire. There is no winning for you. I do not like it.*

"You cannot do that, *piƞe sarnanak*," he reprimanded.

I have every right to take care of you, Ferro. You are my lifemate.

There was surprising strength in her voice. He had done that. He had given her that strength and confidence. He sighed. "Woman, you make no sense. The things I am concerned about, such as whether or not I am holding you back when I should push you to stand on your own—like tonight, among all the Carpathians who have come to celebrate with us— you stay silent about. But this, when I am adamant, you oppose me."

Not oppose, Ferro, she denied, her voice and mind soft. *I will discuss that more with you, but tonight . . . I have given this much thought. Lorraine and Julija are both very powerful women in different ways. They express that power differently. Because they express it differently does not take away from either of them. The way I choose to express my power will not take away from what or who I am.*

"That is true, *sívamet*. You are an extremely powerful Carpathian."

I cannot be anything but who I am. My nature is not like either Julija's or Lorraine's, and although I admire both of them, I am fine with who I am, thanks to you. I will most likely be uncomfortable around many people and I accept that, again, thanks to you. The point I am making, Ferro, is crawling into your mind and hiding away is where I need to be sometimes. It is where I feel safest. You are not forcing me to go there. You are not holding me prisoner or keeping me dependent. I try to hold out because I think it is what you want for me and I even know it is good for me, but it is not always what I want.

He shook his head, dropping his hand to her neck, beginning a slow massage, not really for her, but because he had to do something. Anything. She was killing him. She tried to hold out as long as she could, waiting until she felt bruised and battered, and then hiding that from him in the little compartments in her mind so he wouldn't feel bad.

"You are not going to do that anymore. We are making a new rule. You do not hide anything from me, even if you think it will upset me. Is that understood, *piye sarnanak?*"

Yes, Ferro. She answered immediately, no hesitation, which meant she would obey him.

He bent his head to brush a kiss along her earlobe. "You will allow me access to *all* parts of your mind. Every hidden little cubicle."

He felt her reluctance. *How can I protect you?*

He bit her earlobe in sheer frustration. *I protect you.*

Should it not go both ways?

There was genuine confusion in her voice and that touched his heart. It was impossible not to want to sweep her into his arms and carry her off where he could be alone with her.

"Yes, but not at the expense of your health. You are never to push yourself to the point of feeling bruised or battered or where you think you have to hide how it is affecting you from me. We need to be able to communicate, Elisabeta. I know that expressing your feelings is difficult at times for you, but it is necessary."

She was silent for a few moments and then she capitulated. *Then yes, Ferro, I agree. I will make certain you know where all the various walls I put up with the little cells on them are so you have access to any information I accidentally store there.*

"Thank you, Elisabeta. Traian and Joie are making their way over to us. Are you good with that? I can get us out of here."

He felt her straighten. Again, she tilted her head back and gave him a smile meant only for him. It was genuine, lighting her eyes. "I can talk to them for a few minutes."

Her heart had begun to accelerate and he gently slid his hand down the length of her arm to her wrist, rubbing his thumb over her pounding pulse to remind her to match the steadier beat of his.

"Traian, Joie," he greeted. "I see you both remember how to dance."

"Barely," Traian admitted. "It's all Joie. She has to keep the steps in her mind and I just do what she tells me. She makes me look good."

Joie burst out laughing. "That's not true. He's a really good dancer. Very smooth. Tariq is good, too. Did you see him with Charlotte?"

Ferro answered for them, sparing Elisabeta every chance he could, while she nodded and smiled, her fingers digging into his arm. "It was impossible not to notice. I think everyone watched them. I suppose that is why he owns a nightclub."

Traian flashed a little smile at his sister. "Who would have thought, Elisabeta, that a Carpathian would own a nightclub someday? If they had told us that when we were children . . ."

"We would not have known what anyone was talking about," she finished.

Traian and Joie burst out laughing.

Ferro tightened his arms around his lifemate. Just that small little effort was difficult for her, but he could feel her happiness. Elisabeta was glad she'd made the effort because her brother and Joie were extremely happy that she'd spoken to them, even joked with them.

"Several of the ancients went out to the forest by the lake hunting Cornel and Dorin, but they were long gone," Ferro informed them, to take pressure off his woman. "They cleaned up the traps and put the forest, meadow and lake to rights again so any campers or hikers would not get caught. There were creatures beneath the ground that had to be burned out, and those venomous guardians in the trees were difficult to fully purge, but without guidance from their creators, the brethren were able to destroy them."

Traian nodded. "Tariq feared it would be extremely difficult. He has said he wants that lair as well as the one beneath the city to be watched all the time. Josef is setting up remote cameras, but even that will not be enough. Tariq wants both lairs to be regularly patrolled."

"Will you be taking Josef back with you when you return to the Carpathian Mountains?" Ferro asked.

"I have agreed to escort him once he has completely updated Tariq's system and made certain there are no traces of the infection or any other virus the vampires might have planted."

"You allowed him to kill the vampire with you. He used himself as bait and then the two of you worked together to dispatch the creature," Ferro said. He kept his tone strictly neutral. "The boy has clearly had some experience, but do you think it is a good idea for him to be facing vampires when he does not have the physical strength required? He obviously has the mental strength. And he follows instructions."

"I agree he shouldn't be involved in battles," Traian said. "Josef is . . ." He glanced at Joie, a little at a loss for words. "He never seems settled. He travels extensively. He lives for a short period of time with his adopted parents but he never stays long. He seems restless. They think of him as difficult. His best friend, Skyler, says he's lonely and lost at times."

Ferro nodded. "I would agree with her. I would like him to stay here, even for a short while. The brethren would work with him on his skills. He could work with us on catching up with technology, minus the infection."

Traian narrowed his gaze suspiciously. "Is there something you know that I do not in regard to Josef?" He looked from Elisabeta to Ferro. "I like the kid and I feel responsible for him. If there's a problem, I'd like to know about it."

Elisabeta took a breath. Her hand came up to her throat, her fingers stroking for a minute, as if she were coaxing words to come forth. "There are memories in him that are disturbing. Things that have made him think less of himself."

"There is no place in our world for jealousy." Ferro gestured toward the children flying the dragons. The sounds of laughter drifted down from the sky, blending with music and the conversation of the adults. His gaze followed the rainbow dragon little Jennifer sat on with Josef's arms tight around her, sparkles falling all around them. The little girl clung to him, laughing so hard she looked as if she might fall right off the back of the dragon. Josef didn't look in the least uncomfortable with glitter adorning his hair as the child scattered more of it into the air.

"That is so," Traian agreed. He didn't push Ferro to get on with it. He simply waited to see where the ancient was going with his observations.

"When jealousy is continually displayed to the point that it undermines the confidence of a sibling or adopted sibling, it could be a potential problem later on. The Malinov brothers were very jealous of the Dubrinsky family. They were also jealous of the Dragonseeker lineage. Xavier was jealous of the Carpathian people's longevity. Jealousy leads to darkness, Traian."

Ferro kept his eyes on Josef. The boy whispered in Jennifer's ear and then the rainbow dragon swung its head around and dove over the brown dragon. The little girl giggled hysterically and tossed handfuls of glitter into the air over Danny and Andor. Danny laughed and pointed, covering Andor as best he could. Andor laughed with him and indicated they needed to try to get away because his twin was coming at them from the other direction and there was no doubt she had just as much glitter as Jennifer. The orange dragon was trailing sparkles like a rainbow.

There was no jealousy there. The children played and laughed together. Another dragon, this one green, leapt into the air from the ground. There was a young girl of about twelve or thirteen, with a wild mane of hair, on its back, ducking under the trails of glitter to follow after Josef and Jennifer.

Bella and Lourdes, now adept at flying their dragons in spite of their young ages, also rose, although seated behind them were Tomas and Lojos. Already both Carpathian hunters were doused in glitter. Neither seemed to mind as they rose into the air on the backs of the red and blue dragons.

Emeline flew a golden dragon with brilliant emerald eyes, her daughter, Carisma, in her lap as they took to the sky with the other dragons. Dragomir flew protectively beside his wife and child in the form of a black dragon.

Laughter, music and glitter swirled in the air along with the powerful sweep of dragon wings. It was such a different sight than Ferro had ever seen, and sharing it with Elisabeta was particularly enjoyable. He could feel her happiness spilling into his mind. *I love this, Ferro.*

I do, too, Elisabeta. There are a few things to like about this modern century after all.

I didn't realize dragons were part of the modern century.

He shared her laughter, although his face was an expressionless mask. His joy was for his woman alone.

Traian sat for a long time in silence, watching the aerial show above them, as did many of the other adults. Joie held his hand, her head tipped back, but her gaze was on Ferro's face, and then it shifted to Elisabeta.

"Elisabeta, is Josef at risk? Has someone deliberately put him in harm's way?" She asked the question very softly.

Ferro felt his lifemate go very still inside. She shifted her entire being into him, allowing him to shield her.

"That calls for a conclusion Elisabeta cannot possibly give you. Perhaps if you word your question another way, she will be able to answer you directly. Otherwise, you will have to be satisfied with my interpretation."

"Yes. Of course. Josef seems very lost to me. Have you discovered a reason for this, Elisabeta, when you were working to rid him of this infection? Did you come across information that might aid us in helping him gain self-esteem?"

Elisabeta moistened her lips. She glanced uneasily up at Ferro.

You do not have to answer, piŋe sarnanak. I can do it for you. She was very uncomfortable.

This is invading Josef's privacy. He would not want these things exposed. He did not even say this to his best friends, Skyler or Paul.

"She is reluctant to reveal anything she found in his mind that he has chosen not to tell anyone himself. She regards that as an invasion of privacy, which it is."

Joie nodded. "That is true. I would not want you to reveal anything in my mind, so I perfectly understand. I have to ask one more thing. Do you believe he is at risk because of what you found in his mind?"

Elisabeta bit her lower lip and once more glanced up at Ferro. *He takes chances. Too many, Ferro.*

"You already know the answer to that, Joie," Ferro said gently, not putting pressure on his lifemate. "You and Traian would not be watching him so closely. Traian was not happy that he insisted on setting himself up as bait, yet he couldn't deter him. You both are already worried about Josef."

"But we don't know why he's the way he is. No one knows with perhaps the exception of Elisabeta," Joie said. "And you, Ferro."

"You cannot ask us to reveal his secrets when you would not want us to reveal yours," Ferro said.

Traian nodded his head. "He is right, Joie. As much as we would prefer to know, we have no right to invade his privacy. I do wish you could come to the Carpathian Mountains, even if it was for a little while, Elisabeta, and see home. You might not remember it, but it truly is beautiful. I want to show you all of our old haunts, the places you used to love to go." He sent a quick smile to Ferro. "She loved the forest."

"She still does," Ferro said.

"I loved the memories you shared with me," Elisabeta said. "I will treasure them, Traian, and take them out often and examine them."

Her brother smiled at her. "I'm grateful you're alive and I could give you back some of home. Showing them to you in my mind isn't the same as walking trails with you in the mountains or forest."

"I do love being in the forest," Elisabeta admitted.

"As far as Josef is concerned," Traian continued, "it might be best to leave him here."

"Mikhail wanted him escorted home," Joie pointed out.

Traian sighed. "That is so, although leaving him gives us an excuse to return to see Elisabeta."

Elisabeta turned her head to look at her brother. "You never need an excuse to come to see me, Traian."

"Or perhaps Elisabeta and I will escort Josef back to the Carpathian

Mountains," Ferro said. "We can bring him to you. That would give her a chance to see these places you speak of, Traian."

I think it would be a good thing to go there, Ferro, Elisabeta said. *I would love to see the Carpathian Mountains again, and perhaps even the monastery, but that is where the Malinov piece for the council is hidden. Cornel is aware of it, although he does not know exactly where it is located. He will try to recover it. I am uncertain exactly where it is, either, only that it is not here in the United States.*

When did you remember this bit of information? Ferro tried to keep the challenge out of his voice. Knowing where the Malinov membership piece was was huge. She should have told him immediately.

Just now. When Traian talked about going home. I caught a flicker of it in Ruslan's mind. I could not catch the exact place, but if I am there, it is possible I would be able to find it.

"I would very much like to show Elisabeta the place she was born," Traian said. "It would be a fair exchange to lend you Josef for a short while and then you bring him back to us. I can get word to Mikhail and ask him if this is permissible."

"I think that would be more than fair," Ferro agreed, resting his chin on the top of Elisabeta's head. "It will also give me a chance to meet the prince. Perhaps some of the brethren will travel with me as well so they can meet him, too." He could make up his mind about swearing his allegiance. It seemed that many ancients believed in the prince.

The Dark Troubadours began to play another song, this one slow and haunting, a love song, and Elisabeta turned her head up quickly to look at Ferro.

That is our song. Yours and mine.

He smiled at her. "Yes, it is our song. I gave them the music and lyrics. Come dance with me." He took her hand. "If you'll excuse us, I would very much like to dance with my lifemate."

Ferro took Elisabeta into his arms. Her soft, feminine body molded to his. Fit perfectly. Joy was present. Alive in him. Love surrounded him. Lived in him. All because of her . . . Elisabeta.

APPENDIX I

Carpathian Healing Chants

To rightly understand Carpathian healing chants, background is required in several areas:

1. The Carpathian view on healing
2. The Lesser Healing Chant of the Carpathians
3. The Great Healing Chant of the Carpathians
4. Carpathian musical aesthetics
5. Lullaby
6. Song to Heal the Earth
7. Carpathian chanting technique

1. THE CARPATHIAN VIEW ON HEALING

The Carpathians are a nomadic people whose geographic origins can be traced at least as far as the Southern Ural Mountains (near the steppes of modern-day Kazakhstan), on the border between Europe and Asia. (For this reason, modern-day linguists call their language "proto-Uralic," without knowing that this is the language of the Carpathians.) Unlike most nomadic peoples, the Carpathians did not wander due to the need to find new grazing lands as the seasons and climate shifted, or to search for better trade. Instead, the Carpathians' movements were driven by a great purpose: to find a land that would have the right earth, a soil with the kind of richness that would greatly enhance their rejuvenative powers.

Over the centuries, they migrated westward (some six thousand years ago), until they at last found their perfect homeland—their *susu*—in the Carpathian Mountains, whose long arc cradled the lush plains of the kingdom of Hungary. (The kingdom of Hungary flourished for over a millennium—making Hungarian the dominant language of the Carpathian Basin—until the kingdom's lands were split among several countries after World War I: Austria, Czechoslovakia, Romania, Yugoslavia and modern Hungary.)

Other peoples from the Southern Urals (who shared the Carpathian language but were not Carpathians) migrated in different directions. Some ended up in Finland, which explains why the modern Hungarian and Finnish languages are among the contemporary descendants of the ancient Carpathian language. Even though they are tied forever to their chosen Carpathian homeland, the Carpathians continue to wander as they search

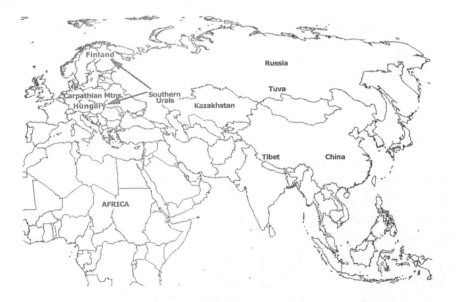

the world for the answers that will enable them to bear and raise their offspring without difficulty.

Because of their geographic origins, the Carpathian views on healing share much with the larger Eurasian shamanistic tradition. Probably the closest modern representative of that tradition is based in Tuva (and is referred to as "Tuvinian Shamanism")—see the map on the previous page.

The Eurasian shamanistic tradition—from the Carpathians to the Siberian shamans—held that illness originated in the human soul, and only later manifested as various physical conditions. Therefore, shamanistic healing, while not neglecting the body, focused on the soul and its healing. The most profound illnesses were understood to be caused by "soul departure," where all or some part of the sick person's soul has wandered away from the body (into the nether realms) or has been captured or possessed by an evil spirit, or both.

The Carpathians belong to this greater Eurasian shamanistic tradition and share its viewpoints. While the Carpathians themselves did not succumb to illness, Carpathian healers understood that the most profound wounds were also accompanied by a similar "soul departure."

Upon reaching the diagnosis of "soul departure," the healer-shaman is then required to make a spiritual journey into the netherworld to recover the soul. The shaman may have to overcome tremendous challenges along the way, particularly fighting the demon or vampire who has possessed his friend's soul.

"Soul departure" doesn't require a person to be unconscious (although that certainly can be the case as well). It was understood that a person could still appear to be conscious, even talk and interact with others, and yet be missing a part of their soul. The experienced healer or shaman would instantly see the problem nonetheless, in subtle signs that others might miss: the person's attention wandering every now and then, a lessening in their enthusiasm about life, chronic depression, a diminishment in the brightness of their "aura" and the like.

2. THE LESSER HEALING CHANT OF THE CARPATHIANS

Kepä Sarna Pus (**The Lesser Healing Chant**) is used for wounds that are merely physical in nature. The Carpathian healer leaves his body and enters the wounded Carpathian's body to heal great mortal wounds from the inside out using pure energy. He proclaims, "I offer freely my life for your life," as he gives his blood to the injured Carpathian. Because the Carpathians are of the earth and bound to the soil, they are healed by the soil of their homeland. Their saliva is also often used for its rejuvenative powers.

It is also very common for the Carpathian chants (both the Lesser and the Great) to be accompanied by the use of healing herbs, aromas from Carpathian candles and crystals. The crystals (when combined with the Carpathians' empathic, psychic connection to the entire universe) are used to gather positive energy from their surroundings, which is then used to accelerate the healing. Caves are sometimes used as the setting for the healing.

The Lesser Healing Chant was used by Vikirnoff Von Shrieder and Colby Jansen to heal Rafael De La Cruz, whose heart had been ripped out by a vampire, as described in *Dark Secret*.

Kepä Sarna Pus (**The Lesser Healing Chant**)
The same chant is used for all physical wounds. "Sívadaba" (into your heart) would be changed to refer to whatever part of the body is wounded.

Kuńasz, nélkül sívdobbanás, nélkül fesztelen löyly.
You lie as if asleep, without beat of heart, without airy breath.

Ot élidamet andam szabadon élidadért.
I offer freely my life for your life.

O jelä sielam jörem ot ainamet és soŋe ot élidadet.
My spirit of light forgets my body and enters your body.

O jelä sielam pukta kinn minden szelemeket belső.
My spirit of light sends all the dark spirits within fleeing without.

Pajńak o susu hanyet és o nyelv nyálamet sívadaba.
I press the earth of our homeland and the spit of my tongue into your
heart.

Vii, o verim soɲe o verid andam.
At last, I give you my blood for your blood.

To hear this chant, visit christinefeehan.com/members/.

3. THE GREAT HEALING CHANT OF THE CARPATHIANS

The most well-known—and most dramatic—of the Carpathian healing
chants is *En Sarna Pus* (**The Great Healing Chant**). This chant is reserved
for recovering the wounded or unconscious Carpathian's soul.

Typically a group of men would form a circle around the sick
Carpathian (to "encircle him with our care and compassion") and begin
the chant. The shaman or healer or leader is the prime actor in this healing
ceremony. It is he who will actually make the spiritual journey into the
netherworld, aided by his clanspeople. Their purpose is to ecstatically
dance, sing, drum and chant, all the while visualizing (through the words
of the chant) the journey itself—every step of it, over and over again—to
the point where the shaman, in trance, leaves his body and makes that
very journey. (Indeed, the word *ecstasy* is from the Latin *ex statis*, which
literally means "out of the body.")

One advantage that the Carpathian healer has over many other shamans is his telepathic link to his lost brother. Most shamans must wander
in the dark of the nether realms in search of their lost brother. But the
Carpathian healer directly "hears" in his mind the voice of his lost brother
calling to him, and can thus "zero in on" his soul like a homing beacon.
For this reason, Carpathian healing tends to have a higher success rate
than most other traditions of this sort.

Something of the geography of the "other world" is useful for us to
examine in order to fully understand the words of the Great Carpathian
Healing Chant. A reference is made to the "Great Tree" (in Carpathian:

En Puwe). Many ancient traditions, including the Carpathian tradition, understood the worlds—the heaven worlds, our world and the nether realms—to be "hung" upon a great pole, or axis, or tree. Here on earth, we are positioned halfway up this tree, on one of its branches. Hence, many ancient texts referred to the material world as "middle earth": midway between heaven and hell. Climbing the tree would lead one to the heaven worlds. Descending the tree to its roots would lead to the nether realms. The shaman was necessarily a master of movement up and down the Great Tree, sometimes moving unaided and sometimes assisted by (or even mounted upon the back of) an animal spirit guide. In various traditions, this Great Tree was known variously as the *axis mundi* (the "axis of the worlds"), Yggdrasil (in Norse mythology), Mount Meru (the sacred world mountain of Tibetan tradition), etc. The Christian cosmos, with its heaven, purgatory/earth and hell, is also worth comparing. It is even given a similar topography in Dante's *Divine Comedy*: Dante is led on a journey first to hell, at the center of the earth; then upward to Mount Purgatory, which sits on the earth's surface directly opposite Jerusalem; then farther upward first to Eden, the earthly paradise, at the summit of Mount Purgatory; and then upward at last to Heaven.

In the shamanistic tradition, it was understood that the small always reflects the large; the personal always reflects the cosmic. A movement in the greater dimensions of the cosmos also coincides with an internal movement. For example, the *axis mundi* of the cosmos corresponds with the spinal column of the individual. Journeys up and down the *axis mundi* often coincided with the movements of natural and spiritual energies (sometimes called *kundalini* or *shakti*) in the spinal column of the shaman or mystic.

En Sarna Pus (The Great Healing Chant)
In this chant, ekä ("brother") would be replaced by "sister," "father," "mother," depending on the person to be healed.

Ot ekäm ainajanak hany, jama.
My brother's body is a lump of earth, close to death.

Me, ot ekäm kuntajanak, pirädak ekäm, gond és irgalom türe.
We, the clan of my brother, encircle him with our care and compassion.

O pus wäkenkek, ot oma śarnank, és ot pus fünk, álnak ekäm ainajanak, pitänak ekäm ainajanak elävä.
Our healing energies, ancient words of magic and healing herbs bless my brother's body, keep it alive.

Ot ekäm sielanak pälä. Ot omboće päläja juta alatt o jüti, kinta, és szelemek lamtijaknak.
But my brother's soul is only half. His other half wanders in the netherworld.

Ot en mekem ŋamaŋ: kulkedak otti ot ekäm omboće päläjanak.
My great deed is this: I travel to find my brother's other half.

Rekatüre, saradak, tappadak, odam, kaŋa o numa waram, és avaa owe o lewl mahoz.
We dance, we chant, we dream ecstatically, to call my spirit bird, and to open the door to the other world.

Ntak o numa waram, és mozdulak; jomadak.
I mount my spirit bird and we begin to move; we are under way.

Piwtädak ot En Puwe tyvinak, ećidak alatt o jüti, kinta, és szelemek lamtijaknak.
Following the trunk of the Great Tree, we fall into the netherworld.

Fázak, fázak nó o śaro.
It is cold, very cold.

Juttadak ot ekäm o akarataban, o sívaban és o sielaban.
My brother and I are linked in mind, heart and soul.

Ot ekäm sielanak kaŋa engem.
My brother's soul calls to me.

Kuledak és piwtädak ot ekäm.
I hear and follow his track.

Saɣedak és tuledak ot ekäm kulyanak.
I encounter the demon who is devouring my brother's soul.

Nenäm ćoro, o kuly torodak.
In anger, I fight the demon.

O kuly pél engem.
He is afraid of me.

Lejkkadak o kaŋka salamaval.
I strike his throat with a lightning bolt.

Molodak ot ainaja komakamal.
I break his body with my bare hands.

Toja és molanâ.
He is bent over, and falls apart.

Hän ćaδa.
He runs away.

Manedak ot ekäm sielanak.
I rescue my brother's soul.

Alədak ot ekam sielanak o komamban.
I lift my brother's soul in the hollow of my hand.

Alədam ot ekam numa waramra.
I lift him onto my spirit bird.

Piwtädak ot En Puwe tyvijanak és saỳedak jälleen ot elävä ainak majaknak.
Following up the Great Tree, we return to the land of the living.

Ot ekäm elä jälleen.
My brother lives again.

Ot ekäm weṅća jälleen.
He is complete again.

To hear this chant, visit christinefeehan.com/members/.

4. CARPATHIAN MUSICAL AESTHETICS

In the sung Carpathian pieces (such as the "Lullaby" and the "Song to Heal the Earth"), you'll hear elements that are shared by many of the musical traditions in the Uralic geographical region, some of which still exist—from Eastern European (Bulgarian, Romanian, Hungarian, Croatian) to Romany ("gypsy"). These elements include:

- the rapid alternation between major and minor modalities, including a sudden switch (called a "Picardy third") from minor to major to end a piece or section (as at the end of the "Lullaby")
- the use of close (tight) harmonics
- the use of *riturdi* (slowing down the pace) and *crescendi* (swelling in volume) for brief periods
- the use of *glissandi* (slides) in the singing tradition
- the use of trills in the singing tradition (as in the final invocation of the "Song to Heal the Earth")—similar to Celtic, a singing tradition more familiar to many of us
- the use of parallel fifths (as in the final invocation of the "Song to Heal the Earth")
- controlled use of dissonance
- "call-and-response" chanting (typical of many of the world's chanting traditions)

- extending the length of a musical line (by adding a couple of bars) to heighten dramatic effect
- and many more

"Lullaby" and "Song to Heal the Earth" illustrate two rather different forms of Carpathian music (a quiet, intimate piece and an energetic ensemble piece)—but whatever the form, Carpathian music is full of feeling.

5. LULLABY

This song is sung by a woman while a child is still in the womb or when the threat of a miscarriage is apparent. The baby can hear the song while inside the mother, and the mother can connect with the child telepathically as well. The lullaby is meant to reassure the child, to encourage the baby to hold on, to stay—to reassure the child that he or she will be protected by love even from inside until birth. The last line literally means that the mother's love will protect her child until the child is born ("rise").

Musically, the Carpathian "Lullaby" is in three-quarter time ("waltz time"), as are a significant portion of the world's various traditional lullabies (perhaps the most famous of which is Brahms' Lullaby). The arrangement for solo voice is the original context: a mother singing to her child, unaccompanied. The arrangement for chorus and violin ensemble illustrates how musical even the simplest Carpathian pieces often are, and how easily they lend themselves to contemporary instrumental or orchestral arrangements. (A wide range of contemporary composers, including Dvořák and Smetana, have taken advantage of a similar discovery, working other traditional Eastern European music into their symphonic poems.)

Odam-Sarna Kondak (Lullaby)

Tumtesz o wäke ku pitasz belső.
Feel the strength you hold inside.

Hiszasz sívadet. Én olenam gæidnod.
Trust your heart. I'll be your guide.

Sas csecsemőm; kuñasz.
Hush, my baby; close your eyes.

Rauho joŋe ted.
Peace will come to you.

Tumtesz o sívdobbanás ku olen lamt3ad belső.
Feel the rhythm deep inside.

Gond-kumpadek ku kim te.
Waves of love that cover you.

Pesänak te, asti o jüti, kidüsz.
Protect, until the night you rise.

To hear this song, visit christinefeehan.com/members/.

6. SONG TO HEAL THE EARTH

This is the earth-healing song that is used by the Carpathian women to heal soil filled with various toxins. The women take a position on four sides and call to the universe to draw on the healing energy with love and respect. The soil of the earth is their resting place, the place where they rejuvenate, and they must make it safe not only for themselves but for their unborn children, as well as their men and living children. This is a beautiful ritual performed by the women together, raising their voices in harmony and calling on the earth's minerals and healing properties to come forth and help them save their children. They literally dance and sing to heal the earth in a ceremony as old as their species. The dance and notes of the song are adjusted according to the toxins felt through the healers' bare feet. The feet are placed in a certain pattern and the hands gracefully weave a healing spell while the dance is performed. They must be especially careful when the soil is prepared for babies. This is a ceremony of love and healing.

Musically, the ritual is divided into several sections:

- **First verse**: A "call-and-response" section, where the chant leader sings the "call" solo, and then some or all of the women sing the "response" in the close harmony style typical of the Carpathian musical tradition. The repeated response—*Ai, Emä Maγe*—is an invocation of the source of power for the healing ritual: "Oh, Mother Nature."
- **First chorus**: This section is filled with clapping, dancing, ancient horns and other means used to invoke and heighten the energies upon which the ritual is drawing.
- **Second verse**
- **Second chorus**
- **Closing invocation:** In this closing part, two song leaders, in close harmony, take all the energy gathered by the earlier portions of the song/ritual and focus it entirely on the healing purpose.

What you will be listening to are brief tastes of what would typically be a significantly longer ritual, in which the verse and chorus parts are developed and repeated many times, to be closed by a single rendition of the closing invocation.

Sarna Pusm O Maγet (Song to Heal the Earth)

First verse
Ai, Emä Maγe,
Oh, Mother Nature,

Me sívadbin lańaak.
We are your beloved daughters.

Me tappadak, me pusmak o maɣet.
We dance to heal the earth.

Me sarnadak, me pusmak o hanyet.
We sing to heal the earth.

Sielanket jutta tedet it,
We join with you now,

Sívank és akaratank és sielank juttanak.
Our hearts and minds and spirits become one.

Second verse
Ai, Emä Maɣe,
Oh, Mother Nature,

Me sívadbin lańaak.
We are your beloved daughters.

Me andak arwadet emänked és me kaŋank o
We pay homage to our mother and call upon the

Pōhi és Lōuna, Ida és Lääs.
North and South, East and West.

Pide és aldyn és myös belső.
Above and below and within as well.

Gondank o maɣenak pusm hän ku olen jama.
Our love of the land heals that which is in need.

Juttanak teval it,
We join with you now,

Maγe maγeval.
Earth to earth.

O pirä elidak weńća.
The circle of life is complete.

To hear this chant, visit christinefeehan.com/members/.

7. CARPATHIAN CHANTING TECHNIQUE

As with their healing techniques, the actual "chanting technique" of the
Carpathians has much in common with the other shamanistic traditions of
the Central Asian steppes. The primary mode of chanting was throat chanting using overtones. Modern examples of this manner of singing can still
be found in the Mongolian, Tuvan and Tibetan traditions. You can find an
audio example of the Gyuto Tibetan Buddhist monks engaged in throat
chanting at christinefeehan.com/carpathian_chanting/.

As with Tuva, note on the map the geographical proximity of Tibet
to Kazakhstan and the Southern Urals.

The beginning part of the Tibetan chant emphasizes synchronizing
all the voices around a single tone, aimed at healing a particular "chakra"
of the body. This is fairly typical of the Gyuto throat-chanting tradition,
but it is not a significant part of the Carpathian tradition. Nonetheless, it
serves as an interesting contrast.

The part of the Gyuto chanting example that is most similar to the
Carpathian style of chanting is the midsection, where the men are chanting the words together with great force. The purpose here is not to generate a "healing tone" that will affect a particular "chakra," but rather to
generate as much power as possible for initiating "out-of-body" travel, and
for fighting the demonic forces that the healer/traveler must face and
overcome.

The songs of the Carpathian women (illustrated by their "Lullaby"
and their "Song to Heal the Earth") are part of the same ancient musical
and healing tradition as the Lesser and Great Healing Chants of the

warrior males. You can hear some of the same instruments in both the male warriors' healing chants and the women's "Song to Heal the Earth." Also, they share the common purpose of generating and directing power. However, the women's songs are distinctively feminine in character. One immediately noticeable difference is that while the men speak their words in the manner of a chant, the women sing songs with melodies and harmonies, softening the overall performance. A feminine, nurturing quality is especially evident in the "Lullaby."

APPENDIX 2

The Carpathian Language

Like all human languages, the language of the Carpathians contains the richness and nuance that can only come from a long history of use. At best we can only touch on some of the main features of the language in this brief appendix:

1. The history of the Carpathian language
2. Carpathian grammar and other characteristics of the language
3. Examples of the Carpathian language (including the Ritual Words and the Warriors' Chant)
4. A much-abridged Carpathian dictionary

1. THE HISTORY OF THE CARPATHIAN LANGUAGE

The Carpathian language of today is essentially identical to the Carpathian language of thousands of years ago. A "dead" language like the Latin of two thousand years ago has evolved into a significantly different modern language (Italian) because of countless generations of speakers and great historical fluctuations. In contrast, many of the speakers of Carpathian from thousands of years ago are still alive. Their presence—coupled with the deliberate isolation of the Carpathians from the other major forces of change in the world—has acted (and continues to act) as a stabilizing force that has preserved the integrity of the language over the centuries. Carpathian culture has also acted as a stabilizing force. For instance, the Ritual Words, the various healing chants (see Appendix 1) and other cultural artifacts have been passed down through the centuries with great fidelity.

One small exception should be noted: the splintering of the Carpathians into separate geographic regions has led to some minor dialectization. However, the telepathic link among all Carpathians (as well as each Carpathian's regular return to his or her homeland) has ensured that the differences among dialects are relatively superficial (e.g., small numbers of new words, minor differences in pronunciation, etc.), since the deeper internal language of mind-forms has remained the same because of continuous use across space and time.

The Carpathian language was (and still is) the proto-language for the Uralic (or Finno-Ugric) family of languages. Today, the Uralic languages are spoken in northern, eastern and central Europe and in Siberia. More than twenty-three million people in the world speak languages that can trace their ancestry to Carpathian. Magyar or Hungarian (about fourteen million speakers), Finnish (about five million speakers) and Estonian (about one million speakers) are the three major contemporary descendants of this proto-language. The only factor that unites the more than twenty languages in the Uralic family is that their ancestry can be traced back to a common proto-language—Carpathian—that split (starting some six thousand years ago) into the various languages in the Uralic family. In the same way, European languages such as English and French belong to the better-known Indo-European family and also evolved from a common proto-language ancestor (a different one from Carpathian).

The following table provides a sense of some of the similarities in the language family.

Note: The Finnic/Carpathian "k" shows up often as the Hungarian "h." Similarly, the Finnic/Carpathian "p" often corresponds to the Hungarian "f."

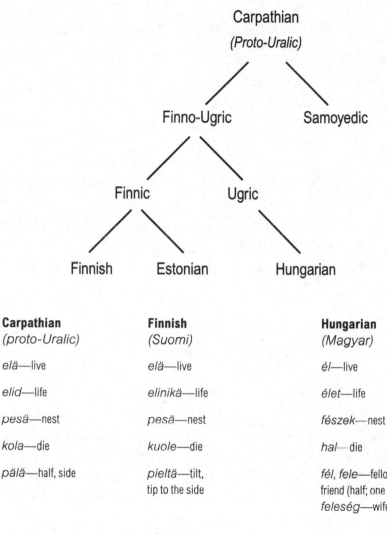

Carpathian (proto-Uralic)	Finnish (Suomi)	Hungarian (Magyar)
elä—live	*elä*—live	*él*—live
elid—life	*elinikä*—life	*élet*—life
pesä—nest	*pesä*—nest	*fészek*—nest
kola—die	*kuole*—die	*hal*—die
pälä—half, side	*pieltä*—tilt, tip to the side	*fél, fele*—fellow human, friend (half; one side of two) *feleség*—wife
and—give	*anta, antaa*—give	*ad*—give
koje—husband, man	*koira*—dog, the male (of animals)	*here*—drone, testicle
wäke—power	*väki*—folks, people, men; force	*vall-vel*—with (instrumental suffix)
	väkevä—powerful, strong	*vele*—with him/her/it
wete—water	*vesi*—water	*víz*—water

2. CARPATHIAN GRAMMAR AND OTHER CHARACTERISTICS OF THE LANGUAGE

Idioms. As both an ancient language and a language of an earth people, Carpathian is more inclined toward use of idioms constructed from concrete, "earthy" terms rather than abstractions. For instance, our modern abstraction "to cherish" is expressed more concretely in Carpathian as "to hold in one's heart"; the "netherworld" is, in Carpathian, "the land of night, fog and ghosts"; etc.

Word order. The order of words in a sentence is determined not by syntactic roles (like subject, verb and object) but rather by pragmatic, discourse-driven factors. Examples: *"Tied vagyok."* ("Yours am I."); *"Sívamet andam."* ("My heart I give you.")

Agglutination. The Carpathian language is agglutinative; that is, longer words are constructed from smaller components. An agglutinating language uses suffixes or prefixes whose meanings are generally unique, and which are concatenated one after another without overlap. In Carpathian, words typically consist of a stem that is followed by one or more suffixes. For example, *sívambam* derives from the stem *"sív"* ("heart"), followed by *"am"* ("my," making it "my heart"), followed by *"bam"* ("in," making it "in my heart"). As you might imagine, agglutination in Carpathian can sometimes produce very long words, or words that are very difficult to pronounce. Vowels often get inserted between suffixes to prevent too many consonants from appearing in a row (which can make a word unpronounceable).

Noun cases. Like all languages, Carpathian has many noun cases; the same noun will be "spelled" differently depending on its role in a sentence. The noun cases include nominative (when the noun is the subject of the sentence), accusative (when the noun is a direct object of the verb), dative (indirect object), genitive (or possessive), instrumental, final, suppressive, inessive, elative, terminative and delative.

We will use the possessive (or genitive) case as an example to illustrate how all noun cases in Carpathian involve adding standard suffixes to the noun stems. Thus, expressing possession in Carpathian—"my lifemate," "your lifemate," "his lifemate," "her lifemate," etc.—involves adding a particular suffix (such as "*-am*") to the noun stem (*päläfertiil*) to produce the possessive (*päläfertiilam*—"my lifemate"). Which suffix to use depends upon which person ("my," "your," "his," etc.) and whether the noun ends in a consonant or a vowel. The following table shows the suffixes for singular nouns only (not plural), and also shows the similarity to the suffixes used in contemporary Hungarian. (Hungarian is actually a little more complex, in that it also requires "vowel rhyming": which suffix to use also depends on the last vowel in the noun, hence the multiple choices in the table, where Carpathian only has a single choice.)

	Carpathian (proto-Uralic)		Contemporary Hungarian	
person	**noun ends in vowel**	**noun ends in consonant**	**noun ends in vowel**	**noun ends In consonant**
1st singular (my)	-m	-am	-m	-om, -em, -öm
2nd singular (your)	-d	-ad	-d	-od, -ed, -öd
3rd singular (his, her, its)	-ja	-a	-ja/-je	-a, -e
1st plural (our)	-nk	-ank	-nk	-unk, -ünk
2nd plural (your)	-tak	-atak	-tok, -tek, -tök	-otok, -etek, -ötök
3rd plural (their)	-jak	-ak	-juk, -jük	-uk, -ük

Note: As mentioned earlier, vowels often get inserted between the word and its suffix so as to prevent too many consonants from appearing in a row (which would produce unpronounceable words). For example, in the table on the previous page, all nouns that end in a consonant are followed by suffixes beginning with "a."

Verb conjugation. Like its modern descendants (such as Finnish and Hungarian), Carpathian has many verb tenses, far too many to describe here. We will just focus on the conjugation of the present tense. Again, we will place contemporary Hungarian side by side with Carpathian because of the marked similarity between the two.

As with the possessive case for nouns, the conjugation of verbs is done by adding a suffix onto the verb stem:

Person	Carpathian (proto-Uralic)	Contemporary Hungarian
1st singular (I give)	-am (andam), -ak	-ok, -ek, -ök
2nd singular (you give)	-sz (andsz)	-sz
3rd singular (he/she/it gives)	— (and)	—
1st plural (we give)	-ak (andak)	-unk, -ünk
2nd plural (you give)	-tak (andtak)	-tok, -tek, -tök
3rd plural (they give)	-nak (andnak)	-nak, -nek

As with all languages, there are many "irregular verbs" in Carpathian that don't exactly fit this pattern. But the table is still a useful guide for most verbs.

3. EXAMPLES OF THE CARPATHIAN LANGUAGE

Here are some brief examples of conversational Carpathian, used in the Dark books. We include the literal translation in square brackets. It is interestingly different from the most appropriate English translation.

Susu.
I am home.
["home/birthplace." "I am" is understood, as is often the case in Carpathian.]

Möért?
What for?

csitri
little one
["little slip of a thing," "little slip of a girl"]

ainaak enyém
forever mine

ainaak sívamet jutta
forever mine (another form)
["forever to-my-heart connected/fixed"]

sívamet
my love
["of-my-heart," "to-my-heart"]

Tet vigyázam.
I love you.
["you-love-I"]

Sarna Rituaali (The Ritual Words) is a longer example, and an example of chanted rather than conversational Carpathian. Note the recurring use of *"andam"* ("I give"), to give the chant musicality and force through repetition.

Sarna Rituaali (The Ritual Words)

Te avio päläfertiilam.
You are my lifemate.

Éntölam kuulua, avio päläfertiilam.
I claim you as my lifemate.

Ted kuuluak, kacad, kojed.
I belong to you.

Élidamet andam.
I offer my life for you.

Pesämet andam.
I give you my protection.

Uskolfertiilamet andam.
I give you my allegiance.

Sívamet andam.
I give you my heart.

Sielamet andam.
I give you my soul.

Ainamet andam.
I give you my body.

Sívamet kuuluak kaik että a ted.
I take into my keeping the same that is yours.

Ainaak olenszal sívambin.
Your life will be cherished by me for all my time.

Te élidet ainaak pide minan.
Your life will be placed above my own for all time.

Te avio päläfertiilam.
You are my lifemate.

Ainaak sívamet jutta oleny.
You are bound to me for all eternity.

Ainaak terád vigyázak.
You are always in my care.

To hear these words pronounced (and for more about Carpathian pronunciation altogether), please visit christinefeehan.com/members/.

Sarna Kontakawk (**The Warriors' Chant**) is another longer example of the Carpathian language. The warriors' council takes place deep beneath the earth in a chamber of crystals with magma far below it, so the steam is natural and the wisdom of their ancestors is clear and focused. This is a sacred place where they bloodswear to their prince and people and affirm their code of honor as warriors and brothers. It is also where battle strategies are born and all dissension is discussed, as well as any concerns the warriors have that they wish to bring to the council and open for discussion.

Sarna Kontakawk (The Warriors' Chant)

Veri isäakank—veri ekäakank.
Blood of our fathers—blood of our brothers.

Veri olen elid.
Blood is life.

Andak veri-elidet Karpatiiakank, és wäke-sarna ku meke arwa-arvo, irgalom, hän ku agba, és wäke kutni, ku manaak verival.
We offer that life to our people with a bloodsworn vow of honor, mercy, integrity and endurance.

Verink sokta; verink kaŋa terád.
Our blood mingles and calls to you.

Akasz énak ku kaŋa és juttasz kuntatak it.
Heed our summons and join with us now.

To hear these words pronounced (and for more about Carpathian pronunciation altogether), please visit christinefeehan.com /members/.

See **Appendix 1** for Carpathian healing chants, including the *Kepä Sarna Pus* (The Lesser Healing Chant), the *En Sarna Pus* (The Great Healing Chant), the *Odam-Sarna Kondak* (Lullaby) and the *Sarna Pusm O Mayet* (Song to Heal the Earth).

4. A MUCH-ABRIDGED CARPATHIAN DICTIONARY

This very-much-abridged Carpathian dictionary contains most of the Carpathian words used in the Dark books. Of course, a full Carpathian dictionary would be as large as the usual dictionary for an entire language (typically more than a hundred thousand words).

Note: The Carpathian nouns and verbs that follow are word **stems**. They generally do not appear in their isolated "stem" form. Instead, they usually appear with suffixes (e.g., *andam—I give*, rather than just the root, *and*).

a—verb negation (*prefix*); not (*adverb*).
aćke—pace, step.
aćke éntölem it—take another step toward me.
agba—to be seemly; to be proper (*verb*). True; seemly; proper (*adj.*).
ai—oh.
aina—body (*noun*).
ainaak—always; forever.
o ainaak jelä peje emnimet ŋamaŋ—sun scorch that woman forever
    (*Carpathian swear words*).
ainaakä—never.
ainaakfél—old friend.

ak—suffix added after a noun ending in a consonant to make it plural.

aka—to give heed; to hearken; to listen.

aka-arvo—respect (*noun*).

akarat—mind; will (*noun*).

ál—to bless; to attach to.

alatt—through.

aldyn—under; underneath.

alǝ—to lift; to raise.

alte—to bless; to curse.

amaŋ—this; this one here; that; that one there.

and—to give.

and sielet, arwa-arvomet, és jelämet, kuulua huvémet ku feaj és ködet ainaak—to trade soul, honor and salvation for momentary pleasure and endless damnation.

andasz éntölem irgalomet!—have mercy!

arvo—value; price (*noun*).

arwa—praise (*noun*).

arwa-arvo olen gæidnod, ekäm—honor guide you, my brother (*greeting*).

arwa-arvo olen isäntä, ekäm—honor keep you, my brother (*greeting*).

arwa-arvo pile sívadet—may honor light your heart (*greeting*).

arwa-arvod—honor (*noun*).

arwa-arvod mäne me ködak—may your honor hold back the dark (*greeting*).

aš—no (*exclamation*).

ašša—no (before a noun); not (with a verb that is not in the imperative); not (with an adjective).

aššatotello—disobedient.

asti—until.

avaa—to open.

avio—wedded.

avio päläfertiil—lifemate.

avoi—uncover; show; reveal.

baszú—revenge; vengeance.

belső—within; inside.

bur—good; well.

bur tule ekämet kuntamak—well met brother-kin (*greeting*).

ćaδa—to flee; to run; to escape.

čač3—to be born; to grow.

ćoro—to flow; to run like rain.

csecsemő—baby (*noun*).

csitri—little one (*female*).

csitrim—my little one (*female*).

diutal—triumph; victory.

džinõt—brief; short.

ećí—to fall.

ej—not (*adverb, suffix*); *nej* when preceding syllable ends in a vowel.

ek—suffix added after a noun ending in a consonant to make it plural.

ekä—brother.

ekäm—my brother.

elä—to live.

eläsz arwa-arvoval—may you live with honor; live nobly (*greeting*).

eläsz jeläbam ainaak—long may you live in the light (*greeting*).

elävä—alive.

elävä ainak majaknak—land of the living.

elid—life.

emä—mother (*noun*).

Emä Maɣe—Mother Nature.

emäen—grandmother.

embɛ—if; when.

embɛ karmasz—please.

emni—wife; woman.

emni hän ku köd alte—cursed woman.

emni kuŋenak ku aššatotello—disobedient lunatic.

emnim—my wife; my woman.

én—I.

en—great; many; big.

en hän ku pesä—the protector (literally: the great protector).

én jutta félet és ekämet—I greet a friend and brother (*greeting*).

en Karpatii—the prince (literally: the great Carpathian).

én maɣenak—I am of the earth.

én oma maɣeka—I am as old as time (literally: as old as the earth).

En Puwe—The Great Tree. Related to the legends of Yggdrasil, the *axis mundi*, Mount Meru, heaven and hell, etc.

enä—most.

engem—of me.

enkojra—wolf.

és—and.

ete—before; in front of.

että—that.

év—year.

évsatz—century.

fáz—to feel cold or chilly.

fél—fellow; friend.

fél ku kuuluaak sívam belső—beloved.

fél ku vigyázak—dear one.

feldolgaz—prepare.

fertiil—fertile one.

fesztelen—airy.

fü—herbs; grass.

gæidno—road; way.

gond—care; worry; love (*noun*).

hän—he; she; it; one.

hän agba—it is so.

hän ku—prefix: one who; he who; that which.

hän ku agba—truth.

hän ku kaśwa o numamet—sky-owner.

hän ku kuula siela—keeper of his soul.

hän ku kuulua sívamet—keeper of my heart.

hän ku lejkka wäke-sarnat—traitor.

hän ku meke pirämet—defender.

hän ku meke sarnaakmet—mage.

hän ku pesä—protector.

hän ku pesä sieladet—guardian of your soul.

hän ku pesäk kaikak—guardians of all.

hän ku piwtä—predator; hunter; tracker.

hän ku pusm—healer.

hän ku saa kuć3aket—star-reacher.

hän ku tappa—killer; violent person (*noun*). Deadly; violent (*adj.*).

hän ku tuulmahl elidet—vampire (literally: life-stealer).

hän ku vie elidet—vampire (literally: thief of life).

hän ku vigyáz sielamet—keeper of my soul.

hän ku vigyáz sívamet és sielamet—keeper of my heart and soul.

hän sívamak—beloved.

hängem—him; her; it.

hank—they.

hany—clod; lump of earth.

hisz—to believe; to trust.

ho—how.

ida—east.

igazág—justice.

ila—to shine.

inan—mine; my own (*endearment*).

irgalom—compassion; pity; mercy.

isä—father (*noun*).

isäntä—master of the house.

it—now.

jaguár—jaguar.

jaka—to cut; to divide; to separate.

jakam—wound; cut; injury.

jalka—leg.

jälleen—again.

jama—to be sick, infected, wounded or dying; to be near death.

jamatan—fallen; wounded; near death.

jelä—sunlight; day, sun; light.

jelä keje terád—light sear you (*Carpathian swear words*).

o jelä peje emnimet—sun scorch the woman (*Carpathian swear words*).

o jelä peje kaik hänkanak—sun scorch them all (*Carpathian swear words*).

o jelä peje terád—sun scorch you (*Carpathian swear words*).

o jelä peje terád, emni—sun scorch you, woman (*Carpathian swear words*).

o jelä sielamak—light of my soul.

joma—to be under way; to go.

joŋe—to come; to return.

joŋesz arwa-arvoval—return with honor (*greeting*).

joŋesz éntölem, fél ku kuuluaak sívam belsö—come to me, beloved.

jŏrem—to forget; to lose one's way; to make a mistake.

jotka—gap; middle; space.

jotkan—between.

juo—to drink.

juosz és eläsz—drink and live (*greeting*).

juosz és olen ainaak sielamet jutta—drink and become one with me (*greeting*).

juta—to go; to wander.

jüti—night; evening.

jutta—connected; fixed (*adj.*). To connect; to join; to fix; to bind (*verb*).

k—suffix added after a noun ending in a vowel to make it plural.

kać3—gift.

kaca—male lover.

kadi—judge.

kaik—all.

käktä—two; many.

käktäverit—mixed blood (literally: two bloods).

kalma—corpse; death; grave.

kaŋa—to call; to invite; to summon; to request; to beg.

kaŋk—windpipe; Adam's apple; throat.

karma—want.

Karpatii—Carpathian.

karpatii ku köd—liar.

Karpatiikunta—the Carpathian people.

käsi—hand.

kaśwa—to own.

kaða—to abandon; to leave; to remain.

kaða wäkeva óv o köd—stand fast against the dark (*greeting*).

kat—house; family (*noun*).

katt3—to move; to penetrate; to proceed.

keje—to cook; to burn; to sear.

kepä—lesser; small; easy; few.

kessa—cat.

kessa ku toro—wildcat.

kessake—little cat.

kidü—to wake up; to arise (*intransitive verb*).

kim—to cover an entire object with some sort of covering.

kinn—out; outdoors; outside; without.

kinta—fog; mist; smoke.

kislány—little girl.

kislány hän ku meke sarnaakmet—little mage.

kislány kuŋenak—little lunatic.

kislány kuŋenak minan—my little lunatic.

köd—fog; mist; darkness; evil (*noun*). Foggy, dark; evil (*adj.*).

köd alte hän—darkness curse it (*Carpathian swear words*).

o köd belső—darkness take it (*Carpathian swear words*).

köd elävä és köd nime kutni nimet—evil lives and has a name.

köd jutasz belső—shadow take you (*Carpathian swear words*).

koj—let; allow; decree; establish; order.

koje—man; husband; drone.

kola—to die.

kolasz arwa-arvoval—may you die with honor (*greeting*).

kolatan—dead; departed.

koma—empty hand; bare hand; palm of the hand; hollow of the hand.

kond—all of a family's or clan's children.

kont—warrior; man.

kont o sívanak—strong heart (literally: heart of the warrior).

kor3—basket; container made of birch bark.

kor3nat—containing; including.

ku—who; which; that; where; which; what.

kuć3—star.

kuć3ak!—stars! (exclamation).

kudeje—descent; generation.

kuja—day; sun.

kule—to hear.

kulke—to go or to travel (on land or water).

kulkesz arwa-arvoval, ekäm—walk with honor, my brother (*greeting*).

kulkesz arwaval, joŋesz arwa arvoval—go with glory, return with honor (*greeting*).

kuly—intestinal worm; tapeworm; demon who possesses and devours souls.

küm—human male.

kumala—to sacrifice; to offer; to pray.

kumpa—wave (*noun*).

kuńa—to lie as if asleep; to close or cover the eyes in a game of hide-and-seek; to die.

kuŋe—moon; month.

kunta—band; clan; tribe; family; people; lineage; line.

kuras—sword; large knife.

kure—bind; tie.

kuš—worker; servant.

kutenken—however.

kutni—to be able to bear, carry, endure, stand or take.

kutnisz ainaak—long may you endure (*greeting*).

kuulua—to belong; to hold.

kužõ—long.

lääs—west.

lamti (or lamt3)—lowland; meadow; deep; depth.

lamti ból jüti, kinta, ja szelem—the netherworld (literally: the meadow of night, mists, and ghosts).

lańa—daughter.

lejkka—crack; fissure; split (*noun*). To cut; to hit; to strike forcefully (*verb*).

lewl—spirit (*noun*).

lewl ma—the other world (literally: spirit land). *Lewl ma* includes *lamti ból jüti, kinta, ja szelem*: the netherworld, but also includes the worlds higher up *En Puwe*, the Great Tree.

liha—flesh.

lõuna—south.

löyly—breath; steam (related to *lewl*: spirit).

luwe—bone.

ma—land; forest; world.

magköszun—thank.

mana—to abuse; to curse; to ruin.

mäne—to rescue; to save.

maɣe—land; earth; territory; place; nature.

mboće—other; second (*adj.*).

me—we.

megem—us.

meke—deed; work (*noun*). To do; to make; to work (*verb*).

mić (or mića)—beautiful.

mića emni kuŋenak minan—my beautiful lunatic.

minan—mine; my own (*endearment*).

minden—every; all (*adj.*).

möért?—what for? (*exclamation*).

molanâ—to crumble; to fall apart.

molo—to crush; to break into bits.

moo—why; reason.

mozdul—to begin to move; to enter into movement.

muonì—appoint; order; prescribe; command.

muonìak te avoisz te—I command you to reveal yourself.

musta—memory.

myös—also.

m8—thing; what.

na—close; near.

nä—for.

nâbbŏ—so, then.

ŋamaŋ—this; this one here; that; that one there.

ŋamaŋak—these; these ones here; those; those ones there.

nautish—to enjoy.

nélkül—without.

nenä—anger.

nime—name.

ńiŋ3—worm; maggot.

nó—like; in the same way as; as.

nókunta—kinship.

numa—god; sky; top; upper part; highest (related to the English word *numinous*).

numatorkuld—thunder (literally: sky struggle).

ńǔp@l—for; to; toward.

ńǔp@l mam—toward my world.

nyelv—tongue.

nyál—saliva; spit (related to *nyelv*: tongue).

o—the (used before a noun beginning with a consonant).

ó—like; in the same way as; as.

odam—to dream; to sleep.

odam-sarna kondak—lullaby (literally: sleep-song of children).

odam wäke emni—mistress of illusions.

olen—to be.

oma—old; ancient; last; previous.

omas—stand.

omboce—other; second (*adj.*).

ŏrem—to forget; to lose one's way; to make a mistake.

ot—the (used before a noun beginning with a vowel).

ot (or t)—past participle (*suffix*).

otti—to look; to see; to find.

óv—to protect against.

owe—door.

päämoro—aim; target.

pajna—to press.

pälä—half; side.

päläfertiil—mate or wife.

päläpälä—side by side.

palj3—more.

palj3 na éntölem—closer.

partiolen—scout (*noun*).

peje—to burn; scorch.

peje!—burn! (*Carpathian swear word*).

peje terád—get burned (*Carpathian swear words*).

pél—to be afraid; to be scared of.

pesä—nest (*literal; noun*); protection (*figurative; noun*).

pesä—nest; stay (*literal*); protect (*figurative*).

pesäd te engemal—you are safe with me.

pesäsz jeläbam ainaak—long may you stay in the light (*greeting*).

pide—above.

pile—to ignite; to light up.

piŋe—little bird.

piŋe sarnanak—little song bird.

pion—soon.

pirä—circle; ring (*noun*). To surround; to enclose (*verb*).

piros—red.

pitä—to keep; to hold; to have; to possess.

pitäam mustaakad sielpesäambam—I hold your memories safe in my soul.

pitäsz baszú, piwtäsz igazáget—no vengeance, only justice.

piwtä—to seek; to follow; to follow the track of game; to hunt; to prey upon.

poår—bit; piece.

põhi—north.

pohoopa—vigorous.

pukta—to drive away; to persecute; to put to flight.

pus—healthy; healing.

pusm—to heal; to be restored to health.

puwe—tree; wood.

rambsolg—slave.

rauho—peace.

reka—ecstasy; trance.

rituaali—ritual.

sa—sinew; tendon; cord.

sa4—to call; to name.

saa—arrive, come; become; get, receive.

saasz hän ku andam szabadon—take what I freely offer.

saγe—to arrive; to come; to reach.

salama—lightning; lightning bolt.

sapar—tail.

sapar bin jalkak—coward (literally: tail between legs).

sapar bin jalkak nélkül mogal—spineless coward.

sarna—words; speech; song; magic incantation (*noun*). To chant; to sing; to celebrate (*verb*).

sarna hän agba—claim.

sarna kontakawk—warriors' chant.

sarna kunta—alliance (literally: single tribe through sacred words).

śaro—frozen snow.

sas—shoosh (*to a child or baby*).

satz—hundred.

siel—soul.

sielad sielamed—soul to soul (literally: your soul to my soul).

sielam—my soul.

sielam pitwä sielad—my soul searches for your soul.

sielam sieladed—my soul to your soul.

sieljelä isäntä—purity of soul triumphs.

sisar—sister.

sisarak sivak—sisters of the heart.

sisarke—little sister.

sív—heart.

sív pide köd—love transcends evil.

sív pide minden köd—love transcends all evil.

sívad olen wäkeva, hän ku piwtä—may your heart stay strong, hunter (*greeting*).

sívam és sielam—my heart and soul.

sívamet—my heart.

sívdobbanás—heartbeat (*literal*); rhythm (*figurative*).

sokta—to mix; to stir around.

sõl—dare, venture.

sõl olen engemal, sarna sívametak—dare to be with me, song of my heart.

soŋe—to enter; to penetrate; to compensate; to replace.

Susiküm—Lycan.

susu—home; birthplace (*noun*). At home (*adv.*).

szabadon—freely.

szelem—ghost.

ször—time; occasion.

t (or ot)—past participle (*suffix*).

taj—to be worth.

taka—behind; beyond.

takka—to hang; to remain stuck.

takkap—obstacle; challenge; difficulty; ordeal; trial.

tappa—to dance; to stamp with the feet; to kill.

tasa—even so; just the same.

te—you.

te kalma, te jama ńiŋ3kval, te apitäsz arwa-arvo—you are nothing but a walking maggot-infected corpse, without honor.

te magköszunam nä ŋamaŋ kać3 taka arvo—thank you for this gift beyond price.

ted—yours.

terád keje—get scorched (*Carpathian swear words*).

tõd—to know.

tõdak pitäsz wäke bekimet mekesz kaiket—I know you have the courage to face anything.

tõdhän—knowledge.

tõdhän lõ kuraset agbapäämoroam—knowledge flies the sword true to its aim.

toja—to bend; to bow; to break.

toro—to fight; to quarrel.

torosz wäkeval—fight fiercely (*greeting*).

totello—obey.

tsak—only.

t'śuva vni—period of time.

tti—to look; to see; to find.

tuhanos—thousand.

tuhanos löylyak türelamak saγe diutalet—a thousand patient breaths bring victory.

tule—to meet; to come.

tuli—fire.

tumte—to feel; to touch; to touch upon.

türe—full; satiated; accomplished.

türelam—patience.

türelam agba kontsalamaval—patience is the warrior's true weapon.

tyvi—stem; base; trunk.

ul3—very; exceedingly; quite.

umuš—wisdom; discernment.

und—past participle (*suffix*).

uskol—faithful.

uskolfertiil—allegiance; loyalty.

usm—to heal; to be restored to health.

vár—to wait.

varolind—dangerous.

veri—blood.

veri ekäakank—blood of our brothers.

veri-elidet—blood-life.

veri isäakank—blood of our fathers.

veri olen piros, ekäm—literally: blood be red, my brother; figuratively: find your lifemate (*greeting*).

veriak ot en Karpatiiak—by the blood of the prince (literally: by the blood of the great Carpathian; *Carpathian swear words*).

veridet peje—may your blood burn (*Carpathian swear words*).

vigyáz—to love; to care for; to take care of.

vii—last; at last; finally.

wäke—power; strength.

wäke beki—strength; courage.

wäke kaδa—steadfastness.

wäke kutni—endurance.

wäke-sarna—vow; curse; blessing (literally: power words).

wäkeva—powerful; strong.

wäkeva csitrim ku pesä—my fierce little protector.

wara—bird; crow.

weńća—complete; whole.

wete—water (*noun*).